P9-CCW-266

WITHDRAWN

LADY BEWARE

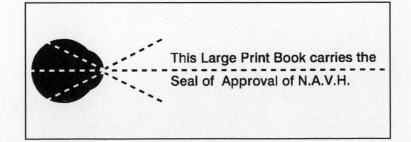

This Large Print Book carries the
Seal of Approval of N.A.V.H.

THE COMPANY OF ROGUES

LADY BEWARE

JO BEVERLEY

THORNDIKE PRESS

An imprint of Thomson Gale, a part of The Thomson Corporation

Mount Laurel Library
100 Walt Whitman Avenue
Mount Laurel, NJ 08054-9539
856-234-7319
www.mtlaurel.lib.nj.us

THOMSON

GALE

Detroit • New York • San Francisco • New Haven, Conn. • Waterville, Maine • London

THOMSON
GALE

Copyright © Jo Beverley Publications, Inc, 2007.

Thorndike Press, an imprint of the Gale Group.

Thomson and Star Logo and Thorndike are trademarks and Gale is a registered trademark used herein under license.

ALL RIGHTS RESERVED

This is a work of fiction. Names, characters, places, and incidents either are the product of the author's imagination or are used fictitiously, and any resemblance to actual persons, living or dead, business establishments, events or locales is entirely coincidental. The publisher does not have any control over and does not assume any responsibility for author or third-party Web sites or their content.

Thorndike Press® Large Print Basic.

The text of this Large Print edition is unabridged.

Other aspects of the book may vary from the original edition.

Set in 16 pt. Plantin.

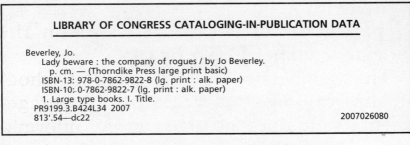

LIBRARY OF CONGRESS CATALOGING-IN-PUBLICATION DATA

Beverley, Jo.
    Lady beware : the company of rogues / by Jo Beverley.
    p. cm. — (Thorndike Press large print basic)
    ISBN-13: 978-0-7862-9822-8 (lg. print : alk. paper)
    ISBN-10: 0-7862-9822-7 (lg. print : alk. paper)
    1. Large type books. I. Title.
PR9199.3.B424L34 2007
813'.54—dc22   2007026080

Published in 2007 by arrangement with NAL Signet,
a member of Penguin Group (USA) Inc.

Printed in the United States of America on permanent paper
10 9 8 7 6 5 4 3 2 1

ACKNOWLEDGMENTS

With thanks as always to my wonderful agent, Margaret Ruley and the Rotrosen Agency, and my super editor, Claire Zion, and all the supportive people at New American Library. Thanks especially to the art department for the great cover on the original edition of *Lady Beware.*

The members of my chat group at Yahoogroups are always ready with encouragement, lively questions, and useful information. Kathy, Lisa, and Joan — thanks so much for shortcutting my research on *cave canem* and Roman traditions. (Anyone can join at http://groups.yahoo.com/group/jobeverley.)

And to my readers everywhere — you're what makes my books come alive.

CHAPTER 1

London May 1817
Lady Thea Debenham wriggled out of her
frothy green gown. "A new gown, Harriet.
Now."

"But *beetroot,* milady!" her maid wailed,
gathering the maroon-stained confection as
if it were a wounded child.

"I know, I know, but I'm sure you can
work some magic. Please. Another gown."

"Which one, milady?"

"I don't care!" But that wasn't true. Thea
whirled to check herself in the long mirror.
Her underwear always matched her gowns,
so she was sea green from stay frill to petticoat hem. "Do I have anything else close
to this color?"

"No, milady."

Thea bit her knuckle — which made her
aware of her green silk gloves. She stripped
them off. "Anything, then. Is there something I haven't worn yet?"

Harriet ran to the dressing room next door.

Thea saw her green slippers peeping out. "Matching slippers!" she called.

She bent to take off the slippers but was caught by the stiff busk of her evening corset. It didn't let her bend at the waist at all. Blast the busk and blast Uffham! She'd felt armored for this difficult evening by the most becoming ensemble in her wardrobe.

In keeping with fashion, the green gown had an extremely low bodice, and that had caused disaster. The Marquess of Uffham had been so engaged in ogling her bosom that the pickled beetroot on his tilted plate had slid off and down her gown.

Two ladies had actually shrieked.

Thea had managed not to, but she'd wanted to. Ruined. The gown had to be ruined — at its first wearing. And tonight of all nights. She paced the room, silk petticoat swishing.

On the surface her mother's ball was to celebrate the betrothal of Thea's brother, Lord Darius Debenham, to Lady Mara St. Bride. Beneath that felicitous froth lurked a deeper purpose. New trouble had surfaced for Dare.

He'd suffered so much. He'd fought at Waterloo, been badly wounded, and been

8

listed among the dead. Thea and her family had believed that for over a year — a long, terrible year. In fact he'd not died, but the woman who'd nursed him had given him too much opium for too long, so that he'd returned to England frail and addicted.

They'd nursed him back to health and now he'd found love. He'd struggled down to a very small daily amount of opium. But now this. As if the Fates couldn't bear to see him happy, a horrid rumor had started. Tongues wagged all around London that he hadn't been honorably wounded at Waterloo, but when trying to flee the battlefield.

It wasn't true! Anyone who knew Dare knew it wasn't true, but there was no one to deny the story. Even he didn't remember much about falling in battle or the days after, and fear that the story might be true was dragging him back down into the dark.

They needed a witness. It had been a battle, for heaven's sake. There must have been hundreds of men nearby. But it seemed that smoke hung like fog around a battlefield, action was fragmented, and everyone was intent on their own part.

So all Thea and her family could do at this moment was present a confident front and use every scrap of their immense influence. This hastily arranged ball was their challenge flung in the teeth of the ton: attend and show you don't believe such drivel; stay away and you are no friend of ours.

Of course, everyone who was anyone had come. The Duke and Duchess of Yeovil were powerful, but they were also universally liked and admired. Everyone had come — but Thea had sensed, and even sometimes heard, the questions simmering beneath the smiles.

Could the story be true? Lord Darius wasn't a trained soldier, after all, but a gentleman volunteer. Not surprising, perhaps, if such a terrible battle proved too much. . . .

Was that why he took so long to come home? Leaving his poor mother so distraught with grief . . . ?

Is that why he still needs opium — guilt?

Thea had smiled, danced, and flirted, showing the world that Dare's family held no doubts, but disaster hovered, and here she was, on the other side of the house in her underwear.

"Harriet!"

"Coming, milady!" The maid ran out of the dressing room, deep red satin trailing from her arms, matching stays and slippers on top.

"Oh," Thea said. "That."

On arriving in London for this season,

she'd learned she'd been tagged "the Great Untouchable." Cold, distant, and haughty. It was so unfair! Was it surprising that she'd not thrown herself into frivolity during her first season in 1815, with Napoleon returning to torment Europe and then Dare rushing off to fight?

As for last year . . . that had been a disaster. They'd still thought Dare dead. Thea had only attempted a season at all to try to distract her mother from her grief. Was it surprising if she'd failed to be all warmth and light? If she'd turned away all suitors?

Hurt by that nickname, she'd ordered a number of bold gowns. The green had turned out well, but the red had been just a bit too much. She never wore red.

But tonight was a battle of sorts, so perhaps it was just the thing.

"Right." She grabbed the stays and threw them on the bed. "There's no time to change those."

"But you're wearing green, milady."

"Which will be covered. Hurry."

Harriet muttered, but she raised the gown over Thea's head. Thea put her arms through the short sleeves and the rest slithered down over her like water. Or blood . . .

Lord! She stared at her reflection. The gown was cut in a new way, making the fabric flow down from the high waist, clinging to her shape. In the mirror, Harriet's eyes were wide.

"It is a bit much, isn't it, milady?" Harriet was in her thirties, but she'd been Thea's maid for only two years and rarely presumed to volunteer opinions, so her comment was significant.

"Lord." Thea said it aloud this time.

"I'll get something else, milady. . . ."

"There's no time." As soon as the gown was fastened, Thea sat on the bench. "The slippers."

Harriet soon had the green slippers off and the red satin ones on, and was crossing and tying the ribbons.

Thea could still see herself in the mirror and she checked for problems. She was wearing pearls. Wrong for a red gown, but all her other good jewels were in her father's safe. The band of white roses in her hair would have to go. She began to unpin it. As soon as Harriet finished, Thea went to the dressing table. "See what you can do with my hair."

As Harriet tidied her brown curls, Thea studied her reflection. In red, her pale breasts seemed to dominate, raised high by the corset, the upper halves exposed. Perhaps she should change to something else. . . .

But Harriet was fixing some red rosebuds and ribbons in her curls. Then the clock on her mantelpiece chimed eleven. Eleven! Thea stood, grabbed her mother-of-pearl fan — also inappropriate with red, but at least it went with the pearls — and headed for the door.

"Milady!"

Harriet's shriek made Thea whirl back. "What?"

Harriet was pointing at her, eyes huge.

Thea spun to the long mirror. A narrow frill of green lace was showing garishly at the edge of her deep red neckline.

"The other stays, milady —"

"Changing will take forever." Thea tugged the gown up and pushed the stays down, wriggling to make things settle into place. "There."

"Milady . . ."

"Don't fuss, Harriet. Do what you can for the green."

CHAPTER 2

Thea hurried out into the dimly lit corridor and headed back to the ball. When she turned the corner, she caught sight of herself in a gilt-framed mirror, illuminated by a wall lamp at its side. That half inch of green showed again.

Peste!

She tossed her fan on a small table and readjusted everything. Lord! Too low! The darker area around her nipples had been showing. Why did fashion have to be so outrageous? Society preached modesty and good behavior, but expected ladies to dress like this.

There. She cupped her breasts and rotated her shoulders, testing the stability of the arrangement. It should stay. . . .

But then something alerted her. She glanced sharply to the left and froze.

In the shadowy corridor, a man watched her. A man with the dark hair and eyes of a foreigner — heavy-lidded eyes that observed her with wicked amusement.

Face fiery, Thea grabbed her fan and flipped it open as a shield. "Who are you, sir? What are you doing in this part of the house?"

If he'd answered, this might be nothing but an embarrassing moment, but he did not.

And she didn't know him.

She knew anyone who had reason to be in Yeovil House tonight, and she certainly wouldn't have forgotten this man after even the briefest encounter.

Though not large or tall, his presence filled the corridor with an air of power and command. She could almost imagine that he'd sucked the air thinner. The light of the lamp beside her hardly reached him, and the next one was behind him, but she could tell his features were well formed and strong.

Dark evening clothes spoke of wealth, as did the flash of jewels in his white neck-cloth. But he wasn't a gentleman. No gentleman would look at a lady as he was doing now.

Who *was* he, intruding into the private part of her home, making her heart thunder?

"Sir?" Thea demanded.

"Madam?" he responded, speaking at last, the one mocking word revealing a surprisingly mellow voice. And perhaps a foreign intonation?

Thea almost laughed with relief. Of course. He must be a new member of one of the embassies. They sometimes arrived with poor English and strange manners. One of the Persian diplomats had constantly invited ladies to join his harem.

"You are lost, sir?" Thea said, speaking slowly and clearly. "This is the private part of the house."

He didn't answer. Instead, he walked toward her.

Thea took a sharp step back. She almost felt she should scream, but that would be ridiculous, here in her father's house.

"Sir . . . ," she said again. Then she thrust out a gloved hand, palm forward. "Stop!"

To her surprise, he did. Her panic simmered down, but all the same, she was completely at a loss. She'd hate to cause a diplomatic incident, but every instinct was crying, *Danger!*

She gestured down the corridor. "May I guide you back to the ball, sir?"

"I believe I can find my way unaided."

She froze, hand out.

His English was perfect.

16

"Then I will leave you to your wanderings," she said and walked forward to pass him.

He moved to block her way.

Thea was caught within a foot of him, mouth suddenly paper dry. She could not possibly be in danger here, within call of family and servants.

But she was not within call of anyone. Her family were all with the guests, and most of the servants were busy there, too. Even Harriet would already be hurrying to the laundry with the ruined gown. She was, she realized, shockingly isolated in the dimly lit silence, in the company of a dangerous man.

She put eight hundred years of aristocratic power into an icy challenge. "Sir?"

He inclined his head. "Madam. At your service. Depending entirely, of course, on the service you desire."

In some subtle way, he lingered on the word "desire," and she remembered the way he'd been watching her.

"All I *require* is that you let me pass."

"I did say it depended."

"You, sir, are a boor and a cad. Step out of my way."

"No."

She glared at him, wanting to force her way past, but physical strength beat out of

17

him like heat. He could control her one-handed.

"Then I will find another route," she said and turned to walk away.

He grabbed the back of her gown.

Thea froze, shock, terror, and fury tightening her throat. Her voice came hoarsely. "If you knew who I was . . ."

"Lady Theodosia Debenham, I assume."

He *knew* her? "Is this some ridiculous joke?" she demanded.

"No."

"Then what are you doing?"

"Trying to talk to you."

Thea inhaled and exhaled twice. "Let go of me."

To her surprise, he did. She was very tempted to run, but he'd catch her easily, so she chose dignity and faced him, flipping open her fan and waving it, trying to make her heartbeats match that pace.

Up close, she saw that indeed his features were regular and could be called handsome — if one didn't mind cold harshness. But she also saw his flaws — a nose slightly crooked by violence, and a number of minor scars.

This was a man who knew danger, and carried it with him.

When faced with a dangerous animal, one

should try not to show fear.

"I do not know you, sir," Thea said, "so how do you know who I am?"

"You have a distinct look of your brother. We were at school together."

Her fear lessened a little.

"You're a Rogue?" she asked. She hadn't met all of Dare's friends from his Harrow school days — the group who called themselves the Company of Rogues — but this wasn't the behavior she'd expect of them.

"No." Something in his flat denial made Thea twitch with alarm.

"Whoever you are, you are too old to behave like a schoolboy. Let me pass."

His dark brows rose. "You often have such confrontations with schoolboys?"

Thea snapped her fan shut. "Let me *pass!*"

He didn't move.

"I will be missed. Someone will come to look for me and then you will get what you deserve."

"But I so rarely do."

Was that a smile? If so, it was twisted slightly by a short scar that cut right through the left corner of his mouth and another that pulled up his right brow. He was truly dangerous, and despite her bold words, it could be a long time before anyone came to

19

this part of the house. Even a scream might not be heard.

Don't show fear.

"Who are you, sir? And what do you want?"

"My name is Horatio, and I want to talk to you."

"You *are* talking to me, but to no purpose that I can see."

"It's making your bosom heave delightfully."

She glanced down. Cursing herself, she fixed her gaze back on him. "Speak!"

"Or forever hold my peace? How suitable. I have a proposal for you."

Thea gaped. "You're asking me to *marry* you?"

Dark brows rose again. "Would you?"

"Of course not! Enough of this. Let me pass, Mr. Horatio Nobody, or you will rue it bitterly."

"Or your brother will."

The words poured over Thea like icy water. "You said you were a friend of his."

"Everyone who went to school with Dare Debenham must adore him? But then, he must need friends now — crippled, broken, and addicted to opium."

"He's not —"

"And accused of cowardice."

"Which is a black lie." She narrowed her eyes. "Are you responsible for that story? If so, sir, you are the most despicable worm ever to crawl the earth!"

"You often talk to worms?"

Thea would have hit him with her fan, but it would shatter a work of art to absolutely no effect. A hammer might not dent him.

Then he raised a hand. The gesture might even have been in apology.

"I had nothing to do with the rumor," he said, "but now that it exists your mother can host a ball a week and command the ton to attend every one of them without wiping it away. You need a credible witness to deny the story, or it will hang over your brother forever."

"You think we don't know this?"

"Sometimes it helps to state the obvious."

"And it pleases you to do so." It was a wild shot, but it hit. "You wish Dare ill," she said, frowning. "No one wishes Dare ill."

"Really? How pleasant it must be to be him. Any pleasure I take in his situation is solely because it will allow me to correct the error."

She distrusted every word he said. "Why?"

"For a suitable reward."

21

"Ah, money." She spat it, and his lip turned up wryly.

"Lady Theodosia, people only sneer at money if they've never lacked it."

This was the most bizarre encounter of Thea's life, but she was beginning to see her way, though she was strangely disappointed that this man proved to be so base.

"So, sir, what do you have to offer? And what is your price?"

He showed no sign of offense. "I can tell the world that I saw your brother's horse shot from under him, in the midst of action, not in flight. In other words, honorably."

Her heart leapt, but she tried not to show it. "Would it be true?" she asked.

"Would it matter?"

A startling question, but it struck home. To save Dare from this burden, she'd lie herself if there were any point to it.

"Then would you be believed? That is crucial."

He inclined his head in acknowledgment. "I fought at Waterloo, and in about the right place."

A soldier. Of course he was. It didn't make him any less dangerous, but at least she understood. Her world had been full of officers all her adult life. They came in all types,

22

but there was something that marked them, even the most lighthearted, as having looked into the eyes of death and delivered it. In this man, it was particularly potent. It sizzled down her nerves and didn't make him safe, but understanding eased her anxiety. Her main comfort, however, came from knowing this was a matter of buying and selling. Her family was very rich.

"So," she asked, "your price?"

"Marriage. Marry me and I will clear Dare's name."

CHAPTER 3

She couldn't help but laugh. "Don't be ridiculous!"

"You care so little for him?"

Put like that, it seemed wrong to refuse, but the idea was preposterous. Then she realized why. "I care too much to place that burden on him — my life's ease for his."

"If you pretended to adore me, he would never know."

Dryly she said, "I am not so good an actor."

"I'm so very appalling?" He was mocking her again.

"You're uncouth, a paltry bully, a foul liar, a greedy swine —"

Something in his face dried her words. All he said was, "I deny the paltry."

"Can you deny mad?"

"I can act the part of a sane man if I try."

"Then try *now*," she snapped.

"I thought I was both sane and clear," he

said. "Marriage for the truth."

"No. But my family would be generous in other ways."

"Perhaps there are no other ways."

He seemed relaxed now, even amiable, but he was looking at her like a predator who has dinner cornered.

Thea waved her fan again, trying to match his manner. "Liars are two a penny, sir, so we will simply find another. One who will accept a sane recompense."

He laughed. "That's probably the only time a Debenham has ever sought a bargain. I'm prime quality and worth my price, my lady."

"Nothing, sir, would be worth tying myself to you for life."

Thea again stepped to go around him. This time he gripped her arm. His bare hand was callused, hot and strong on the skin between her long glove and short sleeve.

"I'll settle for less than marriage," he said.

Thea turned to stare, her face now close to his. *"What?"*

Was he proposing . . . ? He would vindicate Dare for her body . . . ? This was impossible!

But her imagination tested the ground. A few hours, perhaps less. What did she know about these things? Set against Dare's entire life.

"What?" she asked again, demanding clarification now but fearing her legs would give way.

"An engagement," he said.

Thea gasped. *"What?"*

He turned her to face him. "If I clear Lord Darius's name, you engage yourself to marry me. Publicly." When she opened her mouth to object, he put a finger to her lips. "Don't panic. You won't have to go through with it, but the betrothal must hold for at least six weeks."

Thea jerked free of his touch, wanting to grip her head, to rock it back into order. "You're mad!"

"And you are overwhelmed. Think about it. A six-week engagement is not so great a trial compared to the prize it will purchase."

"And after six weeks?"

"You send me off with a flea in my ear."

"You expect me to *jilt* you?"

True humor lit his face this time and his smile carved lines into his lean cheeks. "That's what horrifies you?"

"Yes! A gentleman who jilts a lady is ruined, but a lady who jilts a gentleman is not a true lady — unless she has an excellent and known reason. Are you willing to provide an excellent and known reason why I should not marry you?"

Laughter faded to wryness. "Almost inevitably. So? We are engaged?"

"Of course not. If you truly did see Dare fall, it is your duty to say so without reward."

"But what if I'll have to lie?"

"Then your word is worth nothing."

"Lies, my lady, can be worth fortunes." But he stepped back, clearing her way. "It seems our discussion is at an end."

Thea longed to take the escape he offered, but she found she couldn't do it. Truth or lie, she believed that this man held the key to Dare's future.

A betrothal wouldn't be so very appalling. Except . . .

She still had no idea who he was.

"Who are you?" she asked.

"The man who can vindicate your brother."

"I mean your name."

"Horatio."

"Your full name, sir."

"Why quibble? I'm asking a small price for a large service and you are going to agree."

She wanted to deny that, but couldn't.

"You could be a nobody."

"I'm clearly somebody."

"You know what I mean."

"Yes. You wouldn't lower yourself to marry a tradesman."

"More to the point, no one would believe that I *wanted* to marry a tradesman. If you become Dare's witness and then I promise to marry you, your complete unsuitability as husband for a duke's daughter would ruin everything."

He looked at her in a new way. "I do admire a clearheaded woman. Don't fine tailoring and expensive trimmings tell the story?"

She looked him over, noting again the quality of his dark evening clothes and the emerald glinting in gold amid the snowy linen at his throat. "You could be a rich tradesman."

"You'd never stoop so low?"

"I told you. It would look peculiar!" Clocks began to chime. "Heavens, how much time has passed? I must return to the ball. We will talk more of this tomorrow, sir."

"Now or never. Refuse and I leave this house immediately. You will never see me again."

She stared, appalled. "That's not fair."

"Life rarely is."

"Tell me who you are."

"No."

"Tell me this, at least. Are you a gentle-man?"

"Yes."

"Are you honorable?"

"Yes."

Thea knew that asking these questions was admission that she was going to give in, just as he'd so arrogantly predicted. He'd hooked her like a fish and was reeling her into his net, and she was as helpless as a thrashing trout.

He was an honorable gentleman and a soldier, and handsome in a roughened way. Though his behavior here had been appall-ing, he clearly could do better if he wished. A betrothal might be believed. It might even be tolerable.

But why? Why was he doing this?

"What do you gain from this?" she asked.

"Six weeks of your delightful company," he replied.

She simply looked at him.

He met her eyes but stayed silent.

She sought truth in his impassive features. Perhaps she also sought weakness, or last-minute mercy. She found neither. Instead, she recognized implacable will. He had faced her with a choice and would not relent. There was only one answer that would let her sleep at night.

"If you clear my brother's name," she said, "I will betroth myself to you and it will last for six weeks." When a flash of triumph lit his eyes, she added, "But that is all."

"Except for the sealing kiss."

Thea stepped back. "That wasn't part of the bargain."

But when he grasped her gloved hand, she didn't struggle. Nor when he kissed it, first fingers, then knuckles, his dark eyes holding hers. She could hardly feel his lips through silk, but still she shivered.

When he took her shoulders it was as if he had entranced her, as a snake is supposed to be able to entrance its prey. Did such prey come to *want* to be captured, as she did?

She shocked herself, but their confrontation, their battle of wills, had stirred a passion inside her that demanded some culmination, some final crescendo. As he drew her close and lowered his lips to hers, she swayed. When he finally brushed his lips over hers, a sound escaped her throat.

"You're enjoying this, aren't you, my lady?"

"No." But it came out as a breath.

His lips pressed against hers again. Nothing more, and briefly, but heat sparked.

"Lying will send you to hell," he whispered. "Tell me to stop now and our bargain is sealed."

She should, but it hadn't been enough.

He drew her hard against his powerful body. A sense of raw strength shocked her, but that only made the madness worse. She stared up at him, mouth agape, feeling she should beg for mercy, and then he joined his mouth to hers, his tongue plunging deep.

She jerked back, but she was captured now. She could no more escape than a creature caught in an eagle's talons, but nor did she want to. Sensations were ricocheting through her — *Danger! Danger!* — *Thrill! Thrill!* She thrust fingers into his hair, wishing she were gloveless, and pressed her aching body against him.

Could a kiss truly be endless? Her whole body ached now, pressed to him, burning desperately as she whirled in a passionate storm.

He was the one to break free, having to drag himself out of her demanding hands. He separated slowly and Thea feared she'd topple without his support. She felt as weak and wavery as if she'd been in bed with a fever, and staggered back to lean against the wall, heart thundering, sucking in desperate breaths, staring at him.

"Thus," he said, and perhaps his breathing was unsteady, too, "we are most thoroughly betrothed."

Thea had to swallow to find her voice. "So now, tell me who you are." It came out softly, through her weakness, but also because of a kind of tenderness, even yearning. Being this man's promised wife would not be so bad. Being his wife, in fact, even. . . .

"Your betrothed," he said. But then, eyes watchful on hers, he added, "Viscount Darien."

Titled?

Why didn't she know him, then?

Then it fell into place.

She pushed straight off the wall. "You claimed to be honorable!"

"I did not lie."

"But you're a *Cave!*"

The Cave family — pronounced *cahvay,* like the Latin for "beware" — were notorious.

She shook her head, lost in panic. "I can't betroth myself to a Cave!"

"The bargain is sealed." He turned and walked away.

"No, it isn't!" she yelled after him. When he gave no sign of hearing, she stepped forward as if to pursue, but what good would it do?

"No," she repeated to the dim and now empty corridor, as if that might do some good. "No!"

She was betrothed to a Cave?

She'd just *kissed* a Cave?

She scrubbed at her tender lips. The Caves were villains and debauchers on every branch and twig of the family tree. Not long ago, one of them had raped and murdered a young lady in Mayfair. He'd died in Bedlam instead of on the gibbet because he'd been stark, staring mad.

Such a promise couldn't hold, she thought desperately.

There'd been no witnesses. No one knew about it but him and her.

That felt despicable, but not in comparison to his lies and trickery. She should have known. She'd sensed something foul about him from the first.

But what should she *do?*

Fear could send her running back to her room to hide under the bed. She could plead illness, anything, so as not to return to the ball.

Where he could now be.

Heaven's mercy, he might announce their betrothal in her absence. That would be

33

preposterous for any other man, but he was a Cave!

Thea knew what she had to do. She sucked in breaths, struggling for control, poise, confidence — everything she'd taken for granted until minutes ago. Then she walked swiftly on, the same way he had gone, back to the ball.

CHAPTER 4

Horatio Cave, Viscount Darien, wanted to stop to think, to review, but some points in battle demanded unhesitating action. He'd won the prize he'd come here for. A greater prize than he'd imagined. He had only to grasp it.

He'd invaded the Duchess of Yeovil's ball to acquire a highborn female ally in his campaign to make his family name respectable again. His quarry had been the Duchess of Yeovil herself. The opportunity had fallen into his hands when he'd heard the story about her son, Lord Darius Debenham. Make the mother grateful and she would be wax in his hands.

Perfect wax. He'd spent the day savoring the thought of the Debenhams as his tools. The family of the man he loathed would become his obedient tools. And Dare Debenham would have to acknowledge this in public, with half the world watching.

Just as he'd ruined a boy's life, in public, with half the school watching.

Now it was even better. Instead of a mother forced to be gracious out of gratitude, he had a sister bound to pretend to love him. Sealed by a fiery kiss.

That kiss. . . .

He realized he'd stopped, and within sight of the outer fringes of the ball. Music rippled out of the ballroom — a bouncing, merry tune for doubtless bouncing, merry dancers. Ahead, silk-clad people sparkling with jewels strolled and chattered, all supremely confident of their place in this, the heart of the inner circle.

Unaware of the enemy in their midst.

Not entirely unaware, alas. He'd been recognized earlier, when he'd been searching the ball for Lord Darius.

He'd hoped to avoid recognition by arriving late, but of course there were men here who'd known him in the army. Some of them might have been welcoming in other circumstances, but not here, where his name and title caused horror.

He silently damned his father and older brothers, his uncle and grandfather, and the whole line of Caves who'd lived up to the warning in their name, but then he blended with the ton at play, resuming his search for

Debenham. He needed to get this done before Lady Theodosia recovered her wits. Once his part was played she'd find it harder to balk.

He entered the noisy, packed ballroom and stepped to one side so as not to block the door. His earlier search had failed, and he realized now that Debenham could be changed since the last time Darien had seen him, in the days before Waterloo. He'd been badly wounded since then and become an opium addict.

So now Darien looked for members of the Company of Rogues, that schoolboy clique from Harrow. Wherever the wreck of Lord Darius Debenham was, some Rogues would be hovering nearby. They prided themselves on taking care of each other.

He wished he'd thought of that before. Then, perhaps, he wouldn't have been caught unawares by the sight of some of them and sent running into the quiet parts of the house.

He'd recognized Viscount Amleigh first. He'd encountered the stocky, dark-haired man in Brussels because Amleigh had returned to the army and had been sharing a billet with Darien's friend Captain George Vandeimen. Unfortunately — Rogues sticking to Rogues — Debenham had been sharing the same rooms. That had meant Darien couldn't spend as much time with Van as he'd wished. Another sin to the Rogues' tally.

With Amleigh earlier had been an athletic, golden-haired man. It had taken only a moment to realize it had to be the Marquess of Arden, heir to the Dukedom of Belcraven, arrogant boy become man. He'd attended Harrow with his own retinue of servants.

The mythology claimed that the Company of Rogues had been created for mutual protection. Exactly why would Arden need that? No, it had been a gathering of an elite, too high and mighty to mix with lesser beings, and he'd hated their guts.

Along with Amleigh and Arden had been a man Darien recognized only by his distinctive hair, dark shot with red. Simon St. Bride, who'd recently become Viscount Austrey, heir to the Earl of Marlowe. Good fortune fell into the Rogues' hands.

Observing the group of confident, relaxed men, the past had rushed back on Darien like a tide. Harrow. The worst time of a tough life. Because of the Rogues. Because, especially, of Lord Darius Bloody Debenham.

And so he'd run. It had been a calm, steady walk, but inside he'd been running as he'd once run at school, and he'd hated that. He hadn't paid attention to where he was going as long as it was far away from people. When he'd discovered Debenham's sister alone and vulnerable, he'd seen the opportunity for perfect revenge.

She'd proved to be more than he'd expected — braver, more quick-witted, and infinitely more passionate — though that bloodred dress had been a warning. But he'd captured her. Now all he had to do was find Debenham to clinch his victory.

Where in hell was he? This was his betrothal ball.

Suddenly, he thought to wonder, what if he'd already left? What if he was too frail to last this long? He should have found that out.

Poor preparation.

Poor intelligence.

Dammit. What to do now? He could still tell his story, but he wanted that face-to-face confrontation. He wanted to make Debenham eat his rescue out of Dog Cave's hand.

Leave and come back tomorrow? He needed to do this before Debenham's sister had a chance to block him.

The dance ended, the crowd shifted — and Darien saw him.

He almost laughed aloud.

Where was the addicted cripple?

Dare Debenham strolled toward the ballroom doors, smilingly intent on the lovely
brunette on his arm, and she adoringly
intent on him. He walked without so much
as a limp, and if he bore scars, they weren't
visible. In fact, he looked fitter and stronger
than before.

And completely happy.

He should have been christened Theophi-
lus — beloved of God.

To hell with this. Darien turned to leave
the room. Let's see how long Debenham
smiled with shame hanging around his neck.

But he made himself stop. He'd resolved
to restore the Cave reputation for good
reasons. To retreat now would be another
victory for the Rogues.

Very well, a roll of the dice. If Debenham
looked through him, pretended a Cave
didn't exist, or worse, reacted as if he were
a leper at the feast, Darien would leave him
to stew. If not, he'd play this out. He turned
and stepped into the couple's path.

Debenham blinked, clearly far away, and
then he smiled politely. "Canem."

Only Darien's closest friends called him
that — Canem Cave, a play on *cave canem,*
"beware of the dog." And that rocketed

right back to schoolboy hurt and rage. Damnable. Especially when Dare Debenham had been the one to make that cruel joke.

"Cave Canem," he'd said, laughing, turning Horatio Cave into Dog Cave, leading to —

Enough. The dice had rolled and Darien must pay. He gave his enemy the good news. He even spoke to a couple of military men nearby, but he couldn't linger more than that.

Darien fled the celebration and went straight to hell.

CHAPTER 5

Thea blended with the guests, smiling and hoping no trace of her inner mayhem showed. But she was alert for signs of drama or disaster. There *was* something, something discordant in the air.

What had that man done?

People only smiled and nodded at her, or paid compliments on the ball. If he'd announced the ridiculous betrothal, someone would have to say something. Wouldn't they?

Had it been a trick? Had he terrified her for amusement? Was he now laughing about it with others?

Was he not even a Cave at all?

Hope flared, but shame quenched it. If it had all been a game, Dare would remain burdened.

She couldn't bear not knowing. She wove through the guests, her smile feeling like a grimace, seeking Dare or Darien — what a silly confusion that was! — or anyone else who could tell her what had happened while she'd been away.

"Such a tragedy!"

Thea started and looked at the speaker, Lady Swinnamer. "What's happened?"

"Your poor gown, Lady Thea! Quite, quite ruined, I'm sure."

Thea almost said, "Oh, that," in a manner that would have been bound to raise suspicions, and gaunt Lady Swinnamer was spiteful enough without fuel.

"Not quite ruined, I hope, but a great annoyance. Please excuse me, I must find my brother."

"Lord Darius?" Lady Swinnamer cooed. "Not more trouble, I hope."

Thea blasted a smile at her. "Quite the contrary," she said and walked away, hoping the woman choked on it. Then she halted.

Had someone just said, "Cave?" in a shocked voice, a voice rising on the second syllable? A look around found only bland smiles. She was going mad! She had to find someone she could trust to speak plainly.

She continued on toward the ballroom, sure now of tension in the air. She looked to one side and a woman's eyes slid away, perhaps with a smirk. She challenged a staring Lord Shepstone and the young man blushed. She kept walking, because to stop

43

still in the corridor would give the onlookers even more to talk about, but she wanted to disappear down a hole in the floor. She had never in her life felt so uncomfortable in society.

She searched the dancers, seeing none of her family. She hurried on to check through the line of anterooms, each scattered with people. They smiled, but did some look at her oddly? She saw no one she trusted with this.

Then she spotted her cousin Maddy, typically enthralling three uniformed officers. Blond, buxom Maddy always enthralled, and she had a weakness for a uniform. But she also always knew everything that was going on.

Thea joined the group casually, but after a few minutes of chat she said, "Gentlemen, I'm going to break your hearts by stealing Maddy for a little while. Off you go, sirs!"

They took their congé with good grace, but Maddy wasn't fooled. "What's the matter?" she asked as soon as they were alone.

"I wanted to ask you the same thing. Did anything happen while I was away?"

"Away?" But then Maddy looked at her. "Why have you changed your gown?"

"Uffham spilled beetroot on me. Do you know where Dare is?"

"No. He was dancing not long ago. What on earth is the matter?"

Thea didn't know what to say. Clearly Maddy knew nothing shocking, and she wasn't ready to speak of private adventures.

"Uffham," she said vaguely. "The gown. I thought some people looked at me strangely."

"Not surprising with your stays peeping out."

Thea glanced down and raised a hand to cover the disaster. So that had been it! She turned her back to the room and twitched the dress up again. "I should go and change."

"Nonsense. It's wickedly fetching."

"I don't want to be wickedly fetching!"

"Every woman wants to be wickedly fetching, and that gown should fetch. I wouldn't have thought red would suit you so well. Madame Louise?"

"Mrs. Fortescue."

"I must visit her, though I don't have the figure for that clinging style. Alas, I must make do with bountiful."

"Which you do all too well."

It was meant as a warning, but Maddy grinned. "I do, don't I? But you can't complain. Men positively swarm you."

"High rank and a large dowry ensure it."

"I have both, but prefer to put my appeal to men down to my charms. Oh, Thea, don't give me another Great Untouchable look!"

"Don't call me that."

"Then don't act that way."

Maddy and Thea were like sisters. Maddy's father was an admiral and often at sea, so she, her brother, and her mother had spent a lot of time at Long Chart, the Duke of Yeovil's Somerset estate. As with any sisters, sometimes there was discord. In this case it rose mainly from Maddy's increasingly bold behavior with her coterie of officers and Thea's attempts to restrain her.

"Did you hear that a Cave's here?" Maddy asked.

Praying her high color was taken for alarm, Thea gasped, "No! Truly?"

Maddy's eyes sparkled. "Deliciously alarming, isn't it? The new Vile Viscount. Mother's certain we'll all be murdered or worse. But I ask you, is being raped worse than being murdered?"

"Maddy!" Thea protested, looking around to be sure no one was in earshot. "What does he look like?"

"I haven't met him yet, but I've been on the hunt."

"How can you hunt someone if you don't

know what he looks like?"

"Darkly demonic. That was Alesia's description. He was pointed out to her and now she's in a quake. Marchampton knows him," she said, referring to one of the officers she'd been with. "Dark hair and eyes, he said. Foreign-looking because of an Italian mother. There won't be many like that here, especially with horns, tail, and an odor of brimstone."

"Maddy . . ."

Her cousin laughed. "Well, Alesia was so ridiculous. Cully adores him."

"What?"

Cully was Lieutenant Claudius Debenham, Maddy's brother.

"Desperate case of hero worship. Terrifyingly terrific and at times insane, he says."

"That's adoring praise?" But it seemed frighteningly accurate to Thea and wrecked any hope of the hellish encounter being a joke.

"They even call him Mad Dog," Maddy said with relish.

"Good God. . . ."

"He was wreaking his madness on the *French,* Thea! When did you become so chickenhearted?"

Thea pulled herself together. "Everything's been a bit fraught this evening."

Now there was an understatement. "I must go and find Dare."

"He has enough caretakers," Maddy said.

Thea colored. If she'd niggled at Maddy over her behavior with officers, Maddy had niggled at her protective hovering over Dare. Thea knew that during her brother's recovery she'd become obsessive, she and her mother both.

"I have reasons for needing to speak to him now," she said.

Maddy's eyes sharpened. "You have secrets. Tell!"

Thea said exactly the wrong thing. "No."

Maddy grabbed her arm. "You do! What's going on?"

"I can't tell you. Not now, at least. It's nothing really, but I have to find Dare. Just to make sure everything's all right."

"Very well, but I'm coming with you." Maddy linked arms with Thea. "And keep a weather eye out for dark and demonic. I need to meet the dread Darien."

The thought of Maddy involved with her attacker was terrifying.

They had only reached the door of the room when their way was blocked by a strapping blond officer in scarlet and gold.

"Did you hear?" Cully demanded gleefully, in a voice loud enough for a parade ground. "Dare's cleared! Canem Cave says he saw him fall. No question about it."

People around began to chatter.

"How extraordinary!" Maddy exclaimed.

"How wonderful," Thea said, meaning it, but her heart suddenly threatened to choke her.

"Canem Cave?" Maddy asked. "Do you mean *the* Cave? Viscount Darien?"

"Who else? He says Dare was doing just as he ought," Cully went on, deliberately making sure everyone heard. "Riding hell for leather with a message when a shot brought down his horse and he disappeared under a wave of hooves. Canem says it's a miracle he survived."

"Why Canem?" Maddy asked.

"From *cave canem,* I think," her brother said.

"He's called Dog?" Maddy asked and laughed.

Her brother flushed. "Not in that way. What a stupid creature you are, Maddy."

"Well, really!"

Thea let squabble and exclamations swirl. She was immensely relieved on Dare's behalf, of course, but what did this mean for her?

"Where is Lord Darien?" she asked, trying for a pleased, composed tone. "I'd like

49

to thank him."

"Have to wait," Cully replied. "Said his piece, then left."

"Left?"

"Rum, really. Arrived late, told his story to Dare and a few others, then disappeared. But you never know what to expect from Canem Cave. The House of Lords is in for a shake if he ever bothers to attend. Come on. Dare and his friends are celebrating over supper."

Thea went to join the jubilant party at one of the outside supper tables set in the lantern-lit gardens. When she saw Dare's unshadowed happiness, she was truly thankful and, yes, willing to pay the price if she had to. But as she accepted a glass of champagne for a triumphant toast, she buzzed with panic.

Lord Arden made a joke about the Cave name and there being nothing to *beware* of tonight. Someone else mentioned Mad Marcus Cave, the murderous one. Another said, "The Vile Viscount himself."

She'd promised to link herself to a Cave, to a name that caused shudders, horror, and an expectation of violence. He'd left, but she took no comfort from that. He'd be back, terrifyingly terrific, dark and demonic, to demand his price.

She felt like some character in a folktale — Rapunzel, perhaps? — who made a foolish bargain and then could not escape her promise.

As everyone drank another toast, a breeze rustled through the trees and touched her naked back. It was as if it whispered, *"Beware, lady, beware."*

CHAPTER 6

In a lifetime of crowded army living Darien had found that a well-run gaming hell was the ideal place for a man to be left alone with his thoughts, as long as he played and didn't win too much.

He walked briskly toward a hell called Grigg's, careless of light evening shoes not meant for this work. Mayfair seemed a never-ending parade of tall, narrow houses, packed neatly together in terraces. A strange preference with so many stairs for family and servants. Yet each was a place of comfort, a place of refuge, where people slept easily at night, protected from others by brick walls, locked doors, and bars on the ground-floor windows.

He had such a house now, Cave House, which had been in his family for generations. A tall, narrow collection of empty rooms. He had bricks, locks, and bars, but he felt far from safe there.

Empty rooms should provide peace and quiet, but there were other kinds of noise. Though he had no personal memories of the place, and though all trace of dark deeds had been long since scoured, white-washed, and painted away, the silent house deafened him.

The nighttime noises were the worst, which was another reason to delay his return there. He sometimes woke to grunts, groans, and occasional screams, in a locked house shared only with a few servants. If any house deserved to be haunted, Cave House was it, but the thought of meeting any remnant of his brother, Mad Marcus Cave, made even him quake.

Given a choice, he'd never enter the house again, but he'd made it part of his plan. His living there was supposed to declare to the world that the past was past and that the new Lord Darien had nothing to be ashamed of. He laughed into the dark. His neck still crawled from being stared at and he could remember hearing: *"Mad Dog Cave. What's he doing here?"*

He'd wanted to turn and bite whoever had said that.

Even without words, the subtle avoidance of him had been unignorable. It hadn't been meant to be ignored. It had been meant to drive him away.

He'd seen Van in one room, but by that time he'd known better than to drag a friend into the mess. Later, perhaps, as a reward for victory. For now, clearly a Cave was a Cave, no matter his character and reputation, and ranked somewhat lower than a leper.

At the door of the hell he realized one irony. The warmest welcome he'd received tonight had been from Dare Debenham himself.

Immediately came the never-quite-buried memory of Debenham holding a handkerchief to a bloody nose, saying, *"Cave canem."*

He slammed the door on that. It was over a decade ago, dammit, and since then he'd carved reputation and victory out of a hostile world. And now he'd do the same with the ton.

After all, the Duchess of Yeovil had thanked him tearfully. He had Debenham's sister in his grasp — the lovely, haughty Lady Theodosia. Her name meant "God's gift." God's gift to him.

He knocked on the door of the hell and was let in. Grigg's was the sort of ill-lit place inhabited by men and women whose whole attention was fixed on cards, dice, and the EO table. No music here, or fancy refreshments. Being a Cave didn't matter. Nothing did as long as a visitor had money to lose. Darien had made sure to lose at least as often as he won. He considered it a form of rent for usage of the space.

He sought a simple game and sat at a macao table, where he could play the odds with half his mind as he reviewed his night.

Why hadn't he expected the ton's reaction? Why had he expected them to see Canem Cave, military hero, instead of just another Cave, as vile as all the rest? He remembered the appalled look on Lady Theodosia Debenham's face when he'd told her who he was. The way she'd insisted that he couldn't be honorable. . . .

Why hadn't he expected to have inherited the whole mess along with the viscountcy? His raking, duelist grandfather, who'd been called Devil Cave in an age when it took a lot to summon images of Satan. His brutal father, labeled the Vile Viscount as credit for a lifetime of gross misbehavior. His uncle, "Dicker" Cave, ravisher of any vulnerable girl to cross his path.

He had expected to wear the albatross of the ultimate blot on the family's dirty escutcheon — Mad Marcus Cave, lunatic murderer of Sweet Mary Wilmott — but not in any personal way. Not in women's fearful eyes and men's protective anger.

God.

No wonder his younger brother, Frank, had been rejected as a suitor.

Frank was a lieutenant in the navy, and he'd fallen in love with his admiral's daughter. Admiral Sir Plunkett Dynnevor had warned him off. Not for being a mere lieutenant, but for being a Cave.

Darien had been outraged and had set out on this campaign to prove respectability. But now he understood. If he'd had a daughter, he'd not allow her to be tied to the Cave name for life.

Yet he'd forced Lady Theodosia into that, he thought as he gathered in some winnings, leaving one guinea counter in play.

The lady wouldn't be a Cave for life, however, and a gilded Debenham would survive a brush with muck with little harm. Perhaps, judging by their battle of wills, she might even gain a frisson of illicit pleasure from it.

He'd met that type before and they'd often proved rewarding. . . .

He pulled his mind back to cool analysis.

What would she do? That was the only important point. Would he win the gamble he'd taken tonight, acting on impulse as he so rarely did?

She might be even now complaining of his behavior. No matter how grateful the Debenham family was for his testimony, they'd not embrace a man who had assaulted their daughter. Instead of allies, they would become enemies.

It could even lead to a duel, and the obvious champion was her brother.

Dare Debenham had been changed by his experiences, but if he'd been shattered, he'd mended into a stronger person. The facile glitter had burned away to reveal true steel.

Not a man Darien would choose as an enemy, and definitely not one he wanted to face in a duel, if only because he was damn tired of death. In any case, this was not a matter that required death.

And all because he'd been swept off course and out of sense by a clear-eyed, arrogant, courageous, and fiercely passionate young woman.

"More brandy, sir?"

Darien started and nodded at the servant. The free brandy served here was foul stuff, but he needed something strong and he had the head for it. He knocked back half the glass, welcoming the harsh burn, and glanced at his card. An ace. He drew but was beaten by the dealer's eight. He still had most of his counters in front of him, and played another.

There was a worse possibility.

If Debenham wasn't up to a duel, the next in line would be the lady's cousin, young Cully. In many ways Cully Debenham reminded Darien of his brother, Frank. The same smiling zest for life, unquenched by war, and the same belief in fundamental goodness.

Cully had been someone else Darien had avoided tonight. The lad had an unfortunate case of hero worship.

Darien vowed to flee the country before facing Cully at pistol point.

But this made him realize that he'd better get home to be available if a challenge came, and able to take whatever action was necessary. He rose, only realizing when the dealer urged him to stay that he'd doubled his money.

"The night's young," Darien replied, tossing a handful back to the man. "I'm on to Violet Vane's."

No man could protest his intention to go on to a brothel. He just hoped no one would decide to accompany him. None did. Grigg's was for men who preferred cards to women, except for women who'd combine both.

He walked out into the sort of damp chill

for which England was famous. In Spain and Portugal he'd often missed aspects of England, but never this. It was May, but the night air crept into the bones and felt as if it would grow mold in the lungs. But then, the worthy people in their tall houses were tucked up in their warm beds at this time of night.

Or still dancing at a ball.

What would Lady Theodosia do if he returned and asked her for a dance?

Faint?

Slap his face, more likely.

That made it even more tempting.

He was actually walking in that direction. He shook his head and turned toward Hanover Square. As he walked, he rattled his silver-knobbed cane along railings. His fate for the moment was beyond his control. It now lay in the hands of a lady. Long, elegant hands concealed by gloves. Long red gloves, which suddenly made him think of an army surgeon's hands and arms, crimson up beyond the elbows.

He shuddered at the image. How could those hands, those gloves, have been so damned erotic?

And the pearls.

White, glowing, virginal contrast to bold red.

Was she virgin or wanton? Her courage had seemed the valiance of the young and untried, but her passionate response had knocked him for a loop. But even then, something taut, something frantic, suggested that she had ignited for the first time tonight.

With him.

Lady Theodosia Debenham. Sister to his enemy. Who must hate him now and would hate him more before this was over.

Fate was a wanton, vicious jade.

CHAPTER 7

When the final guests left Yeovil House at dawn, Dare told the family that he'd taken his last opium. Thea knew what this meant. Though he'd tried to hide the agony of past attempts from them, he walked toward torture. And those previous attempts had failed.

This time, she'd make sure he'd succeed. What would she need for instant travel to Somerset?

"I'm going to do it at Brideswell," he added.

"Brideswell?" It had escaped as a gasp before Thea could prevent it. Brideswell in Lincolnshire was the family home of his bride-to-be, Mara St. Bride, but they weren't married yet.

"It's a special place." Dare spoke to her, because she'd let the protest out.

"Of course." What else could she say, but it felt like a betrayal. He would soon marry

61

Mara, but he wasn't hers yet. His true home was still Long Chart. Who would support him at Brideswell?

Then he said, "Mara's coming with me. Her family permits it."

Thea smiled to hide hurt. Her reaction was stupid and unworthy, but the struggle not to show it was agonizing.

She must have failed. As everyone fussed about details, Dare came to her, already looking pale and showing other signs of a lack of his usual dose. "I need Brideswell, Thea."

"Why?"

He found a smile. "Soon you'll visit for the wedding and see for yourself. Feel for yourself."

She wanted to cry, "No, I won't!" like a spoiled child. Instead, she gave him a hug. "I know you'll win this time."

His arms tightened around her. "If not now, never. Thank God for Canem Cave, though I never thought to say that."

She drew back to look at him. "Why not?"

"I'd have expected him to enjoy my discomfort."

All Thea's anxieties came together. "What? Why?"

"Schoolboy nonsense." But then he shook his head. "Not really, but no matter for now." He eased out of her arms. "Whatever his reasons, I'm grateful, so try to be kind to him."

Kind! She clung for a moment, hiding an urge to wild laughter. She'd hoped to talk to Dare about what had happened, even if not in detail, but he was clearly hanging on to control by a thread. She kissed his cheek. "Go. Mara's waiting."

She was rewarded by a smile, but immediately his attention turned to his beloved, to his heart and soul, and Mara St. Bride met his eyes in the same way.

Perhaps Thea's warped feelings were not jealousy over Dare, but envy of that love. She couldn't imagine ever loving so intensely. She wasn't even sure she wanted to. It seemed immoderate. Dangerous. Terrifyingly open to pain.

Like the effect of that man, that kiss.

She shook herself. That had had nothing to do with love!

A footman announced that the coach was at the door, causing a flurry of farewells, embraces, good wishes. Thea went to hug her future sister-in-law. "I know it's not necessary, but I have to say it. Take care of him, Mara."

"Of course," Mara said, but then added softly, "It's probably nothing, Thea, but I'm concerned about Viscount Darien."

Thea came sharply alert. "Why?"

"I don't know." Half or more of Mara's attention was on Dare, and he was leaving the room, glancing back to see where she was. "I sensed *antagonism* in him. And yet he did Dare such a favor. Dare said they had some foolish falling out at school, but that can't explain ill feelings now."

"What do you fear?" Thea asked, going with Mara toward the door.

"I don't know. But . . . your mother is feeling deeply grateful."

"Oh, Lord," Thea groaned.

The Duchess of Yeovil was a wonderfully generous soul — to such an extent that her many causes required four clerks and a secretary to run them. Heaven help them all if the Cave family was the next one.

"Quite," Mara said. "At Brideswell we often don't hear the darkest stories and I thought the Caves merely the usual sort of trouble. Raking, drinking, bullying. But from what I heard last night, well, evil doesn't seem too strong a word. One even committed murder."

"I know."

Dare called Mara's name.

"I must go. My alarms are probably nothing, but . . . be wary, Thea. For all of us."

Thea followed Mara and Dare into the pink dawn and waved until the two coaches were out of sight, sending her most sincere prayers with them. But Mara's words jangled in her mind.

Mara had given that warning without knowing anything of Thea's encounter or the blackmailing bargain, but it made Thea's situation more wide-ranging. Could the man threaten her whole family?

Should she tell her parents?

But she'd made a bargain, and Vile Viscount Darien had done his part.

"You look exhausted, dear," her mother said, putting an arm around her. "Come along to bed."

Thea went. She was too tired to make a rational decision now, and nothing would happen until later.

"Such a night," the duchess said as they reentered the house, "but so wonderful. Everything straightened out, and this time Dare will win, so soon this horrible time will be over."

"It will leave him weak," Thea warned.

"Of course, but he'll soon recover his strength. And then we'll have the wedding. Perhaps two?" Thea's mother gave her a teasing look. "Avonfort, perhaps?"

"No!"

It came out more sharply than she intended, but no wonder her mother shot her a look of surprise. Lord Avonfort was a Somerset neighbor who'd been persistently attentive for over a year now. His home, Avonfort Abbey, was near Long Chart and his sisters were her friends. Thea supposed she would marry him, but she couldn't think of that right now. Besides — she might be betrothed to another!

"If you don't care for him, there are plenty of others," her mother said comfortably. "But you are twenty, and I admit that I've neglected you these past years. Now I can give you all my attention."

Thea escaped to her room.

Heaven help her. She, not Darien, was to be her mother's next project.

Darien stayed in Cave House on Wednesday. No challenge had awaited him when he'd returned last night, but he'd take no comfort from that. Lady Theodosia could well have waited until after the ball to complain of his actions.

If a challenge were to be issued, better it be in private, however, so he stayed in. He had a new problem to consider. In the night, someone had splashed blood on his doorstep. He might not have known about it but for his habit of riding in the early morning, before most fashionable people were about.

He'd left the house as usual by the back, and walked to the mews area that served this terrace. When he'd arrived here a few weeks back, he'd found the Cave section let to others. As he had only one horse at the moment, he'd only reclaimed one box and not bothered to hire a groom.

None of the grooms working in the mews had been particularly welcoming, but one had agreed to care for Cerberus. Darien made sure to visit a couple of times a day to check on the horse and pay his mount some special attention, and he rode him every day. Apart from the pleasure of riding, it was a brief time with untainted affection.

The rides were the best part of his day. He liked riding and he liked morning. Morning presented each day afresh, yesterday's staleness and dissatisfactions washed away, all things possible.

This morning had been particularly lovely and nothing had happened to spoil it, so after his ride, Darien had strolled back to his house the long way, approaching it from the front.

And there, on the step, was a pool of drying blood.

He'd looked around, but whoever had done this was gone.

Hanover Square was still quiet, most servants still abed. He went in quickly and found his domestic staff, the Prussocks, at the kitchen table enjoying tea, bread, and jam. He'd found these three here as caretaking staff and not bothered to replace them yet. They did an adequate job for a man who had no visitors and never entertained, but they were an uncommunicative, unsmiling bunch.

"There's blood on the step," he said. "Has someone been hurt?"

All three — father, mother, and slow-witted daughter — had risen and were now staring at him.

"Blood, milord?" asked Mrs. Prussock. She often spoke for all.

"Never mind. But it needs to be washed off. Now."

"Ellie," said Mrs. Prussock to her daughter. "Off to it."

Lead-footed Ellie grasped the handle of the wooden bucket of water and stumped off with a rag.

"No one's been to the front door yet this morning?" Darien said.

"No, milord. We're just breakfasting. Do you want your breakfast now?"

He ignored that. "Has this happened before?"

More shifty looks. He simply waited. He'd dealt with far worse rascals than these in the army.

"At first," Mrs. Prussock said. "In the days after Mr. Marcus did what he did. Or so I've heard."

He frowned. "You weren't here then?"

"No, milord. We was hired as caretakers when your father died, milord."

He'd assumed they'd been here longer, but of course not. His father, loose screw though he'd been, would have needed better service than this.

"Let me know if anything like this happens again," he commanded. "And yes, breakfast now, please."

He left wondering what it would be like to have a normal household. As pleasant as having a normal family and a normal life, he assumed. And as likely.

The Prussocks had taken on the roles of butler, cook/housekeeper, and maid, but none were trained for their part. Finding better servants to work for a Cave would be difficult, however, so he was thankful for inadequate mercies. They kept the house reasonably clean and tidy and provided plain but edible food, which was all he needed.

He'd made one addition — a valet, necessary to take care of his new wardrobe, which he considered his armor in this battle. Lovegrove was slender, finicky, and skilled. He was also drunk most of the time, but beggars can't be choosers.

As he waited for his breakfast, Darien paced, considering the blood. It had to be a response to his invasion of the inner circles of society, but who would do such a thing or order it done? The Wilmott family, who still had their town house on the opposite side of Hanover Square?

He hadn't known they still spent the season there. He'd assumed they'd shun the place where their daughter came to a violent end in the green and pleasant central gardens. His presence here could be painful, but the empty house was no easier to bear, surely.

Mrs. Prussock bustled in and laid out fried eggs, ham, bread, and coffee. As he ate, Darien couldn't escape thoughts of that crime. He'd been in Spain when Marcus had murdered sixteen-year-old Mary Wilmott, but the news had traveled fast. Darien had been shocked, but not surprised. Marcus had been strange all his life, but untrammeled debauchery had given him the pox at a young age, and it had gone to his brain.

He probably should have been locked up years before the crime, but their father had had the sort of aristocratic arrogance that would admit no fault. No one even knew why Marcus had seized Mary Wilmott, cut her throat and mutilated her, and left her corpse in open view.

No one knew what the young lady had been up to in the gardens at dusk, but that was a question no one asked about the girl who'd come to be known as "Sweet Mary Wilmott," subject of poem and ballad.

Marcus had been easy enough to arrest. He'd left bloody footsteps all the way back to Cave House and been found there, gnawing on one of his bedposts.

It certainly wasn't an event easily forgotten, but Darien hadn't expected this strong a reaction six years after the crime, five years since Marcus's death.

But Mary Wilmott had been one of the ton's own. They did not easily forget or forgive.

But nor did he.

He'd rise even earlier in the future and make sure any further mischief was cleaned away before people were up to see it.

CHAPTER 8

Exhaustion meant Thea didn't lie awake fretting, but when she woke, all her problems rushed back. Her mother, the Cave, the kiss, her promise. Twist her conscience as she might, she couldn't deny that she had made a promise.

Not Rapunzel, she suddenly realized. Rumpelstiltskin.

The young girl's father had boasted that she could spin straw into gold in order to save his life. When she'd been locked away and commanded to do so, her tears of despair had brought a wizened creature who said he would spin straw into gold for her if she promised him her firstborn child. In desperation, the girl agreed and the gold appeared. The king had been so pleased, he married her, and in due course her first child was born.

Had she forgotten, or thought a queen was safe? The little old man returned to claim the baby. When she wept and begged, he granted her three days in which to guess his name. If she failed, he would take the child.

The queen tried every name she could imagine, but couldn't guess the right one. But then one day she heard him singing gleefully about his name, and thus she was saved.

All in all, Thea thought, sitting up in bed, chin on her knees, it was a foolish story, but the lesson was clear — be careful what you promise, because you might have to pay your debts.

Now she had Mara's warning to add to her burdens. Antagonism. That was the word Mara had used, and it resonated with Thea's experience. She'd sensed antagonism in Lord Darien, directed against her and against Dare. But why? Dare was too good-natured to stir such strong feelings, especially back in his youth. Thea's memories of her adored older brother were all laughter and generous high spirits.

Lurking in bed wouldn't solve anything, so Thea climbed out and rang for Harriet, but then she paused, recollecting something that man had said last night. Something sarcastic about how everyone who knew Dare must love him.

But it was *true.*

There was a mystery here, but if there'd been an incident at school, that meant Harrow, and Harrow meant the Company of Rogues. It was almost noon. By the time she'd dressed and breakfasted, it wouldn't be too early for a ridiculously named morning call. She'd visit Nicholas and Eleanor Delaney, for Nicholas was the leader of the Rogues.

Harriet arrived with washing water and breakfast, and Thea asked about the green dress.

"I did my best, milady, but some stains are right in the lace. I did wonder about putting a new panel in the front."

"A good idea. We'll see if the mantua maker has more of the fabric."

May all the problems from last night be as easily solved. Thea wrote a quick note to Eleanor Delaney, sent Harriet to give it to a footman, and then sat to her breakfast.

By the time she was dressed, a reply had come. Eleanor would be pleased to receive her. Thea summoned the town carriage and was soon on her way, Harriet on the opposite seat.

Though Dare had been a member of the Company of Rogues and Thea had enjoyed plenty of stories about them, she hadn't met many before last night. Simon St. Bride,

Mara's brother, had been Dare's particular friend and had visited Long Chart on numerous occasions. He, too, was in Town, but he'd been in Canada for years and she didn't know him well enough to be comfortable.

Nicholas Delaney, however, had a house within riding distance of Long Chart. During Dare's recovery, he'd visited often, and Thea could almost count him as a friend. Almost, because he was an unusual, often perplexing person. She'd seen less of Eleanor, for Eleanor had been pregnant for most of last year, but Thea felt comfortable enough with her to discuss this matter.

Thea wasn't surprised when Nicholas answered the door himself in his shirtsleeves — he was notoriously informal, despite being the brother of an earl.

"Thea," he said, with all appearance of delight, but added, "You'll have to excuse me. We're in the midst of preparations to return to Somerset. I'll take you up to Eleanor."

Thea sent Harriet to the servants' quarters and followed Nicholas, but she was startled to be taken to their bedroom. Eleanor greeted her warmly, but she was sitting in a rocking chair feeding her baby beneath a large silk shawl. The occasional slurping noises were disconcerting.

Eleanor sent her maid off for tea. "I do apologize. But when a baby needs to be fed it is most insistent about it."

"I suppose so," Thea said, taking a chair, not knowing where to look. Eleanor matched her husband in being simply dressed. Her long auburn hair was still loose, tied back only with a ribbon.

"You must all be very happy with last night's success," Eleanor said, as if nothing was unusual.

"Yes, of course, though we won't completely relax until we hear Dare has won the battle."

"He will this time. Especially with Mara by his side."

"I pray so."

That wasn't what Thea wanted to talk about, but in this situation she was tongue-tied.

Eleanor drew her baby out from beneath the shawl and put him to her shoulder, rubbing his back. Thea couldn't help but smile.

"He looks so stuffed and content."

"Like a drinker rolling home from the tavern, Nicholas says. Cross-eyed and burping." Still rubbing the limp baby's back, Eleanor asked, "Did you have some particular reason for calling, Thea?"

Both Delaneys tended to directness. Thea plunged into her concern. "It's about Lord Darien. Before Mara left this morning, she shared some concerns. He did Dare a kindness, but she sensed antagonism between the two men, and Dare mentioned some incident at school. She wondered about his motives."

"Ah." Eleanor brought the baby down into her arms. He was sound asleep. "Nicholas can tell that tale better than I. Would you ring the bell, please?"

Thea did so and a nursemaid appeared almost immediately, clearly to take the baby. Eleanor kissed him and passed him over. "And ask Mr. Delaney to join us, please."

The tea arrived before he did and Eleanor moved to the sofa and poured.

"Do you know Viscount Darien?" Thea asked as she took her cup and saucer. She badly wanted other impressions.

"Not at all. He's been in the army until recently, I gather, and out of sight since selling out."

"The family reputation is awful."

"Yes, but mine isn't sterling. My brother is deplorable, but thankfully abroad."

Thea sipped. Had she landed among Darien's allies? Had he been a Rogue? No. She might not know them all, but she knew their names, and he'd denied it himself. Sharply.

Nicholas Delaney came in, looking curious.

"Thea's wondering about the ill feeling between Darien and Dare," Eleanor told him.

"Ah. Ironic that their names are now so similar when their natures are so different." He took a cup of tea and sat. "May I ask why, Thea?"

"Mara St. Bride shared some concerns and warned me to be careful."

He took a biscuit off the plate. "She's very astute. All the St. Brides are, despite their famous blissful nature. Bliss requires intelligent wariness. Yes, there was a problem, but it was a long time ago."

"Can you tell me what happened?"

He thought about it, and then said, "Horatio Cave arrived at Harrow with every handicap possible except being a milksop. That, he certainly was not. But he was rough in manners and poorly schooled. I doubt he'd ever had friends of his own age and station, and quite simply, he didn't fit in. Add to that his natural reaction to every affront was to fight, tooth and claw."

"Poor boy," Eleanor said.

Thea sipped tea. The poor boy was a man

now, clearly over any such problems.

"He did a great deal of damage?" Thea asked.

"Mostly to himself. Physically, he was very different to the man you see now. He's still not a giant, but back then he could best be described as a runt — short and scrawny. Some thought him easy pickings, but they soon realized their error. He'd learned to fight viciously. Considering his family, one can guess why."

No pity.

"What happened between him and Dare?" Thea demanded. "I need to know."

He gave her a thoughtful look, but didn't balk. "Cave picked a fight with Dare. Needless to say, Dare had done nothing to offend him, but perhaps Cave imagined a slight, or perhaps he chose Dare to represent the whole hated world. By the time they were pulled apart, Dare was well bloodied and Cave had barely a scratch. But then, as you know, Dare never had a fighter's heart."

"That's why we were all concerned by his desire to fight Napoleon."

"Wellington was inspired to give him a job that mostly required riding. He was always a blistering, fearless rider."

"At your suggestion," Eleanor said, startling Thea.

Nicholas brushed it aside. "Via Con, via Hawkinville. Anyway, Dare always turned away anger with a laugh or a joke, and he did so this time. He said, *'Cave canem.'* He meant no ill by it, of course, but other boys took it up. Horatio Cave became Canem Cave, often accompanied by yapping sounds or silly jokes. And then, inevitably, it was translated into English. When someone called him Dog he ripped into such a ferocious fight he broke Derby Trigwell's arm and was expelled."

No pity.

"How sad," Eleanor said.

"For the boy with the broken arm?" Thea asked pointedly.

"For both of them," Eleanor replied. "Didn't you do anything, Nicholas?"

It would seem a strange thing to say except that Thea had grown up with stories of Nicholas Delaney.

"He would have been an ideal candidate for the Rogues, yes," he said, "but we'd agreed twelve was it. Magic number and all that. And he was a year younger. Looking back, I'm sure there were things we could have done to help, but we were schoolboys and mostly absorbed with our own lives. I confess, once poor Dog Cave left school I never gave him a thought."

No pity!

"How it must have festered," Eleanor said. "I remember one school cruelty to this day, and if I met Fanny Millburton I would be hard-pressed to be polite."

"So would you go out of your way to do Fanny Millburton a favor?" Thea asked.

Eleanor looked at her. "I'd like to think so, but I'm not sure."

"What do you suspect, Thea?" Nicholas demanded.

Thea hovered on the brink of telling him everything, but speaking of her promise would make it more real and she knew now that she must find a way of wriggling off the poisoned hook. The man might have suffered unkindness, but had clearly been wild and vicious from the cradle.

"My parents are very grateful to Lord Darien and I suspect that was his aim. Mara's warning made me wonder if he means us some harm, and now you tell me he has reason."

"A very convoluted revenge," he pointed out. "Simpler, surely, to let Dare stew in scandal."

Thea considered that. "But that way his situation wouldn't be changed. Lord Darien's, I mean. Last night, the ton showed clearly that they were not willing to accept a

81

Cave in their midst. Perhaps he seeks to change that. My family's support would be powerful."

"The ton at its vicious worst can be worse than any mob," Nicholas agreed. "If he seeks your family's support to overcome that, what harm in it?"

"Once he's gained his end, he might intend some subtle malice."

Nicholas's brows rose. "Been reading Minerva novels, Thea?"

"People do plan and execute evil," she protested.

He instantly sobered. "I apologize. Indeed they do. Eleanor, I fear we're going to have to stay in Town a little longer."

Eleanor sighed, but said, "Yes. You failed to help Dog Cave a decade ago, so now you must make reparation."

"You know me too well."

"Of course, and I agree, except that it's really Dare's job. He harmed him. Without malice, that goes without saying, but he did."

"Dare won't be up to it for some weeks, so I and the others must hold the fort."

"And do what?" Thea asked.

"Put right the wrong. If Darien wants to be accepted in society, we'll make it so."

Just like that. Thea put her cup and saucer

on the table because her hands were trembling with relief. She'd come here for information, but now it seemed she was saved. With the Rogues on his side, including the honorary Rogues like the Duke of St. Raven, plus some assistance from her family, Lord Darien could have no need of a mock betrothal.

What's more, she now had a threat to hang over his head. Pester her and she would tell all, turning all these allies into enemies.

"I gather he's still known as Canem Cave today," Eleanor said to her husband. "Why, if that was the problem?"

"Perhaps he was clever enough to turn it to his advantage."

"Is he clever?"

"Really good officers generally are, and his military reputation is remarkable. So, what's our plan?" He seemed mainly to be consulting the wallpaper. "Darien must have friends from the army, but many will be like him, away from England until recently. We need people who carry weight in the ton."

"That absolves me of duties," Eleanor said.

"Try to hide your glee, my love." Nicholas took Eleanor's hand, perhaps without even realizing it. Thea was a little embarrassed by the physical connection between the couple.

"Good thing the Rogues are already here to support Dare," he carried on. "They'll have to stay a while. The Members of Parliament are stuck anyway as long as the debates go on. We have a lot of firepower, but even so, we can't shove Darien down throats by force. We need to seduce the ladies and convert the men."

"I gather he's handsome," Eleanor said.

"Oh, do you?" Nicholas teased.

"In a threatening sort of way."

"Often the most dangerous with you foolish women. . . ."

In their teasing they were taking something for granted. "But what if he is a true Cave?" Thea asked. "What if he's evil? What if he plans some vile attack on Dare and my family because of a petty incident over ten years gone?"

Nicholas turned to look at her. "Then," he said, as if discussing the weather, "we destroy him."

Thea left the house relieved of some of her burdens, but wondering what force she had unleashed. Against all her will, the story of schoolboy torment had stirred pity for that misfit boy.

She'd never gone to school, and Dare's

stories of Harrow had made it seem like fun. She'd heard enough different versions, however, to know that a boy's school could be hell. Sometimes the boys even rose in armed rebellion against their cruel oppressors. That was why Nicholas Delaney had formed the Company of Rogues.

For protection.

Horatio Cave had lacked all protection.

A runt.

Poorly prepared for school.

Grown up needing to be a vicious fighter.

She hardened her heart. This all made him more of a threat to her, not less.

Thea returned to the house to find a message asking her to visit her mother's boudoir. Fearing bad news about Dare, she shed her outer clothing and hurried. When she passed a certain mirror, however, she paused.

This corridor received little daylight, so it still held the oppressive atmosphere of the night before, but how different she looked. Her periwinkle blue gown rose high in the neck and was edged with a fashionable white ruff. "Head on a plate," Dare had teasingly described the style.

Her hair was dressed in a simple knot without any ornament. Her only jewelry was pearl studs in her ears and a silver and pearl brooch.

And yet she glanced to one side, half expecting the Cave man to be there. It was almost as if his spirit lingered to whisper, like Hamlet's ghost, *"Remember me."*

She hurried on, but some trace of him pursued so that she began to wonder if Lord Darien himself awaited her in her mother's room. This summons wasn't normal, especially in the afternoon. Her mother should be on her usual round of morning calls.

Darien could not possibly have already approached her father to claim betrothal.

Could he?

CHAPTER 9

Thea entered her mother's boudoir braced for trouble, but sunlight shone on elegance and order, and her mother smiled. She was a very ordinary-looking woman for a duchess, of average build and with plain brown hair, but her kindness formed her features into the sort of loveliness that would last her lifetime.

She was sitting at the linen-covered table, china tea service and cups in front of her, and she had a guest, the always composed and elegant Lady Vandeimen. Maria Vandeimen was a distant cousin of her mother's, but she wasn't a common guest for tea.

"Thea," Maria said, smiling, "how lovely you looked last night. That gown was quite wicked."

"You mean my corset," Thea said, kissing Maria's cheek. "I should have changed it when I changed my gown."

"I mean the cut, dear. If I still had a long,

slim figure, I'd order one on the same lines."

There was no trace of regret in her tone. Maria had remarried last year and given birth in February after years of believing herself infertile. She positively glowed.

Thea sat and accepted a cup of tea, wondering what was afoot here. "I hope Georgie's well," she said, sipping.

"In perfect health." Maria happily described her daughter's many charms, but ceased surprisingly quickly. "Enough of that. I came here to talk about Lord Darien."

Thea's cup only rattled a little. "Why?"

"He's a friend of Vandeimen's."

After the first moment, that wasn't surprising. Maria's second husband — scandalously eight years her junior — was a dashing ex-officer. Though Lord Vandeimen was blond and blue-eyed, and had always been a perfect gentleman in Thea's presence, she recognized similarities.

"From the army, I assume?" Thea said.

"Different regiments, but they found common complaint in their names. Van had become Demon Vandeimen in the army, and of course Darien was Mad Dog Cave."

The duchess tut-tutted. "Such unfortunate names. Maria and I are considering what to do for dear Darien. People can be so unkind. Do have one of these lemon cakes, dear. Cook has surpassed herself."

Thea took one, but tried a warning. "He could be a true Cave, Mama."

"Oh, no. They have always been wicked and selfish to the bone. The old Lord Darien would never have stepped out of his way to help someone. No resemblance at all, I assure you."

"He does have the dark looks," Maria said.

"The Vile Viscount wasn't dark," the duchess said.

"No, but Mad Marcus was. That caused much of the trouble last night. If Darien resembled his father, he might not create such alarm."

"But he looks nothing like Marcus," the duchess protested. "He was a bloated monster."

"Not when young. Before the pox set in."

"Maria!" the duchess protested with a flickering look at Thea.

"I know about the pox, Mama," Thea said.

"Oh, dear." The duchess took another cake.

"Why do they have dark eyes and hair?" Thea asked. She knew she shouldn't indulge her curiosity. It was like sneaking out to visit some scandalous locale, and just as dangerous.

"From their mother," the duchess said. "An Italian. Magdalen something, I think. An opera singer. Or an opera dancer."

Thea noted the difference between an artist and a whore. "Was she accepted in society?"

"Oh, no."

"Opera dancer, then."

"I don't know how you young people know about these things," the duchess complained, but then she added, "I suppose we did, too. But Lady Darien might have been a singer. Merely marrying the Vile Viscount would put her beyond the pale, and she was a foreigner as well. One wonders why she married him. He was never handsome and always unfit for decent company. His brother was worse, believe it or not. Richard Cave had to flee the country. Cheating at cards, and then he killed someone. Not like Mary Wilmott. Some person similar to himself in some back alley. I believe he fled right into the French Revolution and ended up guillotined, which could be seen as some sort of divine justice."

"And wasn't a previous viscount called 'Devil'?" Maria asked. "It really is a sorry saga and won't be easy to overcome, especially with Sweet Mary Wilmott hanging around Darien's neck like the albatross."

"Then we must cut it off," the duchess said. "Such a silly poem. Opium, they say."

She fell silent, and Thea knew she wasn't thinking of Coleridge's "Rime of the Ancient Mariner," but about Dare. It was only afternoon. They wouldn't be at Brideswell yet, but the effects of being without the drug would be biting him. At his worst, in the early days, he'd been tormented by wild visions.

The duchess shook herself. "I'm sure Darien is an excellent man. His military record is exemplary."

Maria coughed.

"And what does that mean?" the duchess demanded.

"We have to face facts, Sarah. He was dashing, daring, and often very effective, but he was no more a pattern card of military propriety than Van. When Wellington tagged him Mad Dog he wasn't being entirely complimentary."

"He did us a kindness, Maria, and we will be kind in return. I assume you and Vandeimen are willing to help?"

"Of course. But it must be approached carefully."

The duchess refilled cups. "Surely the endorsement of people such as ourselves will be sufficient."

"You are above all doubt, Sarah, but I, of course, am a foolish woman under the sway of a wild, but handsome, young man." It was said dryly and with amusement, but it was true.

Thea stirred sugar into her tea. "The Rogues will help. I visited the Delaneys and they said so."

"Good news," her mother said, but frowned a little. "Why rush off to visit there, dear?"

"Because of something Mara said. She detected antagonism between Dare and Darien, and Dare told her there'd been a quarrel between them at Harrow."

"Darien quarreled with Dare?" Maria asked. "That's quite an achievement."

Thea related what she'd been told, and her mother frowned.

"That was not well done of Dare, and he should certainly have repaired the damage. He could have invited the poor boy to Long Chart in the summer."

That was an image to alarm Thea.

"However," her mother continued, "if the Rogues are on our side, success is assured. They can recruit from such a wide range of ladies and gentlemen that no one will detect bias. Sporting men, politicians, diplomats, patrons of the arts and sciences. . . ."

"Don't many people know about the Rogues?" Thea asked.

"Not in that way. That there was a school-boy group, yes. That they are closely bound still, no. And then there are the connections, like St. Raven, Vandeimen, and Hawkin-ville."

"How clever," Maria approved. "It truly will look like an unorganized approval. And Van says many military men will support him."

Thea had to attempt some sort of warning. "But what if Lord Darien has some ulterior motive? Some ill intent?"

"Because of a schoolboy quarrel?" her mother asked.

"Hurts can linger."

"Not through ten years of war," the duch-ess said. "What do we know to Darien's discredit? Not his family, himself."

He assaults women when he catches them alone.

"Mad Dog?" Maria suggested.

"Darien showed absolutely no trace of insanity or rabies."

Thea stared. "You met him, Mama?"

"Of course I did, dear. Would I not seek out our deliverer? Caught him at the door and cried over him, I confess, which drove him out into the night. Very handsome," she said, taking a piece of candied ginger and biting off a bit. "Not in the usual way, but oh, those dark eyes, and such *vigor.* Quite devastating." She licked her lips.

She was doubtless only licking away some sugar, but Thea felt as if she should give her mother a sharp lecture on wisdom and decorum.

She must have showed something, for her mother's eyes twinkled. "Age doesn't blind us to a tasty gallant, does it, Maria?"

"Obviously not, as I married one. But I must point out that you have twenty years on me, Sarah."

"Do I really? I suppose I must." The duchess took consolation in more ginger. "Perhaps the simplest solution is to find him the right bride. One of impeccable reputation, like you, Maria. No more opera anythings."

"An English lady of good birth?" Maria mused. "With an impeccable reputation, but not in a situation to be too choosy." She turned. "Thea —"

"Not me!" Thea protested, straightening with a start.

"Of course not," Maria said, laughing. "You can be as choosy as you wish. I was only going to ask you for suggestions. You know the younger ladies."

"Wouldn't a sensible widow be better?"

the duchess asked.

"As I was?"

"You saw a tasty morsel and gobbled him up, Maria. Sense didn't come into it. I don't suppose Vandeimen minded, but Darien might not want an older bride. Still, someone languishing unwed at, say, twenty-four or -five? Perhaps someone who's given up coming to Town in the season. . . ."

"You're running ahead as usual, Sarah," Maria said. "Before promoting any match, before doing much at all, we must be certain that Lord Darien is suitable for polite society. We know little of him and he is a Cave."

"But Dare . . ."

"One act does not an angel make, and if we endorse him, our reputations will be tied to his."

"What of Vandeimen, then?" the duchess challenged. "You said he wanted to help Darien."

"Van vouches for him in general, but even he admits that army values are different. Extremes that are acceptable among men at war are not comfortable in the drawing room."

"He helped Dare," the duchess said mutinously, "and we must be kind in return."

Thea took a piece of sweet ginger for

herself. Mara's warning had been valid. Lord Darien was now one of her mother's causes and she'd hear no argument against him.

"Even without that," her mother went on, "Darien would deserve our kindness as a veteran of the war. We've seen how hard it is for some young men to settle into peace. Only consider your husband, Maria. A hero, but well on the way to ruin before you took him in hand. You can't deny it."

"I would never attempt to. It's possible Darien is a similar case."

"Or is no case at all. I'm sorry to put it this way, Maria, but Darien has not, to my knowledge, fallen into deep drinking and gaming."

"But as I pointed out, Sarah, we do not know enough about him to be sure."

Thea wondered if they were about to come to blows.

But her mother said, "I've already set Mr. Thoresby to investigate."

"Ah, then," Maria said, relaxing.

Thea relaxed, too. Her mother's secretary was highly efficient and also protective of her good nature and generosity. He'd unearth all Darien's sins.

"He won't find anything to Darien's discredit," the duchess stated. "Cully idolizes him. Perhaps we should invite him to dine."

"Cully?" Thea asked, confused.

"Darien, dear. A carefully chosen list of guests. Bring him into contact with the right people, ones who'll value his army achievements and have power to sway opinion. The duke will drop words of approval around the clubs. I hope Vandeimen will do the same, Maria?"

"Of course, but don't race ahead, Sarah. Wait for Mr. Thoresby's report."

"Oh, very well. I'm sure he'll have a preliminary report in days."

Maria rose, pressing once at her prominent breasts. "I must return to Georgie."

"You should have brought her," the duchess said, rising to kiss her cheek. "I adore babies."

"I will next time," Maria said and left.

"So lovely to see Maria happy. She never made a fuss, but her first husband was a sad disappointment, and not just in the matter of babies. Of course we worried about Vandeimen, but he has turned out excellently. As will Darien." She turned an attentive eye on Thea. "You said you weren't ready to settle on one of your suitors yet, dear?"

"No, Mama," Thea said, heading off

matchmaking on her behalf.

"Good. Then you'll be free to support Darien." Thea's expression must have been revealing. "What's the matter, dear? Does he frighten you?"

"No. I mean, I don't know. I've never even met him," Thea lied.

"Really? You seem to have such strong opinions. I assumed you encountered him last night."

"I encountered his reputation. Everywhere."

"What a strange mood you're in today. Overtired, perhaps? All I'm asking is that you occasionally let Lord Darien give you his arm, perhaps sit by him and engage him in conversation. Partner him in a dance without looking as if you expected to be devoured. Is that too much to ask?"

"No," Thea said. After all, she was supposed to be *betrothed* to the man. How had she ended up in this fix?

"You have such an excellent reputation for virtue and good sense that it will convince people immediately. Now, when?" The duchess opened her appointment book. "Almack's tonight. No hope of getting Darien in there yet."

Yet? Thea wanted to laugh.

"Lady Wraybourne's musicale on Thursday. Very select. That could be difficult. . . ."

"And you intend to wait for Mr. Thoresby's report, Mama," Thea reminded her.

"I'm sure he'll have something by then. We need to act speedily to turn the tide. Once people get fixed ideas they become difficult. Only minor commitments on Friday." She made a firm note.

Thea didn't protest anymore. That gave her three days before she need meet the man again. Unless he brashly invaded, demanding his bride.

She should try to meet him sooner and explain all the reasons why the betrothal was unnecessary, but she could no more seek him out than she would seek out the plague.

CHAPTER 10

By noon, Darien had settled to the never-ending paperwork, secure that Lady Theodosia hadn't complained of his behavior. At least there would be no challenge. She was probably running in circles, however, trying to find a way out of her promise.

He smiled at that. *Oh, no, my lady. You are mine.*

Wicked to enjoy the thought, but if so, ledgers and accounts were his penance. This wasn't work he'd been trained for, but he believed in understanding things for which he was responsible. The hollow rap of the door knocker brought him out of a particularly bewildering column of numbers.

Had he relaxed too soon?

He listened to Prussock's heavy footsteps trudging toward the front door, faint voices, and then footsteps coming his way. A knock.

"Enter."

Prussock did so. "A gentleman to see you,

milord," he said, disgruntled. Clearly visitors were an imposition.

Darien rose, pulling himself into readiness. "Who?"

"A Lord Vandeimen, milord."

The wash of relief blanked his mind for a moment, but then the novelty of the situation struck. Van would be his first guest. Where should he receive him?

The reception room and drawing room were still under Holland covers, as was the sitting room that was part of his father's suite. He'd refused to use those rooms. He'd also rejected the large bedroom that had been Marcus's, even though every trace of the past had been removed.

As a result he was using the third bedroom. It was modest in size and he'd done nothing to fancy it up. Before he could decide, Van appeared in the doorway, lean, blond, and with the long scar down his cheek. "Thinking how to have me thrown out?" he asked, with a smile but not entirely in jest.

Darien laughed and went forward to shake his hand. "Only where to put you. I'm virtually camping out here, but I have supplies. Ale, wine, tea, coffee?"

"Coffee, thank you," Van said, looking around the office.

Darien sent the curious Prussock off with the order.

"I know — Spartan. When my father died, the executor removed all the viscountcy's papers that were here. I haven't bothered to get most of them back. There were some books, but those that weren't out-of-date almanacs and such were thoroughly depraved. I had the Prussocks burn the lot."

"What're the odds they sold them for a tidy price?"

Darien grinned. "A dead certainty. It's good to see you, Van."

Van smiled, but said, "Then I could ask why I haven't seen you sooner. Until I heard you were at the Yeovil ball last night, I didn't know you were in Town."

"Settling in," Darien offered as a vague excuse. "Shall we attempt the drawing room? There is one, but it's still under wraps."

"Then why disturb the shrouds?" Van took one of the saggy-seat chairs by the empty fireplace. "How are you?"

Darien took the other chair, beginning to be wary. Van would be here out of friendship, no question, but he could still be on business connected to last night. Van had his own connection to the Rogues.

"Well enough, all things considered," he

answered. "And you? Marriage suiting you? And fatherhood?" Darien had been astonished last year to hear that Van had married a wealthy, and older, widow. Widow of a merchant, no less. But he'd inherited estates in even worse state than his own.

"Excellently," Van said. "I recommend both."

Before Darien could continue with such distractions, Van asked, "Did you deliberately avoid me last night?"

"Direct and to the point as always. Of course I did. I was the leper at the feast and I'd no mind to contaminate you."

"I never thought you quixotic. But if you were a leper, you're cured. You're the Duchess of Yeovil's darling. Except that you didn't linger to be crowned with glory."

"Put her nose out of joint, have I?"

Van's brows twitched. "Only puzzled her. Why?"

"I don't care to be blubbered over."

"What precisely is going on?"

Darien was tempted to tell Van everything, but only for a moment. He truly didn't want any friend tangled in this, and there might be aspects that he didn't want Van to know about at all.

"For my sins, I'm Viscount Darien. When the regiment ended up back in England and enforcing the Riot Act on a bunch of desperate Lancashire weavers, I realized I was serving no useful purpose in the army. I hoped to be more useful by managing my estates, sorting out the finances, and deciding what to do with it all. Including this damned place."

"It seems a perfectly normal house."

"The hell it is. It's Mad Marcus Cave's lair."

"Good Lord, I suppose it is. Sell it?"

"It's been available for sale or lease for over a year."

"Not part of the entail, then?"

"There is none."

Prussock came in, carrying a tray bearing a tall china coffeepot and other necessities. There was even a plate of biscuits of some sort. Interesting, as Darien had never seen a biscuit here before. He wasn't particularly fond of sweet foods so he hadn't missed them.

He should probably scrutinize Mrs. Prussock's expenditures, especially on the servants' food, but that seemed low on the list. If they required some indulgences to stay on here, that would be cheap at the price.

When coffee was served and Prussock left, Van said, "So there was actually something of value to inherit. You did better than I there."

Darien relaxed into safe subjects. Van might even have useful experience of property law and management. "Astonishing, isn't it? Some of the more valuable items have been sold over the years, but the three estates are intact with only small mortgages. They've been poorly managed, but they bring in a quarterly income that exceeds the essential outgoings, which is more than I expected. Your family's estates were in terrible shape?"

Van smiled wryly. "Drowning in debt. I solved my problems by marrying money. You might want to consider it."

Darien laughed. "What heiress would marry a Cave? I'd find it hard enough to find a healthy, sane female of any kind."

"That's nonsense. . . ." But then Van seemed to accept the truth. "Then last night was fortunate. With the Debenhams' patronage you'll soon be in better shape. Fighting off the ambitious young ladies, in fact. With a title, you'll be like a ten-pointer in stag-hunting season."

Darien laughed. "Is that supposed to encourage me?" He saw another chance to deflect the conversation. "Done any hunting since you got back?"

"Spent a few weeks in Melton over the winter. It's become a world all of its own."

They talked a while about the mecca of fox hunting, making vague plans for the next season. Then Van took another biscuit and asked, "Why did you speak up on Dare's behalf last night?"

Darien recognized that they'd arrived at the subject that had brought Van here, but why?

"Is it so surprising?" he countered.

"Had the impression you hated his guts. In Brussels you avoided him whenever you could."

Darien had hoped he'd hidden his feelings better back then. "We didn't get along at school, and I wanted to avoid discord. With the battle coming."

"We were all trying to be cheerful, weren't we? Sucking life's pleasures while we could. Dare was good at that. What *did* lie between you?"

"Old story."

Van's look was searching, but he didn't insist. "Generous of you to go out of your way to help him, then. It did help. He's off now to stop opium for good, and the fewer burdens he carries the better."

Darien wanted to say something sour, but he'd known other men left with that demon on their backs after lengthy pain. "I hope he wins."

Van nodded. "You have a fight on your hands, too. You want to be accepted in London society?"

"Don't I deserve to be?"

"Of course." But Van's expression didn't deny the challenge. "How can we help?"

"We?" Darien asked.

"Maria and I. You must come over soon. She's keen to meet you."

Darien doubted that. "Not yet. I appreciate it, truly, but I have few enough friends. I'll not embarrass them."

"Instead, you'll insult them? God knows what our social commitments are — women's work — but come to dinner next Wednesday. In the meantime, we'll support you at any public event."

"Your wife —"

"Will agree."

"Have her so firmly under your thumb, do you?"

Van laughed. "You have no idea how absurd that is. She's already agreed to do anything she can. Suggested it, in fact."

"Perhaps she doesn't understand. She's a merchant's widow, isn't she? A foreign merchant."

Van laughed again, throwing his head

back. "You really have no idea, do you? Maria, my lad, was born a Dunpott-Ffyfe. That may mean nothing to you, but the very top of the trees, I assure you. She's cousin to the Duchess of Yeovil and linked on the family tree to just about anyone else of importance, including, I gather, the royalty of at least four countries. She's over at Yeovil House now, weaving plans."

Darien went cold. Van's wife was cousin to Lady Theodosia Debenham's mother? And they were all three in the middle of a web of almost limitless social power? The discovery was like charging down on a vulnerable troop of soldiers and having the entire enemy army come over the crest of a hill.

"I've assured Maria that you're a sound 'un, top to toe," Van said.

Darien put down his cup. "You sound as if you have doubts."

Van's eyes were steady. "No, but you're up to something."

"I merely wish to be accepted in society as a reasonably normal human being."

"Then there should be no difficulty. Leave it to the women. That's my advice." Van rose. "I have an appointment, but Maria will come up with the right invitations for you to accept. Routs and such, I suspect.

They're just a matter of entering the house, greeting a few people, and leaving. You'll have cards for those."

"I do. I'm surprised to receive invitations of any kind."

Van waved a hand. "There are all kinds of arcane rules, but all peers of the realm are invited to any gathering that can't claim to be select. Then there's the theater and perhaps some exhibitions. Being seen with Maria will carry weight."

"It's very kind of you," Darien said, trying to decide if he should accept this sort of help.

"Do you still box?" Van asked.

"Why? Itching to fight me?"

"Always," Van said with a smile. "But it's an activity where you'll mingle with some of the men. Friday afternoon? We could go to Jackson's."

"I'd like that."

Van grasped Darien's arm briefly. "It's good to be back together, Canem. And this time with death unlikely in the near future."

Darien showed Van out, hoping that was true.

He was warmed by friendship but concerned about the new alignment of the chessboard. Three queens in play, and they could be three Fates, deciding if he would live or die.

A moment's consideration told him that he could no more affect that than he could affect the Fates, so he returned to the office and the incomprehensible ledgers. He'd not completed the comparison of two pages before there was another knock.

What now?

Something normal this time — Prussock brought the afternoon post. Darien scanned the three letters, hoping one was from Frank. No. One from his solicitor, another from his new agent at his Warwickshire estate, Stours Court, and a third with no indication of the sender.

He snapped the seal and unfolded the paper to reveal an enclosure — a printed sheet of some sort. When he unfolded that, he found a cheap print of a satirical cartoon, the sort of thing displayed row on row in any printer's shop. He knew this one, however. He'd received another copy, also anonymously, in France within a week of the deaths of his father and brother last year.

In neat engraving, two rotund men sprawled upon a hillside with the mouth of hell open below them. Imps had hold of their booted feet to drag them down to where flames, Lucifer, and a bloated monster of a man awaited.

In case anyone missed the points, the monster was labeled "Mad Marcus Cave" and the two men were labeled "The Unholy Christian Cave" and "Vile Viscount Darien." From thunderclouds above, God hurled a thunderbolt from each hand, with the captioned word, large and bold, *"Cave!"*

At the bottom, the picture was titled *The Wrath of God.*

"Well," he muttered to the sender, "and damn you to hell, too."

The cartoon was accurate in the essentials. His father, the sixth Viscount Darien, and his other older brother, the very unholy Christian Cave, had been found dead on moors near Stours Court. They'd been out shooting and were killed during a thunderstorm.

When he'd heard the news Darien hadn't felt a twinge of grief, but he'd wished they'd died less obtrusively. He wished it even more now. Marcus's foul crime had been six years ago and he'd been dead for five, but the Wrath of God had occurred only last year.

Was this cartoon being reprinted and displayed again? At whose instigation? As he crushed the image in his fist, the knocker hammered again. "God Almighty! What now?" he exclaimed, rising to his feet. Bad things, he remembered, came in threes.

He strode to the door to meet his fate, but it opened to show Prussock again, looking even crosser. "You have a guest, milord," he accused.

"You mean a visitor, Prussock."

"No, milord. The gentleman says he has come to stay."

"Who —"

But the gentleman in question appeared behind the butler, large, round, beaming, and as always resembling a six-foot-tall cherub. "Nice house, Canem," said Pup Uppington, erstwhile lieutenant in Darien's regiment. Darien stared, wondering what he'd done to deserve this.

Pup had been christened Percival Arthur Uppington by parents who'd hoped for a mighty warrior. When he'd turned out to be short of a full dozen they'd sent him into the army anyway. By some miracle he'd survived long enough to make it from cornet to lieutenant, being passed around regiments until he'd landed, confused but willing, under Captain Cave's command.

It had seemed that the whole army had agreed that Pup fit beautifully there, by name if for no other reason. He'd acquired the nickname "Pup" in school, but the prospect of making him Canem's Pup had been too much for anyone to resist.

That might have been why Darien hadn't tried to shuffle him off, and why he'd kept Pup alive over the Pyrenees, through France and the false peace, and even through Waterloo. The unfortunate consequence was that Pup was as devoted as a puppy. Darien had thought he'd shed him when Pup had inherited a godfather's money late last year, but Pup had stayed in the army, devoted as always.

When Darien himself had sold his commission, he'd assumed that would sever the cord, especially as Pup had left at the same time to claim his modest fortune. What in Hades was he doing here?

"Thank you, Prussock," Darien said, rather dazedly.

When the butler stepped to the side and worked around Pup to leave, he revealed an astonishing waistcoat curving over Pup's belly, one composed of blue and yellow paisley. Pup's clothing was all disastrously in the absolutely latest style, including collar points that rose over his ears and a mass of cravat at the front that was probably supposed to be something fanciful like the waterfall knot, but reminded Darien of a cauliflower.

"What are you doing here, Pup?"

"Fancied a bit of London," the young man replied. "Thought, Canem has a house. No wife, no family. Must want some company." His beam showed his certainty of doing a saintly deed.

Yes, indeed. Trouble did come in threes.

"You won't like it here, Pup. I'm persona non grata."

"Persona what?"

"Not welcome. No invitations. No parties. No anything." Hell, he was starting to talk like him. "You'll be more comfortable at an inn. Or a hotel," he quickly amended. The restrained propriety of a hotel would be much safer.

Pup, loose, unaccompanied in London.

Double hell.

"This is fine, Canem. Better than many billets we've had, eh?"

Why the devil hadn't he let Pup drown in the Loire when he'd had the chance? Darien was assembling new arguments when there was another knock.

"Come!" he yelled. This was against the rules. There couldn't be *four.*

Prussock bore a single letter — on the salver this time, and with an air of portent. "From the Duchess of Yeovil!" he declared, loud enough for the residents next door to hear.

Darien took the letter, braced for the judgment of the Fates. He snapped the large crested seal and unfolded the expensive paper — to find a warmly phrased thank-you for his assistance to her son.

Not four. Instead, the first step to victory.

"Duchess, eh?" Pup chortled. "Knew you were funning about grata stuff! Canem Cave, after all. Welcome everywhere! Which room shall I have?"

Perhaps it was the sweetness of the minor victory, or simply that he couldn't toss the moonling out to fend for himself in one of the wickedest cities in the world, but Darien didn't struggle. Pup could have Marcus's old room. His innocent cheer might fumigate it and scare off the ghosts. He carried Pup's valise upstairs while the young man shouldered his trunk without strain.

"No valet, Pup?"

"Had one. Frightened me."

"Use mine while you're here. He's not frightening, but he does drink."

As he put Pup's valise down in the room, an idea stirred. Was it possible to hire the equivalent of a lady's companion for a man? Young men traveling for their education had bear-leaders to guide them and keep them out of harm. Why not a combination of valet and tutor to guide Pup through life?

115

Have to be just the right person. Someone who wouldn't take advantage.

Van might know. Or his Fate-full wife.

He turned to leave, but Pup said, "So, what'll we do now?"

"I'm busy, Pup. Lots of paperwork with a title."

"Tonight, then. I want to visit a London brothel, Canem. The *best* brothel in London."

Darien closed his eyes briefly. "We'll go out and see the sights," he promised and escaped.

He stopped by the drawing room. At this rate, he might need it. He raised one white cotton cover and saw an old-fashioned heavy sofa. Beneath the cloth on the floor was an adequate carpet. The walls were painted a rather depressing buff, but probably with minimum work the room could be usable.

He wondered when this room had indeed last been used. Hard to imagine his father hosting a drawing room affair, and his mother had stopped coming to London early in her married life, unwilling to fight the arctic ton. He himself had never come here. Before going to school, he'd been trapped at Stours Court.

His grandmother? Equally unlikely. Devil

Darien's wife had sued for separation on the grounds of intolerable cruelty, and got it. So her rule here could only have been in the early years of that marriage, long, long ago.

He wondered about the shrouded pictures on the walls and pulled off one cloth. A gloomy landscape with towering mountains and small figures. Another revealed a blank-faced woman in the fashion of the last century. Probably Devil's wife, before escaping hell.

Was there a picture of his mother here? He'd never seen one and his own memory of her was faint. He pulled off more shrouds and found a portrait of his father.

It was a reasonably good oil of a coarse-featured man who looked to be in his thirties. It had probably been painted when he'd inherited the title, long before he married. If the artist had been a flatterer, God help them all.

Even then, the Vile Viscount's heavy face had been blotched and ruddy, his nose bloated, his brown hair thin. Chins hung over a sloppily tied neckcloth and his round belly strained the buttons of a plain waistcoat. All the same, he sat straddle-legged and confident of his power.

The image resembled the older man

Darien remembered, including the slack, reddish lips and pouched, cruel eyes — eyes that seemed to look at him now and say, *Think you're better than me, lad? You're a Cave, too, and no one will ever forget it.*

"Who's that?"

Pup's voice startled Darien. Of course he'd come to find him. Would he know a moment's peace?

"You don't see a resemblance?" he asked.

Pup walked to stand in front of the picture. "Of who? Bit of the regent, perhaps. Remember, when he reviewed the regiment last year?"

Darien laughed aloud. Pup might be good to have around after all. He found a sturdy chair beneath one cloth, carried it over, and with Pup's help unhooked the heavy painting.

That revealed a square of clear yellow paint behind.

Let that be a good sign.

He carried the picture into his father's old rooms and shut the door on it. Pup was hovering, looking tail-waggingly keen to do more furniture moving.

"Have to work," Darien said, and escaped back to his office.

All the same, he felt lighter than he had in eons. Van, the duchess's letter, and even Pup contributed. Exasperating as Pup was, he was the antithesis of everything the Cave name stood for. But then Darien remembered the blood on the doorstep and *The Wrath of God.* Cave House was no place for any innocent. He'd have to sort out Pup's situation soon.

When he sat to his ledgers and leases again, however, his mind wouldn't stick to them. He sat back and reviewed.

The duchess's letter showed that Lady Theodosia hadn't told her mother what had happened. Therefore, she must be willing to go through with the bargain. He hadn't been at all sure she would. Especially after that kiss.

So, he even had something to look forward to — his next encounter with the Great Untouchable.

He laughed at that name. It was as stupid as Mad Dog Cave.

CHAPTER 11

Thea spent the rest of Wednesday fearing a Cave invasion and, against logic, worried that she'd encounter the man at the Almack's assembly. Of course, even he couldn't bully his way past the formidable patronesses, so she flung herself into the delights of a normal evening.

She chatted with friends and danced every dance, and Lord Avonfort proposed. It was the fifth time, and for the fifth time she put him off, but she was in such a good mood that she might have accepted him if not for the Cave business. She wasn't going to betroth herself to the Vile Viscount, but promising to marry someone else right now would be a bit much.

For some reason, Avonfort chose this occasion to persist.

"Why not, Thea? You know we're ideally suited."

"Yes," she said honestly, for she did.

He was a handsome, brown-haired man of twenty-eight and generally acknowledged as one of the most elegant dressers in the ton. He had a lovely house and estate not far from Long Chart. She'd known him all her life, and liked his mother and two sisters. His youngest sister, now Lady Kingstable, was a particular friend.

"I can't make such a commitment yet, Avonfort. Dare —"

"He himself is engaged to marry, Thea, so he can hardly object if you do the same."

"That's not what I mean. It's simply that I need some calm before making important decisions."

"How much time?" he demanded — rather imperiously, she thought.

She wanted to snap, *As much time as I want,* but instead she said, "Six weeks," the term Lord Darien had hung over her head. No matter what happened, in six weeks she'd be free.

"Six weeks!" he protested. "That's the whole season."

"And I want to enjoy the whole season. We'll talk more at Long Chart in the summer."

He frowned, but she saw him take that as a guarded promise. He was probably correct, but it annoyed her. It also made her even more determined to sort out her situation with the Vile Viscount.

On Thursday morning, she asked her mother about Mr. Thoresby's report, but it hadn't appeared yet. In case the Vile Viscount invaded, she went to visit Maddy.

Her cousin was only just out of bed and still in her nightclothes, but she was bright-eyed, with only one subject on her mind. "Have you seen Lord Darien yet?"

Shedding her outer clothing, Thea lied by instinct. "No."

"I haven't either, but last night Caroline Camberley said he's Conrad to the very inch! Have some chocolate." She shouted for her maid to find another cup.

"Conrad? Conrad who?"

"The Corsair!"

"Oh, Byron," Thea said, taking a seat. Lord Byron's dramatic poem, *The Corsair,* had been all the rage a while back. "In what way?"

"In manner, for one thing." Maddy had the slim volume to hand and turned to a marked page. "Listen! *'That man of loneliness and mystery, / Scarce seen to smile, and seldom heard to sigh.'* Isn't that wonderful?"

It resonated, but Thea said, "He sounds very disagreeable."

"You have no romance in your soul. I will

die if I don't meet him, but he doesn't seem to be going anywhere. Mama's saying he'll be thrown out if he dares."

It couldn't be a secret, so Thea said, "Mother is planning his social reinstatement, so you'll probably have many chances."

"Oh, wonderful!" Maddy moved on to another passage. *" 'What is that spell, that thus his lawless train / Confess and envy, yet oppose in vain? / What should it be, that thus their faith can bind? / The power of thought — the magic of the mind!'* The magic of the mind," she repeated, clutching the book to her breasts. "Imagine being powerless before a man's demanding will."

"Absolutely horrid," Thea stated.

"Thea, you're impossible."

The maid returned with a cup and saucer and Maddy poured chocolate. "A pity he's ugly."

"Darien? I wouldn't say . . ." Thea stopped herself and Maddy didn't notice her slip.

"Conrad!" Maddy recited from memory. *" 'Unlike the heroes of each ancient race, / Demons in act, but Gods at least in face, / In Conrad's form seems little to admire.'* I'd love to meet a god."

Thea sipped her chocolate, struggling not to laugh. "An old man with a white beard?"

"Apollo! Adonis!"

"Neptune with seaweed for hair?"

Maddy threw a cushion at her.

"You can't believe Caroline on anything," Thea said, putting the cushion aside. "But Lord Darien doesn't sound to your taste."

"He has a 'glance of fire,' " Maddy said.

"Lord Darien? How alarming."

"Conrad! From dark eyes. Which Darien does have. I must meet him soon. Promise, Thea, if you hear he is to be at any event, alert me!"

"Really, Maddy, he's best left alone." Thea grabbed the book. Like everyone else, she knew the poem almost by heart and it only took a moment to find the passage.

There was a laughing devil in his sneer,
That raised emotions of both rage and
    fear;
And where his frown of hatred darkly fell,
Hope withering fled — and mercy sighed
    farewell.

Instead of dismay, Maddy sighed. "Oh. *Delicious.*"

Thea slammed the book shut. "You're fit for Bedlam."

"Then it is glorious to be mad!"

Thea endured another half hour of Maddy's ravings before making her escape, but that passage of poetry ran in her head. It sounded all too apt. This was the man she expected to see sense? The man who had reason, no matter how distant and warped, to hate her family?

When she returned home, she met her mother in the upstairs corridor.

"How is Maddy?" the duchess asked.

"Running mad over the Corsair."

Her mother put a hand to the wall. "Never say she's taken up with a pirate!"

Thea laughed. "Of course not. The poem. Byron."

Her mother's expression was almost as appalled. "Lord Byron is back?"

"Poem, not poet, Mama. Conrad, Medora, Gulnare, harems."

"Oh, that." The duchess continued with Thea toward the bedrooms. "Such a tale of folly. Medora was in the right of it to point out that her husband had enough money to stay at home and enjoy domestic life. So why sail off again to plunder?"

"Because men enjoy action and danger."

"So true. Did you hear that Cardew Frobisher lies seriously injured after trying to enter the Tower over the wall?"

"Why on earth did he do that?"

"Exactly! Why, when there are perfectly

125

adequate entrances? After surviving the war with hardly a scratch. His poor mother."

"I always thought Medora made a mistake in trying to tempt Conrad with evenings of music and reading," Thea said. "She'd have done better with hearty meals, manly company, and lots of hunting."

Her mother chuckled. "So wise, dearest. You'll make any man a wonderful wife. I saw you with Avonfort last night." Her tone was coy.

"Yes, he proposed again. I'm just not ready, Mama."

"As you said, you deserve a lighthearted season before settling down."

But clearly in the duchess's eyes, too, the match was settled.

At Thea's door, her mother asked, "Do you wish to come out with me later?"

Thea knew she'd be highly unlikely to meet Darien on morning calls, but she'd be safer at home. With both her mother and father out, she could simply refuse to see him if he called.

"I'd rather practice the piano," she said. "I have a new piece I'd like to play after dinner tomorrow."

"That will be pleasant, dear."

Dinner made Thea think of Darien and confrontation, but music did soothe her —

until her mother returned from the social round, still dressed in high fashion and cross. "So tiresome. Such unfair comments about Darien! I moderated them as best I could, but I couldn't yet come out in full support."

"I suppose not."

"Phoebe Wilmott's left Town. Never has a quiet departure been so thunderous."

"You can't blame her, Mama. To encounter Darien would be exquisitely painful."

"*Our* Lord Darien bears no responsibility for her daughter's death. Come along to my room so I can change into something more comfortable as we consider this. Even the Vile Viscount wasn't to blame for Mary Wilmott's death," she said, leading the way briskly, "unless one blames the parent for the child. So unfortunate that they are neighbors."

Thea was having trouble following. "Who are neighbors?"

"Darien and the Wilmotts. I suppose opposite sides of the square is not quite neighbors."

"Cave House is on the same square . . . ?" Thea gasped. "How unbearable!"

"Phoebe's borne it for years," her mother said, with unusual tartness as she entered her bedroom.

"But not *inhabited*," Thea pointed out. "With the chance of meeting a Cave any day."

"That's how the murder came to happen," the duchess said, as her maid helped her shed bonnet and layers. "Mary Wilmott would hardly have been at large in London at night. I suppose she must have thought the square's private garden was safe as only residents have keys. Ah, yes." She picked up a folder of papers. "Mr. Thoresby's preliminary report."

"What does it say?" Thea asked, fingers itching to open it.

"Oh, the usual. Educated at home, Harrow, of course, then the army. I am most cross with Wellington."

Thea stared. "Why?" The duke was everyone's darling these days.

"Would you believe that he was responsible for that Mad Dog name? Fortunately it didn't become Darien's principal nickname. Only think of poor Fuzzy Staceyhume, called that because his hair was wild in his youth, and now he's mostly bald. Or Wolf Wolverton, and he the most gentlemanly man imaginable. Or Mad Jack Mytton. But then," the duchess added thoughtfully, "he truly was mad —"

"Mother!"

"What?"

"The report? It must contain some negatives."

"Not really, but by all means read it." She passed it over. "Darien hasn't paid much attention to his estates, but he's not long out of the army. I'm sure he'll attend to them when he settles down. He'll doubtless apply himself to Parliament and local administration as well, and he may well want a position at the Horse Guards, having military experience."

Thea escaped with the report, feeling she should warn Darien of this onslaught of responsibilities, but also thinking he might be well served for imposing himself on her family.

Once in her room, she flipped through the papers. The closely written pages included accounts and a family tree. She glanced at that, but it was sparse. Four sons in Darien's family. Two in his father's. One in his grandfather's.

In some families the increase could be seen as progress, but not with Caves.

His Italian mother had been called Maddalena D'Auria, and nothing further was said about her. She'd died when her youngest child, Francis Angelo, was three. So Darien would have been seven.

Darien's name was Horatio Raffaelo. Angels, she scoffed to herself. Satan and Lucifer would have been more appropriate.

The oldest son had been named for the Roman emperor and philosopher Marcus Aurelius. That had been a wild stab at optimism, as had Christian for the second. Christian Michelangelo.

What strange aspirations lay behind such names? What lay behind her own? Theodosia — God's gift. She put that aside and settled to reading.

Thoresby had uncovered that Horatio Cave had been expelled from Harrow for fighting, but not why, or anything about Dare and *cave canem.* There were the dates of Darien's army career and his decade-long progression from cornet to major. He'd received rapid promotion to lieutenant because of a battle in which the senior officers of his regiment had been killed or injured. Cornet Cave had taken charge and led the men successfully.

She realized that he'd been only sixteen years old.

She had no trouble in believing that story, or others of courage, decisiveness, and command. She might admire it if she and her family weren't the enemy this formidable man was attacking.

She paused on an incident involving Vandeimen. It seemed Canem Cave and Demon Vandeimen had ended up behind enemy lines, each with a small troop of men. By dash and courage, their combined forces had not only fought clear but captured three French officers and a chest of gold.

She considered the information on Darien's finances and property. He owned three estates — the main one, Stours Court in Warwickshire; a secondary one, Greenshaw in Lancashire; and another, Ballykilneck in Cavan County, Ireland. Mr. Thoresby had been able to discover little about the latter other than that the rental income from it was negligible. Greenshaw was reportedly neglected, having been under the management of Marcus Cave.

Mad Marcus had died five years ago in Bedlam. Time enough for someone to clear up the mess. But then, apparently it was traditionally the heir's property, so it would have passed to the next brother, Christian, whose only superiority over his brother was sanity. He'd died last year, struck by lightning with his father. As her mother had said, though Darien had inherited a year ago, he'd only been out of the army for a short time. She would try to be fair.

At Stours Court the land was all leased

and worked, and Darien had recently appointed a new and better steward, who was beginning to improve the estate. The house needed extensive work, however, or was in danger of falling down.

The last section was on Cave House, and its very blandness showed that Thoresby hadn't known quite how to handle such a touchy subject. He'd clearly decided that there was no point in recounting the lurid details of the murder. Instead, there was the address, including a map of the square, with its terraces of houses on each side and the railed private gardens in the center.

Elevations and floor plans showed a typical house, but Thea pored over them as if they might give a peephole into Darien's life. She caught herself at it and tidied the papers. There was nothing shocking in them, but Thea wasn't reassured. Thoresby hadn't uncovered the truth about Harrow, so what else had he missed? She wasn't surprised, however, when her mother confirmed that she'd sent Darien the dinner invitation.

At least Thea had one remaining night of unpolluted pleasure. The Wraybourne musical evening was one of her favorite events of the season. The company was always select, and there was no attempt at a "crush." The music would be excellent. This year, the boys' choir from Westminster Abbey would perform. It would be glorious.

They attended two routs on their way, passing through crowded houses to fulfill as many social obligations as possible in the limited time the season allowed. Mrs. Calford's rout was a little thin, but Lady Netherholt's was packed. Thea became separated from her parents, but she might have escaped in blessed ignorance if she hadn't bumped into Alesia de Roos.

Alesia grabbed her arm and hissed, "That's the Vile Viscount over there!"

CHAPTER 12

A quick glance showed Alesia was correct, and even worse, Darien was talking to the Vandeimens. If her parents spotted them, they'd be sure to go over.

All three looked at ease, but a subtle space had formed around them even in this crowd. And the man expected her to join him in shunned isolation?

"They call him Canem Cave," Alesia whispered. "It means 'mad dog'!"

"No, it doesn't. The closest translation would be 'dog beware.' "

"Don't be so literal, Thea. It's almost the same thing. He gives me the most delicious shivers. Oh, save me! He's looking at us."

Thea made the mistake of checking on that. Her eyes clashed with his.

"Then don't look back," she said, turning away. "I must go —"

But the Fortescue sisters joined them. "Are you talking about the Vile Viscount?"

Cecily whispered.

"Horrid, isn't it?" Cassandra added, eyes bright. "We can't think of a reason to approach."

"Approach!" Alesia gasped. "He should be thrown out."

"But he's with the Vandeimens," Cassandra pointed out. "Lady Netherholt can hardly offend them."

"*He* was little better," Alesia said. "And Lady Vandeimen —"

Thea interrupted, speaking coldly. "Need I remind you that Maria Vandeimen is a relative of mine?"

Alesia turned red.

"I must go," Thea said, desperate to be out of this mess. "My parents are ready to leave."

If they weren't, they soon would be. That man was a menace. He was harming Maria's reputation and causing discord between Thea and her friends.

Cassandra Fortescue called after her: "Where do you go on to, Thea?"

Thea turned back. "Lady Wraybourne's. You?"

Cecily replied for her sister. "Lady Lessington's."

Thea waved farewell and found her mother, who was wafting a large silk and

135

feather fan and rather red in the face.

"You look hot, too, dear," said the duchess. "But Penelope Netherholt will be pleased by such a crush. Ah, there's your father. Let us escape."

As they moved into the flow of people leaving, Thea thanked heaven for escape, but she found the man's presence pursued her.

All around people murmured:

"Darien."

"Cave."

"Wilmott . . ."

Her mother's tense smile showed she heard the whispers, too. Thea feared that she'd stop to challenge someone, but the flow of people pushed them toward the stairs. They'd reached them when a voice said, "Duke, Duchess, you're leaving, too?"

Thea's parents turned, so she had to, too. Darien was close behind them, and he'd managed that because people were shifting to let him through — or rather, to avoid contact. If he noticed he showed no sign of it.

"Such a crush," he said pleasantly. "The Wraybourne musicale will be a relief."

"You're going there, too, Darien? May we take you up in our carriage?"

Thea wanted to clap her hand over her

mother's mouth. And how had the outcast gained an invitation?

"It's only a few streets . . . ," he demurred.

"But you may as well ride. Night streets can be so dangerous." The duchess was speaking a little louder than necessary, making sure those nearby heard her. She even tapped Darien's arm playfully with her fan. "Of course you won't think of that after fighting in so many battles."

"On the contrary, Duchess. To survive Napoleon and be taken down by a footpad would be ridiculous."

The duchess laughed and even the duke smiled. Thea didn't know how many people had heard the exchange, but everyone would notice the good humor and perhaps begin to doubt their attitudes.

"I don't think you've met my daughter, Darien," the duchess said, smiling warmly. "Thea, this is Viscount Darien, who was so kind to Dare. Darien, Lady Theodosia."

Thea felt caught wrong-footed in a dance. Her curtsy was a beat late, her smile awkward.

His eyes glinted. The man was enjoying her discomfiture.

Then the situation became worse. As they descended the stairs it was necessary to go two by two and she found herself partnering the one man in London she was desperate to avoid. Darien extended his arm. She had to take it. She didn't know what was worse — the sense of his powerful energy or the novel sensation of society staring at her in horrified disbelief.

She looked ahead, smiling as lightly as she could manage. "The Wraybournes have engaged the Abbey boys' choir, my lord. Are you sure that sort of music will suit you?"

"Bawdy drinking songs would be more suitable, you think?"

She flickered a glance in his direction. "Or opera, given your Italian blood?"

"Such a disreputable thing, Italian blood."

Thea felt her cheeks heat. She'd meant that but didn't relish having it pointed out.

"I have little experience with opera," he said. "Though I've appreciated an opera dancer now and then."

"I'm sure you have, my lord, but that is not a subject a gentleman refers to in a lady's company."

"Lady Theodosia, are you implying that I'm not a gentleman?"

His tone was smooth, but Thea's heart suddenly raced. "Of course not. Mama wishes to help you fit into society, that is all. So I thought I'd give you the hint."

"You think that I don't know how to behave in society?"

"Clearly not," she snarled, still smiling, "when you mention opera dancers to a lady."

"A lady who knows what they are, I note."

"That's . . ."

"I'm not sure I approve of that in my betrothed."

Thea was so alarmed she missed the fact that they'd arrived at the bottom of the stairs and stumbled. When a strong hand grasped her arm, she instinctively tensed to resist. He released her as soon as she had her balance, but she felt as shaken as if she'd tumbled down the stairs, top to bottom.

"Are you all right, Thea?" her mother asked, peering at her.

"Yes, of course, Mama." She pulled free of his arm.

He made no attempt to restrain her. "Strange, how trying to take an extra step seems almost as hazardous as not realizing a step is there at all."

"Expectations," Thea's father put in. "Like taking a fence expecting firm ground on the far side and finding a bog."

Darien and the duke settled into hunting talk, giving Thea a chance to recover.

If she could.

He meant to hold her to her promise. He might speak of it to her parents at any moment.

"Sarah!" The sharp hiss almost made Thea jump out of her skin. She turned to see chunky Mrs. Anstruther leaning close to her mother, her two thin unmarried daughters standing nearby, looking like frightened rabbits.

"Do you know who you have in train?" Mrs. Anstruther whispered, red-faced.

Thea's mother pretended mild confusion. "What? Oh, you mean Viscount Darien, Ann? An old friend of my son's. Did so splendidly in the war, you know."

Ann Anstruther's lips drew in like a purse. "Many of the most gallant soldiers are not quite suited to our drawing rooms, Sarah. Or, to our daughters. You cannot have forgotten Mary Wilmott."

"Of course not, but it would be a sad world if we all had to suffer for our brothers' sins."

Thea bit her lip. Ann Anstruther's brother was a notoriously loose fish.

Mrs. Anstruther straightened majestically. "*My* brother has never murdered anyone, and neither have any of yours. You're being softhearted as usual, Sarah, but this is beyond anything. Come, girls!"

She gathered her two daughters and herded them out of danger. The duchess had spots of color on her cheeks, and though Darien and the duke talked on as if nothing had occurred, they must have heard.

"Outrageous," the duchess said, battle in her eye.

"She does have a point, Mama."

The battle eye turned on her. "We are doing what is right, Thea, and I will be disappointed, very disappointed, to see any shrinking and quivering from you. We owe Lord Darien a debt of gratitude and I would be ashamed — ashamed, I say — if any of my family proved reluctant to pay it."

Now Thea's cheeks flared under a sharper rebuke than she'd earned in years. She deserved it more than her mother knew.

Very well. She had made a promise and she would keep it if she must. But if he had a scrap of mercy, or even common sense, she could talk him out of it. Perhaps this evening would provide an opportunity.

A maid came forward with Thea's heavy silk shawl. Despite being in conversation, Darien noticed and came to take the shawl and hold it. Thea made herself smile slightly as she turned so he could put it around her shoulders. She sensed all eyes on her and a disturbance in the air. Her mother was right. The ton was behaving outrageously. They were just like schoolboys turning on the outsider and taunting Dog Cave to violence.

But the brush of his hands on her bare shoulders blew away pity. She remembered their first encounter. Viscount Darien wasn't a misfit boy; he was a strong and ruthless man who was up to no good. She must guard herself against him, especially when he seemed able to have this physical effect on her at will.

She hurried after her parents, not taking Darien's arm, and plunged into the coach as if it were a haven. Darien came, too, of course, but he and her father took the backward seats, so at least she didn't have to sit side by side with him, their bodies touching.

As the carriage moved off, however, she realized that she would have to look at him. He was sitting directly opposite and she could hardly stare out through the window all the way. She expected to be assaulted by mocking looks or even lascivious leers, but he seemed completely attentive to her mother's inquisitive questions.

"When did you join the army, Darien?"

"In oh-six, Duchess."

"You could only have been the merest child!"

"I assure you, a fifteen-year-old lad doesn't think so."

Both duke and duchess chuckled.

"And you served the whole of the Peninsular Campaign," the duke said, "then into France and Waterloo."

"I was so privileged."

"Why did you sell out?" the duchess asked.

He balked at that one. It was subtle, but Thea caught it.

So you have secrets, do you, Lord Darien? Can I use them to defend myself?

"You disapprove, Duchess?" he countered.

"No, but I suspect you didn't want to."

"The war was over, and other matters demanded my attention."

"Your estates," the duke said. "A fair bit of work to do there, I'd think. I don't imagine your father was attentive."

"But not ruinous, for which I'm grateful. Of course there's the current economic disorder to complicate everything."

The two men fell into talk of agriculture, industry, and trade, which lasted until the carriage halted at the end of a line leading to the Wraybournes' house. Thea didn't know much of such matters, but it seemed

Darien was both adequately informed and willing to be advised. That was either a mark to his credit or of more clever scheming.

In either case, it made him a formidable enemy.

Darien and the duke left first to be ready to assist the ladies. Thea took Darien's hand and stepped down, but then her mother insisted on his escort into the house.

Thea took her father's arm, puzzled. But when they entered the house and their names were announced, she caught a frozen expression on the young Countess of Wraybourne's face and understood.

Of course the Vile Viscount hadn't received an invitation. He was an unwelcome invader, but Lady Wraybourne could hardly forbid him entry when he arrived as escort to the Duchess of Yeovil.

CHAPTER 13

The conniving wretch! He'd overheard her calling back to Cassandra that her party was going on here, and then claimed to be invited to the same event. Her mother must have guessed the truth, but instead of tossing him out of the carriage she'd assisted in the invasion.

Did Darien understand what a coup he'd achieved? Being at such a select party did not only imply acceptance by her parents and herself. Lady Wraybourne's other guests would assume he'd received an invitation, and thus feel obliged to be polite to him. Anything less would be an insult to their hostess.

Thea looked around for the Earl of Wraybourne, wondering if he would intervene and insist that Darien leave. That would be a disaster. She and her parents would have to leave, too.

She saw the earl note the situation with

steady, assessing eyes, then turn his attention back to Lord Canning. There really was nothing he could do short of social cataclysm. She, however, was furious that Darien had forced her family into this position.

Why? How could social acceptance be worth this? As they mingled with the company, people reacted with variations on smile-cloaked alarm. No matter how thick-skinned he was, it had to be acutely uncomfortable. Could her wilder fears be true? Was this some convoluted attempt to ruin her family's reputation?

If so, she thought, he'd misjudged. Her parents' eminence was built on rank and wealth, but buttressed by genuine nobility. They both worked hard to serve their country and their fellow men. Everyone liked and admired them, and she and her brothers had not diminished the family name.

Yes, the Debenhams could be embarrassed by the Cave connection, especially if Darien turned out to be as vile as the rest. But they wouldn't be ruined. Society would merely shake its head and say that Sarah Yeovil's generous heart had carried her away again, and hope that perhaps this time she'd learn.

Thea had to greet friends and acquaintances as if all was normal, but she observed. Yes, Darien was clever. He was accepting introductions with polite reserve, subtly acknowledging the reservations of others rather than attempting greater familiarity. He didn't try to impose or linger, but moved on with her parents to the next helpless victims.

In his wake, people whispered, exchanging puzzled, questioning looks, and Lady Wraybourne's charming poise seemed stretched thin. She was only in her twenties, after all, and didn't deserve to have this inflicted upon her.

"Surprised Lady Wraybourne invited the likes of him."

Thea turned to find Lord Avonfort by her side. "My mother brought him."

"Good Lord, why?"

"He supported Dare. The other night, at the ball."

"No more than his duty. Doesn't call for this."

Because of her mother's scold, Thea had to support Darien. "He's probably not as bad as people say. Cully served with him and admires him."

"Army manners," Avonfort dismissed.

"Easy to sneer when we spent the war comfortable at home," Thea protested.

He flushed. "I had responsibilities."

"Yes, of course, I didn't mean that. But we should make allowances, Avonfort."

"Only to an extent. One man from my estate came back all wrong in the head. Had to be put in an institution. Nothing for it. He tried to murder his mother, dreaming he was in battle. Probably what this one'll come to. It's in the blood, after all."

Thea was becoming truly upset at the unfairness of this. "Only *one* of the Caves committed murder."

"There was another a generation ago." But then perhaps he saw her anger, for he smiled. "Typical of you to be so kind-hearted, Thea. It's one of the many virtues I admire in you."

Thea sensed another proposal coming and said, "Come and be introduced, then." That sent him scuttling off with a mumbled excuse. There, now Darien had driven away her prime suitor, too.

Then she saw the Earl of Wraybourne walking toward her parents and Darien, and other concerns fled. The earl had a stalwart, sandy-haired officer by his side — to assist him in removing the intruder? Thea hurried over, though what she could do to prevent disaster she had no idea.

But the officer smiled at Darien and

148

introduced him to the earl, who accepted the introduction with grace.

Army manners, she thought, her heartbeats slowing. And thank God for them.

"What a splendid hound you have at heel." Thea started to find Maddy and Aunt Margaret by her side. Maddy was eyeing Darien with relish. "Do introduce me."

"No. The dog bites."

Maddy laughed and towed her reluctant mother over to Darien. Soon Maddy was flirting with disaster and disaster was flirting back, while all around people surreptitiously watched and commented. Thea joined the group, hating to be part of this.

The performance was announced then, and Thea saw Maddy angling to become Darien's partner. Thea would happily have allowed it, but Aunt Margaret steered Maddy toward the sandy-haired officer — Major Kyle, Lord Wraybourne's brother.

Darien turned to Thea, extending his arm. She took it and they joined the procession toward the drawing room.

"Your cousin is delightful," he said.

"And more innocent than she appears." Thea knew the warning was nonsense. She didn't think Maddy had gone beyond the line, but innocent she was not.

"Ah. I have stumbled into another of those

social niceties. Never praise one lady to another? Especially when the other is my betrothed."

Thea spoke quietly but firmly. "We aren't betrothed yet, Darien."

"Then when?"

"We need to talk about that."

"Your given word means so little to you?"

"No, but —"

"But?"

It was a flat challenge that implied no mercy at all.

"We are too newly introduced for it to be believable."

"I'm all eagerness to become better acquainted."

"We need to talk," she repeated, smiling as they entered the large drawing room filled with rows of chairs.

"Whenever and wherever you wish, Lady Theodosia. I am entirely at your command."

Then disappear in a puff of smoke.

He didn't, so Thea took her seat without further words.

He was willing to talk, however, and that was precisely what she wanted. But they needed a safe and private place. Might there be one here tonight? The sooner the better, for her nerves' sake.

The scrubbed-faced boys in their cassocks

filed in and soon heavenly harmonies were combing through the air and mind, banishing petty cares. Thea relaxed and enjoyed.

Applauding at the end of the first piece, she glanced to her side, hoping to catch Darien in a yawn. Sacred music should have shriveled the Vile Viscount to dust, but he, too, was applauding. The angelic voices began again, but now Thea surreptitiously observed her partner, trying to detect whether that pleasure had been acting. He appeared truly absorbed.

From this side, she realized, his profile might belong to a different man. The lines were elegant because the crook in his nose hardly showed, and the scar that twisted his lip was invisible. She noticed another one, however — a puckered, glossy scar along the line of his jaw, half hidden by his collar. A burn, she assumed. It must have been painful.

As if alerted, he turned to look at her. She met his eyes because to look away would admit weakness, and they were enemies.

After a long moment, he turned his attention back to the choir.

Thea did the same, but now a fluting solo seemed to carol passion. She could feel Darien's presence beside her as if he gave off heat, and flaming memories rippled through her. If they were alone, she might press against him, press into his arms, even. Kiss him as she had the last time. Then, heaven help her, do more. . . .

A finger stroked hers.

She was gloved, but still she started.

Looking firmly at the choir, she moved her left hand into her lap, covering it with her right. How had her hand ended up so far to the left, almost between them?

When she'd regained her calm she flickered a glance sideways. Darien's hands were also in his lap and he seemed intent on the choir. She focused every sense there herself until the performance ended with a high chord that held for so long Thea feared her mind would shatter, taking all sense and restraint with it.

When silence settled, she applauded with everyone else. All around her people shifted and began to talk as if nothing extraordinary had happened. She, however, felt cracked and in danger of falling apart if she didn't escape.

Lady Wraybourne announced the entertainments available during the intermission — refreshments in one room, cards in another, a lecture on the island of St. Helena, where Napoleon was imprisoned.

As Thea rose with everyone else, he spoke.

"You enjoyed that, Lady Theodosia?"

He wasn't talking about music.

"Choirboys sound like angels, don't they, my lord? The soloist was exquisite."

"But soon he and the rest will become coarse men. Alas that we no longer create castrati."

She gave him a flat look. "Another subject no longer referred to in polite society."

"We poor, wicked Italians. There's no hope for us, is there?"

His eyes were wicked, and hot temptation came off him like a wave. Her weakness had encouraged him. Heaven knows what he'd do next. No private discussions tonight, that was certain. How could she bear ever to be alone with him again?

Thea pushed past him and attached herself to Maddy, Cully, and some other young people. They were going to the refreshment room, and a cool drink was just what she needed. A cool drink and freedom from a Cave. She didn't look back and could only pray that he would not attempt to follow her.

CHAPTER 14

Darien let his prey go. He needed time to regain control. Music had always been his weakness, and tonight he'd found himself wondering what his life would have been like if he'd been sent to a choir school. It was an absurd thought. His father would never have considered it, and he doubted any cathedral choir would admit a Cave.

His mother? She'd ignored her children as soon as they'd escaped her womb.

She had sung, however. Not to him. No lullabies from Maddalena D'Auria. But she sang arias in the ballroom for an invisible audience. The only clear memory he had of her was her desperate, soaring voice. Perhaps the cruelest act his father had ever committed was to forbid his wife to perform.

Darien shook away fruitless memories. By some miracle Frank had survived mother, father, and brothers with spirit intact, and now he wanted to marry the woman he loved. It was Darien's job to make that possible. By another impulsive move, he'd gained entrée here. Now he must milk the opportunity dry.

Excellent luck that Fred Kyle be present. Perhaps fate was on his side after all.

That would be nice, because there'd been blood on his step again this morning. It had been cleaned up early, but the persistence worried him. What would be tried next?

He strolled through the rooms, exchanging nods and words with anyone who'd meet his eye, but he found it damned uncomfortable. At the rout, he'd had Van's support. Van and his extraordinary wife, Maria. It had been their idea and their insistence, and they'd paid the price in being ignored. In some alchemical way, however, they'd created the illusion that they were an exclusive trio with all others mere outsiders.

The plan had been to go on to the theater, where anyone was welcome for the price of admission. He should have stayed with that, but on seeing Lady Theodosia and hearing her destination, he'd acted on impulse. Again.

But now he'd let his shield escape and soon his isolation would become obvious.

Clinging to the duke and duchess wouldn't serve. He needed some other support.

As if summoned, a friendly voice said, "Canem, what are you doing in London?"

Friendly, but he didn't recognize the speaker's voice.

He turned and after a moment realized that the tall, dark, intelligent man in civilian dress was Major George Hawkinville. He had a smiling russet-haired lady on his arm, and the lady wore spectacular jewels. Interesting. Last seen, Hawkinville, like himself, had been living on his officer's pay.

"Being pricked by ice, mostly," Darien said in answer, as if they were old friends, but what the devil was going on? He'd met Hawk Hawkinville about four times, and only because he was a close friend of Van's. Ah. Van had alerted the troops, had he?

Hawkinville laughed. "I'm not surprised. But give them time. Allow me to present my wife. My dear, Viscount Darien."

Darien bowed to the lady, who curtsied, smiling without a hint of reservation.

"You're out, then," Darien said to Hawkinville.

"Once Napoleon was done for there was no reason to stay and I had responsibilities at home. The same for you, I assume."

"Yes."

"Always pegged you as army for life," Hawkinville said with genuine curiosity.

"And I might well have been had my father and older brother not died."

"Ah, yes. *The Wrath of God.*"

He said it so lightly.

"That one cartoon certainly lingers in people's minds," Darien said, hearing bitterness creep in.

Hawkinville might have apologized, which would have made matters worse, but another couple joined them. Colonel Lethbridge, still in uniform, was accompanied by his thin, fashionably dressed, middle-aged wife. Her smile looked as if it were forced out by torture. Even so, she was there, and Lethbridge had no connection to Van that Darien knew about.

Then blue caught the corner of Darien's eye and Captain Matt Foxstall of the hussars joined the group. "Not much entertainment in church music, is there?" he said with his lopsided smile. His lower jaw was twisted to the right, and a heavy mustache couldn't disguise it.

What in Hades was he doing at an event like this? Or in London at all?

Captain Matt Foxstall had been a fellow captain with Canem Cave for four years, and they'd been comrades in arms, if not exactly friends. They shared some tastes in war and women, and could trust one another to have their backs in any fight.

Their comradeship had fractured recently, however. First Darien had made major, then he'd inherited the title. Foxstall had resented both. To make matters worse, in peacetime advancement was hard without the money to buy a higher rank, and Foxstall didn't have it.

Darien had last seen Foxstall in Lancashire when he'd left the regiment, and he'd known then that he was a powder keg. Foxstall needed bloody action as much as he needed food and drink, and if it didn't come naturally, he'd create it.

After introductions, Darien asked, "Has the regiment come south, then?"

"Not yet, but we're ordered to India. I'm here to speed up some administrative matters."

"India, eh?" Lethbridge said. "Plenty of opportunities there. Was there myself with Wellington. Wellesley then, of course."

"A most insalubrious climate," his wife said. "I was unable to accompany my husband."

"What a shame," said Hawk's young wife. "Such fascinating customs and art. The Duchess of St. Raven has some remarkable

158

Indian artifacts, and in fact her parents have returned there."

Talk swirled around India until the Hawkinvilles and Lethbridges moved on.

"How did you get through these sacred portals?" Darien asked Foxstall.

"Met Kyle and angled for an invitation. You?"

So easy, if one wasn't a Cave.

"The Duchess of Yeovil."

"Flying high. Good for you, not but what there's muttering in the ranks."

"I'm not surprised. Why are you here, though? I wouldn't have thought the music to your taste."

"Someone said the food was good," Foxstall said. "Didn't know it'd be choirboys and everyone expected to listen. But having paid the piper, let's find the reward."

Darien went with him, but Foxstall was a handicap. He was acceptable here, but the military men, the ones Darien needed for support, might have reservations. Foxstall, for all his fighting prowess, was not the sort of man you wanted to introduce to susceptible ladies. Despite his looks, he attracted them and he had no conscience about how he used them.

Surely he'd show some sense at home and in high circles, however.

They entered the supper room to find, indeed, a bountiful supper table — whole fish, roasted birds, pies, pasties, cheeses, and a mouthwatering selection of cakes, jellies, and fruit dishes.

"Think of the times we were scrounging for vegetables and glad of a meat bone," Foxstall said, grabbing a slice of cold veal pie. "So eat, drink, and be merry."

"For tomorrow we die?"

Foxstall bellowed with laughter.

Three young officers looked across the table and then said, almost in unison, "Canem!"

"I say, sir," said Cully Debenham, bright-eyed. "Be honored if you'd join our table for supper. You too, sir," he said to Foxstall, but with less enthusiasm.

The other young lieutenants, Marchampton and Farrow, echoed the invitation. It was positively embarrassing, but Darien needed impeccable company.

They joined the others in gathering plates of food to take back to whatever ladies they were partnering. After supper, he'd track down Lady Theodosia and insist she partner him for the second half of the performance. It wouldn't do to give the impression that the Debenhams were backing off.

No need. As he followed the younger men

through the chattering tables, he saw her waiting with three other young blossoms of the ton. Her eyes met his, and clearly if she'd had her way, he'd have been stuffed and roasted, too.

There had been three gentlemen to four ladies, he noted. Given Lady Theodosia's rush to escape him, she would be the odd one out. If not for Foxstall, his arrival would have restored balance and paired him with his quarry without effort.

Damn Foxstall.

Thea had been alerted to danger when Miriam Mosely gasped, "Oh, no!"

Following Miriam's stare, she'd seen Cully, Marchampton, and Farrow in smiling conversation with Darien and a strapping hussar officer.

"They won't bring him here, will they?" Miriam whispered. "Mother told me to avoid being introduced to him at all costs."

"Don't worry. Maddy and I have both encountered him and survived."

"But . . ."

"I wonder who the other one is," Maddy said, frankly ogling. "I hope *he* joins us."

"He's ugly," Delle Bosanquet said.

Maddy put on a superior air. "Nobly wounded in war, Delle."

For once, Thea was in agreement with her cousin. The poor man could never have been handsome, for his features were lumpy and his skin coarse, but he'd clearly received a terrible wound across his lower face. The dark slash of it cut down his cheek to his mouth, and the whole of his lower jaw was awry.

She could also see why Maddy was interested. Apart from his size, this man could be the Corsair. Nothing to do with the power of the mind. It was all physical — a kind of animal vigor.

As the men approached, Thea realized there'd be five men to four women. But no. Miriam had slipped away. Now they were an awkward five to three.

"Here's Canem Cave," Cully announced as if he'd towed home a prize. "Lord Darien now, of course. And Captain Foxstall. Dog and Fox. Always together!"

Darien's face was so unreadable that Thea knew he was concealing a reaction. Lord! Cully had just called him Dog. She braced for some outburst, but he put his plate of food in the center of the table as the other men did, then politely waited for March, Cully, and Farrow to claim their seats.

Foxstall didn't. He sat next to Maddy and Maddy smiled. Marchampton, tight-lipped,

162

took the seat on Maddy's other side. The poor man was desperately in love with Maddy and she treated him abominably. Farrow was Delle's partner, so he took the chair between her and Thea. One chair remained, between Foxstall, now putting food on Maddy's plate, and Thea, who had decided he was a boor.

Cully gestured to the empty chair, saying, "There you are, sir," and Darien sat.

Cully captured a chair from another table and inserted it on Delle's other side. Neither a sister nor cousin would thrill him, but Thea would much rather not have had to eat her supper with her nemesis by her side. She would certainly have preferred not to have to face the disgusting sight of Maddy making a scandal of herself over "Fox," as she was already calling him.

"Were you at Waterloo, Fox?" Maddy cooed.

She couldn't have forgotten that poor Marchampton and Farrow had missed the great battle. Like so many regiments, with Napoleon apparently defeated, theirs had been shipped to the war in Canada and they still gnashed their teeth over it.

At the first gap in Foxstall's boasting, Thea asked Farrow about the march from Spain into France in 1814, and dragged conversation from there to the Peninsular Campaign.

She did it for her own reasons, but soon she was fascinated. Before 1815 she'd paid little attention to the details of war. After Waterloo, she hadn't been able to bear mention of it. Because of Dare's experience, she'd assumed any soldier's memories would be grim, but clearly that wasn't so.

"Weren't you involved in the Muniz affair, Canem?" Marchampton asked, eyes bright. "Lord, I remember the fuss about that."

"Rollicking grand affair," Captain Foxstall declared. He was definitely a man who liked to be the center of attention. "Couldn't do anything official so we acted on our own."

Cully demanded details and Foxstall supplied them. Something to do with an unauthorized liberation of a Spanish town made more difficult because of the behavior of Spanish troops that were supposed to be allies.

"I'm surprised you got off scot-free." March directed his comment to Darien.

"Nothing anyone could do," Darien said, sipping wine. "Unlike the affair of the ten pigs. That almost had me court-martialed."

He told a story of the capture of some pigs from a German regiment, which led to similar stories from the rest. All the ladies were suitably admiring of their heroes, but did Maddy have to press up against Foxstall quite like that?

But then Darien laughed. Thea blinked, realizing how different he seemed. Was he drunk? She didn't think his glass had been refilled more than once. He might be drunk simply on friendly company after so much hostility. More than friendly. Cully and March in particular seemed to regard him as a god.

". . . when you and Demon Vandeimen escaped the whole French army," Cully was saying, his plate of food scarcely touched.

"Not the whole of it," Darien corrected, lips quirking.

"A division, at least. Mad Dog and Demon, and not a man lost."

"And a chest of French gold acquired!" March declared. "Wish I'd been there."

"We were only there by accident ourselves," Darien pointed out, "and would much rather not have been. That was a mistake on my part, and but for Vandeimen's arrival, might have been disastrous. As it was, the gold saved my skin and the men's feet."

"The men's feet?" Thea asked.

"It purchased a boatload of boots." She didn't know what he saw in her face, but the mask slid back into place. "You don't approve of war exploits, Lady Theodosia?"

She dug her fork into a forgotten pastry. "I don't know enough to approve or disapprove, my lord, but it's shocking that our soldiers had to go to such lengths to get supplies."

"Someone wrote that an army marches on its belly, but that tends to slip the attention of those in power. Half the army fought Waterloo hungry."

"That's appalling. Something should be done."

"Really?" He looked cynical, but Maddy said, "Oh, Thea, not another cause!" She looked around the men. "She and Aunt Sarah are always scurrying around trying to assist returning soldiers."

"And your contribution, Miss Debenham?" Darien asked.

Maddy actually flushed. "I amuse them!" She turned to Foxstall. "Don't I, sir?"

He raised her hand and kissed it. "Delightfully, Miss Debenham."

Maddy blushed in a way Thea knew all too well. *Not a friend of Darien's, Maddy, please!*

"Are all you gentlemen fixed in Town for the season?" Thea asked.

"Seems so," Cully said despondently. How

men could long for military action she didn't know.

"Not me," Foxstall said. "We're off to India before summer's out."

"That's most unfortunate," Maddy said with a pout.

He still had her hand. "Marry me, Miss Debenham, and I'll forsake the houris."

Maddy laughed, everyone smiled, but Thea noticed what very red lips Foxstall had, lurking beneath his dark mustache. She truly did not like or trust this man.

"Well?" he demanded, reminding her of Darien demanding his bargain.

Even Maddy looked taken aback. She laughed. "I'm quite incapable of making any decision so quickly, Captain."

"Then I can only gather English rosebuds while I may."

Loose red lips smiling. Eyes sliding down to the posy of pink buds between Maddy's breasts. Maddy immediately pulled one free and offered it. He took it, kissed it, and tucked it inside his braided jacket close to his heart.

Thea's teeth were gritted and so, she thought, were March's. She glanced at Darien, silently berating him for bringing this wolf among them. She might pity Foxstall's deformity, but every instinct said he was a rake. A very dangerous rake, well beyond Maddy's usual playing fields.

CHAPTER 15

Lady Wraybourne's butler broke an awkward silence with the announcement of the second choir performance. As they all rose, Thea looked for a chance to separate Maddy from her fox, but Maddy had a firm link to his arm. At least Marchampton stuck close.

Lieutenant Farrow offered his arm to Delle, who good-naturedly invited Cully to her other side. Thea smiled and accepted Darien's arm back to the music. It was all part of the plan, she reminded herself. Her mother expected her to show support.

As they strolled through the house, she thought the plan might be working. Though she was sure many people were maneuvering in order to avoid the Cave in their midst, no one turned their back and she heard no whispers. When Avonfort didn't meet Thea's eyes, she was tempted to march over to him and force him to be polite to Darien.

She found herself comparing the two, and

not to Avonfort's advantage. His elegance, which she'd always admired, looked effete against Darien's plainer style. His carefully arranged hair, high shirt collar, and blue moiré silk cravat seemed overdone.

What was she thinking? She *liked* men who shared her taste for fine dressing, and especially her taste for elegance and the gentler arts. She could honor the courage and sacrifices of war without admiring the coarse results.

"No conversation?" he asked as they began to climb the stairs.

"We could talk about why you are doing this."

"Doing what?"

"Forcing yourself upon my family and upon society."

"Perhaps for the delights of your company, my lady."

She sent him a flat smile. "I am here by duty to convey the Yeovil blessing, Darien, but if you pretend to be in love with me I shall probably be sick."

His lips twitched. "More likely the potted shrimp. I forswear love, then, but cannot deny admiration. You must know you're beautiful."

"Now what is a lady to say to that? If I agree I sound vain. If I say no . . ."

She'd walked into a trap.

"You will feel foolish?" he completed, eyes dancing. "There's no dishonor in claiming an attribute. I am brave, strong, and an excellent fighter."

"Men are allowed to claim things like that. Women are not allowed to claim beauty."

"Instead you have to wait for others to tell you and then coyly demur. A shame, don't you think? Say it. I am beautiful."

"No." Why wouldn't people walk faster and cut this conversation short?

"Then what attributes may you claim?"

"Virtue, sound principles, and Christian charity. Perhaps some household skills."

"Do you have any household skills?" he asked.

"Of course I do. In order to run a great house I must know everything about its working. Cleaning, linen management, accounts, food preparation."

"I look forward to seeing you kneading bread with flour on your nose."

Damning him silently, she confessed, "I have never actually made bread."

"Theoretical knowledge is often deceptive. . . ."

She met his eyes. "I've confessed my folly, Lord Darien. There's no need to belabor the point."

At last they'd arrived at the drawing room again, but she'd swear he laughed. Infuriating, wretched man! She saw people startled to see him in such good humor. They were probably blaming her for it.

She saw Maddy and her two swains and navigated to a seat directly behind them, ready to poke her cousin in the back if she behaved too badly. Maddy distributed her smiles and comments evenly, doubtless hoping to provoke jealousy.

Because of Maddy, Thea couldn't truly enjoy the second half of the performance. All in all, this was turning out to be the most unpleasant ton event she'd ever experienced. And according to her mother's plan, she had more of the same to look forward to.

But not as the Vile Viscount's betrothed. That would be a hundred times worse.

Lady Wraybourne thanked the choir and then offered her guests yet more amusements, including an opportunity to visit Lord Wraybourne's new chamber, built to display his noted collection of ancient pottery.

That seemed safe, so Thea said, "The collection sounds interesting, Maddy. Shall we go there?"

But Marchampton said, "Kyle warned me

off, Lady Thea. Just a lot of old pots." He held out an arm. "Cards, Maddy?"

Maddy took it, but then linked her other arm with Foxstall's, and the trio set off for the card room. Without Darien, Thea could have made a fourth and possibly even distracted Foxstall from Maddy. In fact, she could still do so.

"Cards, then," she said.

"Pottery," Darien said.

"I wish to play cards, sir."

"You said the collection sounded interesting. I do hope you're not flighty."

"I'm allowed to change my mind," Thea said, teeth gritted.

"Only about some things."

It was a warning. Before she could find a pithy response, he smiled slightly. "I thought you wished to speak to me. Old pots seem more likely to provide an opportunity than the card tables, don't you think?"

She wanted to refuse on principle, but he was right, and she needed to clear up confusion. Urgently. And Maddy couldn't get into serious trouble in the card room, especially with March on guard.

So Thea took Lord Darien's arm and together they followed directions through the hall and down a corridor toward the back of the house.

"Not the most popular event of the evening," Darien remarked. Two couples walked ahead and there might be more behind, but there certainly wasn't a crowd.

"Perhaps Major Kyle has been warning the ton in general," Thea said.

"You might warn your cousin that Foxstall is not a safe plaything."

"Really? I had the impression he was your friend, my lord."

"The army makes strange bedfellows. Speaking of which, when do we announce our intention of becoming bedfellows?"

Thea felt heat rise in her cheeks. "Really, my lord!"

"It's what marriage amounts to. I know — it's not what people say. I prefer plain speaking. So, is there any reason I shouldn't speak to your father tomorrow about our commitment?"

"Yes," Thea said sharply.

"What?"

"It's too soon."

"Lady Thea —"

"You do *not* have permission to use my name like that."

He raised his brows. "You prefer to be Theodosia, gift of the gods, rather than Thea, a goddess in your own right?"

The man was infuriating. "I've no idea

174

what you're talking about, Darien, but please address me formally at all times."

"I invite you to call me Canem."

"Or Dog?" she fired at him.

"Don't."

They'd arrived at the door to the room in which about a dozen people had gathered. He gestured her to proceed him and Thea hurried in. Safety in numbers. She wondered if her shivers were noticeable.

She pretended to be fascinated by the room, strolling around the circular walls of glass-fronted cabinets, all full of pottery, whole and in pieces. A central plinth was tiered for special displays and sat beneath a glass dome that would let in excellent light in the daytime. At this hour they had to make do with lamps, and perhaps that accounted for the dullness of the items on display there.

"Old pots indeed," Darien murmured, and despite everything Thea had to bite her lip. That was exactly what the items on the plinth looked like — the plain sort of cooking pots used in a kitchen, except that most were so chipped they'd have been thrown out long ago. Some items were merely shards.

Lord Wraybourne picked up one broken pot and showed it to some of his guests, turning it tenderly in his hands. He was a handsome, urbane man and Thea wondered what had pulled him to this interest, to this obsession, even. It must have cost a great deal of money to create this room. He clearly saw a beauty in his collection that escaped Thea and probably most people.

Rather like love, she thought. People could fall in love with the most unlikely people. Alesia was giddy over a serious-minded clergyman, and one of Avonfort's sisters was happily married to a widower twice her age. Kingstable was an old pot, though actually still a fine-looking man, and Catherine was ecstatically happy in her marriage.

As Lord Wraybourne spoke to the whole group about his collection, Thea wondered if she'd ever experience romantic ecstasy. It hadn't happened yet — not even the sort of infatuation most of her friends flew into again and again.

Her eyes wandered and she wondered who else in the audience was struggling to look interested and who was truly fascinated. One other was distracted, for sure. Lady Harroving was eyeing Darien with a wicked smile. She must be at least ten years his senior! But then, Cousin Maria was eight years older than Vandeimen, and Lady Harroving was a widow.

If you want him, my lady, you're welcome to him, Thea thought. Her mother was looking for a suitable wife for Darien.

Lady Harroving was of good birth, though her reputation was by no means impeccable. No one had ever believed her faithful to her late husband, and she annually hosted a masquerade ball that was only just respectable. But she certainly wouldn't be harmed by the match.

The short lecture ended with Thea hardly hearing a word of it.

Some people gathered around Lord Wraybourne, asking him questions as if truly fascinated. Lady Harroving came over, somehow presenting her large, mostly exposed breasts as her focal point.

"Lord Darien," she said, ignoring all propriety, "I'm Lady Harroving. Maria," she added with a sultry smile. "What an asset you are to a dull season."

It was as if Thea didn't exist.

"I hope to be as dull as the dullest, Lady Harroving," Darien said, with a perfect distant coolness. "Lady Thea, I gather this is Lady Harroving."

His response and introduction were beautifully nuanced deterrents. Red rose beneath the rouge on the older lady's cheeks. "Lady Theodosia and I are acquainted," she said with equal coldness. "I see your reputation is earned."

"I haven't bitten you, yet."

Perhaps to save face, Lady Harroving laughed before turning and leaving the room.

"That wasn't wise," Thea said softly. "You don't need more enemies."

"She insulted you by ignoring you."

She looked at him. "That matters to you?"

"I'm your escort. I take such duties seriously. Old pots do seem to fascinate some, don't they? I suggest we inspect the cabinets a little longer."

He was correct. This room would do for their private talk once the others had left. With the door open, of course. The open door gave a view down the corridor to the front hall. It couldn't truly be considered private.

Thea turned with Darien to inspect the contents of the nearest display case. Sometimes she glimpsed him reflected darkly in the glass, and the other people, farther behind.

Leave, she commanded the chattering group as she moved from gaudy-glazed pots to dull ones and on to a cabinet that held crudely made pottery figurines. The group had moved a little, but paused again. Some kind of tension was building in her. Impatience to get the man to see sense. It must be.

"You have a particular interest in fertility goddesses?"

Thea focused and saw that some of the figures were squat females with huge, pregnant bellies. "Do you think they worked?" she asked, but then blushed.

"Is that the sort of thing a lady talks about with a gentleman?"

She turned to face him. "You started it."

He smiled. "So I did."

It took a moment for Thea to realize that they were alone. That Lord Wraybourne and his companions had left.

Suddenly dry-mouthed and nervous, she said, "So let us talk of such matters."

"You aren't worried about being alone with me?"

"The door is open and we are visible from the hall."

"Stone walls do not a prison make, and open doors do not mean safety."

Thea tensed even more. "You intend to attack me again? I warn you, I'll scream."

He smiled. "You didn't last time."

"You . . . !" But Thea remembered her purpose and controlled herself. "I am here alone with you, Lord Darien, only to talk about the betrothal."

"About speaking to your father."

"No!"

"There is some other first step?" he asked politely.

"Obtaining the lady's true consent," she snapped.

"Then, my goddess, we *are* betrothed."

"No, we're *not!*" Squabbling would get her nowhere. "Lord Darien, you have to see that a betrothal between us would be both unnecessary and unbelievable."

"Unbelievable?" He looked politely puzzled. "If you and your family let it be known that we were to marry, no one would believe it?"

"Of course not. Because you're a Cave."

It brought only a twitch of his enigmatic features, but Thea realized how insulting that had been.

"I'm sorry," she said, both out of fear and pity. Harrow, Dare, and Dog Cave all threatened to weaken her.

They had nothing to do with this strong, successful man, she reminded herself. "I mean that being a Cave, you're not well accepted at the moment. Thus the betrothal would look peculiar. Moreover, you're so new in Town, how have we come to know one another? If I'm to be swept out of my

180

wits by love for you, it would take more than days."

"I've seen it happen in an instant, but I grant you your point, especially when you're known as the Great Untouchable."

"That's —"

"— a ridiculous nickname. I agree. But so many are, aren't they?"

She hated losing so many points.

"How long before it would be believable?" he asked.

"Forever." Before he could retort, she leapt for her main point. "The betrothal isn't *necessary,* Darien. You have my parents' favor and tonight you've entered the inner circle of the ton and not been rebuffed."

A raised brow questioned that.

"Not openly. You clearly have military friends willing to support you, but above all, you are now my mother's cause. Believe me, in these matters she's a veritable Wellington. If you decide you *don't* want to be brought back into the loving embrace of the ton, you have no hope of escape."

Disarmingly, he laughed.

"She even intends to find you the right wife, so you see —"

"But not you, I assume."

"I lack the taste for adventure." Thea

heard the touch of bitterness in her voice.

"My lady in red," he said, "you astonish me."

"I assure you, I do. That dress was . . . I won't wear it again. I want only a quiet, orderly life."

"You're no more suited to tedium than I am."

She looked him in the eye. "We have nothing in common, Lord Darien. Nothing."

"We have that kiss."

"You forced that on me!"

"Then why haven't you complained of it?"

He was taking her silence as *encouragement*? "Because I've no mind to cause a scandal or duel. Do not imagine for one moment that I enjoyed it!"

"Not up to your standards? I apologize and humbly beg a chance to prove I can do better."

He moved closer, and Thea discovered retreat was blocked by the case at her back.

"When pigs fly!" she snapped.

"Put one in the basket of a balloon," he suggested. "Or fire one from a cannon, even."

The image threw her off balance. "That's horrible!"

"A means to an end. I don't let emotions come between me and my purposes, Thea, and you are my means to an end."

"I wish I were the means to your demise —"

He captured her cheek with his hand. "Cease struggling. There is no escape."

Completely still, Thea spoke low and hard. "Take your hand off me, Darien, or I will scream, and to hell with the consequences."

He challenged her and she thought she was going to have to do it, but then he removed his hand and stepped back.

"Release me from my promise," she demanded. "It's outrageous and unnecessary."

"I cannot."

"*Why?* Why is it so important to you? With my mother and the Rogues on your side . . ."

Her words dried because of the look in his eyes.

"The Rogues?" he asked quietly.

"They plan to help you. Because of what happened at school."

Mistake, mistake! She should have realized that he wouldn't want her to know about that.

"I do not like the Rogues," he said, his eyes wide and steady. "And I'm damned if I'll accept rescue at their hands."

"But you supported Dare in order to get help!"

"I *captured* your family. I hold you in my

fist. If I could chain the Rogues and whip them to my will, I would. Are they chained?"

"No." Then Thea found the courage to raise her chin and say, "They feel sorry for you."

He put a hand flat against the glass, barring her escape. "You are a very foolish woman, and we are no longer in sight of others."

She looked toward the door and saw he spoke the truth.

"Foolish to trust you?" she challenged over a terrified heart. "Strange as it may seem to you, I am generally safe alone with a gentleman." His jaw tightened, but she couldn't seem to stop. "But then, a Cave can't be a gentleman. Why not force another vile kiss on me, then? I'm sure that's what you want."

He stepped sharply back. "Oh, no. That's what *you* want. You won't taunt me into destruction. But," he added, smiling coldly, "you have only to beg."

Thea swung to slap his taunting face, but he caught her wrist, and the warning in his eyes froze her. Still, still, beneath ice and terror, all the wicked parts of her body and soul screamed that she beg as he required. That she grovel for another burning, annihilating kiss.

"Perhaps," he said softly, "you only need to ask."

She wrenched free and ran. In the corridor she made herself slow down, sucking in breaths to calm herself. When she entered the hall she smiled, trying to look as if nothing in the world was amiss, but heaven knows what that smile looked like.

"Lady Theodosia, may I assist you?"

She turned sharply and found Captain Foxstall beside her. He was smiling, but the look in his eye was sly.

"Only in telling me where my cousin is, sir."

"Miss Debenham was gathered under her mother's wing." He looked behind her and said, "Ah," as if all were explained. She knew Darien was there.

"Don't let him play you, Lady Theodosia," Foxstall said with those horrid red lips. "That's his specialty, playing with well-protected young ladies. He usually finds it disappointingly easy. The right degree of danger and fear along with a soupçon of charm and they melt like sealing wax, ready for his stamp."

Scalded, Thea turned and walked away. She loathed Captain Foxstall with all her heart, but she recognized truth. That was exactly the game Darien was playing.

Did he think he could use the thrill of danger to force her into marriage?

When pigs sprout wings.

But now, she must escape.

She found her mother playing cards and leaned down to murmur, "Something at supper upset me, Mama. I must go home."

The duchess excused herself from the table. "You poor thing. I do hope there's no wider problem. So embarrassing for the hostess."

"I see no sign. I don't think shrimp agrees with me."

Shrimp. That was what he'd said.

"No, dear? I haven't noticed that before." The duchess commanded their carriage and sent a message to the duke to say that they were leaving. "He'll doubtless stay. I saw him in a serious discussion about the suspension of habeas corpus. Such distressing times. Do you need to lie down, dear?"

"No," Thea said, uncomfortable with a lie. "It's only a tiny feeling at the moment, but I'd rather be home if it develops."

"Oh, yes, certainly. I was glad enough to leave. Partnered with Mrs. Grantham, who is such a silly player. I think this went rather well, though."

"The choir was lovely." Thea wanted to race down the stairs, but it would take time

186

for their carriage to arrive.

"I mean Darien, dear! You were very generous with your attention and that can only do good. And I was so happy to see him enjoying himself with his army friends at supper."

"He does have many army friends, Mama, and the Rogues intend to help him. Perhaps he doesn't need our help."

"Thea," her mother chided. "Gentlemen never have the same cachet as ladies. Except in the clubs, of course. I wonder if your father can get him accepted at White's. . . ."

Only by a miracle, Thea thought as they arrived in the hall and servants hurried off to find their cloaks.

"The carriage won't be long, dear," the duchess said. "Why don't you sit down?"

Thea wanted to pace, as if that would speed their escape, but she did as expected and tried not to fidget. Her mother turned to talk to a friend who was also leaving, so Thea watched the stairs, though what she could do if Darien came down them she had no idea.

Oh, Lord. After all that, she'd achieved nothing in her attempt to escape the betrothal.

She'd have to try again.

Without losing her temper.

Without mentioning the Rogues.

She should have realized how he'd react to her knowing that story. Any man would hate it.

But now her fears were confirmed. His actions were fueled by hatred.

When their carriage was announced Thea hurried into it. As the carriage rolled away, the duchess said, "I do hope you're well by tomorrow, dear."

"What?"

"Our dinner for Darien. Tomorrow night." She broke off because Thea had moaned. "I forgot that you're unwell, dear. Do you want the smelling salts?"

Thea shook her head, speechless.

CHAPTER 16

Darien didn't pursue Thea Debenham, but he followed in her wake and saw her speak to Foxstall. Damn Foxstall. His presence in London was inconvenient, and his attentions to Thea's cousin potentially disastrous. Something about his exchange with Thea set off warning bells as well.

Of course his own exchange with Thea Debenham left a lot to be desired. She seemed able to deprive him of his wits with a fiery look from her clear blue eyes. Then she'd mentioned the Rogues.

Damn it all to Hades, he wouldn't have them meddling in his affairs.

He'd have preferred to leave, but he'd won entrée here and would damn well exploit it. He strolled through the rooms, ignoring any slights and pausing to speak to any army men he knew, glad to see Foxstall leave, doubtless for the livelier amusements of a hell or brothel.

This was the sort of slow, subtle invasion he'd once planned — before he'd met Thea Debenham. Since then, his life had gone to hell in a handbasket. He'd been forced to abandon Pup tonight, so heaven knew where he was. At least the lad was too nervous to go to a brothel on his own.

As he went through the social patterns, he watched for Lady Thea. While talking about the number of naval vessels lying idle, he was alert for the distinctive flower perfume she wore. While discussing affairs in India, he listened for her voice, so light and well modulated.

Except when she was angry.

Or frightened.

He'd frightened her.

He wasn't proud of that, but she was trying to wriggle off the hook and he couldn't allow that. For Frank's sake.

By eleven o'clock, he couldn't take more of the social playacting and set about leaving.

When he took farewell of the Duke of Yeovil, he discovered that Thea and her mother had already left.

"Something in the potted shrimp," the duke said quietly. "Had some myself with no ill effects, but the ladies are more sensitive, aren't they?"

That hadn't been Darien's experience, but then his experience had mostly been of the sort of women who followed the drum. From whores to officers' ladies, toughness was essential.

Besides, he knew what Thea Debenham's complaint had been — an excess of Cave.

He found and thanked his hostess, apologizing for attending without invitation. "The duchess insisted," he said, with some truth.

"I must thank her, then," the countess replied with smiling eyes. "Your presence has livened my sedate entertainment."

"We Caves live to serve."

"I thought the motto was 'beware,' my lord."

"Like pepper, terror can be enlivening in moderation."

She laughed, shaking her head.

He collected his evening cloak and left the house realizing that Lady Wraybourne's playful tone signaled another victory. When he'd arrived, she'd truly been alarmed, perhaps imagining her entertainment ruined by mayhem and violence. Now she was amused and saw no harm in him.

An error, but still a victory in his campaign.

A footman would have found him a hackney, but he was used to an active life and

London stifled him. Perhaps walking the dark night streets also fed some mad urge toward risk. A man could become addicted to that. He saw that fault in Foxstall, but did it live in him, too? Was he capable of living a quiet, orderly life?

He paused in the street, realizing that he'd echoed Lady Thea's words.

No. He was not imagining a future with her, not even in his wildest dreams.

A noise pulled him out of his thoughts.

He'd carelessly taken a shortcut through narrow, dimly lit Cask Lane and now three young toughs were circling him, showing crooked, dirty teeth. "We'll just have your money and trinkets, milord," one said.

Darien launched without warning, wielding his cane. In moments, two were fleeing, one with a bad limp and the other clutching cracked ribs. The third lay whimpering at his feet, hunched against the expected kick.

He only touched him with his toe. "A lesson from an expert," he told the youth. "Attack first, talk later."

He walked on, feeling a little better for the exercise.

CHAPTER 17

Darien entered Hanover Square, which was peacefully quiet at gone midnight, but still the scene of a notoriously bloody deed.

In daylight, the shrubs and bushes of the gardens gave a pleasant aspect, but at night they were dark shapes behind black railings, able to hide any number of monsters. He walked to his house, but then paused to study the opposite row of houses, appearing only as a black square against dark sky, broken only by one curtained window and a couple of lamps beside doors. The Wilmotts' house was over there, and though Lady Wilmott had fled Town, Sir George was still in residence.

Did people point at the Wilmott house as they did at Cave House, as they did at the place in the gardens where the bloody corpse had been found? London people brought country cousins here. Tour St. Paul's, Westminster Abbey, and the Tower of London. Go to Hanover Square to see the scene of Mad Marcus Cave's bloody deed.

One day he was going to have to try to arrange a meeting with Sir George and forge some sort of peace. But he couldn't face that yet. He suspected the man had sent the *Wrath of God* drawing. Who else? He might even be responsible for the blood. He'd no desire to bring the family more distress, but he had his plan to push through.

He turned toward his house, where the family crest sat above the lintel. The snarling black mastiff seemed almost animated by the flickering flame of the lamp by the door. Darien snarled back, ignoring the carved warning beneath. *Cave.*

He should get rid of it, if only because such house crests had gone out of fashion fifty years or more ago. It was carved in stone, however, and set firmly into the brick. Removing it would be the devil of a job, and for all he knew the stone was supporting the upper stories of the house. Causing the place to crumble was tempting, but for now it was his burden.

Taking up residence here had been a mistake, but he couldn't correct it yet. To move now would look as if the blood had frightened him away, and one of his creeds was to never, ever show fear. He'd learned that whenever young Marcus had visited Stours Court. Even before turning mad, Marcus had been the sort of bully who'd feasted on fear like a vampire on human blood.

Hades, he was hovering, reluctant to enter. He unlocked the door and went inside. As always, the house was both silent and loud with malice.

Then Prussock hurried up from the basement. "Welcome home, milord."

This was a change. Was Lovegrove lecturing the other servants on correct behavior in the house of a peer of the realm, or was this Prussock's reaction to the spate of visitors? Darien would rather he not bother, but he supposed the family were anxious not to lose their places here.

Prussock lit one of the two waiting candles and presented it.

Darien took it. "Thank you. Is Mr. Uppington in?"

"No, milord. He went out shortly after you did."

"Do you know where?"

"No, milord."

"He has a key, Prussock, so don't stay up."

"I am perfectly willing —"

"Go to bed, Prussock. That's an order."

"Very well, milord." The butler walked away stiff with disapproval. Darien wondered if he was breaking some other arcane rule, but Prussock had a way of looking disgruntled about everything.

Darien mounted the stairs to where Lovegrove would be waiting to care for his finery — in spirit if not in flesh. Very much in spirit, judging from the amount of brandy disappearing.

There was nothing wrong with this house, he told himself. It was close to identical to the others in the row. Yet every time he entered, a foul atmosphere fell around him like a damp, rotting blanket. He'd slept among corpses with greater ease than here.

A flicker to his right made him turn. It was nothing, but he knew something hovered here, wishing him ill. Perhaps he should have the place exorcized. Did the Church of England do that, or would he need a Catholic priest? A Romish ritual might do more harm than good. There were enough people who still thought Catholics sacrificed babies on the altar.

The majority of people were bloody idiots.

To his surprise, Lovegrove was conscious and upright, if listing. The man managed to be both thin and flabby, but he knew his business and cared for Darien's clothing as if each item was sacred.

"A pleashant evening, milord?" he slurred as he took Darien's silk-lined evening cloak with trembling hands.

"Choirboys."

A sharp look made Darien wonder about the habits of Lovegrove's previous employers.

"The Abbey choir," he expanded. "At Lady Wraybourne's."

"Ah. A mosht select occasion, I'm sure." But the valet's eyes were wide with surprise. He was also useful for his knowledge of the arcane ways of polite society.

"Very select," Darien agreed, surrendering the overly tight black coat and embroidered waistcoat, but not an explanation for his entrée. "I encountered a number of army acquaintances."

"Mosht gratifying, I'm sure, milord," Lovegrove said, steering a course for the chest of drawers. Darien winced when the valet bumped into one corner of the bed.

The gratification was probably genuine. Darien had been amused to learn that a gentleman's gentleman's status depended on the gentleman. In large houses the personal servants were known by their employer's name, so Lovegrove would be Viscount Darien below stairs. He doubted

197

the Prussocks indulged in that sort of nonsense, but the system added to the reasons he'd found it hard to hire a qualified valet. No one volunteered to become a Cave.

Darien was grateful for Lovegrove's skill and social knowledge, but he'd established from the first that when down to shirt and pantaloons he would fend for himself.

Lovegrove retreated, therefore, sighing. Alone, Darien washed his hands and face, but then wandered the room restlessly, remembering Pup walking in here earlier today, without a by-your-leave, and commenting, "Not moved in properly yet, Canem?"

He poured himself some brandy. The last in the decanter, he noticed. Ah, well, he considered it part of Lovegrove's wages. As he sipped, he considered the room.

He'd grown skilled at moving into a billet and turning it into his own by distributing his collection — the richly woven blanket from Spain, the rug made of the fleece of an Andorran sheep, the chess set with the black pieces Moors and the white the forces of Ferdinand and Isabella.

He'd been here three weeks but not put out any of them.

The only personal item on view was his

scarred wooden trunk, which contained all those things.

On impulse, he unlocked the trunk. He tossed the blanket across the bed and the fleece on the floor, where it would greet his bare feet in the morning. He took out his scabbarded saber, the only part of his hussar life he'd retained. What to do with something he'd worn most of the time for so long?

Perhaps he'd hang it on the wall one day, but for now he laid it across the dressing table.

He took two wooden boxes out of the chest. He put the larger one containing the chess set on the table by the window, but didn't open it. Then he set the slender flute box beside it.

Had he really played no music since moving in here?

He'd learned to play the instrument precisely because his father had considered all music unmanly, but in particular the smaller, delicate instruments. It was a trivial rebellion — the only sort he'd been likely to get away with — but it had provided blessings. One couldn't haul a piano around battlefields, and even a violin could be a burden, but his flute had traveled everywhere with him and had often driven away the dark.

He prepared the instrument, remembering how often Foxstall had complained. He had as little taste for music as Darien's father, and he'd sneered at an officer playing for the amusement of the men, which Darien had often done.

Foxstall had never understood the more subtle ways of gaining allegiance. Darien had learned them mostly from his first captain, Michael Horne. The first real stroke of luck in his life had been to land under that man's command. Horne hadn't been a brilliant soldier, but he'd been steady, conscientious, and truly kind. He'd tolerated an angry lad, but only to a point, and rewarded improvement.

Perhaps he'd truly been fatherly, for he'd been over forty, though why any man should choose to adopt Horatio Cave and his load of violent resentments, God alone knew. Darien knew he owed most of what he was today to Horne, and he'd wept to lose him after only three years.

From Horne he'd learned the balance between strict discipline and easy fellowship, which meant the men would follow an officer into the bloodiest battles, follow orders sharply, but retain the ability to think for themselves when needed.

Not too much familiarity — they'd despise that — but the little touches. The hour spent with them around a campfire in the evening, telling stories and making music. Making sure they were cared for when wounded. A memory for anything special going on in their lives, for their family back home and their special interests. He'd allowed those interested to borrow from his small library of books.

When he'd made captain, his men had christened themselves Canem's Curs. They'd meant well, so he'd tolerated it. Did they still use the name? Did they still use "Ca-ve, ca-ve, ca-ve" as their battle chant? Of course there'd been no battles recently except against desperate working folk. . . .

He started a lively jig, the sort the men had liked most, but then found he'd drifted into a lament.

He didn't like the thought of Canem's Curs set loose in India under Pugh, the man who'd purchased Darien's majority. Pugh wouldn't be able to control Foxstall, and Foxstall was a wild force.

If he hadn't sold his commission, he'd be tempted to abandon his invasion of the ton and take over. But the army didn't work like that, and there was never any point in trying to turn the clock back.

He put the flute back to his lips and determinedly played "Jolly Jenny."

His door opened so forcefully that it banged against a chest of drawers.

"Tootling in the gloom, Canem? Can't have that." Foxstall staggered in, taking most of the weight of a very drunk Pup.

Darien lowered the flute. "What the devil are you doing?"

"Bringing your pup home. He cast up his accounts in your hall."

"How did you get in?"

"Pup has a key."

So he did, dammit.

Even Foxstall had trouble steering the wobbly mass to the sofa. When he dropped him there, the spindle-legged sofa shuddered.

"Why bring him in here?" Darien demanded.

"Don't know which is his room, and he's not saying. Besides, strange goings-on to bring a man into your house and not say a word to you." Foxstall blew out a breath. "Need to wet my whistle after that." He grabbed the decanter, then frowned. "Ring for more, old fellow."

"The servants are in bed."

Foxstall put down the decanter with a thump. "Can this be Canem Cave, this dull,

202

tootling wretch?"

"Responsibilities weigh upon a man. Where did you find Pup? Not at Lady Wraybourne's, I assume."

"The luscious Miss Debenham stirred my juices but balked at going further, so I went on to Violet Vane's."

"What-ho!" Pup came vaguely to life. He grinned glassily around. "That you, Can'm? Bit foxed. Plenty t'drink at Vane's."

"For those with money," Darien said. "It's a bad place, Pup."

"Have money. Have lots of money. Should 'a' come, Can. Little redhead. Shweet as shweet. And the black-haired one. Rolled her merrily." His lids fell. "I think . . ." He sank back into slack-jawed sleep.

"I assume he paid," Darien said.

"Why not? Come on, if he wants to be a big bad boy like us, he can bloody well pay for the privilege. When I finished with my whore, he was rolling drunk and ready to toss up his accounts, so La Vane demanded I remove him. Act of Christian kindness, given that he's a moonling."

"Not quite so bad as that."

"Is he not? Devil only knows how he survived the war. Less sense of self-preservation than a ball fired from a cannon."

"Or a pig."

"What?"

Darien shook his head. "Just a memory."

"You fired a pig from a cannon? I never heard of it. Damn waste of pork."

Darien didn't try to explain.

"Why the devil couldn't I have a godfather who'd leave me his all?" Foxstall complained, kicking Pup's hanging boot. "Mine's a vicar with five children."

"Stop that."

Their eyes clashed. "You're in a damn funny mood, Canem."

"Having one's house invaded will do that."

"Bringing Pup home, that's all." Foxstall ranged the room, touching things dismissively. "I'd live better than this if I were a viscount. Surprised to see you at that choral do, but I suppose you have to grovel to the hostesses. Campaign going well?"

Darien had discussed his plans with Foxstall a bit once. That might prove to be another mistake. "Yes."

He could resort to force to get rid of Foxstall, but it hardly seemed worth it. Without women or drink, he'd soon leave.

"Noticed you weren't exactly welcomed yet," Foxstall said with a touch of a sneer.

"Early days. I'm still testing the waters."

"You can dip your toes in River Ton as

often as you like — the ice'll never thaw."

"I have the Debenhams in my grasp."

Foxstall sniggered. "You certainly had the young one. Juicy piece, if not exactly on warm terms."

Darien's jaw tensed, but he only said, "Spying on me, Matt?"

"Just seeking your company. You think you can make any headway there? Forlorn hope — unlike her jolly cousin."

"Leave Miss Debenham alone."

"Not under your orders anymore, and Miss Debenham doesn't want to be left alone, I assure you. I'd think she'd have a pretty dowry, wouldn't you? But her cousin's will be grander."

Darien sent him a warning look, but instead of backing off, Foxstall laughed. "Thought so! Is it a dark and devious plan or are you smitten?"

The desire to commit murder burned, but this was a fuse better extinguished with cold water. "Plan, of course. She's hardly my type."

"Tight-mouthed virgin," Foxstall agreed.

"Enough." Darien put away the flute before he broke it.

This time Foxstall took the warning. "I wish you well of her, but it'll never happen. You resemble your brother too much."

"Marcus?" Darien looked at Foxstall with true surprise. "I damn well don't."

"That's what people were saying tonight. Thought I'd give you a friendly word of warning. Now, friend, lend me some money."

Still digesting Foxstall's words, Darien said, "How much?"

"Three thousand."

Darien stared at him. "Why?"

"Pugh took pneumonia and died. I can get the majority if I can find the money."

When Darien had been selling out, Foxstall had hinted for a loan that would really have been a gift. At that time, Darien had assumed there'd be little money in the family's coffers, but he wouldn't have done it anyway. Fox in peacetime was a powder keg ready to explode. Now the regiment was off to India, where there'd be more action. But Darien trusted Foxstall even less, and this was Canem's Curs they were talking about.

"Sorry, can't do it."

"Dammit, Canem, we've always shared and shared alike."

"We shared the price of a jug of wine or a whore."

"And this means about as much to you now. You're rolling in it!"

"Establishing oneself in society is expensive."

"I see," Foxstall said, and perhaps he did.

Darien tried to soften it. "Think of India. Nabobs, rubies, and harems."

"I make a bad enemy, Canem."

Darien met his eyes. "I make a worse one. Keep away from the Debenhams."

"I'll do what I damn well please." Foxstall slammed the door when he left.

Darien let out a breath. Matt Foxstall had never truly been a friend. He'd shared no secrets with him, sought no solace. They'd simply drank, whored, and fought. Above all fought, and with a wild brilliant fury that lingered finely in the mind. But everything was different now.

All the same, he didn't have so many friends that he shrugged at the loss of one.

He raised the flute and tried the merry jig again, but it had no effect on the dark. And the dark was his foul, pox-ridden brother. He damn well didn't resemble Marcus. They had the same coloring, certainly, but they were completely unalike. His last memory of Marcus was of a cankered, bloated brute.

But what had he been like before the pox ravaged him?

Marcus had been thirteen when Darien

had been born and he'd been living a bawdy man's life before Darien had any memory of him. Marcus, thank God, had preferred to live in London because their father had let him run wild there, but he'd returned to Stours Court too often for anyone's comfort.

Darien surged to his feet and went to the mirror, bracing himself stiff-armed on the dressing table as he stared at his features, distorted by candlelight and the poor quality of the mirror. Perhaps the light and distortion revealed something.

Same dark hair growing up from the high forehead. Same dark eyes with heavy lids. Same slightly olive cast to the skin. Under Spanish sun, he'd turned as dark as the natives while others had burned.

Same cruelty?

No, but Darien recognized that the scars on his face suggested it, and perhaps something stamped there by the worst aspects of war.

Damn Marcus. But that was superfluous. If ever a man was in the lowest depths of hell, it was Marcus Aurelius Cave.

No wonder the ton shrank from this face. No wonder Thea Debenham shuddered at his touch. And Frank, Frank of the pure spirits and generous smile, he had the look, too. On him, dark hair and eyes gave the look of an angel, but would the supercilious, suspicious ton care?

He grabbed his scabbarded saber and smashed the pommel into the mirror, shattering the image.

Behind him, Pup mumbled, "Bad luck that, Canem. Seven yearsh of it. . . ."

Darien whirled, weapon sliding from the sheath — but Pup was snoring again with the look of a dyspeptic cherub.

He rammed the blade back home and carefully put down the sword. He moved the candle to the floor and gathered the shards of glass. Once he was certain he'd found every glinting bit, he put them in a bowl for later disposal.

He looked at Pup, anger still simmering, at him, at Marcus, at the ton, at the whole bloody torture of fate. But what was the point? The past could not be undone, and some pasts would not be forgotten.

A scar remained a scar.

An amputated limb couldn't be regrown.

A moonling wouldn't become a man of sense.

And a Cave would forever be a vile outcast.

He took the colorful blanket from his bed and laid it over the snoring young man.

Canem's Pup — an object of fun, but Percival Arthur Uppington came from a family of modest but impeccable reputation and thus had a better chance of being accepted by the haut ton than any Cave ever would. A better chance, even, of winning the hand and heart of Lady Theodosia Debenham.

He froze. She was simply a means to an end.

He caught sight of his saber, which had so often run with blood. It was still sharp, still able to cleave a man's head in two with one blow. If a bit of bad news made him draw the blade, it had better be out of sight before the next installment arrived.

He buried it deep in his wooden chest and turned the key in the lock, trying to lock away memories and dreams as well.

CHAPTER 18

Darien woke with a start to a strange rumble, thinking *Ghost!*, but then realized it was only Pup snoring on his sofa. He lay back to allow his heart rate to settle, and remembered the details of the previous night.

The glorious harmonies of the choirboys.

The company of friends.

An angry goddess, a cunning Fox, and the cloaked disgust of people who saw Mad Marcus Cave back in their midst.

He was tempted to give up. None of that. He surged out of bed, dressed without assistance and without waking Pup, and then headed off for his morning ride. As he walked to the stables, tranquil morning air relaxed him and stirred hope. He'd made remarkable progress in only a few days, and tonight he would be guest of honor at a special dinner hosted by the duchess.

Morning was like that — fodder for hope.

He rarely drank the night away because it stole morning.

All too many days had progressed to dirt, blood, and violence, however, and there was nothing so melancholy as dawn rising over a field of death, light touching men who would never again rouse from sleep.

He shook off such memories, but he knew this limpid morning would march steadily into a noisy afternoon and on to a hot, crowded evening in the poisoned thicket he'd chosen to hack through —

Gads, he'd be slitting his own throat soon.

He approached Cerberus's box, then paused to listen.

Someone was in there.

There had been some petty vandalism of his part of the stables, but if anyone had hurt Cerb . . .

He reached the box and looked in over the half door. A pale face turned to him, black patch over one eye. Then the mouth split into a gap-toothed smile.

" 'Morning, Major," the man said in a Welsh lilt. "Didn't expect you up so soon."

Darien unlatched the door and went in. Cerberus turned its head in slight acknowledgment, but the horse was enjoying a thorough brushing too much to stir.

"What are you doing?" Darien asked Nid

Crofter. The wiry, almost bald man had been one of the greatest rascals in Canem's Curs, but where it mattered, he'd been honest. Turned horse thief now?

Nid kept on brushing. "Visiting Cerberus, sir. For old time's sake, you might say."

Darien leaned back against a post. "Thought you couldn't wait to get back to your village. In Brecknockshire, isn't it?"

"That's right, sir, and good of you to remember. I did go back there, sir, true enough, but things change, don't they?"

"Some things are damnably permanent. Not suited to country life?"

"No interest in working in a mine, Major."

"It's Lord Darien now."

"So I gather, Major. Very nice, I'm sure."

"A pain in the arse, actually. Broke?"

Crofter shot him a glance. "Not as such, sir, no. But employment's hard to come by, and that's the truth."

Darien considered, but only for a moment. Nid had always been good with horses. "There's not much work in it, but you can be my groom if you wish."

Crofter grinned. "Very good, sir."

"Then wake him up and get him saddled."

Crofter bustled about, clearly having already explored the place.

"Sleep here last night?" Darien asked.

213

A sliding look. "Seemed someone should look after things. There's a decent space above."

"Very well. You'll eat in the kitchen. My staff is minimal and taciturn, but perhaps they'll be friendlier to you. Given you only have Cerberus to take care of, help out in other ways if you're asked."

Crofter slung the saddle onto Cerberus's back. "Very good, sir."

"And if you filch anything, you're out on your ear."

"I'd never touch a thread from your coat, sir! God's honest truth."

Darien checked the horse himself, and then swung on. "Welcome to the Cave domain, Crofter. I hope you don't regret it."

That big grin again. "I'm sure I won't, milord."

Darien rode out, hoping that was true.

He turned toward Green Park, wondering if he was a benefactor or a gullible fool. He was perfectly aware that someone actually wanting to work for him, the prospect of a cheerful greeting every day, had been like bait. He was probably a fool, but war teaches a man to grasp whatever pleasures come to hand and they'd been thin lately.

When a man pushing a barrow of vegetables called, "A fine morning to you, sir!" Darien echoed it back.

Another person in London who didn't shrink from him. There were probably thousands, but not in the quarters where he chose to live.

No one was forcing him to bludgeon his way in where he wasn't welcome. Perhaps even Frank wasn't worth this. But it wasn't only Frank. He wanted a normal life for himself. He was Viscount Darien, and nothing short of death could change that. The title brought responsibilities from properties to duties, such as his seat in the House of Lords. One day soon he'd have to brave that lion pit. His nature didn't allow him to turn his back on his responsibilities.

As he rode along, he tried to imagine what a normal life might be.

A comfortable home for a start. Instead, he had Stours Court, Greenshaw, and a scrap of land in Ireland. And Cave House, God help him. If he didn't live in it, who would?

A jangling bell alerted him to a milkmaid leading her cow and goat down Park Lane, crying her wares. On impulse, he halted and requested some milk. The sturdy woman — wife, not maid, he was sure — worked the cow's udders to fill a frothing bowl and gave it to him. He drank the rich, warm, sweet liquid. Was it delicious because it reminded a person of mother's milk?

If so, it wasn't his own mother's. She'd never fed any of her children. They'd all been given into the care of a local family with a child of a similar age until old enough to wean.

In a fairy story, he would have a devoted foster brother who'd shared the milk, but he'd suckled the milk intended for a stillborn Lagman child. He had some faint memories of kindness there, but they could be wishful dreams. They'd certainly never tried to protect him from his family.

On his recent visit to Stours Court, widowed Mrs. Lagman had fussed over him in the village. She was over sixty now and weathered by time and living under the Caves, but her smile had been broad. He'd put it down to looking for favor from the new lord, but had he misjudged her? After all, the whole family would have been evicted if they'd tried to protect him. Or worse could have happened, given Marcus's temper. Most people avoided being heroes, and it was damn wise of them.

He returned the bowl and paid the woman twice her price, then rode on. Did anyone have good memories of childhood?

Dare Debenham, probably, damn him.

Van, too. He'd run wild in the countryside with his two friends — now Hawkinville and Amleigh — always certain of a friendly face. Apart from one gamekeeper, Darien remembered with a smile, whose life the three boys had made hell. Van's reminiscences had been both pleasure and pain.

Darien had run wild in the countryside, too, but in order to escape the house. Indifferent servants had made escape easy, so he'd ridden out early every day to fish the streams and snare rabbits for food. He'd often climbed the steep hill to the crumbling ruins of Stour Castle, where he'd imagine himself the great Lord Rolo Stour, defending the keep against the enemy.

Lord Rolo's enemies had been the Empress Matilda's forces in the twelfth century, but Horatio Cave's had always been the imagined images of his father, Marcus, and Christian.

He'd desperately wished he were a descendant of Lord Rolo, but the Stours had died out long ago after picking the wrong side too often in royal squabbles. In the sixteenth century the estate had been given to a royal clerk called Roger Cave, doubtless for sneaking around or keeping dirty secrets.

As soon as Frank had been old enough,

he'd taken him along on his adventures. It had been to remove him from the dangers of the house, but he'd proved useful.

One of the gatekeepers' wives had been childless, and Mrs. Corley, round-faced and kindly, would have adopted angelic Frank if she could. She fed him fresh bread and jam and poured him mugs of creamy milk.

Horatio Cave had never had Frank's beauty or charm, but Mrs. Corley would let no child go uncherished, so he'd received the same nourishing food, the same smiles, and even, sometimes, the same bosomy hugs. He'd probably stiffened like a wild thing when she did that, for mostly he remembered a gentle hand on his shoulder or head.

He did remember, however, her praise. Praise was scarce as hen's teeth in Stours Court, but Mrs. Corley would look at him with her bright eyes and tell him how good and brave he was to look after his brother. Of course he'd told her about Lord Rolo, and she would tell him he was just like that hero and would grow up to be a great man.

Were smiles and words, like fresh bread and creamy milk, nourishing?

The milk.

Perhaps that had stirred these sentimental memories.

Mrs. Corley had tried to protect them. When Darien had been about ten, Marcus had beaten Frank. The kind woman had tried to speak to their father about it, and not long after, she and her husband had left the estate. He'd heard that Corley had taken his wife away for her own safety, and it could be true. It's what Darien would have done in that situation.

As Darien entered the park, he tried to push aside all thought of Stours Court, but his memories were like seeds underground, swelling into growth.

There'd been a stable lad, sly and coarse but happy to show the lord's lad how to trap rabbits and steal beer from the alehouse.

A nursery maid, hard-faced and short-tempered, but quick to hide him and Frank if his father was in a drunken rage, or if Marcus turned up, drunk or sober.

She'd betrayed them once, but only after Marcus had twisted her arm out of its socket. Frank could have been no more than four, but Marcus had dragged them both around the house with ropes around their necks, whipping them if they cried. The devil alone knew why.

Or why he'd abruptly lost interest, tossed them in a wooden chest, and put a statue on top so they couldn't get out. It had been pure chance that there'd been gaps between the old oak planks, for it had taken hours for the servants to pluck up the courage to release them.

Darien laughed wryly.

He should have remembered that most seeds grow into weeds. He inhaled and deliberately focused on the beauty around him. A thrush's beautiful song; the waving daffodils and splashes of bluebells; ducks and swans cruising smoothly over sunshine-sparkled water, leaving a silver wake. The delicious purity of the air.

All real and here for all, even a Cave.

He considered where to ride that wouldn't cross the way of the few tonnish people up and about at this hour. There were a number of briskly walking men, and a few more riders in the distance. Nursery maids were exercising apparently cherished children, and an artist sat sketching on a tablet braced on his knee.

Sketching him.

Darien rode around to see the drawing. The sketch was quick lines but conveyed a great deal. "I look like a statue," he said.

The artist, a young man with shaggy brown hair and threadbare clothes, turned his head. "That's what you looked like."

"What do you work in? Oils? Watercolor?"

The artist swiveled to face him completely, flipped to a new piece of paper, and began drawing again. "Mostly charcoal. It's cheap."

"Show me."

The young man flashed a look, clearly resisting an order, but then he turned the drawing. Head only this time, and very few lines, but again he'd caught something — and it was Canem Cave, not Mad Marcus.

"If I advance you money will you prepare an oil sketch? If I like it, I'll pay for a completed work."

The eyes grew wary. Here was someone else who'd learned about life in a hard school. "Which picture?" the artist asked.

"The mounted one first."

"First?"

"If you're as good at painting as sketches, perhaps I'll make you my official artist."

He'd spoken wryly, so it wasn't surprising that the young man looked skeptical. "And who, may I ask, are you?"

Darien faced reluctance to identify himself and won through. "Viscount Darien."

The expression stayed dubious, but a flicker showed the young man was threatened by hope. The stunning thing was that he showed absolutely no sign that Viscount Darien meant anything to him other than the possibility of patronage or disappointment.

"I'll need five pounds, at least." The young man was working on his sketch again, perhaps to hide his face as he bargained. "Apart from the canvas, paints and the rest, I'll need to rent a place with better light. I'm in a cellar now."

"Your name?" Darien asked.

The artist looked up, and then suddenly smiled. "Lucullus Armiger. Don't think I made it up. I ask you, who would?"

Darien laughed. "What do people generally call you?"

"Luck. Which has not, thus far, been prophetic."

"We can hope that has changed. Present yourself at Godwin and Norford in Titchbourne Street this afternoon and you'll receive your five pounds. I expect to see the preliminary work within a week."

Luck Armiger looked at him, still guarded, and Darien wondered if warped pride would make him balk. But then he said, "Thank you, my lord," with simple dignity, and stood to present the drawing he'd worked on.

It was the sketch of Darien's face, more complete now, though still doing its magic with remarkably few lines. Darien would like to study it, to understand what the artist had seen and decide whether it was true, but he handed it back. "I don't want to fold it. Leave it with my solicitors." He turned Cerberus, but then looked back. "You have too much talent for your situation. Why?"

"God's gift," Luck Armiger said, but then smiled ruefully. "A rebellious temperament doesn't lead to patronage."

"It won't bother me if the work's good." Darien touched his hat with his crop and rode away.

A patron of the arts? He laughed at his own pretensions. What he was purchasing was a new image of himself with which to smother the foul ones.

It was probably all lies. Artists were notorious for flattering their customers. But he didn't think Luck Armiger's nature would permit flattery. He'd clearly been well taught and had natural talent, so he must have offended a great many customers to end up in a cellar able to afford only paper and charcoal.

A valet, a groom, an artist. What an entourage he was acquiring.

And a sycophant — Pup.

But if he were to alter course and intersect with those two gentlemen cantering nearby, the chances were that they'd see Mad Marcus Cave returned and veer away.

He didn't alter into their path, but he looked down the long sweep of grass, then leaned to pat Cerberus's neck. "Come on, old fellow, let's loose Mad Dog Cave on this smug little world."

He signaled a charge and Cerberus shot forward, clearly reveling in action as much as he did. Darien laughed aloud for the hot, familiar thrill of it and wished there were an enemy ahead to shatter with bloody force.

CHAPTER 19

"That's Canem. Look at him ride!"

Thea reined in her mount and looked where Cully was pointing. A gray horse was streaking across the park far too fast for safety or propriety. "He's mad."

"In all the best ways."

"Cully, it's insane to gallop where there could be mole or rabbit holes."

"He'll be all right. He's a magnificent rider."

"Which doesn't give him magical powers!"

Thea instantly regretted her snappish tone, but Cully's idol had come up in conversation far too often this morning already.

She'd woken early after a restless night and desperately needed fresh air and exercise. She hadn't wanted a decorous ride with her groom, so she'd sent a message to Cully's barracks, asking if he were free to escort her. He had been, and they'd enjoyed some brisk canters along the paths. Her mental balance had almost been restored, and now this.

She turned her mount's head away. "Come along. You said you were on duty soon."

Cully turned his horse with hers, but he must have been looking back because he suddenly exclaimed, "God!" wheeled his horse, and kicked it into a gallop.

Thea turned, too, and her heart leapt into her throat. The gray pranced riderless near a figure on the ground.

Idiot! Hadn't she predicted as much? She urged her horse flat out after her cousin, but by the time Cully arrived, Darien was sitting up, hatless but clearly unharmed.

As Darien bounced to his feet to brush himself off, Thea reined in her horse, hoping he hadn't noticed her speed. It was too late to hope to escape his notice entirely or she might have ridden away. Sure enough, he looked around and saw her. But then he turned to his horse.

She approved, of course — his insanity had risked the animal's life — but it stung that she counted for so little. He'd run rampant through her sleepless thoughts, and he probably accounted for some wildly

226

peculiar dreams, but she scarcely warranted a look?

"Is he all right?" Cully asked, already off his horse. He gave his reins to Thea and joined his idol.

"I think so." Darien was testing his horse's gait.

Two other riders came up, but Darien said something — doubtless that all was fine — and they left.

The gray looked like a cavalry mount and even bore some scars as evidence. How did men endure riding such faithful animals into danger? She supposed there was no choice, but perhaps the navy was better. Ships did not have flesh to be torn or minds to feel terror.

"No damage at all, I don't think," Cully said, circling.

"Thank heaven." Darien patted the horse's neck then rubbed his cheek against his mount's head. The tenderness of the gesture caught at Thea's heart. Then the horse gently butted him. Apologetically?

It was his fault, you foolish animal. Don't let him off so easily.

"Mole hole?" Thea asked to remind him of that.

Darien turned to her. "Possibly." He passed the gray's reins to Cully and walked over to her, swooping down to pick up his hat in a fluid way that showed he'd suffered no ill effect. His dark hair was in disarray, however, and dirt smudged one cheek.

Disarming.

Illusion.

"Did my folly interrupt your ride?" he asked. "I apologize."

"You're lucky you and the horse are unharmed. King William died in a similar accident."

"You would have mourned?"

"I would mourn any untimely death."

"I'm surprised you would think mine untimely," he said.

"I don't wish you dead, Darien. In fact, I do not think of you at all."

"And I thought I was the bane of your life." She glared at him and he added, "We must discuss this more tonight."

The dinner. On impulse, Thea said, "I may not be able to attend."

His lips twitched. "Coward."

"Nonsense."

"To live life avoiding risk is not to live at all, Thea."

She met his eyes, enjoying looking down at him. "You want me to take risks? Very well." She let go of the reins of Cully's horse, turned her mount and called, "To

228

the water!"

She set off in a direct line, flat out. The wind whipped at her hat and veil and she knew the man had infected her with his insanity. She could kill herself this way!

She had no hope of winning against two cavalry officers, even when they'd both been dismounted at the start, but she leaned low and tried. When she reached the water unpassed, she wheeled her horse and accused the nearest rider: "You let me win!"

Darien reined in his horse. "You never said it was a contest."

"With you, sir, it's *always* a contest."

His eyes flashed. "How very exciting."

Before she could rage at him, Cully reined up, protesting, "You could have killed yourself, Thea!"

"You were pleased enough at Darien racing his horse about. A lady isn't allowed to take similar risks?"

He stared. "Well, no."

She suddenly remembered who she was and where she was. "I'm sorry, Cully."

"So I should think. Fine show if you broke your leg or worse when under my care."

"Some mad impulse took me."

"Moon madness?" Darien asked.

"It's not a full moon, sir," Cully pointed out.

Cully didn't understand, but Thea did. How dare the wretched man talk of such womanly matters? He did these things deliberately to provoke her, just as Foxstall had predicted.

She turned her horse toward her cousin. "We really should get back. You're on duty soon."

Cully pulled out a pocket watch. "Hell!" he exclaimed, then apologized, blushing. "Canem, could you escort Thea back to Great Charles Street?"

Thea opened her mouth to protest, but Cully was already on his way at a canter, taking compliance for granted. She turned a baleful look on Lord Darien.

He raised a hand. "You can't imagine I arranged this."

"You could have staged that tumble."

"What a suspicious mind you have." He looked around. "Which way to your home?"

"Through there," she said, pointing her crop at a gap between houses.

"A better ride via the Mall, surely."

He was right, and Thea would feel safer in open spaces. As they headed toward the tree-lined ride, Thea realized that she had an excellent opportunity for rational discussion. She was in the open, in public, and on horseback. No wild impulses could overtake her, and even a Cave couldn't harm her here.

"Lord Darien —"

"Call me Canem."

She frowned at him. "No."

"Why not? I call you Thea."

"Without permission."

"Goddess, then."

She inhaled. Squabbling would serve no purpose. "We need to talk. Last night . . ."

"Was most interesting."

"The discussion did not go well," she persisted, "but if you have thought on my words, you must see sense."

"Must I?"

His tone was unreadable, and a glance showed a face that offered no more clues.

"You have my parents' approval, Darien. Last night you were thrust into the inner circle —"

"Thrust?" He sounded startled and amused.

"*Rammed,* if you prefer."

"Oh, I don't think so."

She glared at him. "Why are you laughing at me? This is a serious matter."

He sobered. "Most definitely."

"Thank you. As I explained last night, a peculiar betrothal would be counterproductive. It would swell interest and speculation rather than shrinking it. You agree?"

"To shrinking rather than swelling?" He sounded dubious.

"You can't want even more scrutiny."

"Can't I, Goddess?"

"Don't call me that!"

"You are a most demanding and unreasonable woman."

"I am all reason if you'd only pay attention." She studied him more closely. "Did you bang your head in that fall?"

He laughed, which was enough to throw her completely off balance.

Then he said, "Very well."

"Very well, what?"

"I'm willing to consider your point that a betrothal is unnecessary. But if I release you from your promise — and it was a promise, my lady, don't deny it — what will you give me in return?"

"Why, you . . . !" But Thea knew her opponent. He would require something.

She might be able to get away with very little in return while he was in this strange mood, but she wanted to nail this shut. And she had promised.

"My unstinting support," she said. "I will be your approving companion in public on every possible occasion."

He considered her. "Word of a goddess?"

"Word of a *Debenham*."

"Done."

She laughed with relief. "Thank you!"

"So delighted to jilt me —"

"Not precisely jilt."

"— but your agreeable company will be compensation."

"For six weeks only," she said, wishing she'd made that clear.

"For six weeks," he agreed — so easily that she began to worry. What had she overlooked?

"Good," she said. "Then let's consider strategy."

"I think you mean tactics."

"Do I? What's the difference?"

"Strategy is the overall plan. Tactics are specifics when faced with the enemy."

"I believe we need both, then."

"We have our strategy, drawn up, I think, by your mother, whom you did compare to Wellington. We are the ground troops, putting it into execution. Do you play chess?"

"No."

"Pity. It's an excellent simulation of war."

"This is not precisely war, Darien," she objected. "It's more like diplomacy."

"You, Lady Thea, have not been feeling the sharp edge of the sword."

"Oh, have I not? It's been extremely

uncomfortable, and it's going to grow worse before it gets better. But you mustn't think of it as war. Truly. You can't rampage around killing people —"

"You have a strange notion of war."

"We need to employ subtlety," she persisted. "A slow invasion rather than a violent thrust."

"Or a slow thrust?" he said, and his eyes were bright again.

"There's no such thing as a slow thrust," she said.

"A slow slide, then?"

That fall. He truly was, as they said, dicked in the knob, but she'd take advantage of it.

"If you wish," she said. "You must be gentle as you enter the inner circle."

She heard a choke. "Absolutely. And delightful to contemplate."

What did she do if he started to vomit? "No, Darien, it will be *difficult*," she explained patiently. "There will be resistance, perhaps strong resistance."

"Poor lady."

"I'm glad you realize how uncomfortable this will be for me."

"I wish I could make it otherwise."

She looked at him. He sounded sincere. She might be able to gain more concessions, but it seemed like taking unfair advantage of an imbecile.

"Just do as I say," she instructed firmly.

"Your every wish will be my command." But there was that glint again.

"Are you *drunk,* Darien?" That could explain his fall. Surely cavalry officers were not so easily unhorsed.

He suddenly laughed. "Only on you, my goddess, only on you. You delight me, always."

Something shivered inside Thea, something to do with his casual, fall-roughened appearance and laughing eyes. This wasn't her image of him and she didn't want it to be.

"Don't," she said.

"Don't what?"

Instead of all the reasonable things she could say, "Don't laugh" escaped her.

"You are a most unreasonable goddess."

"I know. I'm sorry. I didn't mean that." She looked at him, bewildered. "I meant, don't flirt with me."

"I wasn't."

"Then what were you doing?"

His humor faded, perhaps into regret. "You're right, I was flirting, and that is inappropriate in our situation."

They turned off the Mall by Carlton

235

House, into streets filling with delivery carts and barrows where their riding needed attention. It was like moving from a magical place back to the noisy mundane, and a good thing, too. Something had threatened to spin out of control back there.

They rode, hooves clattering on cobblestones, to her front door, where he dismounted and used the knocker. The footman came out to hold Thea's horse until a groom came around. Darien came to help her down.

"I can manage," she said, instinctively trying to avoid his touch.

"With dignity?"

"With a mounting block," she admitted.

She could insist he hold the horse so the footman could assist her, but that would break their new agreement. When he reached up to put his hands on her waist, she didn't resist. She placed her hands on his wide shoulders as she would with any man and was brought smoothly to ground, breathlessly aware of his strength and control. She stood for a moment, face-to-face with him, body almost to body. As they had been once before.

His dark eyes were somber. "We're flint and tinder, Thea, with gunpowder stacked all around us."

"Then free me."

He stepped back. "I can't. I only wish we had a safe place in which to explode. Till dinner."

He mounted his large horse so smoothly he almost flowed onto it, and then rode away as if he and the horse were one.

Explode, indeed.

But parts of her knew exactly what he meant.

Till dinner. A part of her, most of her, wanted to plead a headache and avoid the event, but she'd made a promise, this time completely of her own free will. Nothing would permit her to break that.

The unsettling thing was that she no longer feared any dark harm Lord Darien might plan. Instead, she feared the lightness she'd encountered this morning — an ease in his company that could dissolve all the barriers she possessed. She needed every one of them to stay safe.

CHAPTER 20

Thea wanted to think about what had happened, but mornings were the duchess's time for administering her many good causes, and Thea was expected to help with record keeping and decisions. Then she was dragged into a meeting about tattoos with some eminent men from the Horse Guards.

After Waterloo, they'd believed Dare dead because of the evidence of an officer who'd seen him fall, and because he hadn't been found alive. But his body had never been found. They knew why now, but at the time they had assumed it had been stripped of identification by looters and tossed into one of the many mass graves. The agony of that had led Thea's mother to decide that all soldiers should be tattooed. Nearly everyone thought it ridiculous, but no one could ignore a duchess.

Thea plied the three generals with tea, cakes, and charm, leaving the heavy gun work to her mother.

The generals raised the subject of costs.

The duchess shot that down with a list of patrons willing to come up with the money.

General Thraves said it was unwise to put the men in mind of death.

"I don't see how death can be out of their minds," the duchess said, "given their trade."

"But we're at peace now," General Ellaston said smugly.

"Then why," asked the duchess, "have an army at all?"

Ellaston reddened. "India, Canada . . ."

"Do these activities not carry danger?"

"Well, of course. . . ."

"And thus risk of death?"

"Less, your grace, much less!"

"Gentlemen, if you can assure me we will be free of major warfare for the next thirty years, I will abandon my project. But I will also ask the duke to scrutinize army spending very closely."

The men exchanged harried glances, then assured her the project would be considered at the highest levels immediately, and fled. Thea gave in to laughter.

"Dolts," the duchess said, picking up her neglected teacup. "Women should administer the army. We're the ones skilled at feeding, clothing, and caring for people."

"At least we'd make sure they had boots to march in and food before a battle."

"Don't they?" Her mother came alert.

"Only an isolated incident, I'm sure," Thea said quickly. "And supply lines must be very difficult."

"Challenges are made to be overcome. I was not made for a life of idleness, Thea, and nor were you. You should consider that as you choose a husband."

Thea picked up a cream puff. "Choose one who'll be a lot of work?"

"That's not what I mean and you know it. You might be suited by a man with a cause. A Wilberforce or Ball."

"Politics bore me, Mama. I'd much rather deal with practical problems. Hospitals for the sick and refuges for the aged."

"Laws often lie beneath such problems, dear, and politics is all about laws. Women would do a better job there, too. I was speaking to Mrs. Beaumont. A most interesting woman. She and Beth Arden are working toward some changes in electoral policy."

Oh, Lord. Not social revolution now. "What changes?" Thea asked.

"To get women the vote."

"Mother!"

"Tell me one reason why women shouldn't be allowed to vote," her mother demanded with a new and terrifying militancy.

"We don't own property?"

"Even women who do can't vote. Ladies who are peeresses in their own right have no vote and are denied their seats in the House of Lords. What justification can there be for that?"

None, but Thea suppressed a groan at the prospect of her mother on this warpath.

She clearly didn't suppress it well enough.

"We have great privilege and power, Thea. It is our duty to use it."

Thea agreed and escaped to go shopping with friends. Sometimes she envied Maddy, whose mother would never preach such lessons to her.

Her enjoyment of Bond Street was marred by a great deal of chatter about Caves and Darien, about Mad Marcus and Sweet Mary Wilmott. Caroline Camberley wanted to walk to Hanover Square to see the dreadful house. "I wonder if there's still blood on the steps," she asked with a delighted shiver.

"After six years, Caroline?" Thea said. "Don't be silly."

"Since this morning!" Caroline said. "Didn't you hear? A maid on an early errand saw it."

A chill swept over Thea. "There's been another *murder?*"

"Well, no," said Caroline. "Not that I've heard, anyway."

"Then what?" Thea asked.

"A prank," said Alesia. "A way of showing Lord Darien he's not welcome in good society."

"He is dining at Yeovil House tonight." Thea was driven to speak by her promise, but also by natural outrage at all this.

Three pairs of eyes stared at her.

"Thea!" Alesia gasped. "Will you have to be there?"

"Of course, and I won't mind at all." Might as well be wholehearted. "I find Lord Darien pleasant company. And he is one of our noble veterans. He deserves better than this."

"But . . ."

"He's a hero," she swept on, and recounted some of his exploits.

"Very praiseworthy," Caroline said without conviction.

Alesia said, "You'll have much to tell us next time we meet, won't you, Thea? But rather you than me."

Thea seethed all the way home and sought her mother. The duchess already knew about the blood on Darien's doorstep. It was the gossip everywhere.

"So petty!"

"I wouldn't exactly call it petty, Mama."

Her mother sighed. "No, you're right. It sets things back, but that means we must work harder. I hope you corrected any false impression."

"As best I could. I tried to trump it with his military record."

"Excellent."

"I'm surprised Darien didn't mention it, though. This morning."

Her mother stared at her. "This morning?"

Thea blushed — for no good reason. "I went riding with Cully, and we met him. Cully ran out of time, so Darien escorted me home."

If she'd expected concern, she'd been wrong. "Excellent. That will have created exactly the right impression."

"I'm not sure anyone saw us. Anyone in the ton, I mean."

"Someone will have. Someone always does. Now, go and prepare for dinner, dear. You must look your prettiest."

Thea went to her room thoughtfully.

The blood would only be from a pig or such, but she felt as if everything had become much darker. As if the reestablishment of the Cave name had moved from being a danger of embarrassment to being danger in fact.

Nonsense, of course, but she changed her mind about her dress. She'd planned to wear her red silk again, perhaps as some sort of private message to Darien, but the color was too much like blood. Instead she had Harriet find a sunshine yellow one from last year.

It was part of a brief fad last year for "country in Town" and was cut on simple, full-bodied lines with little ornamentation beyond a lacy apron. The aim had been to look as if one was about to wander out with a basket to pick wildflowers, but of course like all fashion the filmy gown would be useless for any practical activity.

It was a silly creation, but it was the antithesis of dark deeds and malicious blood. Thea completed the look with loose hair threaded with a ribbon and simple silver jewelry, bracing herself for the evening ahead.

The company would be a carefully assembled group of people with military, political, and diplomatic connections. People likely to appreciate Darien's qualities and achievements and share some of his interests. That meant, however, that she and he would be two of the youngest there, and thus they were to be partners. Her mother had decided to ignore the convention of pairing by rank.

"Darien will be one of the highest-ranking gentlemen, dear, and would end up with someone much less compatible than you."

It showed no consideration of how she would feel, but Thea was determined to play her promised part.

CHAPTER 21

Darien was aware of Thea as soon as she entered the drawing room. He tried to talk intelligently to Lord Castlereagh about the reconstruction of France while aware of her every move. As she greeted people with easy confidence, he noted the way her yellow dress concealed her figure. It was full, and gathered into the high waistband so that he couldn't see a single curve. Even the bodice rose high, entirely covering her breasts.

Did she think dressing like a schoolgirl made her less appealing?

She arrived at him and smiled. "Lord Darien. How lovely to see you this evening."

Her unstinting support. That's all it was. Her payment for his mercy.

They chatted for a moment and then dinner was announced. She took his arm and they processed downstairs to the dining room. "Loose hair really isn't wise, you know," he said.

A wary look. "Why not?"

"It makes a lady look new come from bed."

She gave him one of her heavy-artillery smiles. "Another thing a gentleman does not say to a lady."

"Not even to warn?"

"No. In any case, you clearly don't know many ladies — in that sense. A lady braids her hair to bed, or confines it in a cap."

He struggled with laughter. "Really? You'll do that on your wedding night?"

"We will *not* discuss my wedding night, Darien."

"I suppose not, now it no longer will be ours."

Her color rose, beautifully. "It never would have been ours."

"We're arguing again. What a shame we're in company. We could kiss and make up."

"When pigs grow wings," she said, putting on a bright smile as they entered the glittering dining room.

He had to work to keep his smile moderate. She'd clearly been waiting to make that retort.

Thea sat to the meal pleased to have had the last word there, but still churning inside under the effect of his very inappropriate words.

Her wedding night.

It was a subject she'd thought about, wondering who her husband would be and exactly how it would spin out. She'd heard promises of pleasure and warnings of horror, but she'd never thought about what to do with her hair.

If Darien were her husband, clearly he'd want her hair loose for some reason.

Of course he wouldn't be, but if he were . . . ?

Stars! Stop thinking about such things. She turned to Viscount Sidmouth and asked about some renovations to his estate.

Under her parents' skillful direction, topics throughout dinner were varied and entertaining, but all comfortable for Darien. They touched on the past war frequently enough to remind everyone that his military record was excellent. No, everyone here did not instantly become his friend, but Thea could tell that many barriers were lowering.

When the ladies went to the drawing room for tea, Thea played the piano as background to gossip. She was expert enough to be able to keep track of conversation at the same time. It only touched on Darien occasionally, and no one mentioned blood or Wilmotts, but then, all the ladies knew that he was one of Sarah Yeovil's special projects.

When the gentlemen joined them — quite quickly — Thea surrendered the piano to Mrs. Poyntings and went to assist her mother in handing round more tea. They always did without servants during this time. She made sure to take Darien's and to smile as she gave it.

The best way to regard him, she decided, was as a friendly ally. Almost a brother.

"Still intact, I see," she said.

"Only nibbled around the edges," he agreed.

"Are you trying to tell me that men really do talk about weighty affairs during their after-dinner conclave? That it's not all horses and loose women?"

"Now that, Lady Thea, is definitely not the sort of thing a gentleman discusses with a lady."

A spurt of genuine laughter escaped and she saw it reflected in his eyes.

She looked away. "You certainly didn't linger."

"And deprive the ladies of their dangerous thrill? I think I'm supposed to circulate and titillate them all with terror."

She looked back at him. "Probably. Do you need a protective escort?"

"I wish I could, but they'd detect fear and tear me apart." He strolled off into the fray.

Thea watched for a moment, fighting a sudden true liking. This would never do. She joined two ladies who were looking titillated and attempted to present Darien as both a dashing military hero and a man tame enough to be tedious. At the same time, she observed and assessed.

The men would come around, she thought. Having spent most of his adult life in the army, Darien must be comfortable in the company of men. He had qualities they would admire.

She wouldn't say he was entirely without the ability to please women. He certainly had qualities they admired, as Mrs. Invamere and Lady Sidmouth were revealing, even with their shock and trepidation at being in the presence of a Cave. As her mother had said — her mother! — danger did lend appeal to a certain sort of man.

Foxstall's words slithered back. But perhaps Darien wasn't deliberately manipulating her. Perhaps that was simply how he was.

"Lady Thea?"

Thea started, smiled, and attempted to pick up a conversation she had completely lost track of. She'd been caught watching Darien.

Mrs. Invamere smirked. "Men like that

make terrible husbands, dear. But then, no danger of that! A Debenham and a Cave." She tittered.

"Especially as I hardly know the man," Thea said, and instantly felt despicable.

She rose and went to join him, where he was talking to Mr. Poyntings. After a moment, she said, "There are some prints of Long Chart on the table over there. May I show them to you, Lord Darien?"

Looking quizzical, he agreed, and they strolled to a pier table where a folio of prints lay.

"Seeking to know me better?" he asked.

She colored again. "You have sharp ears."

"Unusual after years of cannon fire. But useful."

"I thought you might need a respite."

"Thank you." His eyes flickered over her. "Yellow becomes you. And red."

Thea blushed.

"You wear pale colors too often," he said.

"Really, Lord Darien. That's inappropriately personal."

"I thought it was a compliment."

"Framed in criticism."

"But true. Do you attempt to fade into the background?"

"Don't be ridiculous." She opened the folio brusquely and indicated the first watercolor of her Somerset home, sprawled along its rise of land, golden in sunshine. "Long Chart."

"It looks like a coronet."

"I suppose it does." She turned to the next painting, which was similar but from the back, including the winding river and the lake.

"Scenery provided by nature?" he asked.

"Not entirely, but the countryside is naturally lovely."

He turned to the next picture, a side view. "Will you mind leaving when you marry?"

"No." As he turned another page, for the first time she noticed the strong elegance of his hands. Not flawless, not at all, but they were well shaped and the nails perfect oblongs, well cared for.

"What's your country estate like?" she asked, looking up at his profile. "Is it improved?"

"Not at all, and it could do with it."

"The landscape?"

"Everything." He turned to another sheet, this time to swans on the lake. "Stours Court was built during the brief reign of James the Second — a bad omen in itself — and by a poor architect. It's of a grayish brown stone with appalling proportions. As for the estate, it comprises badly harvested woodland and a bog."

She chuckled. "It can't possibly be as bad as that."

He smiled. "Trust me."

That seemed to resonate in ways beyond the obvious.

She turned the next page, to a detail of the gardens. "The gardens of Stours Court?"

"Overgrown."

"I can understand the recent neglect, but there's been over a century in which to correct structural flaws."

He turned from the pictures to her. "No money. The second viscount stuck by the Stuarts longer than was wise. He eventually bent the knee to Queen Anne but had lost the opportunity for plum positions and favor. The third flirted with the Stuarts in 1715 and then flung his support to Hanover, but dithering hardly endeared him to the new King George. My grandfather — Devil Cave — was caught in bed with one of George the Second's mistresses before he'd tired of her. And thus it goes. The Caves are not so much marked by wickedness as by political ineptitude."

"It's a sorry tale," she said, but laughing.

"Isn't it?" He raised her hand and kissed it. She allowed it before remembering the room full of people nearby. Awareness of those people made it impossible to snatch her hand away.

So she drew it free gently, even coyly, as if pleased. But she said, "Remember this is playacting, Darien."

"Is it? Then what is my role?"

"My would-be betrothed."

"I would still be betrothed to you if I could. Marry me, adored one."

Thea flipped open her fan and fluttered it. "Alas, sir, I fear you only want my dowry to restore your decrepit estates."

"Not decrepit, precious pearl."

She opened her eyes wide, fighting laughter. "The bog? The mangled woodlands?"

"Only mismanaged, my cherished cherub."

"Cherub!" she spluttered.

"Seraph. More blinding than the sun."

"Stop it."

"It is having the desired effect."

She looked at him sharply, instantly sobered. All calculation. She should have known.

"Your estates are decrepit. My mother is having you thoroughly investigated, you see. She has a report."

"Very wise of her."

"You aren't worried about what it says?"

He smiled wryly. "My dearest Thea, when a man has been condemned as mad and vile, when people shrink away as if he will savage them at any moment, there are no worse secrets to unveil."

He took her hand and led her back among the party, many of whom were giving her very interested looks indeed.

She hadn't wanted to be amorously linked to the Vile Viscount, but he'd done it anyway, damn him. The talk would be all around Town tomorrow — that the Great Untouchable wasn't so untouchable anymore. That she was smitten by Vile Viscount Darien, of all people.

Thea did the only thing she could — she acted as if nothing was amiss. But when the final guest left, she had a headache.

"That went well," her mother said, smothering a yawn. Was she truly unaware?

"I hope so," Thea said. "I tried to be warm to Darien."

"And very convincingly, too."

Thea couldn't hear sarcasm. Perhaps she'd blown the whole incident up out of proportion. Because she'd been angry. Because he'd fooled her and used her. Again. And hurt her, silly creature that she was.

"We can rely on most of those people not

to encourage nonsense," the duchess said as they strolled toward their bedrooms. "Some may even steer talk of Darien into more positive streams, especially the men. But I doubt any will go out of their way to assist him. We need more active support."

"I'm doing as much as I can," Thea protested.

"You're doing splendidly, dear."

The duchess came into Thea's bedroom with her. Harriet slipped away to the dressing room to give them privacy. Thea longed for peace and quiet, but she tried to pay attention.

"His attention to you may seem a little too much," the duchess said, "and it's not fair for you to carry the burden alone. There's a limit to what I can do, as everyone knows our interest. It's time to have the Rogues take over."

Thea remembered Darien's cold anger. His terse, "I want no help from the *Rogues.*"

"Does Darien agree?" she asked.

"Why shouldn't he?"

"That incident at school."

Her mother waved that away. "All so long ago." She kissed Thea. "Good night, dear. You truly were splendid, but this will allow you to enjoy your season as you deserve."

When her mother left, Thea sighed. She

was no longer sure what enjoyment meant or what she wanted, but she knew Darien would not easily accept the support of the Rogues. She was going to have to persuade him. She sat and wrote a note asking him to escort her riding early the next day.

Chapter 22

Harriet had to wake Thea, and — perhaps an omen — the morning was dull and might even threaten rain. Thea struggled out of bed, however, ate her breakfast, and put on her habit.

As arranged, her horse was waiting, being walked in front of the house, but she didn't emerge until Darien rode down Great Charles Street on his gray. The groom gave her a hand up into the saddle, and she was ready exactly when Darien reached her.

Perhaps he noticed. There seemed to be a slight smile on his lips when he raised his hat to her. They rode off toward St. James's Park, hooves clattering on cobblestones.

"So," he said, "you wish to renegotiate?"

"No."

His brows rose. "You couldn't bear more than eight hours without me?"

"Of course not! Why do you have to be so suspicious, Darien?"

"You did say that it's always a contest between us."

So she had. "Only in some matters. In others, we're allies."

An overloaded cart drawn by two huge but weary horses trundled toward them, the cloth stretched over the top flapping in the breeze. Her horse jibbed, and she appreciated the fact that Darien didn't reach to control it. She managed, and they both sidled the horses well away from trouble. When the cart had passed, they rode on.

"This is a meeting of allies?" he asked. "For what purpose?"

She worked up to it gently, explaining her mother's reasoning, but no matter how she tried, she couldn't see a way to soften the end point — except to make it provisional.

"So she wants to bring in the Rogues."

"No." They were entering the park and he moved up into a canter.

Thea pursued. She didn't suppose he was actually fleeing her, but it felt like it. She caught up and kept pace and eventually he slowed, and then stopped.

"The answer is still no."

"They are the best weapons to hand," she protested.

"No."

A wind had come up and it whipped her

veil around her face. Irritated, she tucked it into the high collar of her habit. "This battle means nothing to you then? If it did, you'd accept any means to win."

That hit. She saw it in the tightness of his lips.

"Think of it as using them, if you want. As chaining them and whipping them."

He laughed dryly. "I try not to indulge in self-deception. They pity me."

"No." But then Thea decided that honesty was best. "They did. At school. But not any longer. They believe that they owe you a debt. They will probably pay it by leaving you alone if you insist."

"Evil woman." He rode on slowly. "What will I be expected to do?"

"That's up to you and them, but mostly be seen in their approving company."

Still tight-lipped, he looked at her. "Why do you care?"

"We made an agreement. I see this as part of my unstinting support. I knew you'd reject the idea, but you need to accept."

"It's important to you?" he asked, seeming to give it some special meaning.

Thea looked away. "It will relieve demands on my time."

"Then a bargain."

She turned back. "Oh, no!"

"You don't know what I want in exchange."

"You have no right to ask *anything* in exchange. I'm doing you a kindness."

"You just admitted that you're sloughing off a burden. My price for your freedom — come with me to an Opera House masquerade."

Thea's jaw dropped. "You truly are mad." She instantly regretted the words and braced for anger, but he simply waited.

"You are aware that they are scandalous affairs?"

"Yes."

"Then you know I can't do it."

"Of course you can. You can choose not to, but that is my price."

"Then go drown yourself."

"I'm a good swimmer."

"Tie stones to your boots."

He suddenly laughed. "Ruthless to the core, but not as ruthless as I. If I manage to endure the Rogues graciously, you will attend the Opera House masquerade with me a week on Monday."

"I will be at the Winstanleys' ball a week on Monday. There are to be fireworks at midnight."

"I could provide fireworks at midnight."

Her skin prickled. "Don't be disgusting."

261

"It seems to be my nature. Eleven o'clock."

"The fireworks will be at midnight."

"A week on Monday, at eleven, I'll be outside your house to escort you to the masquerade."

"Then I hope it pours with rain," she said, and rode off at a canter.

He came alongside. "You wish to get wet?"

"*I* will be at the Winstanleys' ball!"

"Soon to miss the fireworks. Because a cruel goddess ordered rain."

She drew up. "You are a most infuriating man!"

"I try. There's no escape, Thea. This is my price if I'm to do your will."

Her scarf escaped again. She confined it again. "I'm only trying to persuade you for your own good!"

"Then refuse my price and we'll say no more of it."

"The same trick as last time," she snapped.

"I know when I hold a winning hand."

She narrowed her eyes. "You're bluffing."

"Thea, Goddess, believe this. I never bluff."

She believed him. She longed to leave him to sink, but she couldn't. Her mother wouldn't give up easily and her mother's chief weapon was herself. But in addition, he truly did need to do this. And, drat the man, she cared.

She tried reason. "It's not even possible. If I made some excuse to stay home from the ball, do you think no one would notice if I left the house at that hour?"

"Poor imprisoned princess."

"I'm *not* imprisoned. But any house is guarded from intruders. What keeps some out keeps others in. How would you secretly leave your house at night?"

He moved his horse into a walk. "With ease. My servants are few and go early to bed."

Keeping pace, she said, "Ours are many and don't. Not all of them, at least. When the family is out, a footman waits in the hall for our return."

"Back doors?"

"Servants sleep near them, and I suspect that at eleven o'clock some would still be up."

"What about the doors out into the garden?"

"From the Garden Room?" She hadn't thought of that. "But the garden is walled."

"There must be a way through the wall. The gardeners don't tramp through the family's part of the house, do they?"

Resolute. Thickheadedly stubborn, more like. Her arguments felt like pelting a rock with ribbons.

"The back wall of the gardens is part of the stables," she realized with satisfaction, "and some of the grooms will certainly still be awake, waiting for the coach's return."

"I lay odds there's a way of sneaking through."

"I don't care! I'm not sneaking out of my house at night."

"Why not?"

She refused to answer. "I wish I'd never met you."

"A familiar feeling, I'm sure. But you need an adventure. You're trapped by cobwebs that you could easily brush aside if you only believed it possible."

"Why on earth should I *want* to throw myself into danger?"

"For the thrill of it?"

She smiled triumphantly. "There you and I differ, Darien. I see no thrill in danger."

"You haven't experienced enough danger to know."

"I've experienced you."

A glint in his laughing eyes suggested a great many responses not made. He spoke seriously. "I can keep you safe, Thea, even out at night. Do you believe that?"

"From footpads, yes. From yourself, most emphatically, no."

"A point. What if I promise to behave as if I were your brother?"

"Tease me to death?"

"Poor sister. Don't be a coward."

"Now that is a brotherly trick, I grant you. A very young brother."

"You never had a very young brother, so how would you know?"

Thea let out a suppressed scream of frustration and rode off. She *was* trying to escape, but he came up beside and kept pace with a sense of leisurely ease. "If you don't do this, you'll regret it for the rest of your life," he called.

"Absolute nonsense!"

But his words struck home.

When she considered her life thus far she saw nothing but the normal, the safe, the correct, and the sane. She'd not even galloped in the park before she'd met him.

Never before had this seemed a *flaw*.

It *wasn't* a flaw. She intended her future to match her past — normal, safe, correct, and sane. With that in mind, she slowed to a decorous pace.

But Maddy's words returned — oh to be gloriously insane, if only once.

She drew up and eyed him. So handsome

in his strong, scarred way. So . . . powerful. Yes, he could keep her safe. From others, at least.

"If I made an excuse not to attend Lady Winstanley's ball," she heard herself say, "a headache, perhaps, my maid would still check on me."

"At eleven?" There was no hint of triumph in his voice. Oh, he was a clever dog. But mad, mad. And so was she.

"No," she admitted. "If I weren't out, Harriet would probably be in bed by then. But my mother might come in when she returned."

Did she want a reason not to do this, or a reason to do it?

"That would be in the early hours of the morning, and you might be back by then. If not, a bolster beneath your covers should do."

"You're like a hawker, teasing people to buy tawdry rubbish."

"I understand the Opera House masquerades are a mix of people of all classes, tawdry to grand."

"And that is supposed to appeal to me?"

"Come, now, are you really so top-lofty? You must have attended a masquerade before."

"No." It suddenly seemed a shameful confession.

"Poor princess. Escape your tower."

Thea felt as mixed up inside as churned cream. She knew she shouldn't let him tease her into risk by childish dares, but he made her sound so dull.

She saw a compromise. "Next Friday," she said, "is Lady Harroving's masquerade."

"Yes?" There was no way to read his tone.

"I might . . ." She took the plunge. "I would be willing to attend that with you if you accept the Rogues' help. If my mother allows," she added hastily. "I'm not sneaking out of my house."

A glance showed complete inscrutability.

"You're offering pinchbeck for gold," he said at last. "A respectable masquerade is not very daring."

"Only more or less respectable. Lady Harroving is only more or less respectable. My mother put the invitation aside."

"But if you wished to go, the duchess would permit it?"

"Probably. You know you have to do this, Darien. You have no choice."

"Don't overplay your hand, Goddess."

At his tone, she had the sense to fall silent. He really was on the edge of refusing, the stubborn, infuriating man. Which made the fact that he was on the edge of accepting fascinating.

"Why?" she asked. "Why is this so important to you? Why will you do something you truly don't want to do?"

She thought he wouldn't answer, but then he said, "My brother."

"Marcus?"

He laughed. "God, no. My younger brother, Frank."

"The naval officer?"

He looked at her, his expression still withdrawn. "The duchess's research?"

"He's in there, but Maria Vandeimen mentioned him. He's no secret, is he?"

"Not at all. Frank has fallen in love, but his beloved's father will not permit a marriage to a Cave. I admit that not being shunned in every drawing room would be pleasant for me, but smoothing Frank's path to marital bliss is my prime motivation."

"That's why you tried to force a betrothal," she said, suddenly seeing the whole picture. "If you were betrothed to me, this other man could hardly object."

"Admiral Dynnevor. Not only wouldn't he object, he'd probably rush his daughter to the altar, salivating at the idea of a connection to the Yeovils. But I let you talk me out of it."

That, too, was fascinating.

"But it was never real, so wouldn't it have been an underhanded trick?"

"All's fair in love and war, and this was both."

"Then why did you let me renegotiate?" she asked, watching him carefully.

"A moment of weakness. You appear to have hit another one. Very well, I'll endure the Rogues, and you will attend the Harrowing masquerade. But if you enjoy it, you will then attend an Opera House one with me."

"You never give up, do you? How will you know if I enjoy it or not?"

"I'll trust your word."

Thea felt a spit of rain in the chilly wind. She didn't think it was the first. She simply hadn't noticed before. "Very well," she said. They should hurry home, but she had one more question while he was in a mood to answer. "What will you do when this campaign is over? Marry?"

"Too far a horizon. It's going to pour. Let's get out of the park, at least."

He raced toward the gates and she had to follow. They made it into the street before the true rain began, and to the Yeovil House stables before it poured. Grooms ran out to take the horses and one helped Thea down; then she and Darien ran into the coach house to catch their breath, both laughing.

She stared at him. He was such a different person when he laughed, but she didn't know which person was the real one.

"Would you like to come in for breakfast?" she asked.

"And drip all over the house?"

"If you ride home from here you'll get even wetter."

"It won't be the first time. Let me know if your mother permits the masquerade."

"And if she doesn't?"

"Then we'll have to renegotiate." He smiled at her as if he'd say more, but then dropped a quick kiss on her lips before striding out into the rain and remounting to ride away.

She watched him, touching her lips. His had been cool and rain-damp, but the sizzle had been hot. Unfair, unfair, that he was able to do that.

There were umbrellas in the stables and she used one to hurry into the house by the scullery door. Once in her room, she stripped off damp layers, trying to recall the morning, but catching only fragments.

Challenge.

Victory.

Laughter.

She didn't truly want him to spend his

time with the Rogues instead of with her. Then there was the new bargain they'd made. She picked at her breakfast, wishing her mother would rise sooner, but unsure whether she wanted permission to go to the masquerade or the protection of refusal.

Impossible man!

CHAPTER 23

As soon as her mother had breakfasted, Thea went to her room.

"You were out in this rain?" the duchess asked, looking at windows running with it.

"It only started toward the end of the ride. The masquerade, Mama?"

"Did you meet Darien by accident again?" her mother asked, clearly knowing it wasn't so.

"I asked him. I wanted to persuade him to use the Rogues' help. I knew he'd be reluctant."

"Really? You're coming to know him well."

Thea couldn't interpret that, but she returned to the question. "May I attend the Harroving masquerade with him?"

"I don't see why not. Much more amusing for you than dinner at the Frogmortons' and then the Ancient Music Society. And Darien will enjoy being anonymous for once."

Thea hadn't thought of that. Was anonymity his main reason for insisting on a masquerade?

"He'll have to unmask at midnight," she pointed out.

"After being admired by many ladies. It's hard to return to frosty disapproval after a thorough flirtation. He must wear the right costume, though. Something romantic but respectable. Do you think he will?"

"I place no reliance on it. He might not be vile, but he is undoubtedly wicked."

Her mother's brows shot up. "I thought you wanted to do this."

Thea sighed. "I do. I do. To an extent. But I'll need to order a costume."

"A good costume takes time. There are a number of mine in the attics here."

"You've attended masquerades, Mama?"

"Of course. I'll just send a note to Darien about his choice and then we'll see if any suits." She sat at her desk to write a note. As she sanded the ink, she said, "A delightful entertainment when properly organized."

"Which Lady Harroving's might not be."

"Maria Harroving is not quite as she should be, but I doubt she allows extremes in her house." The duchess folded and sealed her letter and then turned to look at Thea. "I'm very sorry, dear. You truly have

273

missed a great deal. I did think of bringing you to London in 1814, but you seemed young then and I never anticipated the problems to come." She tapped the letter with one finger. "Do you think perhaps that our troubles have made you overcautious, dear?"

Criticism from her mother, too? Thea's cheeks heated, partly with anger. "If you mean that I prefer to act with propriety . . ."

"I mean that you restrain yourself at an age where a little exuberance would be more natural."

"In other words, you wish I were like Maddy."

"Good heavens, no." The duchess rose to hug her. "Never that, dear. But I fear that needing to be safe will trap you in a sad life."

"It seems to me that seeking danger would toss me into a sadder one."

Her mother grimaced in what might even be irritation. "You don't understand, but perhaps a masquerade will show you. Let's find you a costume."

The duchess sent a footman off with her letter, then summoned Harriet and two other maids. Thea trailed after, feeling abused. She behaved with good sense and propriety and gained the name the Great

274

Untouchable. It had never been a compliment.

Maddy was outrageous and she was popular.

Now her mother, too, implied that she was overcautious and dull. Very well. She'd pick the most outrageous costume her mother had. She laughed at herself. As if her mother would ever have worn anything even close to outrageous.

But, she resolved, if she did enjoy the Harroving masquerade she'd keep her promise. She'd sneak out of her house and go to a scandalous Opera House one with Vile Viscount Darien. And if it all came to disaster, it would be entirely her mother's fault.

Her mother unlocked a door in the top floor and entered a room stacked with boxes, many labeled "Costumes."

"So many," Thea said, amazed.

"Some are your father's. And some Dare's. Gravenham has never cared for masked events."

"Gravenham's a dull dog."

"Thea!"

The protest was probably only for saying it in front of the servants. Her oldest brother, who had the heir's title of Marquess of Gravenham, was dull. She'd once pointed out that calling a child Gravenham from birth might be an oppressive influence. Her mother had replied that the duke had borne the same burden and not been dull at all.

Thea remembered doubting that, but looking at the costume boxes she wondered if her parents had been exuberant when young.

Had they kissed like . . . ?

Did they still kiss like . . . ?

She pushed those thoughts aside and helped the maids lift down the top boxes, beginning to be excited. This was like a treasure hunt, especially when she found gold coins.

"What on earth is this?" she asked, seeing gold among the unbleached muslin wrapping in one box. She peeled back the muslin and blinked at a bodice of gaudy yellow and green satin with spangles of gold. The coins — light and false — were part of a belt.

"Oh, my pirate wench's costume!" the duchess said.

"A pirate wench?" Thea echoed.

"There was a buccaneer ball at Long Chart. Such a long time ago. That was where I met your father." The duchess sighed happily. "A very sprightly costume — it even has a dagger. Would you like to wear it?"

Thea took out the scarlet satin skirt with golden trim but saw that it would reach only halfway down the calf. "I don't think so," she said and rewrapped it, knocked for a loop by this glimpse into her parents' younger days.

"What about Good Queen Bess?" her mother asked, showing some brocade.

"That sounds hot and heavy."

"Yes, it was, even for a winter event. Ah, what about this?" She pulled a length of white cloth out of a box with one hand and a large silver shape with the other. "The goddess Minerva."

Goddess. That immediately appealed to Thea.

"What is this?" Thea asked, taking the lumpy silver tube. It was surprisingly light and she saw it was made of felt with a very thin layer of metal foil on top.

"Armor," her mother said. "Roman style. For the upper body. You know — Minerva sprang fully armed from the brain of Jupiter?"

Now that Thea knew how to look at the object in her hands, she could see that it was indeed a sort of corset made to fit a woman's upper body — curved to every detail.

"Mama, you *wore* this? Visibly?"

277

Her mother turned pink, but her eyes were sparkling. "The robe goes over it." She displayed the white cloth, which was a long sleeveless robe with a Greek key design around the hem.

"The almost transparent robe," Thea pointed out, "and I'll be naked from the waist down."

"You wear a shift beneath, of course, but there's a metal skirt." The duchess found another garment, this time made of strips of silver.

"That can only come down to the knee!" Thea protested.

"This is a masquerade, Thea, not Almack's." The duchess looked around and pointed at another stack of boxes labeled "Heads." "There's a helmet," she told one of the maids. "Large, silver, and with an owl on top."

"An owl?" Thea echoed.

"Minerva's symbol. For wisdom. I should have been carrying it, but there's a spear to manage as well. Perhaps in that corner," she said to another maid. "So we had the owl put on the helmet. It's well designed. Once on, one hardly notices it."

Thea looked at the bosomy silver torso, the metal skirt, and the filmy fabric that would not hide much. She'd promised herself the most outrageous. . . .

Be careful what you promise. When would she learn?

"Sandals," the duchess said, digging into the empty muslin in the original box and finding them — Roman sandals with long silver ribbons that must wind all the way up to the knees. Which would, of course, be exposed by that ridiculous skirt.

Thea put the armor aside and held the robe against herself. When she looked down it trailed on the ground.

"Belt," said her mother. "There's a chain of silver in the safe."

The robe would cover her, and at least veil the armor and her legs, but it would leave her arms bare. "No gloves, I assume." She said it wryly, so her mother laughed as if it were a joke.

"But bracelets and armbands," the duchess said. "They're in the safe, too. The costume will suit you, dear, for you have natural dignity and are wise as Minerva."

That was meant as a compliment, but to Thea it sounded like dull, dull, dull. There was only one possible decision. "Very well. Let's take it downstairs and have a dress rehearsal."

"You truly did wear this, Mama?" Thea

asked, staring at herself in the mirror.

"Twice," said the duchess, still carrying the long spear as if she liked the feel of it.

Or was it a halberd? There was a hatchet blade as well as a point.

"I have sweet memories of the pirate costume," the duchess said, "but the Minerva was my favorite. So much easier to play the part. You must memorize some clever advice for when people ask you for Minerva's wisdom."

"Beware of duchesses wielding blades?"

Her mother laughed. "I never had to attack anyone with it. That does look very well. Believe it or not, my figure was much like yours when I was young. Such a tiny waist I had."

And a generous bosom, Thea thought. Thea was grateful the bodice fit a little loosely there. It lessened the feeling that her breasts, her shape down to her waist, might as well be naked. To her, accustomed to high-waisted gowns, this appeared much more shocking than the lowest of her low evening bodices. She didn't repeat, *You wore this, Mama?* but she thought it.

Of course in her mother's younger days ladies were accustomed to showing their shape down to their waist, but even so. . . .

She was wearing the skirt now, and the

shift beneath, but both came down only to her knees. Could she really go out in public showing her lower legs?

She sat so Harriet could put on the sandals, but when she stood and looked, the cross-woven ribbons did not provide much decency. She grabbed for the robe. Once she had the flowing robe over all it wouldn't be so bad. Then she realized it was open down the front.

Her mother fastened the silver chain girdle, but the flimsy cloth still fell open above to reveal part of her silver torso and below to show her lower legs as she walked.

You wore this, Mama?

Thea felt shaky, as if solid ground had turned fluid under her feet. She'd always tried to behave correctly, but now she didn't know what that meant.

Maria Harroving had a shady reputation, but she was still accepted everywhere.

Maddy shocked people, but she wasn't excluded.

The Duchess of Yeovil — the epitome of respectability — had attended masquerades as a gaudy pirate wench and a half-naked Minerva.

Very well. It was clearly time for change.

A maid presented the helmet — a ridiculously large silver bowl that would cover her hair and even incorporated a mask of sorts. Bits flared out from the sides to cover her cheeks and met a nasal that ran down to the tip of her nose.

And on top sat a small, silver-feathered owl.

Her mother settled the helmet in place. It must have been made of cork, and it was thickly padded inside so it was surprisingly comfortable. Comfortable, that was, for a large, enclosing bowl crowned with an owl.

"It will be horribly hot. And how do I dance in this?"

"With difficulty, but you take it off for the unmasking and there will be hours of dancing after that." The duchess put the halberd into her hand. "There. What memories it brings back."

Thea turned to the mirror again and suddenly felt like someone different. Someone who could have adventures and perhaps even a little exciting insanity. Someone worthy of another fiery kiss. She realized she was disappointed that Darien hadn't attempted to kiss her since that first time.

Did he not want to?

She wouldn't allow that thought. In fact, she'd demand a thorough kiss as her reward for doing this. Why should he always get to set the terms?

She wished there wasn't nearly a week to wait.

And a very frustrating week it was.

That evening, she and her family went to the theater, with Cully, Avonfort, and his sister Deborah as guests. Darien was present, but in other company. The plan was already in operation and he was in the box belonging to the Duke of Belcraven. It sat on the opposite side of the stage to the Yeovil box, which meant a large distance but an excellent view.

The Duke and Duchess of Belcraven were there, as was his heir, the Marquess of Arden and his marchioness. Arden was a Rogue, though if the plan was working, few would think of that. They would merely see Darien in the approving company of another elite family.

Darien was affably keeping his part of the bargain, and when his eyes met hers across the theater, he bowed slightly, as if saying, "See? I keep my promises." If his teeth were gritted, it wasn't obvious. Hers were because Avonfort kept making snide comments about rabid dogs and bloody doorsteps.

"Gads," he said as they rose at the second intermission, intending to stroll in the gallery. "What's Ball doing there?"

They glanced back to see Sir Stephen and

Lady Ball entering the Belcraven box, clearly to speak to Darien. Another Rogue, and this time a respected politician.

"Perhaps he hopes to recruit Darien to the reformist party," Thea said as they continued out of the box.

"Dangerous nonsense," Avonfort said.

"Recruiting him?"

"Reform."

"All reform?" she asked, genuinely surprised.

"With riot and mayhem in every quarter, it's the worst possible time to be changing anything."

"Perhaps there's riot and mayhem because things need changing," Thea pointed out.

"Typical of a woman to come up with a silly idea like that."

With difficulty, Thea accepted that this wasn't the time for a raging argument. "Bonnets and trimming are *so* much more important," she simpered.

He didn't catch her sarcasm. Instead, he smiled indulgently. "Anything that makes you prettier, my dear."

If her fan were a pistol, she might well have shot him. Darien would have understood, but Darien would never have expressed such narrow-minded ideas. Yes, despite his many faults, he had a quick understanding and an open and flexible mind.

She knew then that she wasn't going to marry Avonfort, but that didn't fill her with joy. It wasn't as if she could marry a Cave instead. Her future had recently seemed solid, stable, and orderly; now she faced uncertainty and even chaos.

She fired the thought in Darien's direction. *My life was all in good order before you came on the scene, you wretched man!*

When they returned to their box, two men were taking their leave of Darien in the Belcraven one. One was silver-haired and slightly rotund, and the other was much younger, dark-haired, and elegant.

"Isn't that Charrington?" Thea asked, pointedly. The Earl of Charrington, an epitome of fashion and sophistication, was more Avonfort's type.

"With the Austrian ambassador!" Avonfort exclaimed. "He won't be pleased at having to talk to Darien."

As if in direct contradiction, the silver-haired man laughed and slapped Darien on the back.

"Probably knows him from the war," Thea said, managing not to smirk.

She was truly impressed. The Earl of Charrington was a Rogue. He'd been raised in diplomatic circles, but even he wouldn't be able to force an ambassador to go where he didn't want to go, or to show genuine warmth when there. It was genuine warmth. As she took her seat, she could see it reflected in Darien.

At the next intermission, three military officers with a great deal of gold braid indicating high rank crammed into the Belcraven box and carried Darien away, chatting and laughing.

Thea glanced at her mother and they shared a smile.

"Very satisfactory," the duchess said.

It was, but from Thea's point of view it had been a dull and disappointing evening.

The next day was Sunday, and she and her parents attended service at St. George's, Hanover Square, which they often did. Despite the name, the fashionable church did not sit in the square, but it was close enough to be a natural place of worship for Lord Darien. The plan was that they again show their favor, but Thea attended church in an unseemly eagerness. She looked forward to discussing last night's triumph and how he was feeling about the Rogues.

She saw him across the church, noting as well the people who were still uneasy. Quite a few would be residents of Hanover Square with good reason to distrust a Cave. One of them could be the person responsible for splashing blood on his doorstep.

She leaned close to her mother to murmur, "No more bloody doorsteps?"

"No, but the Rogues set people to watch the house at night."

"Even before yesterday?"

"Yes."

Thea hoped he never learned of that.

Darien was with a fat young man in ridiculous clothes. Surely not his beloved brother. No, he'd be in uniform anyway. She wondered who he was. He didn't look like Darien's type at all.

After the service, her mother went straight for Darien and his companion, who was introduced as Mr. Uppington, who'd been a subaltern in Darien's regiment. As an explanation, that left a lot to be desired. The young man seemed both willing to please and very stupid.

She had no opportunity for private conversation with Darien. Most people dined country style on Sunday, quietly with family in the early afternoon. Thea's mother invited Darien and his friend, which gave Thea a moment's hope, but he and Uppington were engaged to dine at Maria Vandeimen's house. How very unfair.

CHAPTER 24

Darien had no idea why his goddess looked
cross, but he would have liked to spend time
with her and find out. Having Pup around,
however, was like having a troublesome
child. He couldn't be let out of sight without
some mishap — last night it had been
cockfighting and he'd had his pocket picked
and his watch stolen — but Darien was
busier than ever. He needed a keeper,
preferably a wife, and Maria had offered to
help.

As they walked to Van's house, Darien
tried to prepare the ground. "So, Pup. What
are your plans?"

"Plans?" Pup repeated the word as if this
might be a new game. Then he said, "Astley's?"

Astley's was the theater known for circuses
and spectacles.

"I mean for your future. Now you've had

a taste of London, are you ready to settle down?"

"Settle down?"

Holding on to his patience, Darien laid it out. "You've a neat little fortune now, Pup. You'll want a place of your own. A house. An estate. A wife."

"Wife?"

"A pretty woman to come home to. Someone who'll delight in arranging everything just as you like it." A sensible person who'll take care of you like the overgrown child you are.

"Oh, a *wife*," Pup said, as if it were a novel idea. "Don't know about that, Canem. Ladies don't seem much interested in me."

Darien almost said, *You have money now. You only need to show yourself to be hooked.* That wasn't the image to plant in Pup's mind.

"You're here in London in the season. Lovely ladies hanging on every bough, waiting to be picked."

"Like at Violet Vane's?"

"Ladies, Pup. Respectable women. The sort you marry."

"Oh. Wife, eh?" Pup said, clearly still getting to grips with the concept.

His tone was that of a lad presented with his first hunter — thrilled, but nervous

289

about the animal's size and power. He'd never been a coward, however. Foxstall would say he hadn't the wits to know when to be afraid, and he might be right, but that meant that if the right lady could be found Pup would probably mount her without flinching.

Darien pushed that image out of his mind and steered Pup into Van's house.

Maria greeted Pup with good manners and a motherly touch, instantly putting him at his ease. As they dined, she gently interviewed him, framing questions so simply that he soon relaxed and adored her. Darien began to worry that Pup would try to become Maria Vandeimen's lapdog. He'd not intended to off-load his burden in that way.

She introduced the subject of marriage in a roundabout way, rambling on about her first and second marriages. Both were painted as havens of calm and stability. Darien knew nothing of her first marriage, but if Van provided calm and stability, Canem Cave was a ninety-year-old washerwoman.

Amusement died when Maria turned to ask Darien about his own marriage plans.

"None as yet."

"You will want an heir," she stated, ring-

290

ing for servants to bring the second course.

"Doubt it. Frank may oblige. If not, the Cave line will die. Who will mourn?"

"It deserves to live if only for you."

That startled and perhaps embarrassed him. "We're here to discuss Pup's prospects," he reminded her.

"I am capable of driving two horses at once, Darien."

"In different directions?" he countered, and she chuckled.

"Touché. I will steer one and then turn my attention to the other."

"My head's spinning at the image presented."

She laughed again. "You are very literal, are you not? Ignore images and put yourself in my hands and you will be the beginning of an honorable line."

"You terrify me," he said in complete honesty.

"A familiar sensation," Van murmured.

Maria turned to Pup, smiling and softening her voice. "Mr. Uppington. Arthur, I believe?"

He nodded, frozen with a mouthful of something.

"An excellent name, drawing on an ancient king and a modern hero. You should use it more. You will like to be married?" It was a question, but she somehow managed to make it an instruction.

Pup swallowed. "Think so, ma'am. Better than Violet Vane's," he added helpfully.

Van choked. Maria's smile struggled with outright laughter.

"An older lady, I think," she said. "Not *old,* of course, but a little older than you. Young ladies can be so very demanding, and you will like a wife who can run your house for your comfort and advise you how to go on."

Canem thought Pup might object to this, but whether by force of Maria's will or his own inclination, he nodded. "Yes, I would."

She smiled like a madonna. "I'm giving a small dinner party next week, and I will invite a lady of my acquaintance. If you do not care for her, of course we will say no more about it, but I think you will. She's a widow with two young children, but you won't mind that."

"No," Pup said obediently, but added, "Is she pretty?"

"She's pleasingly plump."

Canem had no idea whether Pup liked plump women, but he could see the seed grow shoots and leaves in Pup's mind. Plump equaled pleasing, pleasing equaled pretty. Maria Vandeimen was a truly terrifying woman.

"Her name is Alice Wells," Maria went on. "She is twenty-seven years old and was married to a naval officer who died two years ago. She comes from an excellent family, but unfortunately there's little money and she is obliged to live on her brother's charity, which is not abundant."

She continued a flow of Mrs. Wells's excellence to such effect that when Canem and Pup left the house, Pup was saying "Alice . . ." under his breath. "Pretty name, don't you think, Canem?"

"Lovely."

"And twenty-seven's not too old."

"Not at all."

"Won't mind a couple of children. Like children. Have children of my own, I suppose."

"It does tend to happen."

That led to silence, whether of trepidation or anticipation, Canem didn't know.

"Marriage," Pup said as they neared Hanover Square. "Best thing in the world, marriage, don't you think, Canem?"

From seed to shoot to mighty oak.

"Absolutely splendid," Canem said as he ushered Pup into his house, but he promptly took refuge in the office, Sunday or not. Here he was, surrounded by apparent friends — Rogues. Gad — and now Pup could be safely settled in days. All it needed was a letter from Frank to say he was betrothed. . . . But it was too early for that.

All the same, the change in his situation in less than a week would be gratifying if it weren't so alarming. He felt as if he were in a runaway carriage, lacking all control over his destiny.

Damn women.

But at this rate he soon might have to return hospitality. Entertain in Cave House? Hard to imagine, but he'd better look over the house with that in mind. He visited the drawing room again. It would do, but it'd need a thorough cleaning, which meant more servants. That raised the problem of the Prussocks. They were doing their best and it went against the grain to dismiss them, but the sort of servants he should have wouldn't work under their rule.

Was it possible to hire some maids for the day? He made a note to consult Maria on this and other matters. His pen wandered into curlicues before running out of ink.

Thea Debenham had claimed to know how to run a house.

No. Far too dangerous to involve her in his domestic affairs.

He summoned Prussock and asked for a

tour of the wine cellars. Prussock scowled, perhaps over doing extra work on Sunday, though Darien had seen no sign of piety.

"Not much left," Darien said a few minutes later, surveying empty racks.

"I gather the old viscount drank a lot, milord."

"I'm sure he did. I'll order more. I might be doing some entertaining. Show me how we stand for china, silver, and such."

Now every line of the man's heavy body showed annoyance, but he gave Darien the tour of cupboards of china and glassware. The stock couldn't be called elegant, and no set was complete, but there seemed enough. Darien had no difficulty in imagining a great deal of china and glass being smashed by his family. But silver did not break. When unlocked, the silver cupboard was almost bare.

"Sold, I assume, milord," Prussock said.

"More than likely, but you should have alerted me. What if I had a sudden need of it?"

"You didn't seem to be in the way of entertaining, milord."

Darien nodded and returned to his office. He had long experience of men, many of them scoundrels, and his instincts were ringing alarms.

Sold, or stolen? By the Prussocks? He couldn't accuse them on such scanty evidence, but the viscountcy of Darien and all its possessions were his to take care of now. He wrote a note to his solicitors requesting the inventories made upon his father's death. He sealed it, and then sat there, realizing that Maria's words about him starting an honorable line had settled in his mind like seeds. No shoots and leaves as yet, but there they lay, full of strange promise.

Line meant wife, and wife fired his mind straight to Thea. But he laughed without humor. Thea Debenham, mistress of Cave House? Mistress of Stours Court? One of the Caves?

His revulsion was so strong he rose. He should probably release her from her promise to attend the Harroving masquerade, but he wouldn't, not least because she needed to do it.

He was going to free her from the cobwebs of formality, set her free, so she could fly as she was meant to fly, high and strong. And he'd told her the truth when he'd said he could keep her safe. She'd be no worse for her adventure, but perhaps she wouldn't trap herself for life with that stiff-rumped clotheshorse, Avonfort.

He could do no more than that for her, however, or for himself.

CHAPTER 25

As the next week progressed, Thea's mother remarked at regular intervals how satisfactorily things were going. Thea had to agree, even though she missed Darien. She hardly saw him, and if she did encounter him at some social event, he was engaged with a Rogue and friends of Rogues.

Military men with Major Beaumont, though that sector was mostly on Darien's side anyway.

Reforming politicians with Sir Stephen Ball.

Diplomats with the Earl of Charrington.

Even when she didn't meet him, she could follow his adventures in the press.

While Thea was enduring an afternoon literary salon featuring Mrs. Edgeworth, Darien was racing horses at Somers Town under the aegis of that famous horse breeder and heir to an earldom, Miles Cavanagh.

While she was at a very dull dinner, he attended a gathering of scientists called the Curious Creatures. She'd never heard of them, but wasn't surprised to discover that Nicholas Delaney was a founding member and that many eminent men of science belonged.

He attended a one-night party thrown by the Duke of St. Raven at his country house called Nun's Chase. The journey there and back was a horse race. Lord Arden won in one direction and Van in the other.

Maddy was the one to tell her that Nun's Chase had been the scene of scandalous goings-on before St. Raven's marriage, and that this one had been tame by comparison.

"Strictly gentlemen only," Maddy said to Thea and two other fascinated young ladies at Lady Epworth's Venetian breakfast.

"How do you know?" Thea asked, feeling dull again.

"Cully was there. Disappointed that there were no Cyprians at all. All riding, fencing, shooting and such, which he enjoyed as much or more, but he wouldn't admit it. Darien's a dead shot, but so is Lord Middlethorpe, apparently. They dueled over it forever."

"Dueled!" Thea said in alarm.

"Only in the sense of contested. Shooting at targets at greater and greater distance."

"No wonder Almack's was thin of company that night," Alesia said. "It really is too bad, and he is, after all, a Cave. I still don't trust him."

Thea managed not to argue, but only because it would do no good. Alesia was a twit.

But then good news swept everything else from Thea's mind.

Dare was through the worst and recovering. He planned to soon travel to Long Chart to complete his recovery there before the wedding, which was fixed for June 24.

He made all sound very well, but Mara wrote separately to say he'd lost an alarming amount of weight and was weak as a kitten, so he would need to rest for a while before any journey. Even so, Thea and her mother hugged each other and even cried a little for joy.

When Thea met Darien at a rout that night, the good news spilled out before she remembered the enmity between him and Dare.

"You must all be delighted," he said.

"Are you?" she asked, surprised to realize she could ask such a question now. "Or is Dare still your enemy?"

"No, I've outgrown that. I truly wish him well."

She smiled. "I'm glad." She wished they could talk longer, in some place other than this hot room, with people all around.

She missed him. That was startling.

"I gather you've been attending scientific gatherings," she said.

"Submarine warfare, no less."

"Does such a thing exist?"

"Yes, actually. The Americans almost got it to work in the late war, and there are records of attempts going back a century or more. Even a theoretical plan for a man to go underwater and apply a bomb to the hull of a ship."

"You needn't sound so enthusiastic," she complained, but smiling. "What if you were on the ship at the time?"

"That's the trouble with advances in warfare. The other side always catches up."

They chuckled together. Thea saw her mother waiting to leave, but she lingered.

Darien was so much more relaxed now than when she'd seen him at the Netherholt rout. She couldn't say he was surrounded by universal approval, but even the members of the ton who were still cool had wearied of shock and horror.

"So, how does the campaign progress?" she asked.

"Well. Your mother's beckoning. Let's

work our way toward her."

"So keen to be rid of me?" she dared to tease.

His look was quick but intense. "Never." But then he smiled at a young man who came over. "Thea, do you know Lord Wyvern?"

Thea had to smile at the young earl when she'd much rather have had a few more minutes of Darien alone. "Yes, of course. He's from my part of the world."

She dipped a curtsy and Wyvern bowed, but rolled his eyes at the same time. "Don't know why I allowed myself to be persuaded up to London. Give me the country and the coast any day. I'm off in search of fresh air, if such a thing exists in London at all."

"His arrival in Town provided an excellent distraction," Darien said, watching him depart, "given the furor over his inheriting the title. As he's brother-in-law to Amleigh, I assume the Rogues arranged it."

"Wheels within wheels," Thea said. "How clever."

The new Earl of Wyvern had been the previous earl's estate steward, unaware that he was the man's legal son. Of course the old earl had been completely crazy, so no one was completely surprised that he'd created a mess even of marriage and offspring.

They'd arrived at her mother. There, Darien took Thea's hand and bent over it, his eyes holding hers. "Remember," he said softly, "I'm dutifully paying my price, and you must do your part."

"I will," Thea said, and he turned to disappear into the crowd.

I can't wait, she thought after him. At the Harroving masquerade, she would have him to herself for a whole evening. But for now she had to go in a different direction, to a poetry reading that held no appeal whatsoever. Tomorrow, however, was Friday.

Only one day to wait until her reward.

Friday itself seemed to plod along, but at last Thea could dress in her goddess costume. She found herself both excited and nervous. Soon he'd be here, but what if he thought this costume absurd?

What if his attentions to her had always been manipulative and he felt no attraction toward her at all? What if he *was* as strongly attracted to her as he seemed, and took this outré costume as encouragement to be wicked?

At least she was armed, though the point and blade of her halberd were sadly blunt.

But how much did she want to fight him off? This could be one of their last encounters. They'd not received word yet that Dare had left Brideswell, but it couldn't be long. She and her parents might leave Town for Long Chart as early as Monday. Her father would return to London for parliamentary business, but she and her mother would stay in Somerset with Dare until going to Brideswell for the wedding. By then the season would be over.

This insane adventure would be over.

Her life would probably return to order and calm. She wanted that, but not quite yet.

She surveyed her appearance one last time, suppressed temptation to back out, and went downstairs, helmet on head, weapon in hand.

Her father waited at the base of the stairs with a twinkle in his eye. "I remember this costume," he said.

The duchess blushed.

Thea turned and saw Darien. He was a cavalier in a blue satin coat, heavily braided in gold, and full breeches with knots of ribbon at the knees. Lace frothed at his wrists and neck, and a long, curling periwig of pale blond hair along with a white half mask gave a completely different look to his features. He swept off his wide black hat and bowed deeply in the court manner.

Truly, she might not have known him.

He straightened and looked her over, eyes bright with something. "Britannia?"

Dry-mouthed, she said, "Goddess." The brightness flared. "Armored," she added firmly.

"So I see."

Harriet came forward to drape a white cloak around Thea for the journey, and they went out to the coach.

"I'm not sure if a gentleman should offer to carry a goddess's weapon," he said.

"I have no intention of surrendering it. I think I might need it."

He laughed as he assisted her into the coach. It wasn't easy, with halberd and helmet to manage, not to mention six inches of silver owl on top.

Once she was settled in the coach, Harriet beside her, he took the opposite seat.

"Lovelace?" she guessed, studying his costume again.

"The warrior or the rake?" he asked as the coach started off.

"Perhaps both. That's an impressive costume. Where did you find it at short notice?"

"Where did you find yours?"

"In the attic."

"Mine, too. In your attic. The duchess didn't trust me and sent this around."

"Lord, that probably means it was last

worn by my father. Or just possibly Dare. That would be suitable, as you promised to behave like a brother."

"Not here," he said, and she realized he referred to Harriet, who was pretending to be deaf and blind, but assuredly was neither.

But he might mean, "My promise doesn't hold for this event."

Which did she want?

They didn't have to travel far, and as she extracted herself from the carriage, she wondered if it wouldn't have been easier to walk. Impossible, of course. Even cloaked, she created a stir as she entered the house, among both other arriving guests and the people gathered to watch.

Once inside, she went to the cloakroom to shed her cloak and have Harriet check that all was in order. She turned to the mirror there, and then wished she hadn't. The robe really was almost transparent. She was committed now, however, so she sent Harriet off to the servants' quarters, where there would doubtless be a merry gathering, and returned to the hall.

Darien was waiting, looking relaxed and so very dashing. She didn't know if his ornate, beribboned sword was sharp or not, but he looked well able to use it. As he doubtless was. She could almost wish there'd be a duel so she could see him in action.

He saw her and smiled. She returned the smile brightly and took his hand in the old style to stroll with him into one of a series of reception rooms. She knew that during this part of the evening guests were supposed to parade, showing off their costumes and admiring those of others. Everyone was also supposed to act their part, so she had, as her mother advised, memorized some wise sayings.

She found the costumes fascinating. She saw a sultan, a clown, and a number of Robin Hoods. The latter all carried bows and arrows, and she hoped they wouldn't attempt to fire them.

There were ladies in costumes of all periods, many looking very strange, as the wearers had kept to the current fashion for a high waist. One lady wore the Indian draperies called a sari and Thea wondered if it might be the Duchess of St. Raven. A number of guests merely wore dominoes — hat, mask, and concealing cloak.

"I think that very cowardly," Thea said.

One of the men in a domino stepped in front of her and said in a gruff voice, "And which fair goddess are you?"

"That is for you to guess, sir."

"Only when you guess who I am."

"But you give me no clues," she said rather disdainfully. "Do I not?"

She saw laughing blue eyes behind the mask and said, "Cully?"

He grinned and said in his normal voice, "I have to attend a military do, so I have my uniform on, but I wanted to drop by. This is supposed to be tremendous fun. Is that really Canem with you? More or less with you, anyway," he added.

Thea turned and saw her cavalier being distracted by a bold Nell Gwyn. She grabbed his arm and dragged him, laughing, back to her. She already felt a difference — in her, in him. In everyone around them, because no one knew who they were.

No one was casting him suspicious looks — though any number of ladies were sending interested ones. No one was whispering of old, dark scandals or recent dark reputations.

"You're anonymous here," she said.

"Until midnight at least. You're incognito, too. How does it feel?"

She tested it. "Liberating." Here, she realized, she could be bold as she pleased.

But no. At midnight, less than two hours away, she would be cognito again, with anything she did here stuck to her reputation. Alas.

A Roman centurion tried to steal her by right of nationality, but she parried by saying a goddess could not be commanded.

Another Nell Gwyn tried to tempt Darien with an orange, but he said his goddess commanded his escort.

A medieval lass with long plaits offered them a wild rose from a basket. Darien tried to give it to Thea, but she said it would spoil her costume and tucked it into one of his ornamental buttonholes.

He kissed her bare hand. No gloves with this costume, which was excitingly peculiar in itself.

"I believe I could manage to kiss your lips," he said, "despite the helmet."

Aware of the consequences, Thea turned away, but she did notice a number of other couples who were not being at all discreet. Perhaps no one would remember who did what. . . .

They went upstairs, passing servants in skimpy oriental robes, who presented wine. They drank as they entered the ballroom, which was dimmer than any Thea had ever seen. The center of the room was lit by two great chandeliers, but the fringes of the room were shadowy with only small glimmers of light.

There was music, but few were dancing. Some clearly would have trouble in their costumes, but most were enjoying this stage of playing their parts. Two men were actually sword fighting. She hoped their weapons were as blunt as hers.

One spotted Darien and turned to challenge him.

He immediately whipped out his rapier and set to. Thea had no idea if the fencing was skilled or not, but the swift moves and clashing blades made her heart race. But after only a minute, Darien stepped back, grinning, saluted with his sword, and returned to her side.

"You're mad," she said.

"Of course I am." He drew her swiftly into the shadowy edge of the room and she found herself in a leafy bower lit only by a tiny lamp. "Ideal for trysts," he said.

"Behave like a brother?" she reminded him, dry-mouthed but thrilled.

"That was the promise for an Opera House masquerade."

Thea angled her spear at him. "Behave, sir. At midnight, everyone will know who we are."

"But they'll not know what we do in here." He grasped the spear and easily twisted it out of her hands. In truth, she

310

didn't try hard to prevent him.

Then he tossed his hat to the ground and kissed her. She put a hand to her helmet to hold it in place and kissed him back. This was a taste of what she wanted tonight. Except that the helmet meant lips only. He put his arm around her and met armor, not body.

He laughed. "Armored indeed."

"Inviolable," she agreed.

"Not here, however." He put his hands on her bare arms and rubbed them up and down, over silver bands but also over skin that no man had ever touched before. She rested her hands on his chest, over the rough gold braid on his coat, over his heart.

Their lips met again, so chastely, so very hotly. His hands moved to her shoulders and then down her armored back until his fingers found the laces that tied her bodice. "What is done," he whispered, "can be undone."

The robe was between his fingers and the bow, but she stiffened her arms to hold him off. "No."

"Not even at midnight?"

"Especially not at midnight. I'm wearing nothing beneath but my shift."

He smiled. Even in the dim light she could see that, and sense interest, amusement, and challenge. Despite a flare of hunger, perhaps because of it, she stepped back and grabbed her halberd.

He raised his hands. "You won't need that."

"I know. But . . ."

"Flint and tinder, yes. We could, of course, slip away before midnight and then no one would know who we were."

"Slip away?" she asked, shocked.

"To the gardens, to a secret part of the house. Into the street and far, far away."

"You're mad."

"So it is said. Escape with me, my goddess, to places where there are no restrictions and no rules."

He might even be serious. She shook her head, swallowing. "I can't."

"Of course not. You're the goddess Minerva, ever wise. Why," he asked wistfully, "couldn't you have come as wanton Nell Gwyn?"

"I could have been a pirate wench," she admitted.

"But lack the criminal instinct." He swept his hat up from the floor with an athletic grace that melted her. She'd come to see beauty in him before, but now in the dashing clothes of yesteryear he was designed to drive a lady mad.

"Those clothes are most unfair," she said.
"And yours aren't? Come, let's escape into safety."

Chapter 26

He steered her out of the bower and into the ballroom, which seemed quite bright in contrast.

More people were dancing now and some had already abandoned the cumbersome parts of their costumes. Thea realized a significant disadvantage of her own — she couldn't take off her helmet without being recognized, but it would be hard to dance while wearing it.

"Who are you?" she asked as they strolled the perimeter.

"What do you mean?"

"You didn't say earlier. Are you Lovelace, or simply a nameless cavalier?"

"I'm Prince Rupert of the Rhine. He went to war at fourteen, commanded Charles the First's cavalry at twenty-three, and the entire army by twenty-five."

"Which makes you a sluggard."

"He did have royal birth and nepotism on

his side," he complained.

"And you had only Caves. But you have other things in common. Wasn't he called the Mad Cavalier?" She couldn't believe she was taking such risks, but here, now, her words didn't seem risky at all.

He showed only mock indignation. "I have never taken a poodle into battle with me."

"For which poodles everywhere are grateful, I'm sure."

They laughed together, two anonymous people in a careless crowd. Thea had never felt so free. "You and my mother are right. Masquerades are wonderful. This was once her costume, you know."

"Do you think your father had more success with the laces than I did?"

"No!" Flustered, Thea turned toward the dancing and sought distraction in the conventions of the masquerade. "What happened to you after the death of Charles the First, my lord prince?"

"Various enterprises, including piracy in the West Indies, then glory in England after the Restoration of my cousin, Charles the Second."

"Raking, along with the rest of his court?"

"What do you think?" His fingers raked down her back, down her lacing, sending a shiver all the way to her toes. "Men will be men, and fighting men are lusty."

Thea swallowed. "Did he marry and live happily?" she demanded.

"You equate marriage with happiness?"

She turned to face him, removing her lace-knot from his fingers. "Why not?"

"There's a great deal of living evidence against it, our hostess, I gather, being a prime example."

"And my parents evidence of the opposite. Did he? You?" she corrected.

"What?"

"Marry and live happily?"

"Only a mistress," he said, abandoning his part, "but he stuck with her long enough to suggest at least contentment."

"He didn't marry her?"

"She was an actress."

"That's no excuse. Hal Beaumont just did. He's one —"

"— of the Rogues. Typically quixotic."

"It's nothing to sneer about. I like Blanche, and my mother is learning Wollstonecraftian revolution from her."

He hooted with laughter, and then grabbed her hand. "Let's dance."

"Wait!" she cried and jabbed her spear deep into a potted plant before running with him to join a seemingly continuous long dance. She had to use a gliding minuet step to avoid bouncing her helmet, and her posture was probably more perfect than ever, but she certainly wasn't the Great Untouchable tonight. Tonight she was dancing in the dark with a very dangerous man, and she intended to enjoy every moment of it.

Even incognito, training and manners compelled her to pay due attention to each man and woman she danced with, but her true awareness was all on Darien. Aware of his grace again — and of the eager warmth many other women showed. Some would clearly sneak off with him without hesitation. Not without a fight from her, she resolved.

He was hers. For tonight, at least.

As they turned together halfway down the line, she asked, "How do you dance so well, you a rough officer?"

"Did I ever claim to be a rough officer? Lisbon. Paris. Brussels. Officers are expected to do their duty in all areas."

She danced off thinking sourly about women in Lisbon, Paris, and Brussels, and he a dashing hussar officer in that fanciful uniform of blue, braid, and fur, with scarred good looks and graceful body, and wicked eyes, and all the other things that made him fascinating.

That made him lethally desirable.

"Thea?"

Thea focused on the lady she was paired with now. Another Nell Gwyn with a particularly low bodice and a lot to be exposed by it. Then she looked again. "Maddy?"

Her cousin grinned. "I didn't expect to see you here."

"Well I am," Thea said rather snappishly before dancing back to Darien. Did everyone think her deadly dull?

When she turned with Maddy again, her cousin said, "Who's the cavalier?" with the same hot interest other women were showing.

"That's for you to find out." Thea looked at Maddy's partner — a monk she couldn't identify. "Who's yours?"

"Staverton," Maddy said with a moue. "I'll do better as the night wears on. Keep an eye on your cavalier, coz, or I'll steal him. He and I are of a period, after all."

The pattern of the dance separated them before Thea could warn her off, and she was glad of it. Maddy would tease her for the rest of their lives. But now a lush lady in a Spanish mantilla was brushing up against Darien in a completely inappropriate way and making inviting kissing actions. Thea thought it might be Lady Harroving herself.

Darien turned back to Thea, then said, "Do you have a headache?"

"No."

"That helmet must be a strain."

"The only strain is watching the shameless attention you're gathering."

"Jealous?" he asked. Before she could retort, he added, "I am devotedly yours, my Thea. For tonight, at least."

She knew this was only for tonight. So why did his words hurt?

Inevitably the dance brought her together with Maddy again.

"That's *Darien,* isn't it?" Maddy whispered.

"Yes."

"Oh, my. You do carry duty to extremes, don't you? Will he stay for the unmasking?"

"Of course."

"What fun!" Maddy said, laughing as she moved on.

When the music finally stopped, Thea was hot, damp, and strangely cross. "One thing my costume lacks is a fan," she said.

Darien took off his hat and fanned her with it.

"Clever to have worn a blond wig," she said. "It took Maddy a while to recognize you."

"Your cousin?" He glanced around.

"Which is she?"

"The bounteous Nell Gwyn in yellow."

"Ah."

Thea didn't like his tone at all. Armor-plated breasts didn't seem any competition for generous, jiggling, mostly uncovered ones, and the felt-lined foil was stifling.

"I need fresh air," she said.

"Come, then." He held out an arm and they began to work their way out of the increasingly packed ballroom.

A large man in black, wearing a hood that covered his entire head other than eyes and mouth, stepped in their way. He was probably pretending to be an executioner. "Minerva, offer me wisdom."

Thea thought his disguise horrid, but she spoke one of her prepared lines. "Short is the time which you poor humans live, sir, and small the corner of earth that you inhabit."

" 'Struth, but you're a melancholy goddess. I'm off to find a jollier."

"A justifiable complaint," Darien said, chuckling.

"He's come as a headsman, so he deserves something gloomy."

"What advice would you offer me?" Darien asked.

"Eschew distractions and hasten to the

end you have envisaged."

"Interesting. Whose wisdom are you stealing?"

"Marcus Aurelius."

There was a beat of startled silence, and then he asked, "Do you know that was my brother's full name?"

She stared at him. "No. Or I'd forgotten. I'm sorry. I didn't mean anything by it."

He touched her chin. "Of course not. It was just strange. You should try Poor Richard. He puts things more simply." His thumb brushed her lower lip. " 'If you love life, do not squander time, for that is what life is made up of.' Do you want to squander our time here, Thea?"

There were layers to that, and dangers, but Thea said, "No." She took his hand and led him out of the ballroom.

"Where are we going?" he asked, unresisting.

"Somewhere private. Where?"

He smiled, his lean face beneath the pale mask drying her mouth and weakening her knees. "I suspect privacy is in short supply, but let's try."

Now he led and Thea followed, fighting off a return of good sense. This was insane, but wasn't that what she wanted? A brief moment of glorious insanity. Just a kiss, but a full, passionate, mind-absorbing kiss.

They slipped down a corridor toward the back of the house, past flirting couples and kissing couples. One unmasked lady appeared to be flirting with and kissing two men at once. And one of the men —

"Eyes front!" Darien commanded.

Thea giggled as she obeyed, but willingly hurried on until they came to the dark window that signaled the end of the passageway. He opened the door on the right.

"Stairs," he said, pulling her through and closing the door, steeping them in total darkness. "Up or down?" he whispered.

They were close enough here, private here.

"Up," she said. "The kitchens will be busy."

"Down," he corrected and led in that direction. "Always do the unexpected. Like this."

He halted and brought his lips close to the cheek guard of her helmet. He blew through the space so his warm breath teased her skin, then his lips slid sideways to find hers.

She collapsed back against the wall, arms limp at her sides, and surrendered. It was almost as if he spoke against her lips, though what he said she did not know. Only that it was temptation incarnate. His fingers found her laces again, this time sliding beneath the robe.

"We mustn't," she breathed, speaking convention, not meaning it.

"We must. Our days are numbered."

They were, and even their hours here were brief.

She raised her hands to take off the helmet, but he said, "Not yet," found her hand and set off down the stairs, cautious in the dark but not nearly as cautious as she would be without him.

He opened a door and they looked out into a narrow corridor. She heard noise and laughter nearby — the busy kitchens and the servants' hall where the guests' attendants were enjoying themselves.

"I wonder what they get up to?" Thea whispered.

"No, we're not spying on them," he said, laughter in his voice. He drew her into the corridor and away from the noise, trying each door, opening those that weren't locked.

Thea was surprised by the number of those, but at such a busy event the housekeeper wouldn't want to be scurrying around to unlock the less valuable stores.

"What's in there?" she asked about the second one.

"I don't know, but it doesn't feel welcoming."

"I doubt any room down here will. We're intruders." *And I'm impatient. I'm finally ready for another searing, mind-blanking kiss. Choose a room!*

CHAPTER 27

Then he said, "Ah," and pulled her through a door and closed it behind them.

Darkness slowly softened because of three small windows high in the wall to her left. They showed only squares of gray but were enough for her eyes to slowly perceive a long narrow room and shapes on either side, dark and pale. The smell of the room sorted this out — lavender, pennyroyal, and mint, and that distinctive smell of clean sheets.

"Linen room?" she whispered.

"Linen room."

She heard a click. He'd locked the door.

"There was a key on the inside of the door?" she asked, suddenly nervous despite herself.

"There was a key left carelessly on the outside." She heard humor and warmth and that mellow timbre that had struck her at first meeting but become so familiar that she'd ceased to be aware.

He came toward her, found her helmet, and gently raised it. "Not as good as a bed," he said, "but a distant relation, perhaps?"

"We don't need a bed for a kiss."

"We don't need a room like this for a kiss, Thea." He lifted the helmet away.

She nervously fingered her pinned hair. "That's such a relief. It's not so much uncomfortable as oppressive."

"And a goddess should never be oppressed."

She reached for him, but he unhooked her girdle so that it tinkled to the floor. Her robe slithered after it. He turned her and felt for her laces again. Thea knew she shouldn't permit this, but how could they truly kiss with a solid barrier between them?

He found the bow and tugged. The knot came loose and then he patiently loosened the cross-lacing all the way up, his fingers sending shivers of pleasure up and down her spine.

Thea braced her hands on the wooden shelves in front of her, inhaling the smell of clean sheets and herbs, aware of every touch and of him, behind her in this tight room. His costume must have been stored for many years. It, too, retained a hint of herbs, blending with the essential smell of him. A smell she recognized, though she'd been unaware of that, too, before this darkly mysterious moment.

The bodice came loose enough to remove. She raised her arms and he lifted it off. She turned, feeling shockingly naked with only the silk shift covering her upper body, especially when her nipples brushed against his braided coat.

He unfastened the ties holding up her armored skirt and it fell to the floor with a rattle. His hands lingered on her waist, strong, warm, and a little rough, catching on the silk.

His mouth pressed against hers then, a brief greeting before complete possession. She grabbed for his jacket, found it wasn't there. He'd shed it, and his waistcoat stood open. Her hands clutched cotton lawn, smooth and fine over his muscular torso. She had never felt such a potent body before or pressed her own almost naked body to one. What a tragedy that seemed.

And they kissed and they kissed and they kissed.

She'd built such hunger throughout their sparring encounters, and then through the long days of brief or nonexistent meetings. Now every part of her leapt for this, for this, for more. She wouldn't care now if she were in the ballroom, observers all around —

Yes, she would!

She tensed and resisted.

"Hush," he said, or gasped, his breathing ragged. He drew her into his arms again, but tenderly, holding her, rocking her. He stroked down her back and she arched slightly.

"Like a cat," she gasped in surprise.

"Don't scratch," he said as his strong hands settled on her bottom, circling hands drawing the silk high and higher. Exposing her.

Legs quivering, even fearful, Thea knew she wasn't going to object or try to escape. She simply couldn't. If ruin was the price, so be it.

His right hand trailed up beneath the shift to her front, to her breast, to cup, to gently squeeze, to thumb. She jerked in shock, in pleasure, and in recognition. She gripped his hand and held it there, savoring the feverish pleasure of her most wicked dreams.

Clever hand still playing with her, he kissed her again. A whimper escaped and she gripped his waistcoat for support, moving her knee restlessly up and down his satin breeches, aching deep inside, thrusting her hips.

He froze, head against hers, breathing as

deeply as she. Then he stepped back. Before she could protest or grab for him, she realized he was pulling sheets off the shelves and throwing them to the floor.

"Oh, the poor laundress," she gasped, but she helped and then they sank down onto the nest of cool linen.

His waistcoat had gone. His shirt was out of his breeches. Her hands could invade and touch his hot, silky skin.

His hand teased her other breast as he kissed her, but then his mouth traveled to where his hand had been, nibbling at her through silk. Her head seemed to be floating, far away from her hot, hungry body. He found the edge of her shift and drew it up, his fingers teasing up her thigh.

And then between.

Thea tensed, but then her driving hunger opened to him and his touch there was everything she'd ever wanted.

"The Great Untouchable . . . ," she whispered on a laugh.

"Ridiculous," he agreed. "Relax, Thea. Trust me. I won't ruin you."

"*This* isn't ruin?"

His laughter was warm and gentle. "Only if we're caught, and the door, remember, is locked." He pushed her shift all the way up, so her breasts were uncovered, and then he cradled one and kissed it, then licked and sucked.

"Oh, dear heaven."

He laughed again and his fingers slid between her welcoming thighs.

This was not what she'd expected. From her rudimentary knowledge of the matter of a man and a maid she'd expected something more forceful, more violent. Something involving pain. Not this gentle, almost teasing attention and this building fever of desire.

Won't ruin her.

Not take her maidenhead.

What was he doing, then? She didn't care. Astonishing sensations swirled within her, then tightened throughout her, more and more. She was gasping, almost panicked.

Violence. Ah, now it was. And pain of a sort, that built and built . . .

Into explosion.

She found his mouth and kissed him with all the fiery lights going off in her head, kissed him with all the rippling, seething wonders of her body, entangled sweatily with his.

She slid off the kiss, not exhausted but replete, and simply lay there. Until he took her limp hand and pressed it against something hot and hard.

For a moment she wanted to pull away, but he said, "A goddess might be grateful."

Heat and smells cocooned them in their nest, and darkness permitted anything. "What would gratitude involve?" she whispered.

"A return of favors? Explore me."

She cautiously curled her fingers around the wood-hard shape. Why had she never thought about the mechanics of all this?

"It can't be like this all the time," she said, feeling the length of it. Good Lord!

"No. It needs reducing."

"How? You said you wouldn't ruin me."

"Your hand can do it." He felt relaxed beneath her and sounded as if he were talking about whether she should bake a cake or not. "Or mine. But I thought you might enjoy a new adventure."

"Will I?" She ran her palm up and down.

"I don't know."

She was fascinated by the warm hardness of him, but alarmed by the idea that this was designed to penetrate a woman. Forceful and violent, indeed. Perhaps she wouldn't marry at all. Her hand tightened and he shivered, a ripple throughout his whole body that she recognized as violent pleasure and need.

She snatched her hand away.

"It's all right," he said. "I can do it for myself."

But he wanted her to do it. He would enjoy it, perhaps as much as she'd enjoyed what he'd done for her. She curled her hand again. "Show me."

He pulled her hand from him and pressed it between her own thighs, to the place still exquisitely sensitive and, she felt, very moist. He rubbed her there and that potent pleasure stirred again.

Not now.

Not yet.

He drew her hand back to him and now she was slick against him. When she moved her hand, it slid. He moved her hand up and down, and then at the top he pushed her thumb to go over the smoother tip, where she felt new moisture.

He shivered again.

"You like that?" she whispered.

"Exceedingly."

He lay back, a sprawled shadow against pale white sheets, but she knew dark eyes were looking at her. Could imagine them beneath heavy lids. Could feel the need in him.

She leaned down to kiss his parted lips, continuing the actions he'd shown her. "Am I doing it right?"

"You are, as always, perfect, my goddess."

She played her fingers up and down him, as if playing the piano. "And that?"

"Too gentle for now, Goddess."

So she gripped him tighter and moved faster, sensing his tension, hearing his breathing, imagining that building, feverish madness. It built in her, too. She hooked a leg over his thighs so she could press against him as he thrust against her.

He grabbed part of a sheet and pushed it over himself and her hand. Spurts hit the sheet, some splashing hot on her hand. She rubbed that fluid onto him, eager to carry on, but he captured her hand, stilled it, and drew it away. She collapsed over him, both of them steaming with heat and sweat and surrounded by a heavy, musky smell.

If he'd wanted to put himself into her then, she'd have rejoiced.

Breathing calmed, heat simmered down.

"We must be making a terrible mess," she said.

He laughed. "Don't be a lady, Thea. Not tonight."

He played sweet magic down her back, massaged her bottom, teased down the back of her thigh.

She squirmed, but lazily. "I never knew

how many sensitive places there were on a body."

He stroked up again and slid between her legs from behind. "Especially here. Yes?"

Her body leapt and she rolled off him onto her back. "Oh, yes."

His mouth found her breasts again and his hand that sensitive place. She arched instantly to him, repeating, "Oh, yes!" and this time he was forceful and violent, shooting pleasure through her, burning her up, driving her to pound against his hand. She would have been shrieking if she'd had breath. She only knew that she was going to die soon and wanted to.

And then she did.

She came to on his chest, in his arms, warm, safe, the perfect place to be.

I want to marry you.

The thought didn't make it into words, and she was glad of that, but it was true. She'd never thought the physical act a very important part of marriage. Liking, admiration, suitability of temperament, shared interests, and a comfortable equality of social standing — those had always seemed the necessities for a good life.

She didn't discount them, but now these earthy matters were important, and they were for him and her.

And she did like him. She liked the feel of his skin beneath her stroking hand, and his callused hand on her, but she liked his company and admired his virtues — his courage, his resolve, his staunch dependability. They weren't alike in temperament, but perhaps they complemented. The thought of life by his side, even with the challenges of his family history, was good. So she must make it so.

"What do I call you?" she asked, tracing a circle on his shoulder.

"Lord and master?"

She poked him. "I am a goddess, sir, and have no master."

"Tell that to Zeus."

"You want me to call you Zeus?"

He simply laughed. She remembered thinking about a cat, and that's what he seemed like now, here in this hot darkness. A big cat, content to be stroked, enjoying being stroked.

"I need a true name for you," she said, stroking down his flank, his thigh. "Darien doesn't seem suited to a situation like this."

"You intend there to be many situations like this?"

Yes. Don't you? But she said neither. This was a delicate joy, needing tender care.

"I don't like Canem," she said. "It's fine

for your friends. . . ."

He captured her hand and raised it to his lips. "I had hoped we could be friends."

"Your men friends." She inhaled, savoring his deep, warm smell, their deep warm smell, rubbing her thigh against his stronger one. "Doesn't Canem remind you of that incident? It has to carry pain."

He nibbled gently at her fingertips. "I've made it my own, and I have no warm feelings for the name Horatio."

"What did your mother call you?"

"Horry. I wish I'd heard her call my older brothers Markie and Christie."

Thea chuckled, but said, "Your mother must have had a hard life. She seems to have been ostracized." She wanted to know about his childhood. About all of him.

"It was of her own choosing."

She didn't like his harsh tone. "Is that fair?"

"She chose to marry my father. No one forced her. She often complained of her own stupidity. She thought being a viscountess would make her grand, but the Cave reputation trumped any rank. She left her own world of the theater and was not allowed into the new one. She couldn't strike back at my father, so she punished servants and every child she bore." Abruptly, he rose to his feet, pulling her up with him. "We'd best return to the real world."

Cool air and harshness shocked. "Because I mentioned your mother? Friends are closer than that."

He stilled, and then rested his head against hers. "Because of memories, Thea. I have a great many of them, all bad. Leave them be."

"Of course," she said, cradling his face. "We'll make new ones."

"We just did. But that doesn't change reality."

"We've been busily changing reality recently."

"Some reality is tougher than that. My nature, my family, the Cave reputation, are all stone monuments." He moved back from her and bent, and then her body armor was put into her hands.

"This was real, too," she argued.

"But like sunrise and sunset, lovely yet fleeting. This was precious to me, too, Thea. I'm weak enough to repeat it any time you want, but . . ."

"But it wouldn't be right?"

"Right isn't a word I'm used to, but yes. It wouldn't be right."

She grasped her courage. "We could make it right." When he said nothing, she stated it. "We could marry."

"Because of this?"

"No! Well, yes, but not in the way you mean." She shouldn't be attempting this in the dark where she couldn't see his expression.

"This was not unique, Thea."

"It was for me."

He stepped away and she knew he was beginning to dress.

"Oh, very well, *don't* talk about it." She bent to fumble for the rest of her costume, but he pulled her upright.

"Don't talk about what?"

"The weather!"

She wouldn't say it, so he did. "Marriage. Thea, Goddess . . . You want your children to be Caves?"

She turned to him. "Things are better already. By then —"

"It will be a name of honor and grandeur?"

She gripped his shirt. "We can *make* it so. Canem Cave's already stamped honor all over it."

"Pardon me if I haven't noticed."

She let him go. "If you don't want to marry me, just say so. I've embarrassed myself enough."

The silence slowly shriveled her soul.

CHAPTER 28

Though her throat ached, Thea made her voice light. "It's all right. You don't have to say it. I understand. This was an amusement, the sort men enjoy. And as you promised, you haven't ruined me. Not really."

She turned and groped her way toward the door.

"You need to dress," he said, "and I have the key."

She turned, her back to the door, facing a dark shadow in the gloom. *Are you trying to make me hate you?* She didn't say it, for all she had left was scraps of pride. She felt her way back, almost tripping on some sheets, sheets still holding a trace of their bodies' warmth.

She found the bodice, sorted out which way was up, and shrugged into it. Then she turned her back. "Tighten the laces, please."

She sensed his tension as he moved behind

her. It filled the narrow room and his presence burned before he touched her. She would not cry. She knew how men were. She'd been warned all her life. Why had she let herself imagine this one — this Cave one! — was different?

She adjusted the shell to her body at the front. He tugged, tightened, and then knotted the laces in the small of her back. He gave her the metal skirt and she tied it on, blessing darkness. When she put on the robe, she used an edge to dry her eyes. When she clasped the silver belt around her waist, she reminded herself of who and what she was.

Lady Theodosia Debenham.

A goddess.

The Great Untouchable.

So she would be, body and soul.

She replaced the helmet on her head and returned to the door, saying, "If you have any money, leave some for the laundress."

"I already have."

She'd made a mistake in going to the door first. In the narrow room, he had to brush against her in order to turn the key in the lock, and even that slight touch sent a weak tremor through her. She stumbled out, desperate for light and space. The corridor was dim, but she could see. The dark-walled corridor was narrow, but it was the path to escape.

Laughter and music from the servants nearby put her back in her real world; a cloying medley of smells from the kitchen reminded her that reality wasn't always pleasant.

Lingering sensitivities in her body . . .

Never again.

"I want to leave," she said.

"You have your entourage to collect," he pointed out, his voice level.

Why could her life never be simple? Harriet was at the servants' party. The groom or coachman might be, too. Wouldn't someone have to stay with the coach? She'd never thought of such things before. A coach brought her to an event and reappeared when she wanted to leave. She hated not knowing.

She hated being in an unfamiliar place.

So much for the delights of adventure.

She longed to slip out into the dark and run all the way home. In anything close to normal clothing, she might even have done it. As it was, she could only repeat, "I want to leave."

He was silent behind her and she imagined his impatience with this demanding, pampered lady.

"I'll find your maid," he said, walking past her toward the noisy room.

From the back he could almost be a stranger, with the blond curls tumbling and the full-skirted coat changing his shape. But she knew his walk, his posture, that animal grace.

And she'd known his body tonight. Not quite in the biblical sense, but the wonders of its vital strength and its response.

Never again, she reminded herself, her face, her whole head going hot inside the devilish helmet. She leaned back against the wall, rubbing cool hands up under the cheek guards of the helmet.

"Alone?"

She started and saw the executioner she'd met earlier.

"Go away."

He came toward her, grinning.

She shrank back, but the wall gave her no retreat. She could call out, but the fewer people who saw her down here the better. This reminded her horribly of her first encounter with Darien. Why hadn't she heeded the warning in that?

"My victims would always like me to go away," he said, tapping the axe hanging from his belt. She hoped it wasn't real. He was drunk, but not nearly incapacitated.

She tried to look sideways for Darien, but the helmet got in the way. "Go away," she repeated. "I'm unwell. My escort has gone to find my servants."

"A fine story. I know what you want." He grabbed for a jutting breast.

And found only armor.

His gape made her laugh and then all her misery and tension peeled wildly out.

Fury replaced his grin and his hand went straight under her short skirt. She pushed him with both fists, but he was like an ox. He dragged her away from the wall and got one beefy arm around her, crushing her flimsy armor.

"Let me go!" Thea cried, and it was as much warning as plea.

Darien had run into the corridor, his expression now pure murder.

"Obey her," he said with deadly command.

The executioner turned, but he took Thea with him, holding her like a shield. "Finders keepers. Push off, curly boy."

He must be *very* drunk.

Servants were pouring out of nearby rooms, but what could they do? Thea struggled, but she was like a child in his one-armed hold. He began to back away with her.

Darien stalked, looking for his opportunity.

Thea remembered her helmet. She bowed herself forward, then whipped back. She felt a solid thunk. Her captor yelled and let her go.

She fell to the floor and scrambled toward Darien on hands and knees, but he launched over her, and when she turned the two men were grappling.

"Stop it!" she cried. The hangman had huge arms and a barrel chest and landed a blow that could break ribs. But then Darien had him in some sort of hold. His wig had gone, his hardness revealed.

The whispers started.

"It's Lord Darien."

"The Vile Viscount."

"Mad Dog Cave. . . ."

So much for restoring his family's reputation.

The grimacing hangman caught sight of her and shot her a look of such pure hate she scrambled away on her bottom. Blood was running from his nose and she hoped she'd done that.

She bumped into something. Looked up. Into the grinning face of some sort of kitchen boy. Realized most of her legs were exposed.

She struggled to her feet, thanking heaven for her helmet. Could anyone know who she was? This was going from bad to worse and worse to hellish. Soon the whole world would know what she'd done in that linen room and Darien was going to be killed!

The two men were knotted together, both faces contorted with effort. With a sharp twist the knot parted and the hangman kicked. Darien took it on his hip and was locked with the other man again.

Thea whirled to the servants. "Stop them, someone!"

"Be quiet." The snapped command was from Darien. She turned back to glare at him, but he was intent on his fight. On murder, she realized. She couldn't allow him to *kill* someone.

The hangman swung, but Darien blocked, then hammered blows to the man's chest, driving him back. Then he fired his fist to the man's jaw.

The man's head snapped back and his eyes crossed, but he still didn't drop. Swaying, he lurched forward again, bellowing blue murder.

If Thea had a pistol, she might have shot him.

Darien hooked the man's leg from under him, however, sending him crashing to the ground. He was on top instantly, bashing the hooded head against the floor.

For a moment, everyone watched, but then men ran forward to drag Darien off.

He resisted, clearly wanting to keep on punishing, but then he shrugged them off. He flexed his hands and rubbed at his face. His lip was bleeding and he must be badly bruised, but he looked almost untouched, while his opponent sprawled on the floor.

Had he killed him? Though the man looked coarse, the guests here would all be from the inner circles of society. There'd be a trial. Oh, dear God.

Darien shrugged his clothes into order and then picked up his wig. He didn't bother to put it on. He was already known.

Not murder. Servants were helping Darien's opponent to his feet, but he looked as if he'd have trouble standing on his own. The only blood, however, was from his nose. Her work.

She swallowed the bile rising in her throat. She'd done that. And she was in danger of ruin! Think, think! No chance at all of keeping their identities secret, but no one must connect them with the linen room.

"What an awful man," she said, trying for a tone of distaste. "Thank you for rescuing me, Darien. Harriet? Harriet, where are you?" Her maid hurried forward and Thea grasped her arm. "Help me to remove this helmet. My head's splitting."

"Yes, milady."

Even before the helmet came off, she was known through Harriet.

"It's Lady Theodosia Debenham," someone whispered.

"The Duke of Yeovil's daughter!" another gasped.

Thea put a hand to her head. "I couldn't bear the heat and noise of the ball, Harriet. I came down to see if I could get to my coach from here. Do say I can."

The black-clad housekeeper bustled forward, shooing servants back to their work. "Of course, milady. You just come and sit quietly in my parlor while it's fetched."

Thea didn't look back at Darien. She had no idea what to say and feared what her expression might show. Their time together had been wonderful, but she'd give her all to not have done it, to not be in this situation. She couldn't wipe away the image of his rage, his violence, his attempt to kill, and she still faced complete ruin.

As soon as her coach arrived in the lane at the back of the house, she, Darien, and Harriet were guided through a small garden to it. She had to take Darien's arm and tried to sense through that contact what he was feeling.

She had no idea.

They traveled in silence at first, but Thea needed to make sure that she wasn't linked to that linen room. The servants had their own ways of spreading information.

"Such a headache," she said, eyes closed as if in pain. "I *had* to escape the masquerade."

"You should have sent for me, milady," Harriet said.

"It was so hard to find a servant, so Lord Darien took me in search of you. We'd hardly arrived before that horrible man . . ."

"Disgusting drunk, he was," Harriet said. "But all the same . . ."

She shut up, but Thea knew she, too, was thinking of Darien's violence. If he'd been in some blind fury it might be excusable, but he'd been cold, intent. A punishing machine.

She cracked her eyes open to look at him. He was gazing out at the passing dark, apparently calm, the only sign of that fight being his swollen lip. She needed his help.

"Do you think that man followed us downstairs, Darien?"

He turned to her, assessing her as she had him. What did he see?

"More likely he'd been engaged in a tryst with some wanton wench in one of the storerooms and was looking for another willing partner."

The perfect cover.

"Well, I never!" Harriet exclaimed. "And begging your pardon, milord, but you shouldn't go mentioning things like that in front of a lady."

"My deepest apologies, Lady Thea. It's my Italian blood," he remarked, and resumed his observation of the passing street.

Such a terrible thing, Italian blood.

But it wasn't his Italian mother that was the problem. It was his Cave side, the angry, violent, insane side.

When they arrived at Yeovil House, he escorted them inside. He kept her hand for a moment. "My apologies, Lady Theodosia. I shouldn't have left you unattended."

Lady Theodosia. A declaration of distance. She should want that.

"There was no reason to think —"

"Anticipating the unexpected is the point, isn't it?" he said. "You are unhurt?"

Her lips wobbled. "Yes, of course, though I fear the costume may be dead."

"Especially the owl," he said with a wry look at the helmet Harriet was carrying. The silver bird tilted on its perch, broken feathers sticking out. He gently straightened and smoothed it. "Good night," he said, and left.

It sounded horribly like farewell.

Wasn't that as well? Thea asked herself as she went up to her room. Clearly she truly didn't have the temperament for a tumultuous life. She hated having done something she was ashamed of, no matter how ecstatic it had been at the time. She felt sick at the violence she had caused. If she'd never been there it wouldn't have happened. She certainly couldn't live like this.

The duke and duchess weren't yet home, so Thea didn't face any questions. As Harriet helped her out of the costume, she could only pray that it showed no evidence of what she'd done. Harriet would have whipped off the shift, but Thea held on to it, realizing there might be marks on her body.

"Please, Harriet, go and get a tisane. My head is torture. I'll ready myself for bed."

The maid hurried away and Thea quickly took off the shift. A check in the mirror showed nothing. How could there be nothing from such a powerful experience?

Such delicious pleasure.

The musky, dark intimacy.

The tender exploration —

She slammed that door shut.

She washed, put on her neck-to-toe night-gown, unpinned her hair and brushed it out. Then she paused, silver-backed brush limp in her hand, struggling again with tears.

Harriet came in. "Oh, you poor dear! Get to bed, milady, and drink this up. There's a bit of poppy in it to help you sleep."

Thea climbed into bed and sat propped up by pillows to sip the drink. It was sweetened, but she could still taste the bitterness beneath. A bitterness of herbs, but above all, of opium — Dare's demon, but such a blessing in small, occasional amounts.

Was Darien like that? Safe only in rare small doses?

Had she taken too much, too often, and become an addict?

How right he'd been — marriage wouldn't work for them. Thus, she'd have to endure the torture of withdrawal as Dare was doing.

As Thea returned the cup, Harriet said, "I'll get your nightcap, milady."

"Don't bother." She slid down under the covers and Harriet arranged the pillows.

"You go to sleep, now. It'll all be better in the morning."

Harriet extinguished the candles and left. Thea lay in the dark, knowing it wouldn't all be better in the morning. It would be bleak and painful, but in time, if she was strong, she'd have her orderly world back again, and once there she'd find it was just what she wanted.

As the poppy claimed her, a scrap of memory floated through her mind.

"Loose hair isn't wise, you know. It makes a lady look new come from bed."

"A lady braids her hair to bed, or confines it in a cap."

"You'll do that on your wedding night?"

"We will not discuss my wedding night."

Tears leaked, even as she fell into sleep. Perhaps she wept in her sleep, for she woke with gritty eyes and a smothered feeling.

Harriet brought her washing water. The duchess arrived not much later to check on her health, clearly disappointed that she hadn't enjoyed the masquerade.

"Ah, well," she said, a cool hand on Thea's forehead, "you never were one for adventures, dear. No need to repeat the experiment."

I was outrageously adventurous. And look how very unwise it proved to be.

Thea did tell her mother about being in the servants' area, with the reason she'd given out, and about the fight. She expected horror, but though upset, her mother only

said, "How fortunate you were with someone like Darien, dear."

"Except that he went too far. The man
was down, defeated, but he carried on."

"Men do get carried away, but his anger is
understandable when he'd seen you so vilely
assaulted. I trust his opponent wasn't seriously hurt, though. That could set back his
reputation. A shame that you didn't stay for
the unmasking. Then people would have
known we trusted you to his care. But the
story of the fight will spread," she said
cheerfully, "and have the same effect."

Trusted, Thea thought, feeling out of
humor at this cheerful view of things.
They'd not been trustworthy at all.

"I can see you're still under the weather,"
her mother said. "Have a quiet day, dear. If
you feel up to it later, there are some letters
from the girls' homes to be answered."

When her mother left, Thea pulled a face
over her mother's idea of a quiet day, but
she'd welcome a routine task. The headache
and fight gave her some excuse for being
quiet, but if she moped all day her mother
might become suspicious.

She took a bath and dawdled through her
breakfast, but eventually she sent for the
stack of letters and the big orphanage record
book and settled at her desk. Her mother

supported orphans in refuges around the kingdom. On each child's birthday they received a small gift and they were expected to write their thanks. Those too young, or too new to the home to be able to write, were assisted by others.

As encouragement, each letter received a reply and commendation from one of the family. As the number of needy children grew, however, these responses took a lot of time. The men in the family were supposed to reply to the boys, but they often shuffled it off to a clerk or secretary. Thea and her mother tried to keep it up themselves. Probably the children would never know or care, but it seemed important.

The task soon soothed her, and an hour later, when she sealed the last reply, Thea felt a degree of peace. Each letter had shown true gratitude, and the brief records revealed the children's difficult beginnings. This was what was important in life, not masquerades and dangerous men. She wanted a life similar to her mother's, using rank for good.

Her mother burst in. "Excellent news, dear! A letter from Dare to say he's on his way to Long Chart. He started out yesterday, and of course he won't travel on Sunday, and he's taking it by easy stages so he probably won't do more than forty miles a day. We should be able to get home in time to welcome him. We *could* travel on the Sabbath with this excuse. . . ." She shook her head. "First thing on Monday, however, so make sure your packing is done. Oh, and purchases! There are any number of requests from our country friends that aren't filled yet. How improvident. I'll send you the list. You won't mind shopping, will you? You girls love that."

She rushed away and Thea rang for Harriet, chuckling over her even less quiet day. Being busy was just what she needed, however. By Monday morning this dreadful season would be over. And she would probably never see Lord Darien again. Whatever he decided to do once his brother was able to marry, she couldn't imagine him becoming a regular member of the ton.

She went through her wardrobe with Harriet, deciding what to take to the country and what to leave here. Then she read through the list of purchases requested by country friends. Material, ribbon, hat trimmings, items from a druggist and a perfumer. Books. There was always so much more choice in London than in the country, but this was a Herculean task for one day.

She wrote the book list on a separate sheet

and sent it to Mr. Thoresby, requesting that a clerk do that search. Then she set off with Harriet and a footman. For the food items, at least, she could rely on Fortnum and Mason's.

CHAPTER 29

Darien hadn't slept well, even with the help of brandy. Prussock's statement that it was the last bottle had led him to rebuke Lovegrove, who'd staggered away weeping without even putting away the borrowed costume.

His morning ride hadn't lightened his spirits, and the fact that the artist wasn't in the park had him gritting his teeth even as he knew he was being illogical. Luck Armiger hadn't been there since that first meeting. He'd either run off with the five guineas or was working on his commission.

When he returned, he sat at his desk to write a stinging note to the young man and realized he had no idea of his address. He sent the note to his solicitors, but he doubted that would do any good. No one could be trusted.

Especially himself.

How had he slipped into temptation last

night? He knew Thea wasn't the type to take that sort of amusement lightly. Of course she'd leap to marriage. Which was completely bloody impossible.

He took the inventories out of the locked drawer in a good mood to pin down Prussock's guilt, but today the infuriatingly tiny writing made his eyes ache.

Pup wandered in, glowing with health and good spirits. "Thought you was going to that masquerade last night, Canem."

"I did," Darien growled.

"Didn't see you."

Darien focused on him. "You went?"

"Fox took me. Didn't see you. Left early. Going for a toddle."

Darien knew he should probably go with him, but dammit, he wasn't Pup's keeper. "Enjoy yourself," he said, and returned to the page, which still didn't make any sense.

He'd done the right thing in the end.

Not to begin with. Preserving her virginity was a minor grace. He'd taken Thea Debenham's innocence, but he damn well wouldn't drag her deeper into the pit.

Pit.

Cave.

Perhaps he should change the pronunciation of the family name.

He abandoned the records, grabbed his

hat, gloves, and cane, and strode out to go to Van's house. As soon as Van came into the reception room, Darien said, "Jackson's."

Van's brows rose, but they were soon both walking to Jackson's boxing establishment.

They'd often boxed and wrestled in the past. Outside of the most active times of war, they'd both needed ways to expend energy. Weaponless fighting, fighting with no intent to kill or maim, had been a recreation. In the past week, however, it had been part of the plan, part of increasing Darien's acceptability with the upper-class men. It had been the part of the effort that Darien had most enjoyed and Van had enjoyed the excuse.

"Maria doesn't like the goods marked," he'd said. He'd clearly been joking, but Darien guessed only to an extent, so he'd tried not to leave too many marks.

At the sweaty establishment, they stripped down to shirts and breeches, pulled on the big gloves, and set to. Darien had to hold back. Some fire still burned from last night — from the fight, but mostly from the damned mess of it all.

It was good that Thea had seen him fight, that she knew who he was.

A punishing machine.

A killing machine.

Mad Dog Cave. He hated the name, but he knew he deserved it.

It wasn't as if she needed someone like him to keep her safe. Lady Theodosia Debenham would tread through life in golden security as long as she had nothing to do with men like him.

Jackson stood watching them for a moment, calling a few instructions, then stripped down himself and waved Van aside.

"To what do I owe this honor?" Darien asked.

It was an honor, but he could read the man.

"You look as if you need to let loose, my lord."

True enough, with Jackson he didn't have to be careful. With Jackson, he had to fight for his life. He held his own, just, but it was as well he had no woman who'd be upset over marked goods.

Van complained and Jackson sparred with him — much more as a scientific lesson than a bout.

They washed off sweat and redressed, then relaxed with ale in the parlor.

"Are you going to tell me now what happened?" Van asked.

"Everything, nothing," Darien said. "Thea

Debenham and I were at the Harroving masquerade last night."

Van's brows rose. "A bit of a change for her, wasn't it?"

"She wanted an adventure." Darien gave Van a brief account, framing it in Thea's quick-witted context. "I only stepped aside for a moment, and this brute forced himself on her."

Van took a deep draft of ale. "So you tried to kill him out of guilt at letting him touch her. Very understandable."

Darien didn't answer. It was true. "At least it's killed any inconvenient enthusiasms she might have been developing," he said.

"Not necessary anyway. The Debenhams leave for Somerset on Monday."

It settled like cold stone into Darien's belly. "Dare Debenham's fit again?"

"Fit enough to be on the road, taking it slowly. Is it a problem? You're far enough up the hill to do without them."

"With the beneficent assistance of the Rogues."

"It really is time to let go of that, you know."

Darien pulled a face, but said, "I have. Mostly. I don't know. Things have run fast."

"So what are your future plans?" Van asked. "For summer, for example. You'd be welcome to spend some time with us. . . ."

He broke off because four men came in, laughing loudly.

Lord Charles Standerton saw Van and Darien and came over. "Did you hear about the incident at Lady Harroving's?"

Darien tensed.

Van shot him a glance, but then said easily, "I gather my friend here pummeled an executioner who'd offended a lady."

"Was that you, Canem?" Standerton said and laughed. "The man picked the wrong opponent there. No, I'm talking about Prinny."

"The regent was there?" Van asked in surprise.

More laughter from the group. They grabbed flagons of ale from a servant and pulled chairs up at the table.

"He was indeed," said Lord Pargeter Greeve. "Dressed as a Roman emperor, laurel leaves and all!"

"Pretending to be incognito," Standerton said, "but everyone knew him. Didn't you see him, Canem?"

"Must have been after I left."

"Quite early on. But the real joke was the other Prinny. Someone went dressed as him!"

"Dressed as the regent?" Van said rever-

362

ently. "Did they meet?"

More laughter was the answer.

"Face to fat face!" gasped Sir Harold Knight, pounding the table with his fist. "I tell you," he went on when he could speak again, "the faux regent was true to life and more. Must have been pretty plump to begin with, but with two or three pillows on his belly and more wrapped around his thighs. Probably cheek pads, too."

"Had some tawdry imitation orders glittering on his chest," said Standerton, "and his hair all teased up like the regent does."

"Must have been drunk as a monk," said Lord Pargeter. "Didn't seem to realize what was going on. There was the regent, red in the face, eyes bulging, and the man says something like, "Roman, eh? I'm the Prince Regent."

The three men collapsed again, wiping their eyes. Darien laughed, too, but he had a horrible suspicion. As soon as possible, he claimed need to leave. As he and Van walked down the street, he said, "How are Pup's marital adventures going? I'm sorry I've not had much time for that."

"Maria has it in hand. He came to tea with Alice Wells on Tuesday."

"Will the lady take him?"

"We think so. They walked in the park

with her children yesterday and then went to Günter's."

"I must have been too busy for him even to tell me. I feel like a neglectful parent."

"You're not his father, Canem."

"No, but if anything's to come of it, someone will have to steer him into a proposal. It's not unfair to her?"

"No. It won't exactly be a love match, but she appears to be truly fond of him. I gather her first husband, who was a love match, was a dramatic, dominating type given to jealousy. Someone amiable and easy to manage and also able to provide security and comfort is just the ticket."

"I hope that's true. It feels like an imposition, but I need him settled."

"Any particular reason now?"

"I suspect Pup was the spurious regent."

Van stared. "What? Why? I mean, why would he do that?"

"He'll do almost anything that's suggested, but the description fits. I detect Foxstall's hand behind it."

"He's a bad man, Canem."

"Fox is just restless without someone to fight. Like me, perhaps."

"No. He has a nasty streak. I've heard tales. If people cross him, bad things happen to them. Deadly ones, sometimes."

"Then why was nothing done?"

"No evidence, and in wartime it can be hard to tell quite how a person is wounded or killed."

Darien wanted to defend Foxstall for old time's sake. "I've crossed him and he hasn't wreaked his malice on me. Anyway, he'll be off to India soon. But he is a bad influence on Pup. Best to get him settled in someone's loving care."

When Darien arrived home, Pup was still out. He returned midafternoon, whistling untunefully. "Been to Tatt's," he announced with pride.

The famous horse-selling establishment.

"Buy anything?" Darien asked with dread.

"Couldn't quite work out how to bid."

Thank heavens.

"What did you get up to last night?" Darien asked, pouring them both wine. He expected some awkwardness or even a lie, but he should have known better.

"Went to the masquerade. The same one you were at, Canem. Fox took me, but I didn't see you. Splendid costumes. I was the Prince Regent."

"Not the wisest thing, Pup. Have you told anyone?"

"Fox said it was a secret."

"He's right. It would be very bad to tell

anyone who you were at a masquerade."

"Oh, all right. I didn't get to play my part for long, anyway. Met this fat man dressed as a Roman and he seemed cross. Probably wished he'd thought of my costume first. Fox hurried me away. Before I'd had a go at the supper, too."

Feeling his responsibilities, Darien took Pup to the Egyptian Hall, where the exhibits were exactly the sort to appeal to him. When they returned, there was an invitation for them both to dine with the Vandeimens after church the next day, with the casual note that Mrs. Wells would be there.

"That'll be nice," Pup said. "Lady Vandeimen keeps a good table."

"And Mrs. Wells?" Darien asked.

"She probably keeps a good table, too. Or would, except that she's short of money."

Darien abandoned subtlety. "Which is why you'd better marry her before some other man snaps her up."

It took a moment, but then Pup said, "Do you think that could happen?"

"Definitely. What you need to do, Pup, is ask her tomorrow."

Pup pulled at his enormous cravat, as if it was suddenly tight. "How do I do that, Canem? Want to do it right, you know."

"Of course you do." Keep it simple,

366

Darien reminded himself. "You ask for a moment to speak to her in private. Maria will take you both to a reception room."

"Before or after dinner?" Pup asked anxiously.

"Whichever seems best." Immediately, Darien knew it was unwise to offer choices.

But Pup said, "Before. Worrying about it might turn me off my food."

"Excellent. When you have her alone, you say something like, 'My dear Alice, I have come to like and admire you very much. Will you be my wife?' "

Pup moved his lips, rehearsing his lines. "I can do that," he said.

"Of course you can. Easy as easy. You can go together on Monday to buy the ring, and there's no reason to delay the wedding, is there?"

Pup surprised him with an original thought. "Need a home, Canem. Married man needs a home. Have to wait."

"You can rent something. I'm sure Mrs. Wells is anxious to leave her brother's roof. You and your wife will enjoy looking for the perfect place at your leisure. In the country, probably. Children need the country."

"Right-ho," Pup said. "We can always toddle up to Town now and then. What are we doing tonight?"

Darien wanted to lurk in the Cave cave licking his wounds, some of them real. He was turning stiff from last night's bruises, and Jackson's would set in soon. But by this time tomorrow, Pup might no longer be his burden, so he promised a trip to Astley's, where grand effects, performing monkeys, and pretty equestriennes would be a treat for him.

Talk of marriage had reminded him of Frank, however. Even with the fight, the campaign had gone pretty well. Some of Viscount Darien's social activities had been reported in the newspapers and those accounts would make their way to Gibraltar. Darien wrote to his brother, telling him to keep an eye on the wind and be prepared to approach Admiral Dynnevor again at the right moment.

CHAPTER 30

Thea had almost completed her commissions when she met Maddy in Mrs. Curry's Lace Emporium.

"Were you really involved in a fight in the servants' quarters of the Harroving House?" Maddy demanded.

"Hush!" Thea said, looking around. Quietly, she added, "It wasn't as that sounds."

"Pity. You were dressed for war so I hoped you'd whacked someone. Though I must say that costume looked uncomfortable."

"It was. It gave me a headache, which is why I was down there."

"Why? Oh, do let's go to the pastry shop next door. I'm quite fagged with searching for bugle trimming."

Thea still had a few items to buy, but giving in for a little while would be easier in the end. She gave the list to Harriet and the footman and asked them to try.

When she and Maddy sat to tea and cakes,

Thea realized she truly was hungry. She'd picked at her breakfast. As she ate, she told her story.

"I hear Darien almost killed that man," Maddy said. "How exciting."

"How horrible, you mean —"

"But never say you missed Prinny and Prinny!"

Thea recognized that Maddy had been bursting with this news all along. "What do you mean?"

"You did!" Maddy took a maid of honor and bit into it. Before she'd fully cleared her mouth, she related a hair-raising encounter between the real regent and someone dressed as him.

Thea covered her mouth in horror, but she was laughing, too. "No!"

"Yes!"

"So who was it? I hope for his sake he's never identified."

"I don't know. I'm sure I've never met him. I think Fox might know, but he won't say."

"He was there, too?"

"Oh, yes. Mama doesn't like him, so I had to go with Staverton, but Fox and I had arranged to meet."

"You should listen to Aunt Margaret. He's an undesirable man."

"He's very desirable," Maddy said, smirking and licking crumbs from her lip. "And besides, you can't preach. You were there with Darien."

Thea sighed. "Yes, I know."

"So, are you going to marry him?"

Thea's face flamed. She was grateful outrage might explain it. "No, of course not!"

"Silly you. He looked delicious in all that satin and lace."

"I doubt I'll even see him again. We're leaving for Long Chart on Monday."

"No! Poor you. Why?"

"To be there when Dare arrives. He's already on the way."

"Dare doesn't need you all to wipe his brow and feed him pap."

"Mama and Papa are going, so I can hardly stay here."

"Come and live with us. We'll have lots of fun."

Maddy, day in and day out? Thea couldn't bear it. "I want to go, Maddy. Truly."

"Oh, well. If you're abandoning the Vile Viscount, perhaps I'll play with him. Mother might even permit it now. You've managed to move him from the outer wastes into the fringes of acceptability, and he does have the title. Mother is desperate for me to marry a title. I do prefer a bigger man, of course, but I suppose in bed it doesn't matter too much. . . ."

Tea and cakes threatened to rise from Thea's stomach. She rose. "I have to finish the shopping and organize my packing, Maddy. If I don't see you before I leave, I'll write."

Once home, Thea plunged into packing as if that would remove her from Town and temptation the sooner. Maddy's words had been disgusting, but they'd ignited pure, searing jealousy. She'd recover once she was away. She had to.

Harriet began to mutter, and Thea realized that she never packed her own clothes. She was probably doing it all wrong. She went off to the piano, but for once that didn't soothe her nerves, especially as she kept hitting wrong notes.

She attended a concert that evening, but Darien wasn't there. Thea berated herself for noticing. On Sunday she and her parents attended St. George's again, but Darien wasn't there, either. Was he avoiding her?

By afternoon, Thea's willpower broke. She sought her mother.

"I was wondering . . ."

"Yes, dear?" The duchess looked up from

a list of some sort.

"As we're leaving tomorrow, shouldn't we try to make one last show of support for Darien?"

"It's Sunday, dear."

"What about a walk in the park?"

"That would be possible, but there's so much to do. . . . Oh, you mean just you. To the park? Perfectly respectable. How kind of you to think of it, dear. I think the poor man feels he let you down. He wrote a note to me to apologize."

For what in particular? Thea wondered, blushing. "It wasn't his fault."

"But you felt he had reacted too strongly."

"I was probably overwrought."

"I do think so, dear, so you should put his mind at ease. I'll write a note asking if he's free."

Thea returned to her room in turmoil. She had permission, but now she wasn't sure she should meet him again. In fact, she knew she should resist temptation. But once her family left Town, she probably wouldn't return until late in the year. Anything could happen by then. Just one more meeting wouldn't hurt. And perhaps they could part on better terms.

More likely, he'd make an excuse. He was clearly avoiding her.

But he replied to say he would call at three. Thea flew to choose the perfect outfit, but of course most of her favorites were already packed. In the end she picked a dusky pink dress and spencer from last year. It had been a favorite, and Darien wouldn't know it had been worn many times.

Just a walk in nearby St. James's Park, she thought, adjusting the tilt of a satin beret trimmed with flowers. A chance to reassure him that she wasn't upset, and make a gracious farewell.

But as soon as he entered the reception room where she waited, her heart stampeded and she couldn't stop looking at him. His lean face, his dark eyes, his hands. Those hands . . .

He seemed to search her appearance, too. "Good day, Lady Thea. I hope you are recovered?"

She couldn't bear the yards between them, but felt rooted, unable to bridge them.

"Yes, thank you. Busy, of course. Because we leave Town tomorrow."

"I heard."

Their eyes locked, but nothing of their deeper thoughts could be spoken. For the sake of servants beyond the open door. For the sake of sanity. The desire between them was like a power in the air, but so was the impossibility of any future together.

There was one thing she had to say. "I don't hold you responsible, Darien. For anything."

"Thank you. But my own assessment is harsher." He gestured toward the door. With a suppressed sigh, she walked past him and out of the room.

They were walking down the street in silence, which was intolerable. "I hope you won't miss my family's support," she said.

"I believe I can manage. With the help of the Rogues."

His tone was as unreadable as an ancient manuscript. "You don't mind?"

"Anything for the cause."

She suppressed another sigh. "Have you heard from your brother?"

"No. But then, he could be at sea chasing Barbary pirates or some such."

Why had she suggested this? They couldn't even converse. "How long do you intend to stay in Town?" she asked.

"As long as I can work toward my purpose here."

"Parliament may sit for a long time. . . ."

They continued in this horrible manner until they entered St. James's Park. Then, as if something cracked, he said, "I'm sorry, Thea. I never meant to hurt you, but I warned you from the start."

"You didn't exactly hurt —"

"Don't lie." It was said gently. "Your feelings show."

At least they were talking. Her smile was wobbly, but genuine. "Are you saying I'm out of looks, sir?"

"Another thing a gentleman never says to a lady? You know by now I'm not that sort of gentleman."

She had her hands clasped in front, and they went tight on each other. "I like the sort of gentleman you are."

Like. So tame a word.

"I like the sort of lady you are, Thea. The sort who feels guilty over what we did."

"I don't feel guilty. I don't. To do it again, to plan it, would be wrong, but I can't regret what we did."

"We should walk," he said, touching her arm gently.

He was right, so she obeyed, strolling along the tree-lined path as if only out to take the air.

"Guilt and the fear of guilt can be protective," he said.

"You *want* me to feel guilty?"

"I want you safe, Thea. From physical harm, from all discomfort. From me."

Thea grabbed on to the simplest safety.

"Association with you isn't dangerous. At the masquerade, that could have happened to anyone. It had nothing to do with who you are."

"The way I handled it did."

"You rescued me."

"You rescued yourself. I punished the wrongdoer. You were disgusted."

"I was *shocked*," she protested. "I've recovered."

"You no longer think what I did bloody and vile?"

"You are an infuriating man," she said balefully, stopping to glare at him. "Very well, why did you do it? Why carry on like that?"

"Because I was angry and wanted to hurt him."

Take it or leave it, his flat tone said. *This is who I am.*

And his intention was that she leave it.

She turned and marched on, prattling about preparations for the journey. About which gown to wear on the first day of the journey. About which bonnets were more suitable for country wear and which best left in town. About slippers, sandals, and half boots. About leather gloves and lace mittens.

It was the sort of tedium she'd never

inflict on anyone, but he deserved every boring moment of it. She continued it for a full circuit of the park, only glancing at him now and then. He seemed attentive. She was sure he was thinking about horses, or weapons, or something, so she stopped again to confront him. "Tell me what you're thinking. Now."

"That you would be a very expensive wife."

"Infuriating!"

He laughed. "Not really, Thea, though you would be."

"I know how to be frugal," she protested.

"About as well as you know how to make bread."

"You're not poor," she pointed out, wondering frantically if they really were talking about marriage. Their marriage.

"No, but a season of your gowns might make me so. Thea, my land needs money ploughed back into it, for many years. There'll be little for fripperies. And in truth, I'm not much interested in them."

"Horses?" she challenged, and he smiled. It was a true smile, without restraint.

"Are never fripperies," he said. "I'll want a few good ones, yes, but not like St. Raven, who has dozens and buys a new one on a whim."

"He's a duke."

"And you're a duke's daughter."

"I'm tempted to marry you simply to prove that I wouldn't drive you into debtor's prison," she said.

It was so very dangerous to dance around the subject like this, but what if he was thinking of marriage? Might she not think of it, too?

"But what if you did send me to the Fleet? You'd doubtless abandon me to my fate."

"No, I'd live there with you and hang out a basket to beg pennies from my rich friends."

"You're not taking this seriously, Thea, but you should."

She stopped as if to look at the water in the reservoir and the birds swimming there. "You don't think very highly of me, do you?"

"You are my goddess, but —"

She turned on him. "If you say goddesses lie around in idleness, demanding to be worshipped, I shall hit you."

"You and your mother certainly don't, but you have your sphere and I have mine. I could not bear to drag you down."

"Aren't gods and goddesses always invading lower spheres?" she challenged.

"You've been reading naughty books again."

"The classics aren't naughty books."

"Oh, but they frequently are. Consider the swans," he said, "and think of Leda."

"Or think of feathers," she murmured.

"Broken feathers," he reminded her.

She turned to walk on into the trees that overhung a long dip in the ground. "Do you know this spot? It's still called Rosamund's Pond, even though the pond was filled in long since. It proved too popular for suicides."

"A pond remains a pond when dry. A Cave remains a Cave. A goddess remains a higher being." But he pulled her against him and kissed her as he had the first time, but with no trace of resistance from her. But then, too soon, he set her away from him, his hands still on her shoulders. "There is a magic between us, my Thea —"

"Yes."

"— but the seeds of our destruction, too."

"You're a warrior, Darien. Aren't you willing to fight for us?"

"I fight too much and too well. Isn't that the point?"

"It doesn't matter!" And it didn't. Everything was suddenly clear. "I don't mean I don't care about it, but I know now. I'd rather live with the warrior than without you. Does that make sense?"

"Too much. I can't permit —"

She stepped back out of his hold. "Why do you get to say all the time? I have a new agreement for you."

He turned watchful, and she could see him building defenses. "What?"

"We leave for Somerset tomorrow," she said. "We probably won't be back in London until autumn. The first part of the agreement is this. Neither of us shall commit to another before then."

"And the second part?"

"When we meet again, we discuss the situation."

"*Discuss.* We're on the brink of explosion, here in a public park —"

"In the trees," she countered.

"Even so. And in four or more months you expect us to talk?"

"Perhaps by then we'll see the folly of our excitement."

"And if we don't?" he asked softly.

Thea looked down, almost unable to say it. But then she met his eyes. "Then we marry. Are we agreed?"

He considered her, lips tight. "I assume that by then you'll have come to your senses, so very well, if you wish."

It was ungracious, but Thea had to suppress a smile as they walked back to her house. It wasn't perfect, but she wasn't sure what perfect was. It was a promise, however. And they kept their promises.

CHAPTER 31

The Yeovils left Town, and Darien continued his busy social activities without them. He couldn't resist a tiny flame of hope. He knew he wasn't the right husband for Thea Debenham, and that even if she persisted in her madness, he'd have to stop her from ruining her life. But a small part of him clung to a belief that he could restore his family's reputation beyond tolerable to honorable, and thus be worthy of her.

He was shocked by how badly he missed her. Even when they hadn't met for days, he'd known she was nearby — that he might encounter her. That if he needed to, he could seek her out. Now she was completely, thoroughly absent.

At least Foxstall was, too. He'd finished his duties and had to return north. He'd dropped by to complain about it. "Just as I was making headway with Miss Debenham, too."

Darien would stop that union if he thought it had any chance of happening, but he didn't see the need.

"With some women, I'd think absence would do the trick, but not with her," Foxstall complained. "A true butterfly."

"I don't know why you bother."

"Fifteen thousand and her family's solid gold influence! Don't know how you let the other one slip through your fingers. Especially after getting her to that masquerade."

"It was Lady Thea's idea to attend."

"I hope you made good use of it."

Was there something malicious in Foxstall's tone? No one seemed to suspect what had happened.

Darien had visited Lady Harroving the day after the masquerade, ostensibly to apologize for the fight on her premises, but in fact to find out what was being said about the linen room. Nothing, as best he could tell, though he'd learned his opponent in the fight had been the Earl of Glenmorgan. Glenmorgan was known for his belligerence, and he had apparently tried to send a challenge but had been dissuaded by his friends.

"Her family's opposition might do the trick, I suppose," Foxstall said. "She's willful enough to insist on her way. So you might find me nestled in the bosom of the

Debenham family yet. Nice juicy sinecures. Seat in Parliament. House in the best part of Town."

Over my dead body.

"Won't going back to Lancashire hamper you?" Darien said, neutrally.

"I'm a dab hand with letters. Wish me well, old friend."

"Bon voyage," Darien said, *and good riddance.*

But in Foxstall's absence, Maddy Debenham decided to amuse herself with Darien. He was grateful to be busy.

The fight with Glenmorgan had done his reputation no good. Some men admired the directness of his action, but many thought it uncouth. If there was affront between gentlemen, a properly organized duel was the appropriate action, not a brawl in the kitchens. Therefore, he had to work even harder to make up lost ground.

Morning, noon, and night he was with one or more Rogues — at coffeehouses, scientific meetings, boxing parlors, and gaming parties. When female influence was required, he had the company of beautiful Laura Ball, quiet Cressida St. Raven, spirited Clarissa Hawkinville, and even Middlethorpe's alarmingly trenchant aunt, Arabella Hurstman.

On seeing the plain-faced, plain-dressed woman he'd silently doubted her usefulness, but a walk with her through the park at a fashionable hour had been like a social tonic. Under her firm look, the still reluctant smiled at him for the first time. With the more stubborn, she marched him straight up to them and ordered them to support the innocent victim of spite and malice. Not quite in those terms, but in effect, and absolutely no one denied her.

They were probably as terrified of her umbrella as he was. It went everywhere with her and had a sharp point.

He liked her. He did not like the cool, distant Lady Cawle, but gathered that her deigning to speak to him for a few moments was a seal of approval.

He'd even been received by royalty. Various heavy levers had been brought to bear, and two weeks after the Yeovils left Town, he'd been summoned to Carlton House for a private audience with the Prince Regent. His principal sponsor was the regent's brother, the Duke of York, commander in chief of the army, who'd been genuinely warm.

The regent seemed merely forbearing. Darien had appreciated the honor and what it would mean in his campaign, but his self-control had been stretched. In his extreme girth and fashion, the regent had a distinct look of an older Pup. He regretted missing the now mythic encounter.

Even art was recruited. Luck Armiger had not run off with the money, but worked hard on his commission. His oil sketch had proved his skill, for he'd turned the look of a statue into one of action, with horse and rider raring for battle. Darien had paid for the complete picture. Maria had decreed that when it was finished it would go on display in a gallery, a pictorial representation of a glorious Cave.

Darien thought the idea ridiculous, but anything for the cause.

In the midst of all this, Pup had married his Alice, enjoyed the enormous wedding breakfast he'd arranged himself, and rolled off to honeymoon at Lord Arden's cottage ornée in the country. Darien actually missed him. The gloom of Cave House lowered on him again and the ghosts returned.

But apart from that, all was well. Amazingly so.

Darien wasn't sure, therefore, why he was skulking in his study on a sunny morning, papers untended all around him, drinking too much brandy. The silver feather might be a clue.

He picked it up and twirled it. He'd found it clinging to the braid of the cavalier costume. It was weakness to keep it, but it was all he had of her, and all he would have for many months, perhaps even forever.

There was one solid problem. He hadn't heard from Frank in over a month, which concerned him, especially as inquiries at the Admiralty turned up no particular campaigns he could be involved with. Short of sailing to Gibraltar himself, however, there was little he could do.

He put aside brandy and turned his attention to the books and paper before him. He'd shelved his attempt to understand the inventories in order to prepare to take his seat in Parliament. Before doing so, he wanted some understanding of the myriad subjects he'd be voting on. Having Greek and Latin beaten into him at Harrow had been less work, but it was part of his struggle for acceptance, his striving to be worthy of Thea. He'd give it his all.

Thea didn't hear from Maddy for weeks, but then a letter arrived. She took it onto the terrace to read in sight of the calming lake and swans, but expected only salacious gossip. Instead, it was a wild rant.

I am so ill-used, Thea! Mama has taken against Fox, and for no good reason. How can it matter that he has no fortune or title? I have a handsome portion, and our family influence can provide lucrative positions and I'm sure he'll gain a title anyway one day. As if I care for such things.

Yes, he does want to marry me! I am completely aux anges, or would be if he wasn't in horrid Lancashire, and Mama wasn't forbidding me to write. As if I care for that. I send letters daily.

But she's written to Father, and he's written to me forbidding all contact and it is more worrying to cross Father, so I pray he never finds out. I would use you to pass on letters if you were in Town. Can you not come to London? I'm surprised you've not trailed Dare back here.

True, after three weeks at Long Chart, Dare had been completely recovered and restless, and had decided to return to London. Thea couldn't argue with his reason. Canem Cave's problems were in some part his responsibility and he must do what he could to help. The duke had already returned to continue parliamentary work.

Thea could have gone, too, but she'd said she preferred the country and the duchess had approved.

It had been possibly the greatest test of willpower she'd ever faced. Not because of Dare — now that he was completely recovered, she found the ties loosed. She still loved him, but he had his own life to live and he clearly missed Mara like a severed limb. The daily letters they wrote back and forth had become a loving joke. Her temptation came all from Darien.

Now she was rewarded a little for her willpower. In London, Maddy would constantly try to entangle her in deceptions. It had happened before. She thanked heaven to be out of that, but the sting in the tail of her cousin's letter hurt.

Lord Darien is seen everywhere and truly does seem to be extinguishing his family's shame. Lacking Fox, I amuse myself with the hound whenever I can.

Thea glared at carefree swans, trying not to think of Leda.

She managed to resist the urge to race to London and fend off danger. He'd promised and she'd promised. She had to wait and see where their feelings led.

Darien returned home from a session at Jackson's to find a message asking him to visit Nicholas Delaney. In all the Rogues' support, he'd seen little of Delaney. He gathered he didn't much care for the ton's amusements, but he suspected the man was staying out of his way because he thought Darien found him particularly irritating.

That could be true. He'd been particularly irritating at Harrow.

It hadn't been anything he'd done. He'd simply been relaxed and confident in a way no fourteen-year-old boy ever should be. It hadn't been the confidence of an Arden, certain of his wealth and future power, or a Ball, bulwarked by brilliance. He'd simply been happy to be himself, and he hadn't changed. Darien had accepted help and the responsibilities that came with that, however, so he obeyed the summons.

He'd not visited Delaney's home before. He wasn't surprised to find it much like his own architecturally, as most London houses were, but inside the atmosphere was the extreme opposite to Cave House. Light, life, but a kind of peaceful harmony.

Delaney greeted him warmly and took him to an extremely well-stocked library. So well stocked, books were piled on the floor. One thing the house wasn't was tidy.

"Sorry about this," Delaney said. "The longer we stay here, the more books I buy. Eleanor prays nightly that we can leave. I'm trying to decide which to take to Red Oaks and which to leave here." He saved one from sliding off the corner of the table, glanced at the spine, then handed it over. "You may like that. *The Century of Inventions.*"

"Which century?" Darie asked, simply for something to say. Delaney should have been a fusty scholar, but he glowed with vigor.

"As in one hundred. A frustrating number of forgotten devices. Dare's here. He'd like to speak to you."

It took Darien a heartbeat to catch up, and another to think of a response. "He thinks the dog will bite?"

Delaney's eyes sharpened at the choice of words. "He probably thinks he deserves it."

"Good God, am I supposed to give him absolution?"

"I told him he should simply call on you, but he doesn't want to force a meeting if you don't want it."

For some reason, it mattered that Dare Debenham was Thea's brother, but Darien couldn't decide in what way. He didn't want to talk to the man until he knew, but this was ridiculous enough as it was.

"I have no objection," he said.

"Then I'll tell him. He's talking to Eleanor, but I'm sure Francis will want to feed again — he might as well be a leech at the moment — so she'll appreciate rescue."

He left. Darien opened the book in his hands and puzzled over a strange diagram. When the door opened, he took his time about closing the book, putting it down, and turning.

Dare Debenham looked very well indeed. He'd been physically fit when Darien had seen him at the ball, but freedom from opium had completed him.

"Will a long-overdue apology embarrass you?" Debenham asked.

"Probably. Do you need to make it?"

Debenham smiled. "A good question. Yes, I think so. Not for the words. If I hadn't come up with *cave canem,* someone else would have soon enough. But for hardly noticing the results and not caring at all. I would wish that undone, which is what an apology is about, isn't it?"

"I suppose so. But I'm hardly in a position to cast stones, am I? I made everyone as miserable as I was able, and maimed poor Trigwell. I did write to him and apologize a few years back. He was gracious, but then he is in Holy Orders."

"Is he? I suppose he was the type."

An awkward silence threatened.

"Your family's been very good to me," Darien said. "I think any debt has been paid."

"My debt, paid by others." But then Debenham said, "Did you really see me fall?"

Darien stared at him. "You think I lied?"

Debenham colored. "Apology again. I just found myself thinking. Opium does strange things to the mind."

"If I hadn't witnessed it I might have lied. If that makes sense."

"I follow it. Thea said you've gone through all this in your brother's cause. Is it won?"

Even her name caused a moment of paralysis, but then Darien found his voice. "I don't know. I've kept Frank informed, but it's in his hands when to try his luck again. A good part of me wants him to tell the Dynnevors to go hang themselves, but love knows no reason, does it?"

"I thought it was 'love knows no laws.' "

"That frequently proves the case," Darien said, suddenly realizing that he'd worked through his problem. Dare Debenham was Thea's beloved brother, therefore to be cherished. "There is no enmity between us," he said. "From what Austrey says, you can't help but be happy with Lady Mara, but I offer you my good wishes anyway."

He held out his hand, and they shook. If Debenham looked a little puzzled, so be it.

"What will you do in the summer?" Debenham asked, as they both turned toward the door. "I know my mother would be delighted if you visited Long Chart."

Such temptation, but it would break the pact.

"Impossible," Darien said lightly. "First I must see out this sitting of Parliament, which looks likely to last till Christmas at this rate. Then I go on to pummel Stours Court into civilized shape. If I have any life left in me after that, there's a godforsaken spot in Lancashire that's mine to deal with."

"I often rejoice," said Dare as they strolled into the hall, "in being a younger son."

"I was one once," Darien said, but he made it light and they parted, smiling.

CHAPTER 32

When it came time to travel to Lincolnshire
for the wedding, Thea recognized a flaw in
her bargain with Darien. She'd forgotten
that the journey would take them through
London. It was the only sensible route, and
they had to gather up Dare and the duke
there and stop for the night.

They arrived in the late afternoon and
would leave the next morning, and did not
plan to attempt any social event, so Thea
thought she was safe. Except from her own
ravening temptation.

She hadn't counted on her mother sum-
moning Darien for a recounting of events,
nor had she any warning. If she had, she
wouldn't have been with her mother in the
small drawing room when Darien was announced.

His eyes met hers — and lingered.

Hers ate him up.

How could he be different? She hadn't

forgotten him, but it was like seeing him for the first time, but now more relaxed, easier in his smiles. More handsome.

He bowed. "I hope you enjoyed your time in the country, Lady Thea."

"Yes, thank you, Darien. Will you go into the country when Parliament prorogues?"

Their eyes, the air between them, said other things. He still cared and so, by all that was holy, did she. If her mother hadn't been present, all questions between them might have ended in violent explosion.

When the footman returned to say that Miss Debenham was below, Thea seized on that and escaped. She found Maddy in a reception room in evening finery.

"When I heard you were here I had to stop by. You could have told me!"

"We're only breaking the journey."

Maddy grasped Thea's arm. "You have to persuade your parents to speak on Fox's behalf. Everyone's still fussing over Darien, and he's a Cave! There's nothing disreputable about Fox's family other than lack of title and money."

"You know Mother doesn't put huge weight on things like that."

"Then she'll take up his cause, won't she? I mean, when the poor man was wounded so horribly to protect us all, it is atrocious to be shunning him!"

"I don't think anyone's shunning him, Maddy. He's in Lancashire."

"It's the same thing!"

Thea shook her head. "Sit down. Calm down. Would you like tea?"

"Tea! How can I drink tea? Do you have wine?"

"Wine?" Thea echoed in surprise.

"Why not? Oh, you're so *dull!*"

"Then I don't know why you're here," Thea snapped.

"To seek your help! I'm dying for love, Thea. *Dying!* Fox is the only man I could ever marry. You can't imagine how it is to feel such passion."

"Thank you."

The dry tone made an impression. Maddy frowned at her. "Well, you can't," she said in a less high-flown style. "Some people have grand emotions and others don't. I'm sure it's more comfortable. *Please* say you'll talk to your parents. If they lend their weight, you know mine will give in."

Awash in her own forbidden longings, Thea wanted to help, but she said, "Will he make you a good husband, Maddy?"

"The perfect one!"

"But his regiment's going to India. I'm not sure —"

Maddy laughed. "Silly! He'll sell out once our wedding is allowed, but there's so little time. Please!"

Thea had taken Foxstall in dislike, but she really had no reason. She'd been deeply prejudiced against Darien, and he was not at all as she'd thought.

"I'll try," she promised.

Maddy kissed her and hurried away. Thea sighed, but then her thoughts flew to Darien, who might still be with her mother. She could return. But no. Better not. Because she kept her promises, she raised the subject of Maddy and Foxstall the next morning over breakfast with her mother.

Her mother grimaced. "In this case, Thea, I fear Margaret is correct. Of course she wants a title for Maddy, and a comfortable income. Why not, indeed? Poverty is not at all romantic. And there's Marchampton, smitten. But now it's said Marchampton's father opposes it because of her behavior. I don't know what will become of that girl."

"Perhaps Foxstall is the man for her, then."

"Sadly, no."

"Why?"

"It's not really suitable for maidenly ears, but you're sensible enough to understand, dear. At Margaret's request, we had inquiries made. Captain Foxstall's string of conquests is long."

Thea tried to be fair. "Most men are not religiously virtuous, Mama, and can reform with marriage."

"Yes, but there's a matter of extent." The duchess sighed. "Even while paying attention to Maddy in London he was involved with other women."

"No!"

"Very distasteful. Most were women on the fringes of society, but one — for your own ears only, of course — was Maria Harroving."

"Good heavens. But he was at the masquerade with Maddy."

Her mother shrugged. "He was also spending much time with Lady Harroving there."

"I remember Maddy saying she'd gone with someone else but had planned to meet Foxstall there."

The duchess shook her head. "No sense of decorum. If Margaret had asked, I would have advised her not to allow Maddy to attend. You could be trusted to keep the line, but given any opportunity, Maddy exceeds it."

Thea felt horrid guilt and it made her try harder. "But if that is Maddy's nature, might not someone like Captain Foxstall be the right husband?"

"Not at all. He drinks, he games, he is cruel. He'll make anyone a terrible husband, but especially someone like Maddy. She doesn't have an obliging nature. She'll demand too much of him, and he'll punish her. If Maria Harroving would marry him, it might suit, for she's worldly wise and has ample money, but she has too much sense. His regiment goes to India soon, so it will all blow over and then we'll look for a more suitable match. A firm older man who'll treat her well but put up with no nonsense."

"Mama . . ."

"It's that or she truly will ruin herself, Thea, believe me."

Thea gave in. She'd done her best, but didn't relish explaining that to Maddy, so she was relieved to leave London after breakfast, even though every turn of the wheels took her away from Darien.

Despite what she feared was a broken heart, Thea was able to fling herself into the merry wedding celebrations. Dare claimed Brideswell was magical, and perhaps he was right. Everything felt lighter there, and even her future seemed promising. Thea found herself dancing around the bonfire hand in hand with two village swains. She wore her

401

yellow dress and her hair down, amused by how astonished the villagers would be to learn that it was "country wear."

She thought of Darien the whole time and didn't try to stop herself. She even imagined, during the ceremony, that she was saying her vows to him. For better or worse, for richer or poorer. That was what marriage was about, not the careful safety of equal fortunes and perfect security. Yes, now she truly knew her heart and mind.

Because of this, she didn't struggle against her mother's decision to linger in London awhile on the return journey. After all, she hadn't promised not to return until autumn. She'd simply assumed it.

Thea arrived back at Yeovil House in a nervous fizz and she'd rather not have wasted it on Maddy, but her cousin arrived only hours after they did.

"Thank heavens you're here!" Maddy declared as soon as they were in Thea's room. "I'm at my wit's end."

"What's happened?"

"Mother won't let me see him!"

"See who?"

"Don't be provoking. Fox! Who else?"

"But he's in the north."

"No, he's here! A fortnight's furlough before they sail." Maddy untied her complicated bonnet and tossed it on the floor. "We are determined to marry."

"Oh, dear."

"Don't be like that. I know you don't like him, but that's because he's strong meat for a delicate bloom like you."

Thea held her patience. "Maddy, if you want a kindly listener, don't insult me."

Maddy stared at her. "No need to be vinegary, Thea. I'm desperate. I'd run off to Gretna, but then Father would probably not pay my full dowry. It's most unfair that only part of it is fixed by law. The rest he added only by promise as he became wealthier."

"He might be persuaded after a while. When your marriage is happy and Foxstall proves admirable."

"Oh, for pity's sake. Can you imagine living under that scrutiny, afraid to act boldly or have a quarrel?"

Thea shook her head. "Maddy, what do you want from me?"

"Sympathy. But I see the well's dry."

"I truly do sympathize, but I don't see what I can do. No words of mine will persuade your parents to see things differently, and my parents feel as yours do. He is not obviously an ideal husband."

"He's the one I want," Maddy said mutinously. "Mother's just hoping I'll give in and take March, but I won't."

"Certainly not, if you don't love him."

"I love Fox." Maddy leapt to her feet. "I *adore* Fox. I can hardly bear a moment away from him!"

Thea watched this volcanic performance, recognizing her own feelings, though she'd never behave so wildly.

"*Promise* you'll help me," Maddy said.

"To do what?" Thea asked cautiously.

"I don't know yet, but when I think of something."

"I'm not going to help you to elope."

"You are *such* a dull stick. But as I said, that wouldn't serve. Just promise."

Thea wanted to get rid of her. "If I can, I will."

Maddy grabbed her bonnet and put it on. "I *will* marry Fox. I thought of having your hound instead. But really, in comparison, he's almost as dull as you are. You two really should make a match!"

"Dull?" Thea asked with a laugh. "When he almost murdered a man before my eyes?"

"I'm sure it was a very dull murder," Maddy said and flounced out.

Thea hoped that meant she wouldn't see her again for a long time. She did spend a few moments wondering if she should warn her mother or aunt — but of what? Maddy said she wouldn't elope, and her reasons made sense. She was underage, so there was no other way for her to marry Foxstall. She could write secret letters and even slip out for clandestine meetings as much as she wanted. Thea was sure she'd been doing such things for years. And if Maddy felt for Foxstall as she felt for Darien, Thea truly, deeply sympathized.

When would Darien visit?

He didn't come that evening. When he didn't come the next day, Thea set out in the afternoon to wander fashionable London with Harriet in the manner of an angler trailing a fly across water. She went to Hatchard's to peruse the latest novels, and walked the length of Oxford Street until Harriet was beginning to mutter. She saw no sign of Darien other than a painting in a shop window.

That certainly absorbed her for a while. He was truly splendid in full hussar magnificence, on a prancing gray horse, ready for battle. Others paused to admire it, too, and Thea even heard one woman say, "Brother to that madman, you know, but this one, Lord Darien, he's a regular hero."

Everything was going so well and she wanted to share that with him. That night she and her mother went to the theater, but again, Darien was nowhere to be seen. By then, Thea thought it safe to ask her mother.

"I believe he's visiting the Duchess of York at Oatlands."

"Excellent," said Thea, and she meant it. Not only because that was another sign of his social progress, but because there was a reason she hadn't encountered him.

But the next day he returned to Town — there was a brief note in the *Gazette* — and still didn't call at Yeovil House. That evening, before dinner, where the French ambassador and some other diplomatic people were to be her mother's guests, even the duchess noted his neglect.

"I do hope to see Darien soon. But it is excellent that he's so busy, and with eminent company."

Busy avoiding her, Thea had to conclude. It was possible that he was being noble, but what if he'd realized he didn't want an extravagant duke's daughter for a wife? She couldn't stand the uncertainty, but she could hardly march round and knock on his door, tempting though that was.

CHAPTER 33

The next day, after a fruitless morning spent waiting for some sort of news of Darien, Thea received a plea from Maddy.

Dearest, dearest Thea,
I'm so sorry for losing my temper, but I truly am suffering, and it's made worse with Fox in Town. I'm allowed to go nowhere without escort, and of course my maid doesn't count. Mama says if you accompany me she'll allow an excursion. Thank heavens for your golden reputation! There's an interesting bookstore I've heard of, quite within walking distance of our house. Do say you'll come and escort me there or I'll slit my throat.
                        Your loving cousin,
                                Maddy.

Thea shook her head, but she might as

well be useful to someone. She told her mother, ordered the carriage, and was soon on her way to Maddy's house with Harriet in attendance. Once there, she sent the coach home with orders to return in two hours.

Maddy truly was finding restriction difficult. She was ready and in a fever to be off. "It's like being in prison," she complained as soon as they were outside. "Thank you, thank you!"

For a prisoner, she was in fine looks. Her bright blue outfit suited her to perfection, her color was high and her eyes bright.

"You haven't brought your maid?" Thea asked.

"I knew you'd bring Harriet, and Mama doesn't trust Susannah. With reason," she added with a giggle.

"So what is this special bookshop?" Thea asked as they walked down the street.

"Thicke and Stelburg. Not a fashionable place, but I'm told it carries books that are just a little bit naughty."

"Maddy!"

"Oh, don't fuss. This isn't some great scandal. They're like Minerva novels, but the imprisoned heroines and lusty heroes get up to a little more than kisses. Caroline has one and it's great fun. If I have to live in durance vile, I need amusement."

Thea resisted the urge to exclaim "Maddy!" again. This was harmless enough, and if it distracted Maddy from Foxstall, it would be worth it.

Maddy shared society gossip all the way, but when they arrived at the address, Thea paused. The shop was not appealing. The front was narrow and the windows so dirty it was hard to see what few books were on display in there. Maddy walked in, however, so Thea had to follow.

It took a moment for her eyes to adjust to the gloomy interior. To her right, a morose-looking man hunched behind a small desk, absorbed in a book. In front of her, long rows of shelves stretched toward the dim back of the building, lit occasionally by smoky lamps. Maddy had disappeared.

The place stank of wood rot and moldy paper, and Thea wanted to find these books and get out of there. She crossed the shop, floorboards creaking, peering down each aisle.

There were customers — all male, but at least they looked respectable. She saw young men who were probably students, and older ones who looked like scholars. One was a clergyman.

Thea didn't feel afraid, but where was

Maddy? Sometimes these shops were warrens, but this one looked simple enough, and Maddy's blue gown should shine like a beacon.

She was tempted to call Maddy's name, but the silence was so firm she couldn't quite bring herself to, so she went down an empty aisle looking for cross-aisles or unseen parts of the store. The only crossway was at the very end.

She walked back up another aisle, having to squeeze by a disapproving scholar, until she arrived at the front again. She gave up and went to the desk.

"My cousin, sir. A lady in blue. Do you know where she went?"

The man looked up, sniffed, and silently handed her a folded, sealed sheet of paper.

Heart suddenly thumping, Thea snapped the seal. A glance showed her Maddy's flamboyant writing and the first words.

Do forgive me, Thea.

The wretch! Aware of the man's interest, she went out into the fresh air before reading further.

Do forgive me, Thea, for the ruse, though I do think it a very clever way to gain my freedom. Don't worry. Your part is over. You may do as you please for the

410

next two hours and then pick me up at the bookstore and take me home, with Mama none the wiser.

And I will be with Fox, ensuring our future!

I know you will help me, but if you think to do otherwise, remember that the pot shouldn't call the kettle black. Silver feathers were found in the Harroving linen room. No one knows of it yet other than Fox and me. I'm sure you want it to stay that way.

Your loving cousin,
Maddy.

Thea wondered if her eyes were bulging. "Loving cousin"? Maddy was *blackmailing* her.

But then her knees turned weak. Dear heaven, had silver feathers really been found there? She had noticed that the poor owl had been a bit the worse for wear.

Found by whom? Presumably by the laundress, who'd told Lady Harroving, who'd told her lover.

Clearly her own connection had gone no farther yet, but it only needed someone to make a point of it.

"What's the matter, milady?" Harriet asked. "Where's Miss Maddy?"

There was no hiding it. "Gone, Harriet. Oh, dear. . . ."

"Kidnapped? Shall I get help?"

"No! Hush, I must think." Thea started walking so as not to attract attention. "She's slipped away. Up to one of her tricks. But what should I do?"

"Go right back and tell her mother, milady."

Thea hadn't truly been asking for advice. "No, I can't do that. Hush."

Had Maddy decided to elope anyway? She had to prevent that. But if she told Aunt Margaret, Maddy would ruin her. Yes, she might actually do it.

Maddy could simply be enjoying a tryst. That was wrong, but not worth taking risks to prevent. If she knew where Foxstall was lodging, she'd go there and find out. If they'd left in a post chaise, she'd know the worst and she'd have to act. If Maddy was there with him, it would simply be embarrassing.

"Milady . . ."

Harriet's complaint made Thea come out of her thoughts. "What?"

"Where are we going, milady?"

Thea looked around. She was in a new street, and if she wasn't careful she'd get lost. How could she find out where Foxstall was staying?

Darien. He might know. But she couldn't go to his house.

But then she remembered him taunting her about being confined by cobwebs. Very well. She'd brush this one aside.

"Harriet, how do we get from here to Hanover Square? It can't be very far."

"I don't know, milady."

"Ask that man."

Harriet rolled her eyes, but she asked a respectable middle-aged man, who gave directions. Thea set off briskly.

"Where are we going, milady?"

"To Lord Darien's."

Harriet grabbed her arm. "Not to *that* house, milady! It were covered in blood!"

Thea didn't know if Harriet was referring to the murder or to other events, but she said, "I doubt it still is. Come or not. I'm going because I need some information." She marched on and Harriet kept up, muttering.

When they entered the square, however, Thea paused to bolster her nerve. What would he think? How would he react? She couldn't turn back now.

The square looked so calm and elegant, the central garden orderly, and the four terraces of well-maintained houses promised prosperous, decent inhabitants. She didn't know the number of Darien's house, but knew it had an escutcheon over the door featuring a snarling black dog. People had talked of that with disapproval.

She found it. Other than the dog, it looked unalarming. There definitely was no sign of blood. Yet as Thea climbed the shallow steps and rapped the knocker she felt as if every window in the square held a staring witness to this witless female entering the mad dog's lair.

No one responded, so she rapped again. The house couldn't be deserted. She plied the knocker a third time, vigorously.

The door opened a crack and a round-faced girl stared out at her. "Yes, mum?"

The maid looked ready to shut the door in her face so Thea pushed hard and marched in. The girl gave way, gaping.

"I wish to see Lord Darien."

The bug-eyed girl scuttled off, but not to a nearby room or upstairs. She ran toward the back of the house, doubtless to the servants' area. What sort of establishment was this? Would a body of servants arrive to force her out?

There was no spacious hall here, but rather a wide corridor that shortly narrowed where the staircase rose. Open doors on either side of her showed a reception room and a parlor. Another door was visible farther down the corridor.

She could search room to room. Instead, she went to the bottom of the stairs and called: "Darien! It's Lady Thea. Where are you?"

He came out of the closed door on this floor, in waistcoat and shirtsleeves, frowning. "What the devil are you doing here?"

So cold. So angry. That answered one question.

"Dealing with devilish matters," Thea snapped to hide a spear of pain. She turned back and pointed to a wooden chair in the hall. "Harriet, stay there." Then she marched into his room, using anger to fight tears.

It was an office of sorts, with a desk and empty bookshelves. He appeared to have been poring over densely printed books.

She turned to face him. "Where does Captain Foxstall lodge?"

"Why?"

"None of your business."

"You're in my house."

Their eyes locked. Perhaps he wasn't angry, or not in that way. Or indifferent.

He was half dressed, without cravat and with his shirt open. A vee of chest showed, making her have to swallow. His hair was disordered, as if he'd run his hand through it again and again. She wanted to smooth it.

She pulled herself together. "Maddy is with Captain Foxstall. She expects me to provide her with an alibi, but I can't. She could be making a terrible mistake."

"What mistake do you think she's making?"

In his presence it was hard to think. "Perhaps only a dalliance, but I have to stop her. What if she's eloping?"

"Is the case as desperate as that?" he asked.

"My family is strongly against Foxstall. He's been investigated."

"Poor old Fox. But yes, it must be stopped. It will serve neither of them well." He took his coat off the back of his chair and shrugged into it. His hat and gloves were on a small table by the door. "I'll go and find out what's going on."

"You know where he's lodging?"

"Yes."

"I'm coming, too."

"No."

He turned to leave so she grabbed his arm. "I need to."

I need to be with you.

His muscles turned rigid and sensations rippled from there through her body. She snatched her hand free and stepped back.

His face twitched, but his voice was steady. "Let me handle this, Thea. It could be unpleasant."

"That's the point. Maddy's capable of making an awful scene."

"You can stop her?"

"Probably. And what if" — she bit her lip — "if she's in distress?"

"If he's raped her?" he said bluntly. "That wouldn't serve his purpose, and he's never had need to. He has a way with women."

"They're moved by his war wound, I assume," she said bitterly.

"Often, but it's not a war wound. He tells them a touching story, but the scar is superficial. He was born with the wry face."

"A liar? Even more reason to save Maddy. Why aren't we already on our way?"

He sighed, then gestured toward the door, but neither of them moved.

"Why haven't you come to see me?" she asked.

"Our bargain was for late in the year."

"Or for when I was next in London."

A brow rose. "I don't remember that."

"Then perhaps your memory is weak."

His lips twitched, they did. Hope unfurled.

417

"We're here for the duration of Parliament," she told him.

"And our bargain?" he asked softly. "We haven't had enough time, Thea. You know it."

"Do I?" She stepped closer, she had to, and raised her hand to cradle his strong neck. A pulse beat rapidly against her palm. "I haven't changed. Have you?"

"No."

She moved her fingers to his lips. He kissed them, but then he took her hand. "Come. Let's rescue your cousin, though I confess I have some sympathy for those driven mad by . . . by desire."

Had he almost said "by love"?

He was tugging her out of the room, but she held back. "Wait. I must tell you something. Darien, Maddy threatened me."

"Threatened you? With what?"

"With exposure. She implied that she knew. About what we did." She dug the letter out of her reticule. "Here, read it."

He scanned it quickly, lips tightening. "It could be cunning guesswork."

"But what if it's *true?* Mama told me Foxstall's been . . . That Lady Harroving has been his mistress, even while he's been wooing Maddy. Another reason Maddy mustn't marry him, but that must be how he knows about the feathers. But how could he tell Maddy without revealing . . . ?"

He took her into his arms. "Calm down. If there were feathers there, the story hasn't spread. Lady Harroving might not have made the connection, but if she has she would hesitate to offend your family. In any case there are probably many similar incidents at her masquerades. If they became the tattle of the Town, she'd soon have no guests."

Thea rested against him, where she'd so longed to be, but she felt like weeping. "I hate her knowing. Despite everything. . . ."

"You wish you hadn't done it. I know."

She looked up at him. "I don't regret you. I will never regret you."

He kissed her gently. "I hope that's true. But come, we should ride to the rescue."

They parted reluctantly and walked to the door.

"If we find them, leave him to me," Darien said. "He's not a good enemy."

"He'd be less likely to strike back at me than you," she said.

"I place no reliance on that. He's capable of anything he thinks he can get away with."

Thea shuddered. "We have to free Maddy from him." She walked out into the hall. "Harriet, Lord Darien's taking me to retrieve Maddy. You'd best stay here."

Harriet bounced to her feet. "You're not leaving me in this house, milady!"

"I'm taking the monster with me," Thea snapped, then wished to heaven she'd not. She looked at him in horror, but he seemed to be fighting laughter. She smiled back — and wished Maddy to the devil. But without Maddy's mischief she wouldn't be here.

What should she do now? She didn't want to take Harriet because they might find Maddy alone with Foxstall, which would be a scandal if known. But if she sent the maid back to Yeovil House, there'd be questions.

"Is there anywhere you'd like to spend an hour, Harriet?"

"And leave you alone with *him,* milady?"

"I am perfectly safe with Lord Darien," Thea said icily. "Where would you like to wait for me?"

"In Westminster Abbey, milady," Harriet said, with a silent, *Where I can pray for you to come to your senses.*

"Very well. I think." Thea looked at Darien. "How do we get there from here?"

"A hackney," he said, smiling, but she knew he was noting her ignorance of all the practicalities of life.

CHAPTER 34

They left Cave House and walked out of the square. Again, Thea thought of how many people were watching and wondering. She didn't mind now, however. His feelings hadn't changed, so she wanted to be seen with him, to be connected to him in the mind of her world.

It wasn't very far to the nearest hackney stand. She'd seen the lines of battered carriages in certain places and understood that they were for hire, but she'd never thought about exactly how. Darien stopped by the first in line and handed Harriet into it, then spoke to the driver and gave him money. Harriet was carried away, but not without a strong look at Thea saying, *Be careful!*

Darien assisted Thea into the next one, which was a much sorrier affair. The seat sagged so badly Thea worried she'd fall through, and the straw on the floor was dirty.

"I'm sorry," Darien said, taking the opposite seat as it lurched off, "but if one doesn't take the next in line, there'll be a riot."

"It's all right," she said. "And if it's not, this is my problem, not yours."

"Any problem of yours is mine," he said simply.

Their situation was uncertain and Maddy was being a pest, but here in this unpleasant vehicle Thea felt in a perfect moment, simply because she was alone with Darien. Of course being alone with him was a scandal on its own, though she'd never understood why closed carriages were supposed to be such dens of wickedness. It would take acrobatics to even kiss in this one, especially with it rattling her bones over cobbles and swaying madly when going around corners.

She suddenly giggled.

"What's amusing?" he asked, clutching a leather strap, but his eyes gleamed with humor.

"Oh, everything. Why the gilding?" There were traces of gold paint on the inside panels.

"Most hacks are retired gentlemen's carriages. This one must have been grand once — a very long time ago."

"I wonder what stories it could tell."

They fell silent, but it was a good silence. The coach lurched to a halt, springs groaning, and Darien handed Thea out in front of a timbered inn. The sign above the door read THE CROWN AND MAGPIE and held a picture of a magpie with a crown in its beak. A thieving bird, but it seemed a solid, respectable hostelry.

Thea had never entered a London inn before, but when she did so, it seemed little different to the ones she'd stayed at on a journey. A frock-coated man came forward to welcome them.

"Captain Foxstall," Darien said. "Which room?"

The stocky, red-faced man pursed his lips. "Perhaps I may have your card sent up, sir?"

"No." A guinea changed hands.

"Number six, sir. Upstairs and to the right."

They went up, but at the top of the stairs Darien touched Thea's arm. "Are you sure you want to be there? If your cousin's with Foxstall, she might not welcome interference."

"She probably won't, but I have to be there. In case . . ."

"If he's harmed her I'll kill him for you."

She gripped his arm. "No. No violence."

"There are times for violence."

It was still an issue between them, but this wasn't the time or place to attempt to deal with it. "Then with the minimum of violence. Please."

"It will always be as you command."

He turned and approached the door painted with a six and she hurried after. She didn't hear any voices beyond it. Surely the innkeeper had implied Foxstall was in. If Maddy wasn't here with him, where was she?

Darien raised his hand to knock, but then instead he turned the handle and walked in.

Thea swallowed a protest, but in any case they entered a comfortable but empty private parlor. Thea heard voices now, from beyond an adjoining door. This was hers to do, so she walked forward and opened it — to freeze, gaping.

In a big, rumpled bed, Maddy and Foxstall were lounging and laughing. As best Thea could see, both were naked. Laughter froze as she had frozen, and Maddy pulled the sheet up over her breasts, red-faced. Then her brows rose, and she smirked.

Darien grasped Thea's arm and pulled her back, but she twisted free and surged forward. "Maddy! Are you *mad?*"

Her cousin's laugh peeled out. "Puns,

Thea? At a time like this? Oh, wipe that sanctimonious horror off your face. If you'd done as I asked, you'd not be here to be upset."

Thea swayed. An arm came around her, a strong body supported her. She couldn't stop staring at Maddy, and at Foxstall's knobby, muscled shoulders and chest heavy with hair. He grinned, looking demonic with that twisted jaw. Which wasn't a noble war wound. . . .

"You needn't look so very shocked, coz," Maddy said, turning slightly to snuggle against Foxstall's bare shoulder. "You must have guessed or why rush over here?"

"I thought you might be eloping . . . Maddy, I won't let you do this to yourself."

"It's already done."

Thea feared she might be sick. "I mean marry him," she said.

"And how are you going to stop me? Tell the world?"

"Tell your father and mine."

"Who'll insist we marry, if not immediately, as soon as I get with child. That's what I want. What a fool you are, Thea."

She was. She'd never imagined that Maddy would cold-bloodedly plan something like this, but it was disastrous. She was sure of it. The man himself proved it.

There was no tenderness in his expression, only sneering triumph. He showed not a trace of protective concern for the young woman he'd just despoiled.

"I won't let you do this," Thea cried, to him as much as to Maddy. "If you wed, I'll make sure Uncle Arthur ties up your dowry with strings so tight that Foxstall never has free use of it. Never."

"Bitch," Foxstall spat.

Darien stiffened, but he said, "Come away, Thea. There's nothing to be done here."

But Thea couldn't. "Look at him, Maddy. Look at him. He doesn't want you on those terms."

Maddy turned, but Thea rushed on.

"He'll be a horrible husband. He's all lies and cheats. Even his noble war wound's a lie, and he's been sleeping with dozens of other women in London while pretending to woo you. He won't change. He's rotten, and will always be so."

"Fox?" Maddy said, her voice small.

Foxstall, however, was looking at Thea with flat malice in his eyes.

"Fox, don't worry. I don't believe her."

He looked down and then pushed Maddy away. "The game's up, Maddy, so on your way. With your cousin stirring up your family, we'll never have a feather to fly with."

"That's not true! My portion's large —"

"Not large enough for me."

"Once we're married, my parents will come around. Don't listen to her!"

"Are you going to be boring?" he asked. "She's right about the other women, the sanctimonious prig. I'm not a man to be satisfied by a virgin's teasing for weeks."

Maddy gasped and then scrambled off the bed, clutching the counterpane around her. "You cur, you lout!"

She grabbed and hurled a water glass, a bowl, and then the candlestick. The latter hit him, but her throw was weak and he blocked it with his arm, laughing.

"You'll suffer for this, Foxstall," Maddy hissed. "I'll crush you, I'll ruin you. . . ."

But then she turned and hurled herself against Darien's chest. He had no choice but to let go of Thea and catch her. He drew her away, into the other room, saying to Thea, "Come."

But Maddy's clothing was scattered around the room, so Thea scurried around gathering it. She wished she didn't have to look at Foxstall, but she did, sensing he was like a feral animal, keen to kill. She stumbled over his scabbarded saber and was tempted to seize it, draw it, for protection.

When she was sure she'd collected everything, she backed out, clutching the clothes
in front of her.

"You'll pay for this," he said, lips twisted
as always, but perhaps truly smiling in a
horrid, malicious way. "Silver feathers. How
much are they worth in London these
days?"

Acid rose in Thea's throat, but she met
his eyes. "Not one penny," she mouthed.
Darien mustn't hear or murder would be
done. "I'd rather walk the streets in peniten-
tial sackcloth and ashes."

Then she shut the door between them. It
took a moment to gather herself and turn
to where Maddy was still in Darien's arms,
clinging, weeping, and wailing about wickedness and betrayal.

"Oh, stop it," Thea said, dragging her
cousin away. "You may have been betrayed
about some things, but you came here of
your own free will with this wickedness in
mind."

Maddy turned on her, clutching the counterpane. "What do you know of *passion,* you
cold fish?"

"Silver feathers?" Thea replied tartly.

"I don't believe that. I never believed that.
You've always been jealous of me. Always!"

Darien put his hand over her mouth. "You

said she'd make a scene."

Maddy was goggle-eyed, but she couldn't get free without dropping the counterpane, and even she balked at that.

"I'd go into the hall while she dressed," Darien said, "but I don't trust Foxstall. So I'll station myself watching that door." He let Maddy go and did so, watching the door to the silent bedroom most conscientiously.

Maddy, for the moment, seemed speechless, and Thea wondered if this terrible event had finally shocked some sense into her.

But then she recovered and dropped her cover, brashly revealing bountiful hips and breasts, and a remarkably slender waist. Her deep pink nipples jutted. "Ripe" was the word that came to mind, in look and odor. Perfume, sweat, and that something else rose off her. Thea almost gagged.

"Yes, look," Maddy mouthed. "You'll never know."

"Silver feathers," Thea mouthed back, handing over Maddy's shift.

This was petty, but she was so furious she couldn't stop herself. But, oh God, what would Foxstall do, and what should she do to prevent it?

As she played maid her mind spun around it, always lurching back to Darien. Darien would silence Foxstall. Darien would kill him if she asked. A duel. But that would ruin his hard-won reclamation. If he killed Foxstall, he might have to flee the country.

And what if Foxstall killed Darien? He had to be a formidable fighter.

When Maddy was wrapped in the propriety of expensive fashionable clothing she looked her usual self. No tears, no shame. If she was brokenhearted, she was hiding it well. Was she at all concerned about the risk of a child? Thea didn't know this Maddy at all, but her heart ached. What would become of her now?

Maddy paused, looking at the door Darien guarded, and something rippled over her face. Only for a moment, however. "I'm dressed," she said, "so we can be off."

Darien went to open the door to the corridor. Thea and Maddy went through and down the stairs, Maddy flicking down some veiling from her elaborate hat and thus covering her face. Thea had done nothing wrong, but she blushed as they left the inn, feeling every eye upon her. A hackney happened to be nearby, and Darien summoned it.

Once in the coach, Maddy said, "Well, what's the sentence? Do I hang?"

"If you've given up Foxstall, I see no need

to tell anyone," Thea said.

"But what if I'm with child?" It was tossed as a challenge. "What do I do if I can't marry the father?"

"You should have thought of that."

"I *did!*" Maddy snapped. "That was the idea, and now you've ruined everything. I wish I'd never involved you."

"So do I."

"Where shall we go?" Darien asked calmly enough, but Thea could feel his tension. She knew he burned to go back to the inn and fight Foxstall, but she'd made him promise to avoid violence. Should she release him? *Let loose the dogs of war,* she remembered.

"Back to the bookstore, I suppose," she said, "where my carriage should return soon."

They traveled in silence and found the Yeovil carriage waiting. They changed into it and rode the short distance to Maddy's house.

Aunt Margaret appeared anxiously at the door. "Oh, you're back safely! But no books, dearest?"

"They had nothing suitable," Maddy said, completely in her normal manner. "But we acquired Lord Darien as escort. Isn't that delightful?"

"Of course," Aunt Margaret said, but

431

doubtfully. Clearly she was one of the unconvinced. "Do come in. Tea, perhaps. . . ."

"No, I really must get home," Thea said. "Good day, Aunt, Maddy." Thea sent her cousin a smiling wave. Behind her mother's back, Maddy pulled a face.

Thea returned to the carriage with Darien. "I suppose now we should go and find Harriet."

He gave the direction and the carriage moved off, so much more smoothly than a hackney, but nothing was smooth anymore. A tear escaped.

"Don't," Darien said softly. "Don't weep for her. She's . . ."

She's not worth it.

"She's the closest to a sister I have," she choked out. "What am I to do for her?"

"Sometimes there's nothing you can do. But I can get rid of Foxstall."

"No. No violence."

"Thea, I can't let this stand."

"Because of the feathers?" she asked, looking into his resolute eyes. "But Maddy knows, too. Silencing him won't solve anything."

"You really think she'll betray you?" He sounded shocked.

"I hope not, but . . ."

He sighed. "Listen, she can't do anything

without risking exposure, whereas Foxstall won't care. And he smashes things out of spite."

"He might smash you."

"No," he said flatly.

"You can't be sure of that! I can't bear the thought of you dead. Or of you killing him."

He brushed his knuckles down her damp cheek. "I know. But I must destroy Foxstall, for what he did to your cousin and for the threat he holds over you."

"What does it matter?" Thea asked, trying for a Maddy tone. "We'll simply have to marry. Will that be so bad?"

He smiled slightly, but without softening. "Yes. Do you imagine that I'd allow you to face scandal and shame when I can prevent it?"

Tears were pouring now, and not graciously. She pulled out a handkerchief and tried to stop the flow. "But we deserve scandal and shame. We did much the same. Why should anyone die over this?"

"He's not going to die for taking your cousin to his bed."

"What if *you* die?" she cried.

He simply drew her into his arms and rocked her, gentle but implacable.

The carriage stopped outside Westminster Abbey. They parted, but neither of them moved to get out. Ignoring the liveried footman who'd appeared outside the door ready to open it, Darien took out a handkerchief of his own and wiped away her tears.

"This is like a battle," he said. "Some wives wept and the truly weak even begged their men not to go. Tears can never change duty, only make it harder. Please, Thea, don't weep."

She blew her nose. "That's not fair. I *want* to change things."

"You can't."

"You put yourself at my command," she reminded him.

"No longer."

She knew he wanted to kiss her, but with the footman there, even standing statue-still and looking away, he couldn't.

"If I return to you with his blood on my hands, what will you do?"

She wanted to say that it wouldn't matter, that it couldn't touch her love, but at a moment like this, she could only give him the truth. "I don't know."

CHAPTER 35

Darien delivered Thea and her tight-lipped maid back to Yeovil House, but left before the duchess could appear. He returned to the Crown and Magpie as quickly as possible, but found Foxstall had already cleared out for good. The innkeeper had no idea where he'd moved to, only that he'd left shortly after Darien and the ladies, but not seeming to be in a hurry.

Darien considered a search of London, but if Foxstall wanted to keep out of sight, he would. Unless the search was widespread. The Rogues? They seemed to have a network of useful servants and others.

He went to Delaney's house but found they'd finally left Town. The nearest alternative was Stephen Ball's place. He was out of Town, too, as was Arden. So much for the Rogues' support.

Darien went to Van's. "At least you're here," he growled.

"There's a gathering of Rogues at Marlowe in Nottingham. Do you really still need nursemaids?"

"Be careful," Darien snapped, and Van's brows went up.

"What's happened?"

Darien couldn't tell anyone the details, but he said, "Foxstall's crossed the line. I need to deal with him, but he's made himself scarce."

"I did warn you about him."

"You were right. Set the word around, will you, that if anyone sees him, I need to know."

"Very well. Are you still coming to Rathbone's tonight?"

A card party. "Give my excuses. I wouldn't be good company."

Darien spent the next two days hunting Foxstall without success. He avoided Thea, but he did write her a vaguely worded reassurance that all would be well, hoping he could keep that promise. As part of that, he visited Lady Harroving.

The lady was far too interested in him for comfort, but by engaging in some flattery and flirtation, he discovered that she saw no connection between Thea and the feathers. Certainly someone had been naughty in her linen room, and feathers had been found there, but a little teasing conversation had proved his reassurance to Thea correct. Lady Harroving's servants knew that gossip about the goings-on during the masquerade meant instant dismissal without a character.

The lady made no secret of her association with Foxstall and revealed how he might know all. The feathers had been lying around her boudoir when Foxstall visited her and she'd told him where they'd been found. She hinted that they'd been used in some sort of love play and could be again. Darien had eased out of her presence, and breathed a sigh of relief.

There was still danger, however. The fight had placed Thea close to the linen room. A large enough bribe would loosen the servant's tongue. If Foxstall put it all together and waved it in the world's face, it would be undeniable. Therefore, he had to be stopped.

Despite the treasured note, Thea spent two days braced for scandal, duel, or both, but also tussling with her reaction to violence. She had to come to terms with it to marry Darien. She wished she could lie to him, but when she told him she loved him, loved all about him, it had to be the truth.

Her mother drove her to distraction by

asking too often why Darien hadn't stayed long enough to speak to her, and wondering why he still didn't visit, but on Saturday, she said, "Ah, well, he'll be at church tomorrow."

So he would. Thea spent the day in a mindless daze.

When they arrived at St. George's, however, Darien hadn't yet arrived. Thea tried not to watch for him, but she found so many excuses to turn to look that her mother asked if she was all right. The service was about to begin. Was he truly so determined to avoid her?

Then a verger passed a note to her father, who read it, then murmured, "Darien won't be able to attend." His lips were tight.

Thea's heart beat with fear and she needed details, but the organ played and they all rose. Instead, she prayed. Had Darien found Foxstall and fought him? Was he fleeing the law, or lying wounded?

She prayed as never before for his safety, and for another chance. Her blind terror finally convinced her that she could not live without him.

Once they were out of the church, she demanded, "What happened to Darien, Papa?"

"An unpleasantness at his house." Her

father was attempting to appear relaxed as they strolled toward their waiting coach, but Thea knew something was terribly wrong.

Surely, however, he wouldn't speak of a death as an unpleasantness? And "at his house"? That couldn't mean a duel. She wanted to hurry there, but as usual they had to pause every few steps to exchange greetings.

Then Thea noticed whispers that felt horribly like those first days.

"A bloody corpse!" someone hissed.

She turned, trying to guess who'd said it. Darien's corpse?

"Thea."

The sharp reprimand made Thea turn back and replace her smile. But they'd been waylaid by Lord and Lady Rotherport now, an older couple but eagle-eyed gossips.

"Quite horrible," Lady Rotherport was saying, bright-eyed, "but given the family, perhaps understandable."

Murdering the current Viscount Darien?

"I don't see the relevance," the duchess said. "Darien's family has nothing to do with someone killing a pig."

"A pig?" Thea gasped.

"Shocking," her mother agreed, but with a sharp look that commanded Thea to control herself.

"It took place in the Hanover Square gardens," Lady Rotherport protested. "At night. In the exact spot where Mary Wilmott was found."

Thea might have turned faint except for relief that Darien was unhurt. Physically, at least. This must be horrible for him. "Who would do such a thing?" she asked.

"A trail of footprints led from the carcass to Cave House," Lord Rotherport said with relish. "Just as before. The poor Wilmotts."

"Fortunately they've left Town," the duke said, sounding bored.

"Only Lady Wilmott, Yeovil. Sir George is soldiering on."

By killing pigs in the garden? Thea wondered. Mary Wilmott's still-grieving father might be driven to such extremes. She'd known Darien shouldn't be living in that house.

Thea's mother took charge. "Come, Yeovil, we must go and offer our support to Lord Darien. Such a tiresome inconvenience for him." She led the march to the waiting carriage. Thea followed, feeling something would burst from her effort to appear as if bodies and blood were simply tiresome.

As soon as the carriage moved off, Thea's father said, "Sarah, dear. . . ."

"If we don't go, it will look as if we're abandoning him."

He sighed. "Very well."

As they rolled into Hanover Square, however, they heard angry voices. The duke leaned to look ahead. "A mob. No, Sarah, it will not do." He instructed the carriage to continue along a quiet side of the square and leave.

"But Darien . . . ," Thea protested, craning to see his house.

"Is well able to take care of himself."

"Maria's house isn't far from here, Charles," the duchess said. "We shall go there and send someone back to find out what's going on."

The duke agreed to this and gave the order.

Thea had seen no sign of Darien in the square, thank heavens. She was frightened, but as much by the mob as the vile act. These days, with such hardship in the country, a mob seemed to form over any little thing, and they could rapidly get out of hand. Innocent people had been hurt and even killed, and often the rich and powerful seemed a natural target. A mob didn't heed whether the inhabitants of a private coach were careless oppressors or those who worked hard to ease suffering.

■ ■ ■ ■

There'd been no blood-splattering for weeks, but Darien had kept up the habit of checking the front of the house before his ride each day. There'd been no mischief at all until today, when there'd been blood. Only traces this time, but a bloody handprint on the door.

He'd gone to the kitchens to tell Ellie to clean it up and continued on to the stables. Why hadn't he looked around and found the bloody footsteps? He could have had the whole mess cleaned up before anyone saw it. As it was, he'd returned from his ride to a tense atmosphere in the stables. He'd shown nothing, but he'd signaled to Nid without getting off Cerb.

Nid had come alongside and told him the gruesome story. "Load of idiots, sir, thinking you've gone stark mad and taken to murdering pigs. But the mood's ugly."

Darien's instinct was to confront, to fight, but he knew when caution was wisest. He'd no mind to be trapped in his house by an angry mob, perhaps stirred up for some particular purpose. Foxstall? He was sure the man would want to do him harm.

"Go to the house," he instructed the

groom, "and tell the Prussocks to get out if they can. If not, they're to stay away from windows, and not put themselves in danger to protect the house. You, too. I'll be back soon to restore order."

He rode to Van's. He only remembered when he got there that he was supposed to be at St. George's, cementing his reputation of worthy piety and friends in high places. He laughed bitterly. However this turned out, Sweet Mary Wilmott and Mad Marcus Cave would be on everyone's lips again, and he'd be back to the beginning.

Was this Foxstall's revenge? He was capable of it, but it was too mild. He'd not think social embarrassment punishment enough.

He found Van and Maria about to leave for church, but they discarded that to hold a startled analysis of the situation. A couple of their servants were sent off to discover more, and a message was sent to the Yeovils at St. George's.

Speculating did little good, and when Van's servants returned, they could only report that the mob was growing in size and turning nasty. Even though the remains were of a pig, it had been roughly dressed in a woman's blue gown, so some still insisted it was a person. Even some of those who believed it was a pig were saying that it had been killed to hide human blood.

"With talk of mad Caves, I assume," Darien said, head in hands.

"They'll soon discover no one's missing," Maria said, "which will put an end to that, at least."

"How?" Darien demanded, looking up.

"They'll not find anyone missing from Hanover Square, I hope, but I'm sure some woman went missing in London last night, so why not assume she was my victim? The only difference between me and Marcus being that he was too insane to cover up his crime."

"Then we have to discover who did do this," Van said, "and why. The family of the girl? The Wilmotts?"

"No, I can't believe that," Maria protested. "They're decent people. Lady Wilmott is out of Town and Sir George isn't that sort of man. If he took any action, he'd confront you in the street, Canem, or even spit in your eye. Nothing sneaking like this. This," she added, frowning, "is *peculiar*. Do you have any enemies?"

Darien laughed.

"I mean personal ones."

He decided not to mention Foxstall. "Not of this dimension, no."

444

"Then who would want to wreck your attempt to restore your family's reputation?"

"Admiral Sir Plunkett Dynnevor?"

"This isn't a joking matter," she said severely, "and he's in Gibraltar."

"And he'd hardly go to such lengths to prevent his daughter marrying your brother," Van pointed out.

"Why not? I would if I were him."

"Let's keep our tempers," Maria said. "People don't do things for no reason. What was the reason?"

Darien rose to his feet. "Perhaps it's not a person. Perhaps it's Marcus's cursed spirit." The others stared and he added, "I'm not entirely joking. I think the house is haunted."

" 'Struth," Van said. "You really must abandon it. Move in here."

"After this?"

"Especially after this."

"No."

"He's right, Van," Maria said. "To move without clearing this up would look very bad. In fact —"

The door knocker rapped. They all fell silent, perhaps all feeling the same wariness. But how could trouble follow Darien here?

The footman came in. "The Duke and Duchess of Yeovil are below, ma'am, and

Lady Theodosia Debenham."

Maria smiled with relief. "Bring them up, Simon."

They all rose to greet their guests, but Darien felt this was another straw on his breaking back. He didn't want the Yeovils involved in this sordid mess. Especially Thea. He risked a look at her and caught an expression of furious militancy.

Don't, love. Don't side with me.

The details had to be recited again.

"A dress," the duchess said, shocked.

"A pig," Thea said, but thoughtfully. "Wouldn't it be hard to acquire a live pig in Mayfair?"

"And transport it," Maria said. "They squeal."

"Or get it into a dress," Van pointed out. "There might be some line of inquiry there."

"But not yet," the duchess said. "Darien, I fear it is necessary for you to return to Hanover Square. Your absence could be seen as guilt or flight."

"It could be dangerous," Thea protested.

"Your father and Vandeimen will go with him and take the coach, and I would hope the magistrates will have matters in hand by now."

If the duke looked wry, he obeyed his

orders, but Thea rose, too, and came to Darien.

"I'm so sorry this has happened," she said, offering her hands without hesitation. "Take care."

He wished she'd stayed aloof, but he took her hands. As she'd ignored their audience, he did, too, and kissed each. "Your belief in me means a great deal."

Her features relaxed a little — disastrously. Her lips quivered until she bit them. He bowed and left before she broke. That would break him.

Chapter 36

The arrival of the Duke of Yeovil's carriage in Hanover Square, complete with liveried servants, provided new excitement for the throng.

Soldiers were preventing people from entering the railed garden, but the circumference was lined with gawkers. More were gathered around the bloody footsteps and threshold like ants around jam spots. Others simply hung around in chattering groups waiting for the next excitement.

Darien's emergence from the grand coach raised a cry. Someone shouted, "That's the Cave! He's already under arrest!"

The duke simply stared around, and silence slowly settled.

"Viscount Darien is not under arrest," he said, clearly, but making no attempt to shout. "We are here to discover the truth of this tasteless prank."

Darien admired his simple dignity, and it

had a general effect. Those who had not heard what he'd said received it murmured back through the crowd. There was no more shouting but the air was almost electrical.

Two men came out of the gardens and approached — a military officer and a burly gentleman in civilian dress. They turned out to be Lieutenant Waring of the Horse Guards and Mr. Evesham, the magistrate.

"Glad to have some assistance here, Your Grace," Evesham said. "Nasty business, and they're all out for blood, but there's not really a crime, see? Not even a bylaw against killing a pig here, and nothing about being careless with the blood. But this lot" — he tilted his head toward the ear-stretched crowd — "I was afraid they'd string Viscount Darien up if he came here unprotected. Why I sent for the military."

He turned, and despite what he'd said, Darien could tell he thought he should arrest him for something. "What we need to do to pacify them, my lord, is search your house, if you'd be so kind as to give permission. Your staff won't open up."

"On my orders. But I have no objection to an orderly investigation. Perhaps we can call upon a couple of the more worthy people from the onlookers, and if the duke and Captain Waring were part of it, all would be satisfied."

The magistrate turned and pointed to two men, both well dressed and sober. They turned out to be a Mr. Hobbs, a shoemaker, and Mr. Linlithgow, a banker's clerk.

Evesham bellowed out what was going on. He added a request that all go about their business, but no one took the suggestion. Everyone waited expectantly for the search party to report.

Evesham stood by Darien's side and Darien was glad of Van's presence. The magistrate and the crowd resembled well-trained guard dogs — quiet, but ready to tear him to bits if he tried to make a run for it.

In about fifteen minutes, the four men returned and reported, and Evesham bellowed it.

"There is no sign of blood in Cave House, nor any sign of disorder or violence, and certainly no additional corpse. This has been idle and wicked mischief, and if the perpetrator is found, he will be punished. Now go about the Lord's Day or I'll have you dispersed by force."

That did cause a shift, and slowly people began to go back into their houses or out of the square.

Darien went with the duke and Van into

the garden to see the victim of violence. The blue dress was disconcerting, but the corpse was simply a pig, throat cut, and already a feast for flies.

"Quite young," Darien said.

"Not even a year," the duke agreed.

"Easier to handle," Van pointed out. "What do you think? Fifty pounds? A man could carry it without too much trouble, but as Maria said, it'd squeal."

"Drugged?" Darien suggested.

"There's a thought," Van agreed. "At least it would die happy. . . ."

The magistrate broke in, seeming annoyed by the practical discussion. "But what are we to do with it, my lord?" he asked Darien.

"It's nothing to do with me, sir, but I'll pay for it to be butchered and distributed charitably." He moderated his tone. No point making another enemy. "Thank you for your excellent handling of this, Evesham. It could have turned destructive."

The magistrate warmed. "Indeed it could, my lord. And I'm pleased to see you cleared. These notorious crimes do linger, however."

It was a warning, but as the man went to make arrangements for the disposal of the pig, Darien wondered what he was supposed to do with it. He turned toward his house. "I'd be glad never to enter the place

451

again, but I don't run away."

"You could remove that damned dog from over the door," Van said.

"It's carved in rock."

"Have it hammered off."

"So simple," Darien said with a sharp laugh. "Very well, but not right now. Anything I do immediately will be seen as uneasy conscience."

"Then let's get back to my place and sort this all out."

"Just give me a moment to talk to my staff."

Darien found the Prussocks in the kitchen, drinking tea that clearly had brandy in it. He supposed they were entitled to it. "Where's Lovegrove?" he asked.

"Left, milord," Mrs. Prussock said with a tight smirk. "Couldn't take the strain, he said. Took the silver standish from the office, milord, and I don't know what else."

"You couldn't stop him?"

"We were a bit at sixes and sevens, sir."

Darien reined in his temper. "Thank you for following orders. I'll be out for a while. Needless to say, continue your vigilance. No one is to enter."

Could Lovegrove have staged the drama as concealment for thievery? It seemed unlikely for such a weak sot of a man.

Darien went quickly up to his room. Nothing obviously missing there, but when he went down to the office, indeed the silver standish was gone. He kept his cash on hand, jewelry, and important documents in a safe here, which was concealed behind one set of shelves. Lovegrove shouldn't even have known about it. Darien himself hadn't until his solicitor had informed him. There were only two keys. He kept one on his person and his solicitor had the other.

He swung the section of shelving open, unlocked the metal door, and found, as expected, nothing disturbed. It had been a wild idea, anyway. He knew enough of chronic drunkards to recognize a genuine one, and they weren't up to complicated planning. He really wouldn't have thought the valet a petty thief, though, either. A coward, yes, but not that sort of thief. Brandy, now.

He was sure the Prussocks had used the valet's flight as excuse for more thievery. Simply fire them or call in the Runners to investigate their crimes? That would certainly have to wait another day.

But he decided not to abandon the place. He told Van, and then settled to study the neglected inventories. At least this meant he could avoid Thea.

With Foxstall out there somewhere and this insane prankster up to mischief, the farther away she was and remained, the better.

He didn't make much headway with the records because of constant invasions. It seemed that every man he'd developed good terms with came by to show support. The crowding reduced him to laughter at one point, especially when St. Raven ruthlessly removed all the Holland covers from the drawing room and demanded tea. When it arrived, Prussock's hair looked as if it was standing on end.

If Marcus's damned spirit truly did linger here, by midnight, when the last guests departed, his hair would be on end, too.

After all that, Darien wasn't entirely surprised to return from his ride the next morning to find the Prussocks gone. With, of course, some other bits and pieces of value. He returned to the stables to talk to Nid.

"Don't go to the house in the morning, sir. Take me breakfast here with some of the other grooms. Well I never, but I'm not surprised. A peculiar lot." He scratched his nose for a moment. "Don't like to cast suspicion, sir, but I did get a glimpse of Prussock two nights since. Thought he had a woman, I did, which surprised me and that's no lie. But now I'm wondering if it was a pig, see?"

"A pig? It was Prussock . . . ? But why? I've been more tolerant than they deserve."

"Ah, but they were none too happy having you there at all, see? Had a nice little spot, all to themselves, and with the place's reputation and all, they thought to have it for a nice long time. So I think they've been trying to scare you away. I suppose I should have said something, but I never dreamed it'd come to this."

"Nor I. They've been stealing from the house, too. Living like lords when they had the chance, I've no doubt. It'll have to be the Runners, but they're probably crafty enough to be far away by now."

"You'll be right there, sir. Do you want me to help out? Cook or something?"

Darien remembered Nid's attempts at cooking in the army. "No, but here's some money to get yourself food from a chophouse. I'll see about hiring new people, though the pig's put the house's reputation back a bit."

He returned to the house and checked for losses. Any remaining silver had gone, plus some smaller vases and even a pair of brocade curtains from the drawing room.

Then he found the safe had been broken open.

He cursed his own stupidity. He'd suspected the Prussocks, so why hadn't he been on guard? Yesterday, one of them must have followed him as he checked the house. Most safes got their security from being unknown. A short time and brute strength and they were vulnerable. He sent Nid for a Bow Street Runner but didn't think much of his chances of getting his property back.

He stood in the hall, testing the feel of the truly empty house. Not even a ghost, yet it still felt foul. What was he to do with it?

He was tempted to move in with Van, and lack of servants would provide an excuse, but he'd stick it out for a day or two, until the latest furor calmed.

But he wasn't going to attempt to make this his home.

CHAPTER 37

"A message for you, milady."

Thea looked up from breakfast, which she'd only picked at. Her spirits weren't low, not after the way Darien had taken farewell of her yesterday. But she was completely focused on overcoming all obstacles.

All the trouble at Cave House was now explained as mischief by Darien's servants, and that was being spread around Town by all possible means. She'd suggested that he be invited to move in here and had an hour's delicious anticipation until his reply had been received — a polite refusal.

She'd even found herself fretting about his care and housekeeping, but he could invite himself to eat at any one of a dozen houses, and an army man could live simply if he must.

So all in all, things weren't so bad. She simply needed a private, unhurried moment in which to convince him that she loved him and must marry him.

A glance had shown her that the letter was from Maddy, tempting her not to read it at all, but she snapped the seal. Inside, the writing was cramped and Maddy's pen must have been atrocious, for the ink went rapidly from dark to pale and there were inkblots all over the page. She struggled to read the letter, frowning.

Thea, dearest Thea, I know I was horrid to you, but I was so hurt by Fox's betrayal. Now I've done something really stupid. I sneaked out to Darien's house to ask him not to kill Fox. I know that's foolish, but I can't stop loving him.

Was that a teardrop? Maddy!

But Darien was so horrible to me. I can't tell you. He hates me because I threatened you, and he hurt me until I promised never to speak of the feathers, and now he's left to kill Fox anyway. I have to get out of here before he returns, but I have no clothes.

No clothes! Thea gasped, trying to comprehend.

Yes, she knew Darien had been angry with

Maddy, but she also knew he wouldn't hurt her.

Yet, she had seen him when that punishing rage consumed him. He'd not behave like that with a woman, she was sure of that, but he might do something to frighten Maddy so she wouldn't reveal what had happened at the Harroving masquerade. Nothing truly terrible — no clothes? — but enough to cast his reputation on the dung heap if discovered.

She rubbed a hand over her face, glad Harriet had returned to the servants' area.

One thing was sure. She must get Maddy out of his house before she was discovered there, half naked and in a wild state. She read through the rest of the letter, struggling at times with the scrawl.

Please, Thea, you must help me. There's no one here. No servants or anyone. He must have sent them away so he could do this to me. I've unlocked the front door, so you can just come in. Please don't betray me to anyone! Just bring some clothes and get me away from here. I have to warn Fox!

Thea sat there, her mind in a fog. Was that the truth of the missing servants? But —

459

she reread to check — Maddy said she'd gone there of her own accord, so how could Darien have planned this? Typical of Maddy. Muddle and exaggeration. Darien would have done no more than scare her. . . .

She'd achieve nothing sitting here like a ninny. She ran into her dressing room, wondering what of hers would fit Maddy. None of her shifts or corsets. She hunted through drawers and the armoire until she found a loosely cut dress with a drawstring waist. She added a full-length cloak and a pair of slippers. That would have to do.

She bundled it all up, then paused. Should she tell her mother? It would be wiser, but the fewer people who knew, the better.

What if he had lost his temper and gone too far . . . ?

No, she wouldn't believe that.

She brushed away tears and put on a simple cloak herself. She was about to test Darien's suggestion of a way to leave her house secretly. She went downstairs, praying she not meet anyone who felt able to question her. She slipped into the Garden Room and through the doors into the gardens.

The mystery was the entrance from the stables, but when she walked through the winding paths and clever hedges designed to create the impression of a much larger space, she found the high wall that was part of the stables. In the wall was a door. She tried the handle, and the door opened. So simple. Cobwebs, indeed, but there could be a roomful of people beyond.

She was Lady Theodosia Debenham, she reminded herself. If she wanted to wander to the stables this way, who could object?

The room beyond the door was empty of people, though full of a bewildering amount of wood and leather, all doubtless to do with the carriages. She heard voices, but none nearby. A window showed her where she wanted to go, and when she peered into the corridor, she saw an open door to the lane.

In moments, she was walking away from her house, alone in London for the first time.

Before emerging onto the street, she pulled up her hood and then hurried in search of a hackney stand. She felt sure the driver knew she was a young lady who shouldn't be out alone, but he took her shilling without comment and soon deposited her by the side of St. George's church.

She walked from there, entering the square cautiously. She saw no sign that anything was amiss. In fact, Hanover Square looked too ordinary and orderly. A cloaked woman carrying a bundle might attract attention. She had no choice, however, so she walked at a steady pace up to Darien's house. When she mounted the steps, the nasty black dog seemed to be snarling directly at her.

Her feet froze in place. Until this moment, it hadn't crossed her mind that Darien could harm *her*.

And he couldn't. If she didn't believe that, her world lay in ruins. In fact, Maddy would have exaggerated the whole thing. She continued to the door, turned the knob, and, as promised, it opened.

She went into the house, eyes and ears on full alert. She didn't think she'd ever entered an empty house before. There were always servants, even if the family was away. Of course Maddy was here somewhere, but the hair was rising on the back of her neck, as if evil spirits were around.

"Maddy?" she whispered, closing the door behind her, feeling worse when daylight was blocked.

Only silence. For the first time she wondered if this was a trick. Maddy wouldn't.

Would she? If it was a trick, Thea couldn't imagine how to do anything to her cousin that was sufficiently painful.

"Maddy," she called more loudly.

"In here." It was a terrified squeak from

the parlor to her left. Thea's heart immediately raced, and mentally apologizing, she ran in.

A hand covered her mouth and a strong arm encircled her.

A man. A big man.

Not Darien.

In the mirror across the room, she caught a flash of blue and silver, but then a hood was dropped over her head, blinding her.

A hussar uniform. Foxstall!

New terror beat. But Maddy. Surely Maddy wouldn't have . . .

Instantly, Thea realized Maddy hadn't. Her cousin hadn't written that letter. She wasn't even here. She'd been lured here by Foxstall alone. By Foxstall seeking his revenge.

She struggled wildly, but the big hand came around her throat and squeezed. She clawed at it but couldn't find breath. As darkness closed in on her, she knew this was to be Foxstall's revenge on Darien as well as on her.

Another murdered lady, and this time actually in Cave House.

CHAPTER 38

Darien entered his house from the back, passing through the empty servants' area and into the hall, wondering what the hell was going on. For days he'd been wary of some malice from Foxstall, and now he had it. But it was pointless.

On returning from his ride, Nid had given him a letter that had come to the stables. It was an incoherent plea from Pup to meet him at an inn across the river in Putney. He'd gone straight there, of course, but found Pup enjoying an enormous breakfast and believing Darien had arranged the meeting.

The message to Pup had been delivered by Foxstall, who'd also offered to return the key to Cave House. Pup had passed it over. So casually, a weapon given to an enemy. But to be used for what?

Darien had explained it away and sent Pup back home; then he'd returned to Cave

House as quickly as possible. Now, he stripped off his gloves and tossed them, his cane, and hat on the hall table, looking for trouble.

He found it.

Blood on the floor of the hall.

Bloody footprints by the look of it, just like the ones outside yesterday. He knelt and touched fingers to the dark liquid, raising them afterward, but he knew. He was familiar with blood and this was recent. It might be wisest to leave and find help, perhaps Evesham, the magistrate, but if Foxstall had left a body in the house, he'd have done his best to make Darien look guilty of the killing.

He looked up the stairs, seeing smears of red on the handrail. His heart began to pound. The body of a person, this time, rather than a pig?

He picked up his cane and went upstairs slowly, sensing for danger at every step. Whatever else awaited, he hoped Foxstall was here. More than ever, he needed to kill him.

The smears grew scantier, but they led toward the back of the house.

To his room?

He approached his door listening, but heard nothing.

Not even the ticking of the hall clock.

He realized that no one would have wound it since the Prussocks fled.

But something was in the room. Every instinct he possessed said that. He grasped the doorknob, turned it quietly, and eased open the door.

His bedroom looked completely normal, even to the chess game he'd laid out to study. But the hangings around the bed were drawn. He never drew them in warmer weather. He moved forward as quietly as boots allowed, but froze at a noise. A rustling from behind the curtains.

Not a corpse then. A snake, a rabid dog? That might appeal to Foxstall's warped mind.

Keeping an eye on the curtains, Darien opened his chest, dug down, and pulled out his saber. *Forgot this, didn't you, Foxstall? Whatever vengeful mischief you've created here will come to a rapid, bloody end, and you're next.* He slid the blade out and put down the scabbard, then approached the bed, trying to analyze the slight sounds.

Cautiously, he parted the curtains with the blade tip.

He eased the curtain back. Some cloth on the bed. Another pig in a dress?

No noise at all, now. No hissing or snarling. No movement.

With the blade, he swept the curtain to the right, rings rattling, letting daylight in.

Then he tossed the weapon aside.

"Thea? My God, Thea? What's happened to you?"

She was pale as the pillow — where it wasn't stained with blood. Her blood. Her eyes were huge and blind with terror. She was bound.

He grabbed the saber again to cut the strip of cloth around her arms.

She screamed. By instinct, he clamped a hand over her mouth. "Hush, love. It's me. Darien. I'll have you free in a moment."

Foxstall, Foxstall, death's too good for you. I'll flay you, inch by inch.

She was threshing her head and trying to claw, but he couldn't let her scream. If anyone came, she'd suffer even more. Her clothes were torn half off her. . . .

He cut her hands free, and then her legs, then tossed the blade aside again and gathered her into his arms. She began choking in gasping sobs and he couldn't tell if it was still terror or relief. He clambered up on the bed and held her tightly, rocking her and saying whatever came into his head.

Then he saw fresh blood on his hand. "Thea, stop. You're bleeding again. Let me take care of you."

She pushed away from him, fixated on his bloody hand. "Let me go, let me go!"

He did and she tumbled to the floor on the far side of the bed, her hair wildly straggling, and staring at him as if he were a wild beast.

"Thea," he breathed, his heart breaking. He spoke as calmly as he could manage. "I didn't hurt you. Let me take care of you." He stretched a hand out, saw the blood on it, and wiped it off on his breeches. When she stilled, he joined her on the floor, taking out his handkerchief and pressing it to the wound on her throat. Thank God it wasn't deep, nor was the livid scrape across one cheek, but she was bruised. He'd tried to strangle her?

And her unseen hurts could be worse.

She was still now, but not in a good way. He took off his jacket and put it around her shoulders, then went to pour some brandy. He put it to her lips. "Drink, love. It'll help."

Dark eyes on him, she parted her lips and he tipped some in. Most dribbled away, but she swallowed a bit. She coughed and fell into weeping again, but blessedly in his arms now.

"Oh, love, oh love, I'll make it all right." Thank God he'd remembered not to mention killing, even though it consumed his mind.

He rocked and soothed, unable to ask for details. When he thought she was able, he raised her to her feet, brushing tangled, blood-matted hair off her face. "Come, we must get you home. . . ."

But then a crash downstairs was followed by voices — a wild howling of them coming up the stairs. His mind clicked into the cool clarity that had brought him alive through battle.

The rest of Foxstall's plan.

Catch them here.

He grabbed his saber in his right hand and half carried her out of the room and through the door to the serving stairs. He hated to abandon her, but the alternatives were worse.

"Stay there while I deal with this." No time for more. He shut the door and stepped back into the corridor, saber out just as the invaders poured up the stairs.

"What the devil's going on?" he demanded.

"Devil's right!" snarled the red-faced man at the front of the pack. "Who've you murdered now, you Satan's spawn?"

It was Sir George Wilmott.

Darien was gathering a soothing comment

when someone called, "His bed's all over blood!"

He'd forgotten the state of the room.

The press of fury pushed toward him, but halted when he flicked the saber. He wasn't willing to kill anyone here, but he was even less willing to be strung up by a mob convinced he was another Mad Marcus.

Above all, above all, Thea mustn't be found here, her reputation as shredded as her gown. He fought the need to go to her. He could serve her best here. He faced Wilmott's raging eyes. "I've done nothing wrong. Send for the magistrate. I'll come down in an orderly manner and we can sort this out."

"Sort it out!" Sir George howled with laughter. "We'll sort it out all right, and this time it'll be the noose. That'll put an end to Caves forever."

"Then you'll have to do me in, too."

The new voice was used to calling out orders in a storm.

People turned. Not all of them. Some had wit enough to keep a close eye on Darien. But most swiveled to look behind to where Frank stood at the head of the stairs in his blue naval uniform, not smiling, but still managing to convey clean, honest goodwill and fellowship.

No one asked who he was. Dark hair and eyes and the cut of the jaw declared him a Cave, but as always, the magic of his charm worked.

CHAPTER 39

Bafflement softened the mob's purpose. Sir George muttered something about devil's spawn, but his heart wasn't in it. That didn't mean he glared less at Darien, however. Hardly surprising, given the state of the bedroom.

Darien realized he was smeared with Thea's blood as well.

Frank was looking at him, a question in his eye. Part of it was a willingness to fight free of this mob, so Darien shook his head.

"Whatever the problem here," Frank said, again with that crisp authority, "it will be sorted out in good order. Downstairs, everyone."

The shuffling movement began, but Sir George resisted. "And leave him to slip out a back way? In front of me, Darien, so some of us can make sure you don't run."

Few in the world would dare to speak to Canem Cave in that way, especially when he had a blade in his hand, but the man was right to feel safe at this moment. Darien stalked forward. A way cleared, which could well be because of the naked blade still in his hand, or because of his visible rage.

He hoped to reach Frank and somehow give him the word to take care of Thea, but the mob separated them as they all crowded down the narrow stairs and into the tight hall.

"Outside," Frank ordered.

He was probably trying to reduce the danger of an accident, but Darien would have refused if he could. He didn't want this outside for the whole world to see — him, blade in hand, blood marking him. But then, perhaps the world should see this play out.

As he moved into daylight at the top of the stairs, Darien faced a growing, angry crowd. He was in real danger. If they decided to hang him on the spot, he and Frank alone couldn't stop them.

But then he saw Foxstall at the back of the crowd, lounging against the railings in his hussar uniform, watching his plan work, smiling his twisted smile. Nothing else mattered.

Darien charged down the stairs and across the street. People scattered, crying, "Stop him! Stop him!" but not trying themselves.

For a second, Foxstall still smiled, but then the smile fled and he straightened, dragging his saber free just in time to catch Darien's killing blow with a sparking clang.

"Someone stop this madman!" he cried, parrying and dodging.

No one tried, though Darien heard Frank call his name in protest.

"He did it! He . . ." He choked down details. Thea's name mustn't come into this.

"Did what?" Foxstall asked, alert to avoid his very real danger, but grinning all the same. "I think you truly have cracked at last, Canem. Can't someone hit him over the head or something? I don't want to hurt the idiot."

"I intend to kill you," Darien said, catching a breath.

Foxstall looked into Darien's eyes and saw truth. "You'll hang."

"It will be worth it." Darien slashed for the head again, was parried again, the shock of contact shooting up his arm. He was trained to fight on horseback, but so was Foxstall. They both had to think differently, move differently, but he'd kill him. Foxstall had to die.

"Whichever way, I win," Foxstall taunted, dodging. His plan was clearly to look reluctant to fight and hope someone did intervene. "I kill you or you hang. And I had your woman first."

Roaring, Darien slashed for his legs. Foxstall dodged, but his returning swing tangled in his fur-trimmed pelisse. He ran back a bit to steal time to drag the tie loose and shed it, then turned to swirl the heavy cloth over Darien's sword, following with a stab to the heart.

No more playing now.

Darien swept the cloth aside and twisted, but Foxstall's thrust ran along his ribs. Barely holding his balance, Darien slashed backhanded simply to stop Foxstall following up on his advantage.

His blade sank deep and jarred. He spun to see he'd got the neck.

Blood spurted from the artery. Foxstall's eyes and mouth opened in surprise, and then his legs crumpled. His fall would have pulled Darien down with him if he'd not let go of the saber. Foxstall's mouth moved, but then he died, still looking astonished.

Darien met those eyes, heaving for breath.

Foxstall had been a friend of sorts once.

He'd been a good officer in war but scum in every other way. The world was better without him, especially after what he'd done.

Thea, dear God, *Thea.*

The silence shattered into cries and howls. Wearily, almost past caring, he dragged his blade free and turned. Frank was already at his side, white-faced but resolute, his navy cutlass out.

"This will go to trial," he declared, his voice carrying.

Certainly, with the railings at their backs and the crowd a crescent of gleeful anger around them, there was no escape. Darien knew he'd be lucky not to be strung up or kicked to death. And why the hell did Frank have to be here, possibly to suffer the same fate?

Then a carriage pulled by galloping horses rocked into the square at the same time as a troop of soldiers cantered in from the other side, weapons drawn.

"Magistrate and enforcement," Darien said. "Three cheers."

"Well, I'm damn glad to see them," Frank said.

Darien wasn't so sure. Despite the justification he'd just killed a man. It could be called a duel, but without any of the protocol. In another case, it could be seen as murder in the eyes of the law. Men had hanged for such things before.

If he went on trial it would be in the

House of Lords. A nine-day wonder to add to the Cave load, and Thea might become involved. Would she have had the strength and courage to flee the house alone?

"What did he do?" Frank asked, indicating Foxstall's corpse without much concern.

"You assume I had good cause."

"Yes."

Softly, Darien said, "He raped and harmed a lady of good family, in our house. She may still be in there, on the service stairs. I can take care of myself here. Go to her."

"How?" Frank asked dryly.

True, they were penned in by the crowd, who still looked ready to tear them both to pieces.

The mounted soldiers forced a passage for Evesham. George Wilmott came with him, calm now with a dreadful satisfaction.

"Mad, the lot of 'em," he declared to the mob. "I've been saying so all along. This one did murder in that accursed house, then rushed out to slaughter this noble officer, a mere bystander!"

"No, he wasn't," Darien declared, though he doubted reason would rule here.

"Be quiet," Evesham snapped at Sir George. "We'll have law and order here, not inflammatory speeches. Captain, move this rabble back. At the first sign of violence," he bellowed at the crowd, "I'll read the Riot Act."

That would allow the soldiers to use their weapons on civilians, and had some effect.

"Now," Evesham said, "someone tell me what's gone on here. You." He pointed at a dark-clad middle-aged man, who stepped forward to give a coherent account of sword fight and slaughter.

"Lord Darien was unprovoked, you say?" Evesham asked him.

"I can only attest to what I saw, sir. His Lordship raced out of the house and attacked the officer, who appeared merely to be watching the commotion."

"The man's mad," Sir George declared. "I keep telling you. Caves." He spat.

Evesham glared at Frank. "You a Cave, too?"

"Lieutenant Cave, RN."

"He had nothing to do with it as best I know," Wilmott said reluctantly.

Darien had to appreciate his fairness. The man truly believed history had been repeated and he wanted blood. But only the deserving blood.

Evesham spoke to Frank. "Put up your sword, Lieutenant." To Darien, he said, "Surrender yours peaceably, my lord, or I'll have you shot."

Like a mad dog ran silently through the air.

Darien passed the bloody saber to Frank, who offered it hilt-first to anyone who'd take it. The captain of the troopers rode forward and took it, though he didn't look pleased.

"Viscount Darien, you are under arrest for murder. Will you come peaceably?"

"Of course." The sooner this part was over, the sooner Frank could take care of Thea.

"You will proceed to my coach, my lord—"

"Stop that!"

The high, rather thin cry turned everyone toward the house. Thea stood on the steps, still in Darien's dark green jacket, her clothing obviously torn, her hair all over the place.

Darien stepped forward. The cavalry captain pointed his own bloody saber at his chest to stop him.

"Frank, do something. Get her out of here before she's recognized."

Frank tried to push through people and horses, but Thea was running down the steps in bare feet and across the square, crying, "Stop it, stop it, stop it. It wasn't him!"

The crowd parted, some puzzled, some

479

aghast, some gleeful at the prospect of new drama among the great.

Darien looked up at the cavalry officer, whom he didn't know, damn it. "You have my parole. I'm not trying to escape."

The man looked sympathetic, but shook his head.

Frank reached her, caught her to him, said something.

Thea looked up at him, clearly dazed by someone who looked like Darien but wasn't.

"Get her away, Frank. She needs care. He hurt her."

Thea's eyes shot to his and she pulled free. "Yes, *he* hurt me!" she cried, pointing at Foxstall. "He trapped me, hurt me. He wanted you all to think Lord Darien did it."

"Now, why would that be?" the magistrate asked, not unkindly, but without belief.

She spun to him. "Because he hated him. I mean Captain Foxstall hated Lord Darien. You have to believe me!"

"And your name?" the magistrate asked.

"Is none of anyone's business," Darien said quickly. "Frank, get her away. She's shocked out of her wits, but I hope," he said to Sir George Wilmott, "that you'll believe at least that I didn't murder any lady in my house today."

"Only because we arrived in time."

"He was *helping* me!" Thea pulled out Darien's bloodstained handkerchief. "See. This is his!"

"Frank . . . ," Darien said, but the magistrate said, "The lady's not going anywhere until I know what part she played in this, especially when I don't know who she is."

"I'm Lady Theodosia Debenham," Thea said clearly. "Daughter of the Duke of Yeovil. And Lord Darien is my promised husband."

Frank's eyes met Darien's, wide.

"I'm sure it was an irregular fight," Thea continued, like a stone statue speaking, "but it's hardly surprising that Lord Darien attacked Captain Foxstall after I told him who'd hurt me so badly."

Darien had been staring at her in an attempt to get her to shut up, but now he simply looked at her, humbled by her foolish courage.

"Now," she said with that inborn dignity that had once infuriated him, "may I please go to him?"

A way opened and she walked through it, chin high, as if blind to all around, into his arms. He held her close. "You shouldn't have done that."

Against his chest, shivering, she said, "Yes,

I should. But take me home, Darien. Please."

"You have my parole, sirs," Darien said to the captain, the magistrate, and to Sir George. "I won't try to escape the law, but Lady Thea needs to be taken away from here."

A duke's daughter exposed half dressed to the fascinated eyes of the mob was a trump card.

"Use my carriage, sir," the magistrate said.

"What?" Sir George exploded. "Let him drive off with his victim?"

Thea jerked free to face him. "I am not his *victim*, you stupid man."

Darien almost laughed. "Why don't you come with us, Sir George? Your guardianship will be golden."

That seemed to stump the man, but only for a moment. He demanded a pistol from one of the troopers.

Darien pulled a wry face at Frank. "Welcome home. Take care of things here. There's a slim chance I may be allowed to return later to clean up my own mess."

Frank was clearly bursting with questions, but he nodded.

Darien picked up Thea and carried her to the carriage, ignoring Sir George close behind. It was harder to ignore him when he was sitting opposite, the large pistol ready, clearly longing for the excuse to fire it.

Darien kept Thea on his lap, holding her close, helpless to wipe the horror from her life. The horror he had brought.

CHAPTER 40

At Yeovil House, the groom got down to ply the knocker. Darien eased out of the coach with Thea limp in his arms, though her eyes were open on his, as if he were her savior. By the time he reached the door, it was open, the footman agape.

Darien walked in. "Is the duchess at home?"

It took a moment for the footman to pull himself together. "Yes, sir!"

"Find her."

With servants' instinct, another footman and a maid came into the hall, also to gape. Darien addressed the maid. "Lead me to Lady Thea's room."

The maid hesitated but flinched under Darien's glare and hurried up the stairs.

"The other gentleman?" the footman asked.

Darien glanced back and saw Sir George.

"He can do what the Hades he wants as

long as he doesn't bother us."

He was settling Thea on her bed when the duchess rushed in. "Oh, dear heavens, what has happened?"

"That," said Darien, suddenly adrift, "is a very complicated story."

Thea held out her hands to her mother, who ran to her.

Darien backed out of the room. . . .

He was thrust back into it. The duke followed him in and shut the door.

Thea was sobbing in her mother's arms. The duchess looked at her husband, pale and aghast.

The duke said, "What has happened?" It was not a question to be refused.

Darien pulled himself together as best he could. "She was taken prisoner. By Captain Foxstall. Entirely because of me." He pressed his hands to his face. "It's my fault."

"No!"

Thea's cry made him uncover his eyes to look at her. "If I had never invaded your life, this would not have happened."

"What did this Foxstall do to my daughter," the duke asked, awfully, "and where is he?"

"Dead," Darien said. "I killed him."

The duke exhaled. "That, at least, is satisfactory."

"Thea declared before a large portion of London that she is engaged to marry me, Your Grace."

"That," said the duke, "is not." But his eyes asked a bleak question.

Darien didn't want to answer it, but he supposed his silence was enough.

Thea sat up, detaching herself gently from her mother. "None of this was Darien's fault. I received a note. I thought it was from Maddy. Asking for help. I went and was taken prisoner."

"By this Foxstall?" the duke asked gently.

"Yes." Her eyes flickered around the room and she shuddered. "He tried to hide his identity, but I knew. He was larger. I caught a glimpse in the mirror before he strangled me." Her hand went to her bruised throat and the duke muttered, "Dear God."

"Oh, my poor darling," the duchess said, drawing Thea's hand away to look at the darkened skin and blood-smeared wound.

"I thought he was killing me, but I came to. On the bed. . . ."

The duchess held her close. "It's all right, dear. You don't have to say more."

Thea shook her head. "He'd blindfolded me, and he tried to disguise his voice, to sound like Darien, but I knew. He told me how he hated me. He cut me. On my neck.

My leg. I thought again he was going to kill me, but then he loosened the blindfold. By the time I'd brushed it off with bound hands, he was gone."

After a moment, the duchess asked, "That was it, Thea? He didn't violate you?"

"No! Oh, no."

"Thank God," the duke said, and Darien echoed it. But he wondered at the depth of malice that had lied to him about that, even when Foxstall knew he might soon be dead.

"Very well," the duke said, briskly now. "We need a story to contain all this." He turned to Darien. "Half London, you said?"

Darien pulled himself together to make a report. "Events in the square were witnessed by about forty onlookers, then a magistrate and two officers of the law, then twenty cavalry. Those events included my killing Foxstall in a bloody and completely irregular duel and Thea rushing out to prevent the mob from lynching me on the spot."

"You were quite correct," the duke stated. "Everything would have been a great deal better if you had never intruded into our lives."

"I will belatedly remove myself, Your Grace. I gave my word to return and face the law."

Darien left the room, wondering if he'd ever see Thea again. He realized that the duke had followed and he braced for further scathing remarks. He deserved them.

The duke led the way in silence downstairs and to his offices. No curious, gawking servants were to be seen, but some scurrying suggested they were around every corner. The news would already be flying to all parts of London and beyond. . . .

Once they were inside the businesslike room, Darien said, "I deeply regret Lady Thea's involvement in this and I will do anything to reduce it. Leave the country. Even put an end to my disastrous existence."

"I doubt that would help," the duke said coldly, making Darien feel like an overwrought youth. "I have no idea to what extent you caused this, Darien, but I will find out. It appears my willful niece may have made a contribution, and Thea should never have left the house alone."

"It is not a fault to be kindhearted."

"Can you deny that she was almost certainly attempting to hide some folly of my niece's when she ought to have taken the note to her mother?"

Feeling now like a schoolboy hauled up before an implacably logical, vengeful master, Darien kept his mouth shut.

"There will be no trial," the duke said. "Especially not a sensational one before the House of Lords. I will not have my daughter called as witness in such an event."

"I certainly don't want that."

"How did Foxstall gain access to your house?"

"He had a key from a mutual friend, sir." No point trying to explain the complexities of Pup's part in this.

"Then I suggest you guard the keys to your house better in future. He decided to use your house for his wicked purposes. You caught him at it —"

"Beg your pardon, Your Grace, but he was placidly observing events from the square when I saw him and killed him."

The duke's glare blamed him for the inconvenience of facts.

"When you unexpectedly returned home," he amended, "Foxstall escaped, but lurked, waiting his chance."

To do what? Darien wondered, but he didn't interrupt. If the Duke of Yeovil could tie all this up in a tight little bundle and bury it, he'd not object.

"You saw him, saw his guilt written all over him, and raced to seize him and hold him for the law. He resisted violently and

489

you had no choice but to defend yourself, leading to his death."

"I raced to kill him, sir, for what he had done to Thea, but if your story will hold, so be it."

The duke nodded, studying Darien with an icy eye. As best he knew, the Duke of Yeovil had never been in the army, but at this moment he could give Wellington a run for his money as far as scathing disapproval went.

"Is there anything in this betrothal?" he demanded.

"No, Your Grace. She said it to try to protect me."

"This event is hardly going to improve your family's reputation."

"No, Your Grace."

"But if Thea declared your commitment before witnesses, especially dressed like that, it had better stand for a while. Fortunately, with us having left Town once, Thea and the duchess are able to return to Long Chart without it seeming too peculiar. In view of your happy plans, you will wish to go to your own estates and attempt to put them into good order for your future."

"Of course I will," Darien said dryly. "But having taken my seat in Parliament, I should stay until the session ends, sir."

The duke's tight lips implied he'd sooner see the menace gone, but he said, "Of course. When the fuss has died down, Thea will release you from the engagement. I doubt anyone will be surprised."

Darien bowed, left the room, and walked toward the front of the house, hoping Sir George Wilmott was not waiting to harangue him. His tolerance was almost exhausted, no matter how justified the complaints.

Instead, he found Frank, holding his jacket. Darien had been unaware of being so insufficiently dressed.

Frank passed the jacket over. "The duchess came down and gave it to me. She said to tell you that Lady Theodosia is recovering well and will want to receive you here tomorrow early, before they leave for Somerset."

Darien saw the bloodstain on the lining at the front and wasn't surprised by the sharp smell of blood when he put it on. The hint of Thea's perfume was a different matter.

"She clearly hasn't spoken to the duke yet." He led the way toward the front door, which the very interested footman opened for them. "What happened with the authorities?" he asked as they left the house.

"The magistrate insisted on inspecting Cave House, which seemed reasonable enough. Nothing there, of course, except the mess in the bedroom but he still wants to talk to you and Lady Thea. Pugnacious Sir George has gone off to try to find a crime to pin on you. Are there truly no servants? You're suspected of doing away with them, too."

Darien shook his head. "There's a groom. The others absconded, taking what was left of the silver. We need to get back there."

"No, we don't. They can all wait, and we can't live at that place. There's a perfectly good inn on the next street."

"How do you know that?" Darien asked, amused despite himself.

"The footman told me."

"Such a simple solution. But I'll need my things. Where are yours?"

"At the coaching inn. I wasn't sure you'd still be living at the house. Why are you?"

"From this perspective, I have no idea."

"There's blood on your shirt. Are you wounded?"

Darien remembered Foxstall's blade slicing along his side. He touched the sore spot. "Nothing serious."

Frank took his arm and steered him along. "Come on. We'll retrieve your possessions later. Now, you need food, brandy, and a bit of peace and quiet."

"What chance of that with you around?" Darien complained, but suddenly, despite disaster, loss, and pain, the world seemed better. "And what of your fair Millicent?"

"Millicent? Oh, that's all in the past. She was such a weakling over her father's objections that it took the gilt off the gingerbread, and then the admiral made sure I was busy on patrols. She sent me tear-smudged letters for a while, but when I left she was in smiling adoration of a captain."

Darien began to laugh.

CHAPTER 41

He was soon settled in a comfortable parlor in the Dog and Sun, enjoying the novel situation of Frank looking after him, and very well, too. He hadn't seen his brother for two years, and he was now completely a man. Not surprising when those two years had included all the usual demands of navy life and the expedition against the Barbary States.

He was pleased, but eventually said, "I hope this will stop short of you wrapping a shawl around my shoulders."

Frank grinned. "All right, very well, but it was an alarming situation to come home to. I'd heard some things, anyway."

"Ah."

"What's been going on?"

So over ale and excellent meat pies, Darien told Frank most of the recent events, but left out the original motivation.

"Surprised you wanted to leave the army,

especially to get into this world," Frank said, "but I understand what you mean about the end of the war. I'm feeling a bit that way myself."

"What?" Darien asked, older brother resurfacing. "Because of Millicent and her father?"

"Lord, no. I told you, I consider that a lucky escape. I've no wish to be tied down before I've found my feet. I'm leaving the navy."

Not a question, a statement.

"Already arranged?" Darien asked carefully.

"Floated, let's say. It suited old Dynnevor to send me here in case Millicent wavered, but I did request it. I've hardly been in England beyond Portsmouth for years. I need to know what it feels like. Certainly can't complain of boredom as yet," he joked.

"But why? I thought you enjoyed the life."

Frank drained his glass and refilled it from a pitcher. "Yes, but I'm not mad for it. I would have been as happy in the army, I think, or anywhere else that provided action against the enemy. Many of the other officers are mad for it, though, you see. They love the ships and the sea and it kills them to be shore-based. Doesn't seem fair to take a place that others want so badly."

"I see. But dare I raise the question of money? I'll support you, of course, but . . ."

Frank laughed. "We'd be at one another's throats if I were your dependent. Prize money, Canem, prize money. The navy pot o' gold."

"I didn't realize you'd been involved in rich captures."

"Not the magnificent sort, but enough, and as first lieutenant, my share of last year's hauls was handsome."

"I may tap you for a loan," Darien said, but when his brother looked at him sharply, he shook his head, smiling. "Amazingly, I have enough, and with improved management I'll not want. So, what plans?" Darien asked, still slightly alarmed, even though Frank always landed on his feet.

"I've no idea," Frank said happily. "Isn't that splendid? I joined the navy at twelve, and I've not had substantial say in the ten years since —"

"I'm sorry."

"Do stop that," Frank said with a mock frown. "You talked Father into sending me early and I thanked you and God for it. I've enjoyed the life, but I'm ready for something new. But what about you? Is there going to be a trial?"

Darien marveled for a moment that

Frank's carefree state existed in ignorance of that. Always expect the best.

"Probably not. It's in the Duke of Yeovil's interests for there not to be. The story will be that I was seeking to arrest Foxstall, but he resisted and I killed him more or less by accident."

Frank's expression was politely dubious.

"He didn't rape Thea."

"Malice *and* stupidity?" Frank said. "The world's definitely better without him."

"Yes. But we were friends of a sort. He was a damn good soldier." He felt the need to tell a few stories that showed Foxstall in a good light, and Frank indulged him, but he could see that his brother wasn't much impressed. They both knew that blind courage and the ability to kill were common enough. That honor and integrity were more important in the long run.

"What will you do next?"

Darien rose, taking his glass of ale with him, to wander to the window that looked down on the inn yard. This wasn't a mail coach inn, but it was still busy with comings and goings.

"Go to Stours Court once Parliament ceases the endless talk," he said. "To prepare it for our spurious happy future."

"Why spurious?"

"No one could ever be happy at Stours Court." Darien was surprised to find that certainty in him. He looked back at Frank. "Dry rot, wet rot, deathwatch beetle. And memories."

"Pull it down."

"It's probably your inheritance. I doubt I'll marry."

"Then definitely pull it down. But you could outlive me if you've settled to a peaceful life."

"My ability to live peacefully is signally absent." He told Frank about the masquerade.

"What else could you do? Earl or not, the man was a swine and he'd abused your lady."

Darien smiled. "It's good to have you here, Frank."

"I see it is," his brother said bracingly. "Seems to me you've been letting yourself get blue deviled. It's probably that black dog snarling at you every time you go into the house. That'll have to go. You know what a black dog means, don't you?"

"Nothing in particular."

"Melancholia. Black dogs are ill omens in general. I don't see using the house at all, but that monster still should be removed. Did you see the inn sign here?"

"A dog and a sun, I assume."

"The rising sun and Sirius, in the constellation Canis Major. See. It's always how you look at things."

Darien laughed, but stopped, knowing he was too close to an edge.

"So," said Frank, "you and your Thea will need better homes."

Darien looked at his glass and found it empty. "We won't marry."

"No? I admit the situation was a bit strained, but you both seemed mightily concerned for one another."

"I care too much to let her link herself to me, and after this I doubt her family would permit it."

"And she? Women can be dauntingly persistent. I know that from experience."

"Hound you to death, do they?"

Frank laughed, but didn't reply.

Darien leaned back against the window frame, hearing the distant bustle of normal life all around, seeing before him that Cave didn't inexorably mean outcast.

So it was himself that caused all the problems. He was more like the rest of his family than he'd thought.

"Lady Thea has led a sheltered life, so I excite her, but she's had ample evidence now of the havoc I bring in my train. If she hasn't come to her senses already, she will, given time, so I intend to present that gift. I'll go to Stours Court as commanded. She'll go to beautiful, polished, orderly Long Chart and realize that is her setting. For months, half the country will separate us, and if we do meet again, we'll be polite acquaintances, no more."

Frank said nothing, but he clearly didn't believe a word of it.

"Grand loves do die," Darien said. "You've experienced that."

"I wouldn't say Millicent was a grand love, but by all means attend to Stours Court. Things will work out as they should."

"Dammit, you sound like Candide. 'Everything is for the best in this best of all possible worlds.'"

"But keep an eye on the weather," said Frank. "Let's see what you think after meeting your lady tomorrow."

"I doubt I'll be admitted."

"I'd back the duchess and Lady Thea over the duke any day."

"That assumes Thea wants to see me."

"Lay you a pony she does."

"Have I not always frowned on gambling for high stakes?"

"Not willing to risk your blunt," Frank teased, "being the poor relation?"

"Not willing to gamble on this matter at all."

Frank rose and came to stand by the window with him. "I'm sorry. What will you do if she won't have you?"

Darien shrugged, smiling wryly. "Go adventuring with you, perhaps. But for a present adventure, we'd best go to Cave House to deal with mayhem and collect my possessions."

They walked, for Frank was eager to see as much of the city as possible, but when they entered the square, Darien braced himself. There was no physical evidence of the recent events, however. Someone, perhaps the duke, had arranged for a thorough removal of blood and disorder. But the remnants of death and disorder hung in the air.

A couple came out of a house three doors down, paused, stared, and hurried away.

"Cave, cave," Darien murmured.

"Violent death on the doorstep is a bit upsetting," Frank said, "no matter who you are."

"Will you allow me no drama?" Darien asked as he unlocked the front door.

"Don't see the good in it."

Darien led the way in. "I could wish the ghosts would return, just to show you. But

they, too, were a machination of the Prussocks, I'm sure."

"What?"

"I suppose I haven't told you about my
wonderful collection of servants —" Darien
broke off. There'd been a thump upstairs,
where no one should be. Then an
"Ooooooooooo . . ." floated down. He shared
an astonished glance with his brother, and
then they raced up the stairs.

"I'll tell you something," Frank said as
they reached the top of the stairs, "that's
not Marcus. Far too feeble."

A roar came from the front.

They both halted, and despite the years,
authority, and war, moved toward the
shrouded drawing room with much greater
care.

A guttural moaning now, along with shuffling sounds.

Darien's skin crawled, and as he stepped
into the room he wished he had his saber,
even though it would be useless against an
evil spirit.

A pale shrouded shape loomed.

He realized it was a person an instant
before the Holland cover was thrown off to
reveal a grinning Pup. "How's that, Canem?
Give you a turn?"

After a breathless moment, Frank, eyes

bright, said, "Do introduce us, Canem."

Darien needed a strong drink. "Frank, meet Pup Uppington. Pup, meet my brother, Frank."

Pup came forward beaming, hand out. "Lieutenant Cave, an honor to meet you! Good to see you, too, Canem. Bit worried about the Foxstall business. Thought I should come to see. Nid Crofter told me what happened and there was some man here left a note for you." He produced it and it was from Evesham, who was sternly making an appointment on the next day. Mention of His Grace, the Duke of Yeovil, however, showed that the duke had already begun his work. "Rum do," Pup said. "Everything all right now?"

There seemed no point in going into details. "Being sorted out. What was that with the ghost?"

"Heard you say you wanted some, so I obliged. Pretty good, eh?"

Darien shook his head.

"Anything I can do to help?" Pup asked. "Can't live here without servants. Can come to stay with us, if you like."

"No, thank you," Darien said, "but thank Mrs. Uppington."

"Fine woman. Never minds anything and she's a splendid manager. Always the best food, and just as I like it. And you were right, Canem — wife is better than a whore."

Darien heard a strangled noise from Frank, but didn't dare look.

"I'm sure she's missing you," Darien said, "so you'd best get back to her. Thank you for coming."

"Righto," said Pup. "You can always call on me, and I fancy I know a bit about the married state now." He beamed at them both and left. Whistling out of tune.

Frank collapsed on the uncovered sofa and tried to stifle his laughter in the padded arm.

After a brief struggle, and after the front door shut, Darien joined him, laughing until tears ran. And if there were some real tears mixed in, hopefully Frank wouldn't notice.

They eventually pulled themselves together. Darien showed Frank the portrait of their father. Frank shuddered and covered it again. They went through the house, but agreed in the end that there was nothing in it either of them wanted other than Darien's belongings.

They packed the wooden chest, but with his fashionable wardrobe, his possessions no longer all fit.

Darien put the coverlet on the floor and

tossed his clothing into it to make a bundle. Lovegrove would have fainted. Poor old Lovegrove.

After a final look around, they left, locking up the house. In the stables, Darien told Nid to get a man with a pushcart to bring the trunk and bundle to the Dog and Sun, and then to move himself and Cerb there, too. After that, Darien walked down the lane with his brother, hoping never to set eyes on Cave House again.

CHAPTER 42

There was a message from Van waiting at the inn, inviting Darien and Frank to dine at his house that night. Van and Maria would want to go over every detail, and he might have liked to avoid that, but there was no point.

They found St. Raven and Cressida there, and also Hawkinville and Clarissa. Maria's plumply pretty niece, Natalie, attended, too. Darien wasn't sure that was wise, given Frank's attraction for young ladies, but he was going to attempt his brother's insouciant approach to life.

Over dinner, without servants, the events were discussed.

"We definitely don't want Lady Thea exposed to additional public attention," said Cressida St. Raven, who preferred to avoid attention herself.

"Some ladies enjoy notoriety," her dashing husband teased.

"No lady enjoys notoriety," Maria corrected firmly.

"And thus a large section of the ton is unnobled," said Van with a grin.

"Please," drawled St. Raven, "don't preach that nobility is entirely of the soul or these days we'll have to clap you in irons for treason and rebellion."

There was a brief, serious discussion of unrest and the sensible and idiotic ways the government was trying to deal with it, but then Frank lightened the mood with an account of Pup's ghostly play, and Hawkinville added a story of a brush with Pup that Darien had never heard.

"It was good of you to take care of him, Canem," Clarissa Hawkinville said, "rather than passing him on. It must have been confusing and worrying to be him."

"It was definitely confusing and worrying for everyone else," Darien said. "Don't make me into a saint. Once he became Canem's Pup, what could I do?"

"Let him drown in the Loire," Van said, meeting Darien's eyes for a moment before describing another hopeless subaltern he'd encountered.

There was no more talk of death and disorder, so it was a strange end to a dire day — a pleasant evening among, yes, friends.

Before leaving, however, Darien made an opportunity to talk with Maria. "Do you know how Thea is?"

Her eyes were kind but concerned. "It was a horrible experience. She's badly shaken."

"But her wounds aren't serious?"

"Oh, no. Did no one reassure you on that? They were only shallow cuts, but how cruel to do that simply to terrify her and you. The whole plan was vile. I'm glad you killed him."

"But is Thea?"

Her look was sympathetic. "I don't know. I haven't intruded. What are your plans?"

Delicately indirect. "When Parliament breaks up, I'll take Frank to Stours Court to look around the old place. He suggested tearing it down, and that might be the right idea. I do need to think of something to do with Cave House. I won't live in it again, but it can't be left empty. I've tried to rent or sell it, but no takers."

He hadn't answered her true question, but she didn't press him.

The next morning Darien sent a message to the Duchess of Yeovil, asking if he should call. He didn't want to put anyone to the inconvenience of turning him away at the door. The reply came swiftly. He was expected, and she and Thea were to begin their journey in an hour.

He dressed with particular care, and then walked the short distance, aware of a ridiculous urge to run. Every minute on the journey was a minute less with Thea. But his interview with her would doubtless be short anyway. When he passed a flower seller he bought a posy of fragrant sweet peas, but then felt foolish arriving with them in his hand.

He was admitted to the house by an impassive footman, but it was the same one who'd admitted him yesterday, with Thea in his arms. Doubtless many reactions were spinning behind the professional gloss.

The duchess came out of one of the reception rooms, smiled at the flowers, and invited him into that room. Not good. He was not to be admitted to the family's part of the house.

Thea was there, however, standing sideways to the empty fireplace, as if braced for something. She looked drawn and tired and he longed to take her into his arms.

"Here's Darien," the duchess said, and left, closing the door.

Darien looked at the door for a moment

in surprise, and then turned back to the woman he adored. The woman he must set free. So why the devil had he brought her flowers? The perfume was rising from them, threatening to fill the small room.

She was dressed for travel in a sensible blue-gray gown that did nothing for her color. The bodice was fairly low, but filled with ruched white that ended with a small frill around her neck. Her hair was dressed in a neat knot on top of her head and she wore small pearls in her ears. He remembered her in red.

He could think of nothing to say other than an inadequate, "How are you?"

"Quite well," she said.

He had to go to her and offer the flowers. She took them with a slight smile, raising them to her face to inhale. "Lovely." She gestured toward the sofa. "Won't you sit?"

She did so first, hands in her lap, holding the posy. He took a place at the other end of the sofa, wondering why he hadn't planned this encounter with care.

"Your wounds?" he asked.

"Shallow, but they still sting. And yours?"

"The same."

She looked at him closely. "How are you?"

"Quite well. It's a blessing that Frank turned up." He'd found a subject he could talk about. "He's no longer my baby brother and I'm well taken care of." A few moments later, he realized he was babbling on about Frank like a doting parent. Or like a man desperate not to say what was in his heart. "I'm sorry."

She was smiling, breathing in the flowers again. "Don't be. I'm glad you have family at last. And he was a godsend yesterday."

"Yes."

"So," she said, still buried in blossoms, "we're engaged to marry."

"Your father thought it best."

She looked at him. "And you?"

"It will cover some of the peculiarities. I'm sorry that a bit of scandal will always linger over that event. And that you'll have to jilt me." He attempted a smile, but she didn't echo it.

"Or not," she said.

He looked at her wide, defiant eyes, and said what she was braced for. "It won't work, Thea."

"Don't I get a say?"

"No. You've seen, twice, what I'm like. It's my nature. I've known no true peace all my life and few trustworthy friends. If trouble doesn't come and find me, I'll probably find it and deal with it bloodily. You won't like that."

"Both times you were saving me." She straightened out of the flowers to declare, "I *do* get a say."

"Thea, love —" That was a mistake.

"If you love me it's nonsense to let this go."

He surged to his feet and put distance between them. "Love is not enough."

"Love is precious."

"Love doesn't always survive."

"But what if it never comes again, like this? For either of us?"

He kept his back to her, resisting her plea.

"Darien," she said, "I'm holding you to our bargain."

He turned. "What bargain?"

"That we decide in autumn."

Hope stirred, that struggling, crippled thing in his chest that he should kill. "It was, I believe, until you returned to London."

"I'm holding you to the spirit of the original promise," she said steadily. "To see how our feelings survive. In any case, we have to remain betrothed for some weeks to let the world forget about the origins." She smiled slightly. "You can't stop me, after all. Unless you plan to jilt me, and that *will* ruin the Cave reputation."

He stared at her, speechless.

"Since it's uncertain when Parliament will begin again later in the year, shall we say the beginning of autumn? In September?"

"It appears that I have no say."

She rose, poised and graceful, his flowers in her hands. "You may say no in September. If you wish to."

"As may you."

"Of course. Did you remember a ring?" she asked.

It took him a moment to follow her and understand. A curse almost escaped. "I'm sorry. I'll . . ."

She took one out of her pocket and offered it on the palm of her hand. "You've had many things on your mind. And it really didn't seem fair to have you purchase one on such a hypothetical basis."

He took it. Five small rubies around a pearl. "From the ducal hoard?"

Her lips curled up in a miraculously mischievous smile. "It belonged to a Debenham lady reputed to be a lover of Rupert of the Rhine. Of course, she failed to win her prince."

He turned the ring in his fingers a moment, then took her left hand and slid it on. "I'm neither prince nor prize, Thea. You can do much better than me."

"I'm sure I can, being a duke's daughter

with a handsome dowry. Don't forget that dowry when you make your decision, sir. I believe your estates could use it."

Unwillingly, he was smiling, too. "You are a terrifying woman."

"Remember that, too. They say daughters turn out like their mothers."

He sobered immediately. "What if sons turn out like their fathers?"

"Perhaps it wears off after two. I needed only a moment with your brother, Darien, to know the taint wasn't inevitable."

She stepped closer and kissed him, perfume rising between them with the heat.

He tossed the posy on the sofa and gathered her into his arms simply to hold her close. To his alarm, tears rose to his eyes and thickened his throat. He fought them back before relaxing his hold and brushing his lips against hers. He'd allow himself no more, not even when he saw the glisten in her eyes.

He stepped apart. "I wish you a safe and pleasant journey."

Despite the moisture on her lashes, she was perfectly composed. "I gather you're going to Stours Court soon."

"As your father commanded."

"Don't if you don't want to, but you probably should. You should probably tear it down, too, for its memories if no other reason."

"How on earth do you know my mind?"

She chuckled. "No magic. Maria sent round a note."

"Ah. The three Fates."

She cocked her head. "What?"

"Never mind. If I tear down the house, and if — unlikely in the extreme — you become my wife, we'll be homeless." Dangerous but irresistible to speak of it.

"There's a Lancashire property," she said.

"Worse."

"Ireland?"

"I have no idea yet, but it's an unruly country, and I'm tired of war."

"Then we simply purchase something new. Canem," she suddenly added. "I've decided I should call you Canem, as all the friendly world does. Will you mind?"

He had to swallow again. "No."

"It could be very pleasant," she said, picking up the flowers and turning toward the door. "Choosing a house, I mean. Few people in our station get to choose exactly where to live. Our home could be close to Long Chart, or near Dare at Brideswell." She was watching his reaction. "In hunting country, even. Anywhere you wanted."

He took her hand because he couldn't

help himself. "If it happens, it will be where you want."

"Very well, but you'd better make your wishes clear, because I'll be choosing for you."

She opened the door and they found the duchess there, supervising servants and luggage — but probably really hovering.

The duchess turned, assessed, and beamed. Then she said, "Darien, about your house . . ."

"Lord," Thea muttered. "I forgot to warn you."

The duchess swept over. "I gather you don't intend to live there. Very wise, my dear boy. . . ."

He'd become her dear boy?

"Could I persuade you to donate it to the cause? I have in mind a refuge for some of the most difficult cases among our wounded veterans, and some of our special cases among the orphans and unfortunate women. They could all live together, you see, assisting one another. It won't be quite what the inhabitants of the square are used to, but it will be quiet. And I think they'd be happy to be rid of Cave reminders."

She seemed anxious that he agree.

Darien laughed, took her hand, and kissed it. "You are my savior in all things, Your

Grace. Consider it yours."

"Theirs, Darien, dear. Theirs. So kind of you. Now, Thea, we really must be off."

Thea was swept away to a waiting coach before Darien could come to terms with it. He left the house he had invaded months ago, fighting a new war, one against hope. Time, they said, healed all wounds. He knew that wasn't true, but distance often changed the way things appeared.

In her beloved home, surrounded by the warmth and tranquil order she loved, Thea would come to see him for the dark presence who had caused her so much harm. He shouldn't wish otherwise, but the weaker part of himself did.

He walked through the parks, remembering so many incidents. Here, he'd urged Thea to change, to be bolder, to brush away cobwebs. But our deeper natures were never so insubstantial, no matter how they looked to others.

She had changed. Could he?

He knew he could control his violent side. He didn't regret killing Foxstall, and he'd do it again, but with God's blessing nothing like that would happen again.

Glenmorgan? That could have been handled better, and not even with a duel. There were times for violence and times for other ways. He'd learned that in the army, but he'd never had to apply it when someone offended the woman he adored, cherished, worshipped. . . .

He watched three children running to the water where a pair of swans glided by.

Swans.

If a goddess could come to earth for him, he could make changes of the same dimension.

When parliamentary duties were done, Darien and Frank rode to Stours Court. They traveled at a gentle pace, for Frank wasn't used to horses and he wanted to explore the countryside they passed. They didn't far outpace the cart bringing their personal possessions.

The journey had been enlightening for Darien. He himself hadn't spent much time in England, but he'd never had the wondering appreciation Frank showed.

"Of course I arrived in winter," Darien said, sitting on a bench outside an inn in a small village, drinking summer ale on a lazy afternoon. Bees buzzed around a basket of flowers hung nearby and a pair of kittens chased each other near his feet. "Then the regiment was sent straight to the north, where the sun didn't shine and the rain didn't stop for weeks."

"I mean to explore the whole country," Frank said, scooping up a kitten that scratched his boots. "Rough and smooth." The kitten purred. When Frank put it down, it mewled and attempted to follow when he left.

In due course they arrived at Stours Court, and though summer sun blessed the day, it worked no magic. If there were rough and smooth, this was part of the rough. Darien felt a familiar urge to turn away. Wytton, the new estate manager, had achieved a great deal, but he'd been instructed to concentrate on improving the land and essential building and not to waste time on the house, gardens, or anything impractical.

Wise decision. One glance with clear sight confirmed that the house should go.

"Strange," Darien said, halting Cerb. "When I visited last time, I felt this place was a burden I could never shed, like Prometheus's rock or the mariner's albatross. Now it's simply an ugly, decrepit house plagued by damp. I wonder if Father thought the same. The neglect isn't new. The stables are this way."

"I do remember," Frank said. "I even

came here now and then over the past decade."

Darien had never imagined that he would. "Sure you don't want to try to save it?"

"Lord, no. If it was wood, I'd suggest a bonfire, but that brown stone would just laugh at flames."

"And any wood inside is probably too damp to burn well. Come on, then. I don't suppose it will actually tumble down on our heads."

Wytton had obviously considered the stables practical, for the roof had been fixed and the young grooms who came out to care for the horses looked healthy and cheerful.

In preparation for this visit, Darien had sent orders weeks ago to get rid of the tattered remnants of his father's servants, but he'd provided parting money or pensions, even for the ones he remembered as cruel. Being a responsible custodian of the Cave inheritance was proving expensive. He'd ordered Wytton to find new staff, but had not been sure it would be possible. In the past, few had been willing to work here.

In addition to the stable boys, however, he found a cook and scullery maid in the clean kitchen, who curtsied to him and Frank, looking perhaps cautious, but not afraid. There were two house maids, the cook told them, and they soon met them — sturdy young women bustling about making beds, sweeping floors, dusting and polishing. They, too, seemed wary, but they were here and willing to smile. Twenty-four hours of Frank would have them merry as larks.

But despite the improvements, the house was beyond hope. No amount of cleaning and polishing would remove the smell of rot, and only complete replacement of the roof would correct the many damp areas on the upstairs ceilings. What point in any repairs when the house stood on land so damp it was close to bog? Heaven alone knew why the site had been chosen in the first place.

"I'm reluctant even to sleep here," Frank said, eyeing a distinct sag in the ceiling of the room prepared for him, "but the servants have made a gallant effort, so noblesse oblige."

"It so often does."

They obliged, therefore, settling into bedrooms, complimenting maids, eating dinner, complimenting the cook. At least there was no need to lie. The servants had done their best, but when the house went so would go their employment. It seemed poor reward, but Darien didn't see a solution.

Wytton dined with them. He was a solid middle-aged man, hardworking but not one for small talk, so the meal was businesslike. Darien was amused by Frank's eagerness to learn. He quizzed Wytton at such length that the man excused himself early.

"I think you've wrung him dry," Darien said, smiling as he passed the port.

"It's all fascinating stuff. Drainage. Who'd have thought that was so important?"

"I wish whoever planned this house had considered it."

"Yes, indeed, but everywhere, apparently. And trees. I thought they were just for appearance, masts, or furniture. Coppices, pollarding."

He went on like this at some length so that Darien rose and urged him away from the table, hoping to change the subject. But as they left the dining room, Frank said, "How would it be if I had a go at Greenshaw? Not permanently, I don't think. But I'd like to try my hand at estate management."

Darien was taken aback by this, but said, "It's a bleak spot, but if you want, by all means." Whatever Frank did, he did conscientiously. They had that in common.

In crossing the paneled hall, they both paused by the carved oak chest. Darien raised the lid. As usual, it was empty. But it still bore the scars on the inside from when he'd tried to cut their way out with his small knife.

"Keep or discard?" he asked.

"Keep," Frank said.

"Why?"

"Never show them you're afraid. You taught me that."

He closed the lid. "I wish I'd never had to."

"We are what we are because of what we've been."

That was a startling way to look at it. But then, Frank was Frank, and he was Mad Dog Cave. He'd spent quite a bit of time reviewing his life and found little he repented of.

They spent a pleasant enough time over the next few weeks exploring the estate, with Frank continuing to suck the harried estate agent dry, though he had to go up to London eventually to deal with his final severance from His Majesty's navy. When he returned, a civilian, they went through the house, deciding what should be saved before the place was torn down.

Much of the furniture was old, and though the heavy old stuff was no longer fashionable, it had done nothing wrong. If it was sound and free of woodworm, it was taken off to storage.

They went to church, of course, causing a stir, but then being cautiously welcomed. They even received some invitations. When an assembly was held in nearby Kenilworth, Sir Algernon Ripley rode over to urge them to attend.

"My daughters," he said wryly. "They'll never forgive me otherwise. You are warned, young men."

The Ripley daughters were young and excitable, and along with most of the other females present, all fell hopelessly in love with Frank. In his new policy of optimism, Darien assumed Frank was used to it and could cope. His own reception wasn't quite as warm, which could be caused by lingering doubts about the new Vile Viscount or simply his harsher appearance and manner. But he certainly wasn't ostracized, which was seductively pleasant.

When Frank escaped a bright-eyed trio of maidens, one surely no older than fifteen, Darien passed him a restoring glass of wine punch. "Imagine how bad it would be if you had the title to add to your charms, lad, and thank me for saving you."

"I do, daily," Frank said with a grin. "But I have to point out — you're not being mobbed."

"I have cloaked myself in the frosty dignity of a peer."

"Still Thea?" Frank asked, perhaps with concern.

Darien drained his glass. "Always Thea."

"She's probably at assemblies and parties, too."

"I hope she is. I want her to appreciate the charms of her normal life and the virtues of kindly, undramatic people. If she decides to be sensible, however, you'll have to produce the next generation of Caves, so back to the fray."

Frank smiled as he drained his glass, but he turned serious. "That sounds theatrical, you know. The one and only."

"It's practical. It wouldn't be fair to marry another with half a heart and I don't think I was made for pretence and mediocrity. If my heart changes . . ." He shrugged. "However, if you want optimism, I'm thinking of rebuilding Stours Court. I see the possibility of making a home in this area, though how to solve the damp problem, I'm not sure."

It felt dangerous to put the new idea into words, but Frank said, "I think so, too," as if the choice were a simple matter. "I'm off for another dance, with that shy blonde this time. If you're planning on being part of society here, you'd better dance more, too."

"Damn you, you're right." Darien surveyed the room. "Safely with a wife, I think."

"Canem, Canem! What makes you think wives are safe?"

Darien laughed and went off to ask Mrs. Witherspoon to waltz. She was forty and homely. Alarmingly, she blushed.

CHAPTER 43

Thea could have been happy in cloistered quiet as she waited out the days, but she upheld the implicit promise of living a normal life. It was necessary, anyway. London stories had reached Somerset, and she had to put out fires of speculation everywhere. If she'd seemed changed and reclusive, Canem would be blamed.

Instead, she showed herself to be delighted by her betrothal, and she and her mother mentioned his heroism whenever his name came up, until some had the impression he'd saved Thea directly from the evil Foxstall's clutches. They didn't correct that.

When Parliament finally ended, Avonfort returned to his estate and Thea braced for more trouble. He did not propose again, however. If he seemed chilly and disapproving, Thea could easily ignore that, though she was starving for someone who'd seen Canem recently to tell her about him.

The duke joined them only a day later, but the only thing he said about Canem was that he'd gone to Stours Court as expected.

As ordered, Thea thought, but she couldn't summon the nerve to ask for more information. She knew her father did not think him the husband for her, but Canem, Canem, Canem was her deepest pleasure. She blessed the betrothal because it allowed her, almost compelled her, to mention him whenever she was in public.

She'd found some books in the library that mentioned the Caves and Stours Court, and studied them secretly, as if it were a sin. She read of the heroic Stour family and of the coming of the Caves. She wondered if Canem knew that the Cave who'd been granted the estate had married a widow who had been the last surviving Stour. If not, she looked forward to telling him.

One guide to gentlemen's homes in Warwickshire had a print of the house, which it described as "lacking architectural significance and poorly situated." She stifled laughter, thinking *Poor Canem,* and longing to be there with him to deal with the problem. At the same time, she traced windows, wondering which room he was in now, if he was there at all.

He could be visiting his estate in Lancashire, or even the one in Ireland. She hadn't found any book that mentioned them. He might have gone to Scotland for shooting, or to Brighton for play. He might have taken a ship for the antipodes. He might be dead! No, they'd be sure to tell her if her promised husband died.

The London papers they received here never mentioned him, but why should they? He was no longer a center of attention. She'd worked hard for that but now she'd welcome some snippet of scandal. As long as it wasn't about another woman.

No, she knew he'd keep that promise, but it didn't mean he wasn't changing his mind.

She received nothing useful by letter, for most of her friends were here in Somerset with her. She thought of writing to a Rogue or one of their ladies, but that seemed like prying. If the Delaneys had driven over she might have asked questions, but there was no particular reason for them to visit now, with Dare gone.

She did receive a letter from Maddy, who was in exile in Wales. After the Foxstall affair, Thea's father had asked many uncomfortable questions and Thea hadn't been able to hide Maddy's bookstore ruse and her tryst with Foxstall, especially as Harriet had already spilled part of that to the other servants. Thea had kept the details secret, but that exploit plus some other adventures had been too much for Uncle Arthur. He'd packed her off to a distant relative who lived, by Maddy's account, surrounded by nothing but hills and sheep.

The letter had been a mix of repentance and resentment that left Thea unclear as to her cousin's true feelings — toward her, toward Darien, and even toward Foxstall. But at least Maddy wasn't with child. That was a great blessing. Thea wrote back, trying to say nothing to hurt or to stir resentment, but she wasn't sure they would ever be close again. Maddy had played no part in Foxstall's plot, but Thea couldn't shake the feeling that her cousin's behavior had been at the root of all the trouble.

August began, but autumn was still a long way away. Thea's patience with parties, picnics, and race meetings thinned to transparency, especially with Canem's silence wearing at it day by day. She tried to convince herself that his honor required that he not write. It hadn't been stated, but it was implicit in the agreement she'd insisted on.

But inside, especially in the dark hours of the night, she fretted that his silence meant his feelings had faded. She tried for calm, tried telling herself to have faith, that she only had to wait until late September. But waiting was so hard.

By the second week in August, her patience snapped and she sought an interview with her father. "I need to talk to you, Papa."

She thought he sighed, but he said, "Let's walk in the garden. It's too nice a morning to be indoors."

It was a perfect summer day, though it might become overhot in the afternoon. The estate looked like the one shown in those watercolors she'd gone through with Canem — so long ago. Carefully tended lawns sloped gently to the swan-rippled lake, deer stepped delicately among handsome trees. In nearby flower beds, bees harvested pollen and butterflies flitted.

It was perfect, but it was not what she wanted.

Thea gathered her courage. "If I decide to marry Lord Darien, Father, would you be displeased?"

He walked on for a few paces, hands clasped behind his back.

"Would I forbid it?" he said at last. "No, my dear. By the end of the year you will be of age, and though I'd like to think my mere displeasure would deter you, I doubt that would outweigh true love. But I do have reservations. He will not be a tranquil husband, and you have always seemed a person who dislikes drama and alarms."

Thea tried to match his measured tone. "Perhaps it's like wine, Papa. At first, many people don't like it, and then they find they like it very much."

"But there, too, moderation is necessary. Darien may not be capable of that." But then he shook his head and smiled at her. "Here I am, a father with one daughter. No man in the world would ever be good enough for you, my dearest girl."

They came to a halt beneath the shade of a spreading beech.

"Are you saying I shouldn't look for advice from you, Papa?"

"Is that what you're doing?"

Thea blushed because she wasn't, not really. She was, she supposed, testing the waters, but with every intention of plunging in.

"You are a very sensible young woman," her father said, and then added, "Don't wrinkle your nose as if that's an insult."

"But people always say that about me. And they usually mean I'm dull."

"There is much to be said for a quiet life, Thea."

Thea remembered the costumes. "Did you think so when you were my age?" she challenged.

He laughed. "I'm not sure I was ever your age. And you are not exactly your age, either. Your mother and I trust your good judgment, so we are willing to let you make this decision. Your wish to take time to consider the matter shows your wisdom. And," he added dryly, "no one can say you've only seen him on his best behavior."

Thea laughed, blushing, and then she took the plunge. "So, may I go in search of him?"

"*What?* No, Thea."

"But I'm going mad stuck here," she protested. "I know we said autumn —"

"What?" he demanded.

Thea had forgotten that no one but she and Canem knew the details of the arrangement. Having spilled the beans, she had to explain.

"So," her father said, walking on, "that is why he's made no attempt to contact you. I admit that has given me the impression . . . But is it fair to cut short his time of reflection?"

"One way or another, he will have made his decision by now. I have."

He laughed, shaking his head. "Ah, your mother was as impatient once."

"Mama was?"

"Haven't you noticed she's still impatient when she has a project in mind? When she decides something must be done, she wants it done immediately." He continued to walk down to the edge of the mirror-like lake and stood for a moment in contemplation.

"Very well, my dear. I'd be a poor father to allow you to sink into insanity. If you're sure of your mind, I'll escort you to Stours Court. In any case, I need to see that Darien can provide the comforts you will need."

Thea threw her arms around him and hugged him. "All the comforts and more."

Thea and her father traveled in a post chaise, accompanied by Harriet and her father's valet in a coach with the extra baggage. It took three days to reach Stours Court, but then, finally, they were approaching through countryside much plainer than her home county. As if to test her resolve, the weather had turned cooler as they'd traveled north, and now the sky hung heavy, threatening rain.

She remembered the print called *The Wrath of God* and wondered what nearby hill had been the site of that event. She hoped God wasn't inclined to any active demonstrations today. She was wound tight enough already.

She'd insisted that they not send word of their coming. She cherished an image of Darien's shocked delight to see her, but she'd also been terrified that given notice he'd try to avoid her. In short, she was a mess of hope and fear and might even be sick with it as they finally saw the gatehouse that must belong to his estate.

A woman came out and pulled open the iron gates. Thea scrutinized her as if she might reveal something of importance, but she was merely a sturdy country woman with a square face who bobbed a curtsy as they passed.

"We can always turn back," her father said.

"No! I'm just nervous, Papa. In case he isn't here."

He didn't look convinced by that, which was hardly surprising. Thea unlocked her tense hands and tried to look merely composed.

The post chaise lurched a little as they went down the drive, but the estate wasn't in terrible shape. The grass was kept short by sheep, that practical and common method, and there were some excellent trees and pleasant vistas, presumably all provided by nature. Thea glimpsed the romantic ruins of Stour Castle on a rise.

But where was the house? The drive was ending, but there was no building of substance anywhere in sight.

The coach followed a branch of the drive toward some two-story buildings — a stable block. Then she realized that the large area of muddy, rubble-strewn ground must be where Darien's house had recently stood. Not only was he not here, his house wasn't, either.

She stared out at the stables, completely at a loss, even though some grooms had appeared.

Then a voice said, "Thea?"

She looked around, focused, and there he was — in boots, breeches, and an open-necked shirt, looking almost like a field laborer, his skin darker after summer sun. He seemed as dumbstruck as she'd been.

No longer. A groom had opened the door and she rushed down the steps.

Right into a deep puddle of mud.

She stood there gaping, hiking her skirts up, her feet soaking.

Canem ran over and swept her up into his arms. "God, Thea! I'm sorry. What are you doing here? Now, I mean? I —"

But Thea was laughing at the insanity of this, and for pure soaring joy. She wrapped her arms around his neck and kissed him

536

with all her heart.

They had to stop eventually, though their eyes seemed unable to part. "Where's your house?" she asked, smiling so widely her cheeks hurt.

He was smiling, too. "Gone to house heaven. I hoped to have something built for you by autumn. A Palladian villa or something. . . ."

For you. By autumn.

He hadn't changed his mind. She laughed softly, touching her head to his. "But where are you living?" she asked.

"In a gamekeeper's cottage." His eyes finally looked beyond her. " 'Struth, is that the duke you've brought?"

Thea giggled. "He wanted to be sure you could provide me with suitable comforts."

"I'm sunk then." But he smiled as he carried her to dry ground, where he put her down. If his hands lingered, perhaps her father wouldn't notice. But then, after that kiss . . .

In short order, Canem had the coach moved to drier ground and her father climbed out. The servants' coach, coming along behind, had been more careful. Thea was relieved to see that the duke looked more amused than angry, but she feared he'd want to delay the wedding, and she couldn't bear that.

"My daughter's feet are wet," he pointed out, quite mildly, considering the circumstances.

Canem gathered her into his arms again, saying, "The best I can offer nearby is the groom's parlor, Your Grace." His eyes on hers sparkled with humor as he carried her into the simple room, which was whitewashed and provided only a deal table, wooden benches, and a plain sideboard by way of furniture.

He settled her on a bench and knelt, eyes smiling at her in a different way, to unlace and remove her half boots. Squirming pleasantly inside at the touch of his hands on her feet, Thea wondered if he'd actually attempt to remove her stocking with her father watching. She never found out, because Harriet bustled in, exclaiming and scandalized.

With a blown kiss, Canem rose and went to where the duke was observing the scene outside.

"Well, Darien, you don't do things by half measures."

"I try not to, Duke."

Her father harumphed. "Do you want to marry Thea? After that kiss, your answer had better be yes."

Canem half turned to smile at her. "Yes."

Harriet hurried off with the wet shoes and stockings to find dry ones. Thea saw Canem's gaze settle on her bare toes and wriggled them at him.

"Immediately," he added.

"That would be lovely," Thea said.

"You will be married no sooner than three weeks from now at Long Chart," the duke stated. "By then, Darien, I expect you to have arranged a suitable house and servants for my daughter, here or elsewhere."

"I would like to make a home here," Canem said, still to Thea. "But only if you wish, my love."

Location was irrelevant, but Thea knew neither man wanted to hear that. "It's pleasant land and I like the castle. But did I encounter the bog?"

He grimaced. "I'm afraid so. I'm looking into drainage, but it won't be easy."

"Then why not build on higher ground?"

Canem stared at her. "Like mother, like daughter. Of course. Here I've been trying to build on the same site as if it were sacred, but you see right through the problem. I wonder where." He moved to the doorway to look around.

Thea was becoming irritated by being stuck on the bench, but Harriet hurried back in with stockings and slippers. Not well suited to the situation, but they'd do. As soon as she was shod, Thea rose to go to Canem, but then she paused to look at her father, standing incongruously in the simple room. He shook his head but waved her on her way.

She spent the next hour with Canem, picking her way around — and sometimes being carried, which was no penance — as they sought the perfect location for their house. Their home. Their heaven.

They settled on a spot that would be high enough for dryness without being inconvenient, and Thea turned back, hand in hand with him, to the scar of the old one. "And the boggy land becomes a lake."

" 'Everything for the best in this best of all possible worlds.' "

"That sounds like a quotation. What from?"

"Voltaire's *Candide*. A very silly story."

"It sounds happy, at least."

"On the contrary, it's a string of misfortunes."

"Then we'll have no part of it." They kissed again, but softly. No need for scandal this close to the prize. As they strolled back to the stables hand in hand, she said, "Did I ever tell you that you were likened to the

Corsair?"

"Byron's Corsair? Wasn't that supposed to be based on himself? Are you accusing me of being poetic, wench?"

She chuckled at the thought. "But you have to admit you appeared among the ton as a 'man of loneliness and mystery.' "

"Not by choice." He squeezed her hand gently. "You haven't mentioned such concerns, Thea, but I'm not an outcast here. In fact, the local gentry are so welcoming that I'll be glad of rescue."

"Rescue?"

"From young ladies eager to overlook my faults to become a viscountess."

"What faults?" she asked, but added, "I see it's as well I didn't wait until September though."

He turned her into his arms and kissed her again. "Do you think so?"

"Yes," she said, cuddling close. "But only because I couldn't stand it a moment longer."

Simply being together was so irresistible that they lingered there.

Eventually, Thea looked up at him. "There is the problem of somewhere to stay. Come back to Long Chart, Canem. The house can wait. We'll build it together. Despite what my father says, I'll enjoy a gamekeeper's cottage. For a while, at least."

He kissed the tip of her nose. "I'm glad you qualified that. I was wondering where my goddess had gone."

She laughed, but asked, "Where's your brother?"

"In Lancashire for a while, playing at agricultural management. I don't know where his interest will finally settle. . . ."

They returned to the stables, arm in arm, discussing Frank, their home, their future, and everything. When they reached the stables, however, the duke's patience had run out. He demanded the direction of a decent inn and carried Thea away. But Darien only delayed to dress properly before joining them for an excellent dinner, and the next day, they set off together to Long Chart and their wedding.

CHAPTER 44

If the duke had been uncertain about the match, the duchess clearly was not. She shed tears of joy and plunged into preparations for the wedding of the year. Nothing Thea said could change her mind, and as long as her mother didn't try to delay the event, she didn't care. But she escaped with Darien as often as possible.

They walked, rode, and drove around the countryside as Thea showed him all her favorite places. For the first time, he admitted to playing the flute, but he would play only for her, out in the country. He also had a good singing voice, however, and finally joined her in a duet in front of others.

They would have music in their home.

Their time alone together was limited, however, for the whole county seemed to want to meet him, and it was one social function after another. Some of their neighbors wanted to meet Lord Darien out of horrified fascination and had to be won over, but that was easier now, largely because Darien was different. He still had every scrap of that power and vigor that had first attracted and terrified her, but he was less guarded and lighter of heart.

When Frank Cave turned up the week before the wedding, Thea thought he might be the major cause of the change. The devotion between the brothers wasn't demonstrative, but it was deep. In Frank's company, no one could be cool or guarded.

When she told Canem her thought, however, he said, "No, my Thea. Any improvement in me is entirely your work."

Dare and Mara arrived too, of course, presenting an excellent example of married happiness. Thea was moved to see no lingering anger and resentment between Canem and Dare, though she wasn't so pleased when the two men organized a quarterstaff contest and Canem ended up with a bump on his head.

He lay beneath a tree with her, his head in her lap as she applied vinegar cloths. "It's worth it for this," he said, eyes closed, "but I think a sweet kiss might work better than vinegar. . . ."

The next day Canem challenged Dare to

a saber contest, but both Mara and Thea vetoed the idea. They settled for a steeple race that involved most of the young men of the area. Thea muttered something about Conrad and Medora and had to explain to Mara.

On the wedding eve, the duchess threw a ball. Hundreds attended, and many stayed, so that even Long Chart was packed. Yet again, time alone together was impossible, but tomorrow — ah, tomorrow — and tonight they could dance.

The duchess had wanted Thea to order a new gown, but Thea wore the red. She wore it exactly as she had that night except for one thing — she put on the right corset.

"Pearls, dear?" her mother questioned when she saw her. "My rubies, perhaps."

"No, Mama. This is exactly how I want to look."

Her mother shook her head but didn't protest.

When Canem saw her, his reaction was everything she'd dreamed of and they danced through a magical evening in a world of their own. As they waltzed, she said, "Did I tell you there's to be fireworks at midnight?"

He burst out laughing. Everyone beamed indulgently at the mad lovers.

They watched the magical fire together, she wrapped in his arms, feeling his occasional kisses on her hair as he told her softly that she was his fire, his spark, his beauty in the night. When the explosions were over, they danced again, but not for long. The wedding was set for ten in the morning, so no one could dance till dawn.

Thea did have a new dress for her wedding, a simple white muslin embroidered with forget-me-nots, and silk forget-me-nots in her hair. The actual wedding service was a small affair, held privately in the duke's private chapel with only family in attendance, but afterward there was a fete in the grounds and grand celebrations for everyone in the area.

Thea and Canem did their duty but were delighted to escape in the midafternoon, even if in a flower-decked carriage that was cheered by crowds down the long drive and on the road for a good mile until they'd passed out of her father's lands.

"Phew," Canem said, collapsing back on the seat. "If you'd warned me, I might have fled."

"Really?" Thea asked.

"No," he said. "Come here."

She was wearing a bonnet now, which presented a minor challenge, but nothing,

546

as Canem pointed out, that could make a war hero blanch.

They'd been lent a house only fifteen miles from Long Chart, which was as well. By the time they reached there, they could endure the bare minimum of courtesy from the servants before finding their bedroom.

But once there, Thea found herself ridiculously shy. Sunlight still poured in through the window, which stood open. She could hear birds, but also people somewhere in the garden, and distantly the barking of a dog.

"Perhaps we should wait until night," she said, even though she seethed with hunger.

"If you wish."

She looked at him, knew he felt as she did. "No, but . . ."

"I could draw the curtains, if you're afraid the birds might see."

She fell into laughter and into his arms, and then it was all right.

He found the control to go slowly, to undress her slowly, tenderly unwinding her, it seemed to Thea, from layers and anxieties with kisses and even laughter. And he managed to shed his own clothing at the same time so that he shed the final layer first.

He took off his shirt to stand naked in sunlight, his skin slightly dark all over, his form so beautiful that Thea paused simply to enjoy. But then she walked forward in her silk shift to touch scars — on his arm, on his side, down his belly. . . .

She touched his manhood, too, shy but familiar with its warm hardness.

He drew her last garment up and off, and pulled her to him for a kiss. Then he swept her up and carried her to the turned-down bed to settle her gently on cool sheets. She shivered, but it wasn't from chill. It was from the potent smell of freshly laundered sheets, which set fire to need.

She stretched her arms to him and he joined her, to kiss, to touch, to explore as they had done once before, but this time completely. When he entered she felt the stab of pain, but it was what made this complete. Completely perfect. They were finally one.

After a still moment, he moved. She laughed softly at the sensation and then matched him, reveling in each new, delicious discovery, in her body, in his, until the passion built, the passion she knew, that she'd longed for now for so very long. That was even better than before.

"Fireworks," she said eventually, stretching with languorous delight. "But not at midnight."

He drew her into his arms. "There will be many, many midnights, but sunshine, too. I promise you that —"

But she put her fingers over his lips. "Don't fret, don't strive, beloved. We simply are, and nothing, nothing at all, could ever be better, Canem Cave."

"I might be Canem Cave," he said, "but are you still the Great Untouchable?"

She laughed at that. "Never to you. Never, ever to you. Love me again, beloved."

So they touched again, kissed again, and with birdsong pouring in through the window, he obeyed.

AUTHOR'S NOTE

To Rescue a Rogue (published in September 2006) completed the stories of the members of the Company of Rogues, but their world had become my version of the English Regency world, so whenever I write in that setting, they'll be around somewhere, even if out of sight.

As part of that, I'm weaving in my other Regency fiction. Those of you who have read my very early Regencies will have recognized Lord and Lady Wraybourne, Fred Kyle, and even Maria Harroving, who all appeared in my very first book, *Lord Wraybourne's Betrothed.* We hope to have a new edition of this book available soon, but as it was published in hardcover, you may be able to find it in a public library.

I didn't plan for Lord Darien, however. He merely strolled in toward the end of *To Rescue a Rogue,* ready to play a small but important role, and bristling with antagonism. It took me only a moment to realize that, of course, someone back at school had to have hated the Rogues simply for being themselves, and perhaps also with cause. Young people can be carelessly cruel. The beginnings of the story spun out in my mind.

What if he were to encounter Dare's sister . . . ?

Immediately I had problems, however. This man insisted his title was Lord Darien. Lord Dare and Lord Darien in the same book? I protested. He insisted, and as you've seen, Darien's not someone you can push around.

Then there was the whole business of *cave canem* and the pronunciation of the family name. There are many English names of places and people that are not pronounced as they're spelled. Mainwaring is "mannering," Worcester is "wooster," and they say Featherstonehaugh is "fanshaw," though I've never quite believed that one. So Cave could easily be "cahvay" — I just had to let the reader know.

The phrase *cave canem* dates back almost to "the year dot," as they say. In about AD 20, a Roman called Petronius described the practice of putting a picture of a guard dog on the lintel above the door along with the words *cave canem*. This was confirmed in the eighteenth century when exactly that was discovered in the ruins of Pompeii.

So yes, all those Harrow schoolboys, who were mostly taught the Classics — Greek and Latin — would have been familiar with the phrase.

Apart from that, this story progresses through quite normal Regency pathways — if we allow for scheming servants and a ruthless enemy. I hope you enjoyed it.

If you're open to something different, a few months ago, NAL published a collection of novellas called *Dragon Lovers*. My story there is set in a fantasyland of castles, princesses, and knights in shining armor. Princess Rozlinda is the Sacrificial Virgin Princess of Saragond, which means that when a dragon swoops in to ravage the land, she'll be offered to placate it and send it away. No bit deal, given that the sacrifice is symbolic, and once done, she can get on with her life. Marrying her dream knight, and thus ceasing to be a virgin, is top of her list of things to do. But someone has changed the rules, and Rozlinda discovers that the sacrifice isn't symbolic anymore.

My fellow authors in this collection are my good friends Mary Jo Putney, Barbara Samuel, and Karen Harbaugh. We have a

Web site at www.dragonloversromance.com. You can find out more about *Dragon Lovers* and my other work on my own Web site www.jobev.com. There are excerpts, pictures, and other material connected to my books. There's even some free fiction to enjoy. You can also sign up to receive my more or less monthly e-mail newsletter.

I'm also part of a group of historical authors who blog about life and writing at www.wordwenches.com. We each do one day, and currently I'm the Saturday Wench, though that is subject to change. Drop by.

And you can always e-mail me at jo@jobev.com.

If you're not into the Internet yet, you can still contact me by post. Please send any letters to me c/o Margaret Ruley, Jane Rotrosen Agency, 318 East 51st Street, New York, New York 10022 (SASE appreciated).

What's coming next? A return to the Georgian era, I think. There's this rake and he encounters a nun in distress. But is she really a nun, and exactly who is chasing whom?

Happy reading,
Jo

ABOUT THE AUTHOR

Jo Beverley is widely regarded as one of the most talented romance writers today. She is a five-time winner of Romance Writers of America's cherished RITA Award and one of only a handful of members of the RWA Hall of Fame. She has also twice received the *Romantic Times* Career Achievement Award. Born in England, she has two grown sons and lives with her husband in Victoria, British Columbia, just a ferry ride away from Seattle. You can visit her Web site at www.jobev.com.

The employees of Thorndike Press hope you have enjoyed this Large Print book. All our Thorndike and Wheeler Large Print titles are designed for easy reading, and all our books are made to last. Other Thorndike Press Large Print books are available at your library, through selected bookstores, or directly from us.

For information about titles, please call:
(800) 223-1244

or visit our Web site at:
www.gale.com/thorndike
www.gale.com/wheeler

To share your comments, please write:
Publisher
Thorndike Press
295 Kennedy Memorial Drive
Waterville, ME 04901

Mount Laurel Library
100 Walt Whitman Avenue
Mount Laurel, NJ 08054-9539
856-234-7319
www.mtlaurel.lib.nj.us